Hania Allen was born in Liverpool, but has lived in Scotland longer than anywhere else, having come to love the people and the country (despite nine months of rain and three months of bad weather). Of Polish descent, her father was stationed in St Andrews during the war, and spoke so fondly of the town that she applied to study at the university.

She has worked as a researcher, a mathematics teacher, an IT officer and finally in senior management, a post she left to write full time. She is the author of the Von Valenti novels and now lives in a village in Fife.

Also by Hania Allen

DI Dania Gorska Series
The Polish Detective
Clearing the Dark
The Family Business

The Ice Hotel

THE
MURDER
STONES

Hania Allen

CONSTABLE

CONSTABLE

First published in Great Britain in 2022 by Constable

1 3 5 7 9 10 8 6 4 2

A CIP catalogue record for this book
is available from the British Library.

ISBN: 978-1-47213-168-3

Typeset in Bembo by Photoprint, Torquay
Printed and bound in Great Britain by Clays Ltd, Elcograf S.p.A.

Papers used by Constable are from well-managed forests and other
responsible sources.

Constable
An imprint of
Little, Brown Book Group
Carmelite House
50 Victoria Embankment
London EC4Y 0DZ

An Hachette UK Company
www.hachette.co.uk

www.littlebrown.co.uk

Whoso sheddeth Man's Blood by Man shall his Blood be shed.
Genesis 9:6

PROLOGUE

MAY 1940

The officer sat back in the swivel chair and gazed at the mug of tea his NCO had just placed on the desk. He waited until he'd heard the door close before removing the bottle of Vat 69 from the desk drawer. Almost mechanically, he poured two fingers into the whisky glass. Since the tea was hardly worth drinking and he needed fortification for what lay ahead, a drop of Scotch this early in the afternoon was perfectly justifiable. And, in such strange times, who was going to tell him otherwise?

He'd been pulled off his current duties and assigned this task under instructions that it was strictly top secret. He'd suppressed a yawn. As an officer in one of several intelligence agencies in His Majesty's Service, everything he was tasked with was top secret. Although what he'd been asked to do was surely beneath his rank – he was to make an inventory of the items in a large naval kitbag. But when he'd been told what the bag contained, the breath had left his body.

He sipped the whisky, his gaze straying to the cardboard box on the horsehair sofa. It contained his gas mask, as yet unused. He felt a prickle of anxiety as he listened to the hum of aircraft over

1

London. With Norway and Denmark invaded in April, and now Holland crushed, the phoney war had come to an end.

The officer returned to his work. He was less than halfway through the process of registering the diamonds. The packets were mostly numbered and labelled, and tied securely with string, some even sealed with red wax. However, there were a few which hadn't been sealed. After a surreptitious glance at the door – unnecessary, as his NCO always knocked before entering – he'd opened one of the small bags and emptied the contents on to his blotter. The irregularly shaped and poorly coloured stones told him these were industrial diamonds. It was then that he understood the significance of what he'd overheard on passing his CO's office. At first, he'd caught only snatches of conversation – we have nothing to stop the Germans, who are now sweeping across Europe, it was a close-run thing, thank God they returned safely – but after putting his ear to the door, he'd learnt that a one-day mission had been mounted to retrieve the 'industrials' as well as the cut stones in Amsterdam's vaults, and bring them to Britain. That the new prime minister had even authorised a destroyer to take the agents there and back was testament to how important this mission was. Given the speed with which the rescue had taken place, and the level of secrecy, he doubted the British public would learn of the operation. The officer smiled. In years to come, they'd make a film of the affair.

He counted the stones, replaced them in the packet, retied the string and made the entry on the sheet. He was coming to the end when he noticed a bag considerably larger than the others. It was made of thick velvet and had an elaborate gold crest embroidered into the material. The crest consisted of a shield with a saltire and crossed swords, and a feathered helmet above the shield. A label was attached to the sturdy drawstring, and on it someone had scribbled a name, and an address on Tolstraat.

The officer opened the bag and shook out a few stones. A wave of excitement coursed through his veins. These were not industrials, nor did they bear any resemblance to the tiny cut stones he'd seen in the other packets. These heart-shaped gems were expertly cut, and at least half an inch wide. They were faintly pink, and the large number and arrangement of facets caused them to shimmer and wink in the light that streamed through the window. Although he was no expert, he understood immediately that just one of these stones would be worth a king's ransom. So, how many were there?

He emptied out the bag, taking care not to lose any gems, and grouped them into clusters of ten. After he'd finished, he straightened, and smoothed down his moustache. There were one hundred and thirty-nine. Enough to purchase the moon. He realised he'd been holding his breath. Slowly, he let the air out of his lungs. One hundred and thirty-nine. Was this the entire stock held by the firm? He imagined the scene: the agents arriving, trying to persuade the meneer to part with his diamonds – no, it would be too risky to send them overland to Paris or Switzerland, they would be safe in Britain, we have a destroyer at our disposal. And then the meneer, in despair, hearing shots in the street and the heavy sound of boots on the stairs, opening his safe and emptying its contents into the bag, in too much of a hurry to count the diamonds, remembering at the last minute to scribble his name and address on the label in the hope that his fortune would be returned to him after the war.

One hundred and thirty-nine. The man wouldn't have had time to count them.

The officer picked up the pen and added the merchant's name and address to the inventory. Then, next to it, he added the words: one hundred and twenty.

CHAPTER 1

PRESENT DAY

Eddie Sangster tapped the Morris's brakes as he neared the junction. A pall of snow had shrouded the land since the heavy fall earlier in the day. It wasn't often that Dundee had such weather, but he'd expected the ploughs to have cleared the road by now. Yet, as with so much in life, expectation and reality were two different things. He was now anxious to be home. The sun set early in February, right enough. Although the snow reflected what little light there was, the clouds had long since dispersed, leaving the frozen stars to gleam only faintly, and darkness to settle on the land.

Eddie knew these roads well, the fields corn-yellow in summer and ridged brown in winter, so he'd not bothered buying one of these navigation contraptions because he could find his way easily enough by the landmarks he'd known since childhood – the characteristic stone walls, the rise and fall of the land, the ancient trees, the places where woodland began and ended. But with this endless cladding of snow, one field or tree looked very much like another, and he felt strangely unnerved. However, the approaching junction was one he recognised, and it told him he hadn't far to go. Once back at the Hall, he would settle himself beside the fire with a glass of Balvenie. It was one of the few pleasures left to him. Aye, perhaps the only pleasure. Other than going for his wee drives.

He turned left on to the narrow road, relieved to see that the local farmer had swept away the snow. That was something, at least, and meant he could get his speed up. The Traveller's engine purred into life as he rammed his foot on the accelerator. Ach, that was more like it. The headlights picked out the trees on either side, the snow banked up against the trunks, the branches spectral white.

Ahead was the treacherous bend. But as he slowed and was preparing to rev up to take the curve, he thought he saw something stir in the trees. Aye, there it was – a figure slipping into the woodland. It stopped suddenly, then wheeled round to gaze in his direction. It was a man, Eddie saw then. He seemed to be breathing heavily, the breath condensing into fog that veiled his face. And then the image faded as the headlights slid away, and the car accelerated into the bend.

There was something about the way the man had held himself that made Eddie's throat tighten. He had a sudden presentiment that he'd not been there by chance, that he'd been waiting. But why? For him, perhaps? The thoughts were swirling round his head when he heard a metallic bang. Something seemed to grip the car and yank it off course. He grabbed at the wheel and tried to steady the vehicle, but no sooner had he straightened it than he saw something that made his heart lurch. A looming, amorphous shape blocked the road. He would never pull up in time. He slammed his foot on the brake, simultaneously swerving to the right. The bumper hit the object, causing the car to fish-tail wildly, and in a sweat of panic he knew he'd lost control. And then, in one blinding second, he understood who had been standing watching from the woodland.

A moment later, crashing thunder shook his body and he heard a noise, like the splinter of bones. On the threshold of consciousness, he thought he saw the figure again. Then darkness raced past him.

'Come on, Gorska! You can do it!'

DI Dania Gorska wiped the mud from her eyes, wondering yet again why she'd agreed to take part in the team-building assault course. Climbing the ten-foot wall at speed followed by the twenty-foot net had been bad enough, but then there were the obstacles to jump over and crawl under, to say nothing of dragging herself through pipes and swinging from trees. And this was at night, under the glare of arc lights because the course was used for commando training during the day. At least she didn't have to carry full pack, she thought sourly. And the morning's snow had been shovelled away. That was something, although it had left the ground soggy and slippery. No concession had been made for this by the instructor, Sergeant William Fairbairn.

The course had been the brainchild of DCI Jackie Ireland, a woman who'd started out in the military before moving to Police Scotland. The others in Dania's team, specifically DS Honor Randall, had been enthusiastic. That is until they'd seen what they were expected to do and how little time they had in which to do it. Sergeant Fairbairn, a muscular man with a washboard stomach, had tutored them thoroughly, giving them enough time to master the various stations of the course. After a short break, they then had thirty minutes in which to complete it. Today, it was only Dania and Honor who were on the list.

Dania was less than halfway through when she glimpsed someone running over the turf towards Fairbairn. She was about to start climbing the netting when she felt a firm hand on her shoulder. The sergeant gripped her arm and pulled her to one side.

'Sorry, Gorska, that's as far as you go.'

'Have I done something wrong?' she said, panting.

He smiled. 'Aye, and I never thought I'd hear a copper say that.' He had striking blue eyes and close-cropped hair, which could have been dark, but it was hard to tell in the weird light. 'You're wanted back at HQ.' He released her arm. 'Pity. I thought we could have gone for a wee bevvy afterwards.'

'I'm on duty.'

He had an easy laugh. A wee bevvy would have made the exertions of the day worth it, Dania thought, trying to keep her eyes on his face.

He inclined his head. 'You can come back next week and do it again if you want. I'll keep a place for you.'

She thought of the brutal assault course, the exhaustion, the mud in her hair, and decided she would be tied up with whatever this new case would be.

'Perhaps my colleague would be free for a drink,' she said, watching Honor crawling under the low planking.

'Randall?' he said, following her gaze. 'Aye, maybe.'

She left him studying Honor's wriggling backside and headed towards the main building. After a quick shower, she climbed into the Fiat 500 and was soon heading west on the A92 towards the city centre.

'A car crash?' Dania drew her brows together.

'I wouldn't have pulled you off your course,' Jackie Ireland said, 'but there's evidence it wasn't a simple accident. We had a phone call from another driver, who said he saw the car hit a tree. When he went over to investigate, there was a man leaning in. He ran off sharpish when he saw him.'

'Have the SOCOs arrived?'

'Aye, and Milo's already out there.' The DCI glanced at Dania's wet hair, then nodded at the pegs on the wall. 'You'd better take my woollen hat. You'll catch pneumonia otherwise.'

Back in the Fiat, Dania punched in the coordinates Hamish Downie had texted, and started the engine. She turned the heating to the highest setting, wishing now that she'd grabbed a coffee before leaving the station. Tiredness was settling in her bones, and she wondered if she'd be able to stay awake. The city streets had been cleared of snow – if piling it up on the pavements could be called clearing – but where she was headed was part of Dundee's rural hinterland, and she doubted the snow ploughs had been in action. From what she'd gathered, it was left to the individual farmers to deal with the roads and, if they thought the snow would melt soon enough, they didn't always bother. She would need to be alert. She turned the heating down.

The scene of the accident was north of the A90, but to get there meant negotiating the roundabout at Longforgan and hoping she didn't miss the underpass. She'd never have found it in the dark, but then that was why God had invented sat-navs. It was as she'd expected: the roads were mostly uncleared. She eased her foot off the pedal and shifted down to second gear.

It wasn't difficult to spot the crash site. A number of arc lamps had been erected, their eerie light illuminating the white-suited people wandering around like ghosts. The snow had been shovelled away, which meant that the SOCOs would have a better chance of picking up clues. Assuming there were any.

As she drew near, she caught sight of the blue vehicle, its nose up against a tree. Milo Slaughter, the chief pathologist at Ninewells Hospital, was speaking with someone holding a camera. It could only be Lisa. She had a keen eye for detail and was the photographer of choice of everyone at West Bell Street.

Dania pulled up behind a row of vehicles. Hamish drew away from the group and hurried over with a suit, latex gloves and over-shoes.

'Love the hat, ma'am,' he said wryly, watching her struggle into the suit. 'Correct me if I'm wrong, but doesn't the DCI have one like it?'

Dania smiled. 'I couldn't possibly comment.'

The hat had been the cause of hilarity at West Bell Street. With its bright stripes and cat's ears it was more the kind a child would wear. It said something about Jackie Ireland's standing that no one said anything to her face. And it said something about her personality that she wore it without a trace of embarrassment.

'So, bring me up to speed, Hamish.'

'It looks like an accident, but the professor believes there's something not right about this.'

'A man was seen loitering and behaving suspiciously, I understand.'

'Aye, that's about all we have so far. The witness is a local man, Tam Adie.'

'Adie? I think I know that name.'

'He was fair shaken by what he saw. He said the car swerved and hit the tree.'

'Where was he when this happened?'

'In his car, a black Volkswagen Polo. He was travelling from the other direction, which is how he saw the accident. He left the Polo and hurried across. The driver's door was open, and there was a man bent over, leaning inside. At first, he thought the driver had managed to get out, so he called to him. But as soon as the man saw him, he legged it and disappeared into the woodland.'

'And Adie called the police?'

'That's about the size of it. I came straight over with one of the uniforms. Tam was sitting in his car, waiting for us. I took a statement, then sent him home.'

'I take it he didn't check for signs of life?'

'Aye, he didn't. He assumed, given the force of the crash, that the driver was dead. And he added he didn't want to contaminate the scene.' Hamish threw her a crooked smile. 'Maybe those detective shows on telly have done some good, eh.'

'Okay, Hamish, thanks.'

She ducked under the tape and made her way to the car. It was an old model, she saw then, an estate vehicle with wood along the sides and across the two rear doors.

Milo glanced up. 'Dania, good to see you.' He peered at her over his half-moon glasses. 'I hear you've been training to become a commando.'

'Who told you that?'

'Hamish. He was relieved he had to stay behind and hold the fort at West Bell Street.'

'His chance will come next week,' she said, savouring the thought of the stocky Hamish hurtling through the trees on a zip wire.

She turned her attention to the car. The driver's door was open, giving her a clear view of the heavy figure slumped face down over the wheel, his arms dangling. There was no air bag. What she could see of his dark hair was flecked with grey, and blood had seeped through it and trickled into his ear. His sheepskin jacket was worn and patched in places, although the matching gloves looked new. His head was almost touching the windscreen, which had shattered so completely that the mere touch of a finger would dislodge the webbed glass. She brought her face close to the man's skull, then straightened and gazed at Milo. From the expression on his face, he'd seen it too – the array of wounds to the back of the head.

'I'm about to move him,' he said. He glanced at the photographer. 'Ready, Lisa?' He leant into the car and gripped the man's shoulders. Using no more force than was necessary, he eased him back and rested him against the seat. It was then that Dania noticed he wasn't wearing a seat belt.

Milo stepped back, inviting her to look.

The man's craggy, lined face put him in his sixties, although he might have been older. His eyes were open and their expression of terror made it clear he'd been fully aware of what had been about to happen. The purplish-blue bruise on his forehead and the smashed nose suggested that it was the force of the blow on hitting the windscreen that had killed him.

The photographer took several photos, then picked her way round to the other side, leant in at the open passenger door and took several more.

'That's me done, Prof,' she said, fiddling with the camera.

Trying not to disturb the clothing too much, Dania fished around in the man's pockets. She found only a crumpled white handkerchief, and a small colour photograph of a young woman with fluffy blonde hair. She was laughing as though she'd been caught out by whoever was taking the picture. Dania turned it over, but there was nothing scribbled on the back.

'His daughter, perhaps?' Milo said, peering over her shoulder.

'Or his wife when she was young.'

Dania beckoned to one of the SOCOs, who put the photo into an evidence bag.

She made her way to the passenger side and checked the glove compartment. It contained a single item: a Morris Traveller handbook.

'Is that what this car is?' she said to Milo. 'A Morris Traveller?'

'Indeed. You don't see many of them around these days.'

'There's no indication of who he is. We'll have to get an ID from the DVLA.' She glanced at Milo. 'Do you know much about these cars?'

'I used to drive one, would you believe. I bought it when I was a student. Lovely maroon colour. There was a girl in my class I wanted to impress, you see, and I thought having a car would do it.'

Dania looked at him with curiosity. She knew nothing about his private life. She didn't even know if he was married. 'And did you?' she said. 'Impress her, I mean?'

'Alas, no. She fell for a boy with a motorbike. The two of them dropped out of medical school and went touring round the world.'

Dania smiled. 'I see. And do you happen to know if Morris Travellers come with air bags?'

'Not as far as I'm aware; at least mine didn't when I bought it. Although it may be possible to have them fitted. But don't quote me on that.'

'Kimmie should be able to tell me. What she doesn't know about cars isn't worth knowing.'

'And what's your current thinking? That there's an air bag installed, and it failed?'

'It's possible. But what puzzles me more is that he wasn't wearing his seat belt.'

Milo frowned. 'It never fails to amaze me that even now there are people stupid enough not to buckle up. Right, I'd better get him to the mortuary.'

She watched him leave with one of the SOCOs, then called Hamish over. 'This man that Tam Adie claimed to have seen leaning into the car. Did he give you an indication of where he was headed? You mentioned woodland.'

'Aye, into those trees behind you.'

She stared into the wood. The day-old snow covered the ground as far as she could see. 'What about footprints?'

'We thought of that. Johnty is already in there, following the tracks. He's using his scanner.'

'That must be a thankless task.'

'You know what Johnty's like. When it comes to footprints, he never lets up. He said he'll keep going until he gets to the other side. According to Google Maps, the woodland comes out on to a road. My guess is this unknown man left his car there.'

'I won't even ask if there are traffic cams.'

'Nothing for miles. The nearest are on the A90.'

'I wonder what made the car crash into the tree. Is there ice on the road?'

'If you come this way, ma'am, I'll show you.'

Hamish picked his way through the cluster of SOCOs, Dania following.

She gazed in astonishment at the shape in the road. 'Good Lord, I've never seen a deer *that* big.'

'He's fair bonnie, and no mistake. A red deer, according to SOCO.'

'Why hasn't it got antlers?'

'Aye, well, they shed them in winter, then regrow them.'

'Seems a waste of time and energy.' She glanced back towards the Morris. 'Okay, so he was driving along the road, saw the deer—'

'Hit it and crashed into the tree. Or swerved to avoid it and crashed into the tree.'

'Seems straightforward enough. But there's one thing that bothers me.'

'Aye?'

'He had wounds to the back of the head. Hitting the wind-screen wouldn't have caused that.'

'You think it was this man Tam Adie reported?'

'Possibly.' She examined the deer. 'This animal's been hit, which must have been the Morris Traveller. But the damage isn't enough to have killed it.'

'You think it was already dead?'

'And here's the evidence. See these tracks here?'

Hamish squatted on his haunches and peered at the ground. 'Aye, I ken what you mean.'

'They suggest the carcass was deliberately dragged.'

'Which means—'

'That whoever did it, intended to cause an accident.'

CHAPTER 2

It was close to ten before Dania let herself into her flat on Victoria Road. She was shaking with cold, although she put that down partly to exhaustion. What she needed was a nourishing meal, and a hot bath. But as soon as she stepped into the living room, she knew that something was wrong. It was so icy, she could see her breath clouding the air.

She hurried into the kitchen and opened the door to the boiler cupboard. The machine was stone cold. Pressing the restart button did nothing: instead of the boiler whooshing into life, it sat there, stubbornly refusing to ignite. Was it a problem with the gas supply? She checked the gas fire in the spare bedroom, but it fired up normally. She swore softly. With the boiler dead, the tiny appliance was the only source of heat in the flat, as the other rooms had radiators. But even if she left it on all night, which wasn't a good idea, she'd never heat the place sufficiently to get the temperature up. There was only one thing to do. She pulled out her phone.

A short while later, she was pressing the buzzer to her brother's apartment. She'd had the presence of mind to call him first in case he was entertaining a lady, but she was in luck. Or he was out of it, depending on which way you viewed these things.

The door opened. She was surprised to see Marek dressed more casually than usual in jeans and dark blue sweater. It suggested he'd had the day off. Or, given that his straw-blonde hair was more messy than usual, maybe he'd come back from an undercover investigation. A third possibility, which gave Dania a twinge of guilt, was that he had indeed had a lady with him, and on receiving Dania's call had asked her to leave.

'Danka, come in,' he said, in Polish. His expression changed to one of alarm. 'What happened to you? You look terrible.'

'Thanks.' She stepped into the hall and dropped her overnight bag on the floor.

He seemed to remember himself then. 'Have you had anything to eat?'

'Not since lunchtime.'

'I made soup earlier. I'll heat it up.'

Her spirits lifted. 'What kind is it?'

'*Solianka*. With mushrooms.'

There were three variants of this Russian soup. It could be made with fish, meat or mushrooms, and in all of them Marek used Maggi seasoning, which he obtained in stock-cube form. Her preference would have been for meat, but she was in no position to object and, anyway, everything her brother made tasted good. When it came to culinary talent, she was the polar opposite. She'd discussed this once with her mother. They'd concluded that, with twins and cooking ability, God divides: one twin gets the talent in the kitchen, the other gets it somewhere else. In her case, it was the piano.

She flopped on to the kitchen chair and pulled off the DCI's hat. Her hair was damp and scrunched up, and probably looked awful. But she was beyond caring.

Marek was cutting thick slices of dark rye bread. 'And the boiler's packed in, you said?'

'Completely.'

'Did you check the fuse?'

'No need. The starter-button light was on, but nothing happened when I pressed it.' She ran a hand over her face. 'Thanks for putting me up. I couldn't bear the thought of sleeping in that cold flat. You wouldn't believe the day I've had.'

He glanced at her. 'You look as though you've been in the wars.'

'In a way I have. I was on an assault course earlier.'

'What on earth made you sign up for one of those?'

'It's part of a team-building initiative at Police Scotland.'

'In your case, I don't know why they'd bother. You've built a great team. They'd walk through fire for you.'

Dania stared at him in surprise, wondering what had made him reach this conclusion. He hardly knew her colleagues. Then she remembered the number of times their cases had collided, some of which had nearly led to his arrest by members of said team. As an investigative journalist, he occasionally crossed the line. But then, as a detective inspector, so did she. When her promotion had come through it was not, as she'd suspected, for loyalty and following correct procedure, but for getting results.

He brought the soup and bread to the table. 'Now tell me more about this course. Is it only the brass who get to go?'

'We're all doing it. And there's a test at the end. You have to keep taking it until you pass.' She wondered idly how Honor had fared. And whether she was now on a hot date with Sergeant Fairbairn. Lucky Honor.

'And who catches the bad guys when you're climbing walls and jumping over obstacles?'

'It's staggered. Honor and I were the only ones on today.' She took a spoonful of the *solianka*. 'This is divine,' she murmured.

'There's plenty more.' He studied her. 'And you're back from this course only now?'

'I was pulled off it early,' she said, remembering that, since she hadn't completed it, she would have to return. She could feel her shoulders sagging.

'A case?'

'A car crash.'

'Surely you don't get assigned those. You're in the Murder Squad.'

'Someone went to great lengths to make it look like an accident.'

'I've read so many cases where murderers tried to do that. Either accident or suicide. And they always made a mistake. It could be a tiny error, but it betrayed them every time.'

'Like the rifle fired through the mouth, made to look like suicide, but the arms were too short to reach the trigger?'

'Or the body placed in the driver's seat in a car, which had been driven to a viaduct and shoved over, but on examination the seat had been pushed back and the victim's feet couldn't reach the pedals. So was your case like that? The victim was already dead when the car crashed?'

'His injuries suggested he'd definitely driven the car himself. What raised our suspicions was that there's evidence of trauma to the back of the head.'

Marek cleared away the plates. 'Had it been me, I'd have employed a contract killer.'

'Who would have kept the evidence that you'd employed him and blackmailed you for the rest of your life.' She watched him make coffee. 'Anyway, what are you up to these days?'

'Today's task was to write up my recent investigation.'

'Will I be reading about it in the *Courier*?'

He threw her a strange look. 'You'll be reading about it at West Bell Street. I've sent my findings to the Fraud Squad. One of the local councillors is on the take. He's been getting backhanders from Euan Leslie.'

'The gangster? I mean the property developer?'

Marek smiled. 'You were right the first time. Anyway, I managed to infiltrate the company.'

'Leslie's?'

'Don't look so surprised.'

'What I'm surprised about is that you're not floating in the Tay with your throat cut. I take it he doesn't know who you are?'

'He will do when he reads the article. I used my *nom de guerre*, Franek Filarski, when I worked for him, but he'll know from the details that Franek Filarski and Marek Gorski are one and the same.'

She felt her pulse quicken. 'That was stupid, Marek,' she said, making her voice hard. 'Are you saying your real name will be on the article?'

'Whether it is or it isn't hardly matters,' he said, bringing the mugs to the table. 'Even if my name is withheld, he'll put two and two together. He has the contacts to trace the article's author. And there are plenty of photos of me around if you know where to look. I did disguise my appearance, but it's not too much of a stretch to conclude that Franek Filarski is Marek Gorski.'

'Leslie will be after you.'

'Leslie will be locked up.'

'Don't be so sure. He's managed to stay out of prison so far.' She placed her hands on the table. 'Look, Marek, can you delay publishing?'

'Why would I do that?'

She was tempted to say, 'To give you a chance to leave the country,' but she knew how it would sound. And her brother wasn't the type to go into hiding. It wasn't the first time he'd put himself in harm's way to get a scoop. He seemed to relish the thrill of the chase, the danger even. What *she* didn't relish was having to bail him out, although she was doing less of that these days as her own cases were starting to mount.

She brushed her sleeve across her eyes. 'At least wait to see if the Fraud Squad decide to pick him up.'

'You know I can't do that,' he said, opening the fridge. 'The other papers will get hold of the story and my advantage will be gone. Anyway, it won't come out for a day or two.' He pulled a bottle out of the freezer. 'Time for a nightcap. I thought we'd give this a try.' He set the glasses on the table.

She frowned at the black bottle with the familiar bison on the front. 'Is that what I think it is?'

'Żubrówka Czarna. Black Żubrówka.'

'Here, let me see.'

'I've been reading up on it. The filtration process uses charcoal from oak trees in the Białowieża forest, which of course is where the bison grass grows. They've added two botanicals – mint and juniper. And the water comes from springs in the Białowieża. It's all good.'

'Remember that trip we took there as children, looking for bison?'

'That was a wasted effort. We didn't stumble across a single one.'

What they did stumble across were graves. It was after they'd returned to Warsaw that her father had told them about the Polish and Soviet partisans who'd taken refuge in the forest. And the Gestapo executions that had followed.

She opened the bottle and poured.

'Well?' he said, after a while. 'What do you think?'

'It's hard to say. How do you describe such a subtle taste? It's definitely Żubrówka. But different.'

'Are you giving it a thumbs up?'

'Absolutely.'

'Glad you like it. I wasn't sure.'

They sat in silence for a while. 'Shall I make more coffee?' Marek said eventually.

Dania finished the vodka, then poured herself another shot. 'I think I'll stick with this.'

'Thanks for getting on to it so quickly, Kimmie,' Dania said.

The Australian threw her a dazzling smile. 'No worries. You know I clear my desk when you come calling. Your cases are always the most interesting.'

They were in the large 'garage' under Kimmie's forensics lab. Unlike most garages, it was kept scrupulously clean. It had to be, as the forensic work carried out there could make the difference between a case being solved or being shelved. Cars stood about the place, some with their wheels off, and one with its engine in pieces on the floor.

The Morris Traveller was parked near the front. It looked bluer than Dania remembered, but that was because arc lamps tend to bleach everything. Next to the Morris was a tray holding a variety of power tools. She guessed the girl and her team had spent the morning taking the vehicle apart, and then putting it back together.

Kimmie was the station's chief forensics officer, and someone Dania had enormous respect for. They'd worked together on many occasions and Dania had learnt much from her. The girl's stunning appearance and sunny character were not lost on the men at West Bell Street and, whenever Dania paid her a visit, she had no shortage of volunteers clamouring to accompany her. But this afternoon she was on her own, having left her team with instructions to track down the owner of the Traveller. It didn't help that the DVLA's computer system was down. Honor, back from her triumph at the assault course – she'd completed it in a mere twenty-five minutes – was ringing round the local garages to see if they'd serviced a Morris Traveller. Someone had suggested contacting the many Morris Minor Owners clubs across the UK. Although the Morris involved in the crash wasn't a Minor, the clubs might be able to help. Failing that, if the DVLA wasn't back online soon, they would have to get the photo from the victim's pocket into the media.

'It's a long time since I've seen a beaut like this,' Kimmie said, eyeing the car.

'Is it fitted with an air bag?'

'You're wondering if the bag was tampered with.'

'It crossed my mind.'

'This model never had them, and this one hasn't been retro-fitted. But it's been kept in good nick. The wood can rot easily on Travellers, but not on this one. If anything, it's been varnished recently.' She grinned. 'The sort of people who buy a Morris are enthusiasts, who treat them like their own kids. You know the type. Every weekend is spent attending club events where owners show them off. So they have to lavish heaps of attention on the bodywork.'

'I knew someone like that at the Met. But it was a Lagonda, not a Morris. So, as well as the wood, the rest of the car's in good shape, you said?'

'Take a look.' Kimmie lifted the bonnet.

'I'm not an expert, but this engine looks deceptively simple.'

'Morrises were made before the advent of on-board computers. If you know anything about cars, you can maintain these yourself. This one's been lovingly looked after. Okay, there's a bit of rust, but everything is original, including the clutch and gearbox, which is behind here. There are owners who dislike the fact that not all the gears have synchromesh, so they make changes. But this owner was obviously happy with double de-clutching.'

Dania hoped her expression didn't betray that she had no idea what synchromesh or double de-clutching were. She doubted she'd know even if she looked up the terms in Polish.

'How old would this car be?' she said.

'They stopped making them in the early 1970s. Now, I'm guessing you want to know about the damage to the bodywork. Have a look at the passenger side. First thing to note is that there were two impacts.'

'Two? The deer and the tree?'

Kimmie shook her head. 'The car hit the tree head on. But I'm talking about the damage to the *side*. See the bumper and bodywork? And the smashed headlight? That wasn't caused by the deer. It was something much harder. The driver hit another object first, then smacked into the animal. Time to come up to the lab. There's something there you need to see.'

They took the lift to the ground floor, where the door opened directly on to the main lab. Whenever Dania entered the room, she imagined she was in a mad scientist's laboratory. Instruments and equipment of every kind were set out on the tables. And this was only one laboratory. Kimmie had several more leading off, one of which was used for test-firing weapons.

Kimmie operated the controls on the wide screen, and a

23

schematic of the crash site appeared. The blue Morris Traveller was some distance from the deer. 'Now watch this,' she said. She pressed a button and the vehicle moved forward. Without warning, it jerked violently and veered to the right. Kimmie paused the image. 'It's at this point that the bumper was crushed. And this is the culprit.'

On the table next to the window were three large pieces of weathered stone.

'The SOCOs found them at the side of the road — the passenger side — several metres from the deer. As soon as they saw they weren't ordinary stones, they had them taken straight to the lab.' Kimmie drew on her gloves and moved the fragments together. They fitted perfectly to make what looked like a rectangular headstone. 'The driver is unlikely to have seen it, especially in the dark.'

'So, he hit it and lost control.'

'There'd have been an almighty bang, and the sound of glass shattering. That would have done it for most people. They'd have been too shocked to react in time. However, judging by the wheel marks, he managed to straighten up, but then the other headlight caught the deer.'

'Wouldn't he have swerved to avoid it?'

'There's evidence he tried, but he was too late. Once he hit the deer, all bets were off. Had that blasted tree not been there, he might have survived. But those trees are close together.' She shrugged. 'Miss one and you hit another. We've reconstructed what his final journey would have looked like. I can show you from start to finish, in slow motion.'

Back at the screen, she played with the controls.

Dania watched the Morris move forward, hit the stone, veer

wildly and straighten up. Then it swerved suddenly, but not enough to avoid delivering the deer a massive, glancing blow.

'See these wheel marks all over the place?' Kimmie said, tracing their outline. 'He was well out of control at this point. I'll show you the photos we took of the pieces before and after we scraped off the moss.' She tapped the screen and a series of stills appeared. 'I, too, thought it was a headstone, given its size. That is, until I saw what was carved on it.'

A new image appeared of the reconstructed stone. On it were engraved the following words:

This stone was erected to the memory of Watson Sangster.
Cruelly murdered near here.

Remember – Thou shalt not kill.

'I've never seen anything like it,' Dania said slowly. 'There's no date. How old do you think it is?'

Kimmie rubbed her chin. 'Given the amount of weathering, I'd say twenty, thirty years, something like that.'

Dania returned to the table and examined the stones. The lettering looked modern, unlike the curling script on Victorian headstones.

'Why was the stone erected there?' she said, more to herself.

'Murdered near here, it says. If he was murdered, he'll be in your files.'

'I wonder if this has anything to do with the crash.'

'About that: there's a good case for saying it was a set-up.'

'The deer being dragged into the road, you mean?'

'Those tracks speak for themselves. Yes, the animal was dead before it was hit.'

'Can you tell how it died?'

Kimmie worked the screen's controls. 'See this X-ray? The skull is badly smashed. Some, though not all, of that damage could have been inflicted by the Morris. There are no other marks on the body, except for one. We checked the animal's ear. The tag had been carefully removed, but not carefully enough that we didn't spot the mark.'

'Meaning it was stolen from somewhere like a farm.'

'That's my guess. But killing a deer and dragging it into the middle of a road isn't normal behaviour for lads wanting to do something for a lark. You need a fair bit of planning, including taking the animal. So you have to ask yourself why someone would go to all that trouble.'

'Someone was planning a murder. Possibly the man who was seen leaning into the car.'

'We've still to get Johnty's report on the footprints. He's trying to identify the boots the guy was wearing. You know what Johnty's like,' she added, grinning. 'He thinks he's Sherlock Holmes.'

'Don't we all.' Dania smiled. 'But he's come good in the past, so he's worth the wait.'

'I'll whizz over these video clips and images, then. Before you go, any thoughts on when our glee club's meeting again?'

Dania had been persuaded to join Kimmie's Edith Piaf Singing Society. The group – all women – met fortnightly to belt out the French singer's livelier songs. Fortunately, Dania wasn't expected to sing, just accompany them on the piano. To begin with, there had been six members, and she'd had no problem fitting them into her living room, where she had the Bechstein. But word had soon got around and now there were twenty. Not only was it a crush, but the man next door had complained that he couldn't watch footie with 'that racket going on'. The group's last session had been a month ago, and they still hadn't found a suitable venue.

'I asked my neighbour if he wanted to join the group,' Dania said. 'You know, sort of in the tent pissing out rather than the other way round.'

Kimmie's eyes widened. 'The guy with the orange hair? What was his reaction?'

'Not encouraging. I'll keep my ears open. There might be a church hall we can hire.'

'That'll cost big bikkies.'

'Maybe not.'

As they chatted, Dania wondered what a local might make of their conversation: a woman with a strong Australian accent nattering to one with a strong Polish accent. Maybe they should both learn Dundonian.

When Dania entered the incident room, she found only Honor and Hamish at their desks.

'Any joy with identification?' she said, dropping her bag on the chair.

'Yep,' Honor said, gazing at her screen. 'We've got it.'

'DVLA back online?'

'We found the owner through the car's MOT. The deceased was an Edward Sangster.'

'*Sangster?*'

Honor glanced up. 'You know the name, boss?'

Briefly, Dania filled her colleagues in on what she'd learnt at Kimmie's.

'Seems a bit of a coincidence, ma'am,' Hamish said. 'Edward Sangster hits a headstone with the name Watson Sangster on it.'

'How common is the name Sangster? Maybe there are loads in that area. We should check whether they're related. And have we a next of kin for Edward?'

'He lived in Sangster Hall with his son, Duncan, and daughter-in-law, Grace,' Honor said. 'It's not far from the crash site. I've got the postcode.'

'Right, let's go.'

There was one squad car left in the car park, and Honor signed it out before anyone else did. Dania was relieved they didn't have to take her Fiat 500, as it wasn't fitted with winter tyres. For that matter, neither was Honor's Ford Fiesta.

The sun was close to setting as they cruised along the A90. The traffic was heading west, as commuters left the city to return to the outlying villages, some even travelling as far as Perth. Dania wondered how many of their jobs could be done from home. Perhaps the day would come when something happened that would open their eyes to that possibility.

'You'll have to slow down,' she said, seeing the Longforgan sign. 'I nearly missed the turn-off. And the roads start to narrow. Some have passing places. They're hard to spot normally, but they're almost impossible with this snow.'

'No problem. The sat-nav will keep me right.'

Honor had changed the device's clipped female voice to a husky American male. 'At the next roundabout, honey, take the fourth exit,' he crooned.

'That reminds me, what did you think of Sergeant Fairbairn?' Dania asked.

'A bit of a meatball. But a meatball with gravy,' Honor added hastily.

'And how did you two get on?'

She pulled a face. 'Not brilliantly, if I'm honest. We went for drinkies, but he spent the whole evening asking questions about you. He finds your accent unbelievably sexy. Wanted to know if you're with anyone.' She threw Dania a glance. 'I think you're in with a chance there, boss.'

'Did he say anything about the fact that I was pulled off the course?'

'Oh, yes,' Honor said, drawing out the words. 'He can't give you a certificate until you complete it. And pass the test. Did I tell you it only took me twenty-five minutes?'

'Several times.'

'It's one of their best scores. Most people who pass take just over twenty-nine. Crikey, you're right about these roads,' she added, slowing down sharply.

'The forecast is for more snow tomorrow.'

'We hardly ever see snow here. I bet you have tons in Poland.'

Dania thought back to her childhood, and the bone-piercing cold of Poland's winters. But there were compensations. Once everyone left their dreary, grey communist apartment blocks – known as *bloki* in the vernacular – they took their sledges and headed for Wilanów Park with its colourful Christmas lights. In Warsaw, it was the only show in town.

'What I remember is standing in the snow, singing *kolędy*, or Christmas carols. The cold would tear at the back of my throat whenever I breathed. It was particularly painful when I took a huge intake of air.'

'Do you miss it?'

'Doesn't everyone miss the Christmases they had when they were children?'

'Yep. It's somehow never the same when you're an adult. By

the way, boss, how much are we telling the Sangsters? Are we even hinting that we have our suspicions?'

'Until we hear from Milo, we say only that Edward died in a car accident.'

'What about Watson Sangster, and that headstone?'

'Again, nothing. Not until we've made our enquiries. I don't want the Sangsters jumping to conclusions.'

'A headstone, though, saying someone was murdered. How weird is that?'

'And it's the word "murder" that makes me want to keep it quiet until we see what Hamish digs up.'

'Unfortunate choice of phrase, boss,' Honor said primly.

'Okay, we're getting close. It should be just ahead, according to the sat-nav. Look, there's the sign. On the left.'

Honor slowed to a crawl. A minute later, they found the entrance. The sat-nav voice purred, 'Y'all have reached your destination. Now, you're not gonna leave me all by my lonesome here, are you, honey?'

'You've got to love him,' Honor said, grinning. She cruised through the tall, ornamental gates past the sign with SANGSTER HALL in large letters.

The wide asphalted drive, cleared and salted, was flanked on both sides by trees whose leaves had long since fallen. Through the wilderness of bare branches, Dania glimpsed the snow-covered fields stretching endlessly to the horizon, broken only by the odd shed or farm building. Straight ahead, tiny Sangster Hall slowly grew larger. There was a light in one of the ground-floor windows. In summer, the house would have been swallowed up by the trees, whereas now it dominated the landscape. The drive, which led directly to the front entrance, took them past a slabbed area. Honor pulled up next to a white Kia Picanto.

'Whoa, boss, that's some pile. What would you call that? A manor house? A country house?'

'A mansion.'

It was hard to say whether the three-storey stone building was late Georgian or early Victorian, as architecture had never been one of Dania's interests. It was a sprawling, highly asymmetrical house with an octagonal tower at one end. The steep roof suggested there was an attic you could stand up in, although, from the size and layout, there were likely to be several attics.

Next to the building was a red-brick, modern house, which looked as though the architect had put it in the wrong place.

They climbed out of the car and made their way to the massive wooden door. Dania had the strangest sensation that she was standing outside a prison, except that the entrances to prisons were usually in better condition: the wood at the bottom of this door was starting to buckle. She leant on the buzzer, hearing it echo deep inside the building.

Moments later, there were footsteps, then the door opened with such a loud creak that Dania wondered when it had last been moved. Perhaps there was a better-used entrance round the back.

A man wearing a tweed jacket in a mustard-and-olive tartan stood looking at them enquiringly.

'Mr Sangster?' Dania said.

'Yes.'

'Mr Duncan Sangster?'

'That's right. How can I help you?'

'We're police officers,' she said, holding up her warrant. 'DI Gorska, and this is DS Randall.'

The man drew his dark brows together. He had a squarish face, and black hair with a thick fringe. The high colour in his cheeks suggested he'd been drinking. 'Has something happened?' he said, an expression of alarm in his blue-grey eyes.

'May we come in?'

He hesitated. 'Of course.' He stood back to let them enter.

The dark room was more of a reception area than a foyer. The furniture consisted of a modern-looking desk and chair on the left, and an empty clothes rack with wire hangers on the right.

'Would you like us to take these off?' Dania said, as she and Honor wiped their boots on the coir doormat.

'No need. Our carpets and rugs have been specially treated.'

He opened the door into a wide, well-lit hallway with doors to left and right. It was carpeted in a heavy-duty weave in a nondescript neutral shade.

A door to the left opened, and a worried-looking woman appeared. She was in baggy jeans and a heavy-knit red sweater that was two sizes too big.

'What is it, Duncan?' she said, hurrying into the hall. Her mousy-brown hair framed an oval face, but her most striking feature was her deep, dark eyes.

'These are police officers,' he said, glancing at her. 'DI Gorska and—'

'DS Randall,' Honor said.

'My wife, Grace.'

'Please, come into the living room,' the woman said, her smile wavering.

The high-panelled room was spacious enough to contain several three-piece suites in the same old-fashioned floral material. If Dania had been worried about marking the oak parquet, she needn't have, as it was almost completely covered with shabby, overlapping oriental rugs. They added colour to the room but managed at the same time to jar with the sofas' flower patterns, making her wonder how long it would be before anyone sitting here came down with a migraine. The fireplace was one of those you could stand up in. Logs smouldered on the hearth, suggesting that the fire had only recently been lit, which would explain the chill in the room. The wood suddenly caught and shifted, sending up sparks, the flames briefly illuminating the dull gold of the picture frames. They were portraits, all men, and all with the same thick black hair as Duncan's. One was a uniformed officer, who gazed down at Dania, a sneering smile under his trimmed moustache.

As she moved deeper into the room, she was struck by the lack of ornaments. Other than the old-style red telephone on the sideboard, the only objects were the bottle of Balvenie and the whisky glasses on the coffee table.

Duncan indicated the sofa nearest the hearth. He and his wife settled themselves in the armchairs opposite. 'I must apologise for the temperature,' he said. He rested his hands on his knees. 'We've been out for the day. My father must have forgotten to light the fire, right enough.'

'Aye, we only got it going half an hour ago,' Grace said, glancing at her husband.

There was silence for a moment, then Dania said, 'I'm afraid I have bad news.' She looked from one to the other. 'Your father, Edward, was killed in a car crash yesterday evening.'

'But he can't have been!' Grace blurted. 'He's in his room. You must be mistaken.'

'When did you last see him?' Dania said, wondering if they'd made a monumental blunder and someone other than Edward Sangster had been driving.

Duncan seemed to wake as if from a trance. 'It would have been yesterday morning. He was instructing one of the estate workers to clear away the snow.'

'What about yesterday evening? Was he at dinner?'

'We were out. We didn't get back till late.' He swallowed hard. 'We didn't see him at breakfast today but that's nothing new. He often rises early and takes breakfast alone.'

'We can check his room,' Grace said promptly. She didn't seem to want to let go of the idea that Edward was still alive. Dania had seen this before: relatives for whom the idea of a deceased loved one was too much to take in. The first reaction was disbelief. Pain came later.

Grace was looking pleadingly at her husband. 'I'll phone the room.'

'Phone the *room*?' Honor said.

Duncan ran a hand over his eyes. 'He lives in another wing. There are so many rooms in the different parts of this building that we have an internal phone system. I'll do it, Grace,' he added, as she made to get up.

He walked across to the sideboard and snatched up the red receiver. With a shaking hand, he pressed the buttons on the telephone and waited, the receiver to his ear. 'No reply,' he murmured, after a while. 'And he hasn't got a mobile.'

Dania was about to suggest they go in person to Edward's room when Duncan said: 'A car accident, was it, Inspector? Are you sure it's him?' He returned to his seat.

'He was driving a blue Morris Traveller.' She opened her notebook and read out the registration number. 'There was no identification but we found this photo in his pocket.' She handed it to Duncan.

The light vanished from his eyes. 'That's my mother, right enough,' he said, in a cracked voice. 'She passed away last year.'

Grace made a small sound, and her hands flew to her mouth. 'Och, Eddie,' she said, in a muffled voice.

'Didn't you suspect anything when you saw the Morris Traveller wasn't parked outside?' Dania said gently.

'That's nothing new,' Duncan said. 'He often went for a wee drive around this time of day.'

'Even with snow on the ground?'

'In all weathers.' He seemed to think about this. 'Was that what caused the accident? The snow?'

'We think so. He went into a tree. He wasn't wearing his seat belt.'

Duncan's eyes flared. 'Ach, we told him again and again,' he said, through clenched teeth. 'He never listened.'

'You're saying he was in the habit of leaving the seat belt undone?'

'He thought nothing would happen to him on these country roads. Seat belts are for driving in the city, he said.'

Grace looked searchingly at Dania. 'He used to go out for a wee spin with his wife, but it was always around these parts. Sometimes they went up to Liff, and other times over to Abernyte, to the antiques centre there.' She hesitated. 'He never got over her death. After the funeral, he kept to his room more and more.'

Duncan laid a hand on Grace's arm as if to indicate that he should deal with this. 'After my mother died, he continued his drives, although he didn't stay out as long. He told me he took a circular route, up to Knapp, then Fowlis, Benvie, and then back here.'

'Always the same route?'

'That's what he said. He loved those particular roads. He used to take that route often, even before he was married.' Duncan stared vacantly. 'Where did the accident happen?'

'Not far from here. I can show you on a map.'

Dania was about to pull out her phone when he hauled himself to his feet and marched into the hall. He returned a few moments later with an Ordnance Survey map. After moving the whisky glasses aside, he spread the map on the coffee table.

'Sangster Hall is here,' he said, tapping the sheet.

She studied the map. 'The accident occurred on this road, where the woodland starts.'

'Aye, that's part of his route.' Duncan shook his head sadly. 'If he lost control of the car, his mind must have been on other things. As Grace said, he never got over my mother's death.'

'What sort of a man was he, if you don't mind my asking?'

'What can I tell you? He was a great father. Instilled the ideals of hard work and perseverance into me, and no mistake.'

'Are you an only child?'

'Aye, that I am. I think my mother had problems with the birth and was warned against having more children.'

'And what do you do for a living?'

'I help—' He checked himself. 'I *helped* my father with the estate. But it's been going downhill for years. I don't mind telling you we have a mountain of debt to clear,' he added, with an embarrassed smile. 'Grace and I hit on the idea of leasing out the Hall for events and residential conferences. This house has so many rooms, it's ideal. It's a bit of a rabbit warren, if I'm honest, so we've put up signs in the corridors. There's an east wing, and a west wing, which is where we are now. And several in-between wings, I suppose you could call them.'

'We stay in the cottage next door when there are events,' Grace said nervously. 'We help with things like making breakfast, although the event organisers usually get caterers in. Then when it's over, we employ people to clean the rooms, do the laundry and so on. We have one or two permanent staff, but we've let most of the others go.'

'There's one more thing,' Dania said, after a pause. 'I need you to come in to Ninewells and make a formal identification. We can't conduct the post-mortem until that's been done.'

'Post-mortem?' Duncan said, lifting his head sharply. 'Why?' he added, his voice faltering.

'It's routine when there's an unexpected death, Mr Sangster.'

He considered this. 'Aye, okay.' He took his wife's hand. 'It doesn't need both of us, does it?'

Grace was staring at the detectives with huge, stricken eyes.

'Just yourself would be fine,' Dania said. 'We'll give you a call when we're ready.' She stood up. 'I should add that we may have further questions.'

An uneasy expression drifted into his eyes. 'Why do you say that, Inspector? Do you reckon it wasn't an accident?'

'Questions always come up, even during a routine investigation.'

'Of course.' After a silence, he said. 'I'll show you out.'

As she left the living room, Dania glanced back. Grace was holding a handkerchief over her face, sobbing quietly.

'What did you make of that, boss?' Honor said, when they were back on the road. 'Don't you think it strange that for over twenty-four hours they didn't notice Edward's disappearance?'

'In a rambling pile like that?' Dania stared out of the window. It had started snowing again, although only lightly, with the first snowflakes floating to earth and melting. 'I would have thought if you wanted to keep yourself to yourself you could do it easily.'

Honor switched on the wipers. 'I saw a film once about two families who lived in the same mansion. They met in the middle for Sunday lunch and to exchange news. Other than that, it was as if they were in separate houses.'

'We should have asked who else lives there. They mentioned permanent staff but I'm guessing they come in to do whatever they do, and then leave. I suspect it's just the three Sangsters in that place. Two, now.'

Honor's gaze was glued to the road. 'Not sure I could live in a house that big. I mean, I know the queen does it and all that, but I couldn't.'

'Why not?'

'The wind whistling through the cracks would get on my nerves pretty pronto. And those huge houses creak at night when they settle. I'd be constantly looking over my shoulder to see if anyone was there.'

'I didn't know you were so jittery, Honor.'

'I read Victorian novels at school. That did it.'

'I thought Duncan's wife was a bit highly strung.'

'She struck me as the type who can't function without a man at her back.'

'Just as well she's got one, then.' Dania gazed out at the cotton-wool flakes. 'The snow's getting heavier.'

'I'll drop you at your flat, boss, so you don't need to drive home in this. You can pick your car up from the station tomorrow.'

'Thanks.'

'Good thing you live near enough you can walk in.'

'Actually, could you stop on the Perth Road, at the top of Union Place? You can't miss it. It's opposite that wine-and-whisky shop.'

'I know it. The one with the green paint. Are you visiting your brother?'

'I'm staying with him. My boiler's out of action.'

Honor threw her a grin. 'And I bet he's doing the cooking.'

But as they pulled on to the Perth Road, Dania's thoughts drifted to the Sangsters' living room and its portraits. The thick black hair and pale eyes marked them as Sangsters, if Duncan was anything to go by. So which one was Watson?

CHAPTER 3

'Sorry I didn't have time to cook,' Marek said, as he threw the fish-and-chip wrappings into the kitchen bin. 'I was in the office and didn't manage to get to the Polski Sklep.'

Dania waved a dismissive hand. 'For heaven's sake, don't apologise. Anyway, fish and chips are a good substitute.'

'Did you manage to get through to the boiler people?'

'Are you trying to get rid of me?'

He smiled. 'Not at all. I'm just curious.'

'The good news is that I finally got them on the phone.'

'And the bad news?'

'They've been inundated with emergency call-outs. They said to phone them again on Friday.'

'Do you think boilers have been especially designed to break down when the weather turns bad?'

'Now you're being cynical.'

She watched him bustle about. He moved gracefully with the ease of someone who knows where everything is and doesn't have to keep opening cupboards. She wondered again whether, by staying at his, she was depriving him of a lady's company.

'Remember the car accident I told you about?' Dania said, as he brought the tea glasses to the table.

He pushed across the jar of cherry jam. 'The one you thought had been set up to kill the driver?'

'A deer had been dragged into the road. It turns out that before the driver hit it, he hit something else. It looked like a headstone. The name Watson Sangster was engraved on it, and there was further information to the effect that he'd been murdered.'

Marek lifted his head slowly. 'Watson Sangster, did you say?'

'You know the name?'

'It's not a headstone, Danka, it's a murder stone.'

'A what?'

'A stone that tells you that someone has been murdered. You don't get many here, although England has a few. They were erected mainly in the nineteenth century by the local community, or the relatives. Sometimes the murderer was caught and sent to the gallows. Sometimes not. Charles Dickens wrote a scene in *Nicholas Nickleby* where they come across a murder stone.' He left the kitchen and returned with his tablet. 'So, in *Nicholas Nickleby*, he and his pal Smike come across a stone marking the murder of a man known as the "Unknown Sailor". What's interesting is that this murder stone actually exists.'

'Really? Where?'

'In Surrey. An area called the Devil's Punch Bowl. It's outside Hindhead. Let me read you what Dickens wrote:

They walked upon the rim of the Devil's Punch Bowl; and Smike listened with greedy interest as Nicholas read the inscription upon the stone which, reared upon that wild spot, tells of a murder committed there by night. The grass on which they stood had once been dyed with gore; and the blood of the murdered man had run down, drop by drop, into the hollow which gives the place its name.

41

Marek held out the tablet. 'And here's a picture of that stone.'

'I can't read the words,' Dania said, peering at it.

He tapped at the screen. 'I found the inscription online.'

She read the text:

ERECTED
In detestation of a barbarous Murder
Committed here on an unknown Sailor
On Sep, 24th 1786
By Edwd. Lonegon, Mich. Casey & Ja$^{s.}$ Marshall
Who were all taken the same day
And hung in Chains near this place
Whoso sheddeth Man's Blood by Man shall his
Blood be shed. Gen Chap 9 Ver 6

'So the murderers of this sailor were caught,' she said, glancing up. 'What does being "hung in chains" entail?'

'After execution, the body is put in a gibbet cage and left to rot.'

'Charming.'

'Must have been quite a sight. To say nothing of the smell. A reminder to everyone of the long arm of the law. In Scotland, though, bodies of the executed were sometimes sent to medical schools for dissection.'

Dania added a dollop of jam to her tea. 'How do you know all this about Dickens and the Devil's Punch Bowl?'

'I researched murder stones for an article I wrote for a history magazine. One of the editors informed me that he'd come across a murder stone somewhere west of the city centre. He told me where to look.'

'And it was this same one with Watson Sangster's name?'

Marek shook his head. 'It had a different name. Fraser Sangster.'

'*Fraser* Sangster?'

'Let me show you my article. You'll find it interesting.'

After scrolling through his files, he handed Dania the tablet.

The title of the piece was 'Dundee Murder Stones Baffle Community'. Below were photographs of two headstones. She recognised the one on the left, having seen it in Kimmie's lab. The one on the right was identical in size, shape and inscription except for one detail: the name engraved on it was Fraser Sangster.

Dania read the article slowly. Watson and Fraser were brothers, which was interesting in itself, since the circumstances in which brothers are murdered usually make for fascinating reading. But what caused her pulse to race was that there was a third brother. His name was Edward, and he was the youngest of the three.

'Edward Sangster,' she said, sitting up.

Marek was watching her with curiosity. 'From that look on your face, I'd say that's the man who was in the car accident.' He raised an eyebrow. 'Am I right?'

'It'll be in the papers soon enough.'

'Don't worry about me, Danka. I know how to keep my mouth shut.' He stirred jam into his tea. 'Keep reading.'

According to Marek's research, no one seemed to know who had erected the stones for Fraser and Watson, but they'd first appeared in 1990, not far from Sangster Hall. Edward had them destroyed, but they reappeared somewhere else – always near the Hall. Each time he had them demolished, they sprang up again a short while later. This went on for the best part of a year. Then he gave up and left the stones where they were. And, after a while, Dundee forgot about them. That is until a historian had asked Marek to research them and write an article.

Dania gazed at her brother. 'How did you learn all this?' she said.

He took a gulp of tea. 'I questioned the locals, and I scoured the newspapers from that year and the one following.' He nodded at the tablet. 'If you keep going, you'll see a map of the locations. It took me a while to create that. I was lucky. A few of the people I spoke to had taken photos and were able to give me a clear indication of the stones' locations. It got so they went hunting for the next ones as soon as Edward had them removed. It became something of a game.'

'And each time the murder stones reappeared they were identical?'

'That's right. If you know how to carve stone, it won't take you very long, I discovered.'

She scrolled down until she'd found the map. The positions of the stones and the dates they were erected were clearly marked.

'So, what do you see, Danka?'

'They form a rough circle.'

'And what is at the centre?'

She looked up. 'Sangster Hall,' she said softly.

He held her gaze. 'It's as if the person who kept erecting the stones was trying to tell us something.'

'How were these brothers, Watson and Fraser, murdered?'

'I don't know that they were. I didn't have time to check as I had too much else going on. And the historian was more inter-ested in the stones themselves. But I'm sure you'll find it in the police archives.' He added more jam to his tea. 'If it turns out that they were murdered, and this third brother was too, it might make a good follow-up article.'

'Could I email myself a copy of this?'

'Of course. Take the whole folder. My interviews are there. And the photos the locals sent me.'

She skimmed through the files. One name caused her to pause. 'You interviewed Tam Adie.'

'The artisan potter?'

'*That's* where I know the name. There's an exhibition of his work in the V&A. He was the one who witnessed the accident that killed Edward Sangster.'

'He's an interesting man. He knew all three Sangster brothers.'

'I was at Sangster Hall today. There are portraits in the living room of what I assume are Sangsters going back through the ages.'

'Watson and Fraser will surely be there.' Marek finished his tea. 'As a matter of fact, I'm going to be staying at Sangster Hall for a few days. Want me to see what I can find out?'

She stared at him. 'What are you doing there?'

'Covering an event. It's starting on Saturday.'

'Surely, with Edward dead, the Sangsters will cancel it.'

'I don't think they can afford to. From what I could gather from the locals, the estate is losing money hand over fist. Anyway, the Sangsters aren't directly involved. By that I mean they're not running the event. They're leasing out the Hall to the event organisers.'

'Yes, they told me they stay in a nearby building when there are conferences and things. They'll presumably be keeping a low profile.'

Marek played with the teaspoon. 'If this third brother *was* murdered, and Watson and Fraser were too, then there's something nasty going on with that family.'

Dania thought back to her encounter with Duncan and Grace. They'd seemed normal enough, displaying the reactions you'd expect of people who'd suffered a bereavement. But if her case wasn't a simple accident, then it came to her that the path to solving it must lie at Sangster Hall. And these murder stones held the key.

'Let's go into the living room,' Marek said. He cleared away the glasses. 'You can play something for me. After all, you don't want to get out of practice.'

The living room was scrupulously clean and tidy, making Dania wonder if he had indeed had a lady living with him. Then again, anywhere looked clean and tidy when compared with her own flat.

She lifted the piano lid. Marek's big love was Chopin, but tonight he was in for a surprise.

She waited until he'd stretched out on the sofa, then brought her hands down on the keys.

'What the hell is that?' he said, sitting up.

'It's a song by Edith Piaf. "Mon Manège à Moi". Do you know it?'

'What happened to Chopin?'

'He's still around. But I need to practise this.'

'Why?' he said helplessly. 'I mean, don't get me wrong, you play it brilliantly. As far as I can tell, that is.'

She turned to face him. Only then did she notice how large his living room was. He had told her it had once been two rooms, but the previous owner had knocked down the wall. 'I've joined Kimmie's Edith Piaf Singing Society. I accompany them on the piano.'

'This is Kimmie from Forensics?'

'She's got a great voice. She could sing these songs solo.' Dania chose her words carefully. 'We're looking for a new venue. One with a piano.'

He was frowning.

'And I was wondering.' She licked her lips. 'Would you like to join the group?'

'Aye, that's my father,' Duncan Sangster said, his voice unsteady.

Dania had to admit that Milo and his team had done an excellent job. Edward's eyes were closed and, had it not been for the bruising on his forehead and the broken nose, he could have been sleeping peacefully. Only an insider knew of the trauma to the back of his head.

'Would you like to be alone with him, Mr Sangster?' she said, in a kindly tone.

Duncan shook his head.

Milo nodded to the assistant, a young man with carefully groomed red hair. He pulled the sheet over Edward Sangster's face and stepped back respectfully.

The call that they were ready for the identification had come through early that morning. Dania had offered to pick up Duncan, even though Sangster Hall would be out of her way, but he wouldn't hear of it. He would meet her at the hospital. Part of her was relieved. It had snowed through the night and she doubted the roads around Longforgan would have been cleared. Dundee itself had almost come to a standstill. Fortunately, she'd brought her snow boots to Marek's, and he lived sufficiently close to the city centre that she could trudge into work. But not everyone was as fortunate: there was more than the usual number of empty desks in the incident room.

'Should we get a coffee?' Dania said, when they were in the corridor.

Duncan hesitated. 'Thank you, but I should be getting back.

Grace will be anxious. We had a couple of journalists round first thing this morning, asking questions about the accident.'

Dania wondered how they knew, as no press release had been issued. But journalists had a habit of insinuating themselves into the tiniest crack.

'What did you tell them?' she said.

'Not much. They knew my father's name and that he drove a Morris Traveller.'

'Someone must have seen it being towed away.'

'Aye, and there aren't many of that model about. Whoever it was must have put two and two together, right enough, and contacted the press.'

'I'm afraid it will be in the papers and on the radio soon.'

'I'll warn Grace.' He glanced at his watch. 'I have to supervise preparations at the Hall. We have an event starting on Saturday.' He must have taken her silence for disapproval because he added: 'Grace and I discussed this last night, and we reckon it's not feasible to cancel. We have a number of international visitors arriving, and it wouldn't be fair on them. Not at such short notice. I phoned the event organisers last night and told them we'd be going ahead.'

'And if we need to get hold of you, where will you be staying? Is it that building next to the Hall?'

'Aye, that's the one. But it would be best to phone ahead if you plan to come over. Grace and I might have to look in at the Hall. My office is there.'

'And what is this event, if I may ask?'

'Didn't I say? It's "Magic Week". We're having a group of illusionists and stage magicians staying at the Hall.' He smiled faintly. 'My father was so looking forward to it.'

The momentary silence was broken by Milo stepping into the

corridor. The assistant would have left by the other door, wheeling the trolley back to the mortuary.

Duncan pulled himself up. 'Thank you, Professor. You'll let me know when my father's body will be released?'

'Of course. Either I or the detective inspector will be in touch.'

With a curt nod, Duncan walked away, letting his shoulders slump, no longer having to keep up the pretence.

'Are you free tomorrow morning, Dania?' Milo said, watching him.

'The post-mortem?'

'The procurator fiscal is in Glasgow but should be back by this evening.'

'Tomorrow morning will be fine. Assuming we don't get more snow.'

'I'm sure that somewhere in this hospital we can find a bed for you for tonight. You're welcome to stay for lunch, if you like.' He had a cheeky expression on his face. 'And then you can attend my lectures this afternoon.'

'What are your lectures on?'

'Bone fractures.'

'A favourite subject of mine. But I'm afraid I'll have to give it a miss. I'm needed back at West Bell Street.'

He smiled, brushing back his comb-over. 'I'll see you tomorrow, then.'

CHAPTER 4

Dania arrived at West Bell Street to find it even quieter than before. Hamish was the only officer at his desk. She sank into her chair and pulled off her boots.

'Honor not in?' she said.

'She's away to the canteen,' Hamish said. He must have seen the look on Dania's face because he smiled and added, 'I'll ring her, ma'am, and tell her you've arrived.'

Minutes later, Honor returned with a tray of mugs.

'Cappuccino for you, boss,' she said, setting the mug down in front of Dania. 'And shortbread biscuits.'

'Thanks, lass,' Hamish said.

She threw him a mischievous glance. 'By the way, while you were out the call came in. The date for your assault-course training and test has been set for this Saturday.'

'Braw. I'm sure I'll sleep better for knowing that. Anyway, I can't make it this Saturday. I'm cleaning the flat,' he said, with quiet dignity.

She ripped open the packet of shortbread. 'I gave that up a long time ago. There aren't enough days in the weekend.'

'Right, bring your chairs over,' Dania said, making space at the desk. 'There's something I want to show you.' She pulled up

Marek's files on the murder stones. As succinctly as she could, she filled her colleagues in on what he'd uncovered.

'Cripes, murder stones? First time I've heard *that* term,' Honor said.

A look of disgust appeared on Hamish's face. 'Sounds unhealthy, memorialising murder.'

'But look at where the stones were erected,' Dania said. 'They lay on a circle round Sangster Hall.' She glanced at him. 'What did your research into Watson Sangster reveal?'

'Aye, well, you ladies had better fasten your seat belts. It's quite a story.'

'Hold on,' Honor said, taking another piece of shortbread. 'I need fortification.'

Hamish waited until she'd started munching. 'Now, as Marek has discovered, there were three brothers. Watson, the oldest, was born in 1955. Then Fraser, two years later, and finally Edward in 1960.'

'And they've always lived at Sangster Hall?' Dania asked.

'Aye, they worked on the estate. Which, incidentally, is huge.' He tapped at the screen and a map of the area appeared. 'It's bounded by these roads,' he said, tracing the lines with his finger, 'so there are several ways in and out.'

'What did they do? Farm?' Honor said.

'That's about the extent of it. Fraser dealt with the accounts. And Watson organised the workmen's schedules. You could say he was the manager.'

'Were the brothers married?' Dania asked.

'Only Edward. He married in September, nineteen eighty-five. Here's the wedding photo from the newspapers.'

'Nice dress,' Honor said appreciatively. 'I've always thought lace is best for weddings.'

Dania recognised the woman from Edward's photo. She doubted she'd have recognised Edward. As a young man, he was thinner and had the same shock of black hair as Duncan. His new wife had slipped her arm through his and was gazing up at him adoringly. He was smiling at the camera.

'Now here's where the story hots up,' Hamish said. 'Earlier that same year – 1985 – Fraser disappeared. I found his name on the long-term missing list.'

'Then he's *still* missing,' Dania said.

'Aye, but look at this,' Hamish said, scrolling down. 'A few days later, his clothes were found on the Tay Road Bridge, at the Fife end where the distance between the bridge and water is greatest.'

'Suggesting suicide,' Honor said.

Dania held up a finger. 'Or murder made to look like suicide.'

'Whoa, hold on a tic,' Honor said. 'His clothes were found *a few days later*? Why weren't they found on the day he went missing? That's a busy road. You'd notice a pile of clothes.'

'Fraser was last seen at Sangster Hall on the afternoon of Monday the seventeenth of June. That evening, the Road Bridge was closed to traffic so major repairs to part of the undersurface could be carried out. It reopened a week later, the twenty-fourth. That's when the clothes were found.'

'Who reported him missing? Edward?'

'Aye. He filed a missing persons.'

Honor picked out another finger of shortbread. 'Was there a suicide note along with the clothes?'

'Nothing. This is the police inventory: lightweight jacket, shirt, trousers, pants, socks, shoes, wristwatch – which was later identified by Edward – and a handkerchief in the trousers pocket.'

'Were any estate vehicles or cars owned by the Sangsters missing from the Hall?' Dania said.

'None.'

'So, how did he get to the bridge from Sangster Hall if he wasn't carrying money or cards?'

'Exactly, ma'am,' Hamish said, with an indulgent smile.

'And what did the police conclude?'

'They assumed he'd walked. It's something of a trek, but he was young and fit. And if he was determined to kill himself, he'd walk it, no question.'

'I don't get it,' Honor said. 'Why not kill himself on the estate? There'd be hunting guns around, surely. Or why not take a car to the bridge, and then jump off? And anyway, what's with taking off your clothes? You won't drown any faster.'

'Who was that guy who left his clothes on a beach and faked his own death?' Hamish said, screwing up his face. 'Lord Lucan, was it?'

'I think his name was Stonehouse,' Honor said, after a moment. 'He wanted people to think he'd drowned while swimming. Maybe it was the same with Fraser.'

'Aye, leaving your clothes on a beach is one thing, but you're hardly going to go swimming by jumping off the high end of the Tay Bridge.'

'Did they find his body?' Dania said.

Hamish locked his fingers together. 'They sent in divers, right enough, but there was no corpse. It was a week later, remember. The water could have swept him away. An expert who knew the tides pinpointed the places on the coast where the body might wash up. But it never did.'

'Did the police consider murder?'

'Not immediately, ma'am. But then something happened that changed that.' Hamish worked the controls. 'Look at this article from the *Courier*.'

Dania gazed at the screen. '*Watson* went missing, too?' she said incredulously.

'While the divers were looking for Fraser's body, Edward contacted the police and said his other brother had disappeared.'

'Just a few days after Fraser?'

'Aye. He vanished. No clothes found abandoned anywhere. And no suicide note from him, either.'

Honor took a sip of coffee. 'I don't suppose anyone thought to search Sangster Hall for Watson. I mean, he might have locked himself into one of the rooms by accident. Maybe they didn't have that internal phone system back then.'

Dania cast her mind back to what she'd seen of the Hall. She could well imagine someone in a high attic room beating at the door, screaming to be let out, the screams growing fainter as the days went by. However, it was unlikely that anyone would lock themselves in accidentally. Although that wasn't to say someone else couldn't have done it for them.

'There's a report on file that the police searched the house and grounds,' Hamish said. 'It was a wasted effort.'

Dania ran a hand through her hair. 'What about Watson's personal effects? Were they still in his room?'

'Aye, the room was untouched, according to Edward. His passport was there, as was his wallet with his money and cards.'

'Two brothers disappear within a few days of each other,' Dania said half to herself. 'Was there an appeal in the media?'

'All the usual, ma'am. Photos, where they were last seen, et cetera. Edward even offered a reward for information leading to their being found alive.'

'Then he didn't believe either Fraser or Watson was dead.'

'There's a recording of him being interviewed on a prime-time chat show. Hold on, let me find it.'

A few seconds later, a woman with honey-blonde hair cut in a short bob appeared. She gazed into the camera and her face took on a serious expression.

'We come now to the strange case of two brothers, Watson and Fraser Sangster, who went missing the week before last. Their brother, Edward Sangster, joins us in the studio.'

The shot widened to reveal a man sitting on the other side of the table, an untouched glass of water in front of him. He looked distinctly nervous, and was playing with his tie. The physical resemblance to Duncan was noticeable, although now that Dania had a close-up view, she could see the differences. His face was thinner and his complexion more pallid.

'Mr Sangster,' the interviewer was saying, 'what do you think has happened to your brothers?'

'I've absolutely no idea,' he said, spreading his hands helplessly. 'I'm hoping the public will work with the polis to find them.'

'Do you think they've simply left home?'

'If they have, I can't understand why they'd go without telling us. My father is frantic with worry, and no mistake.'

The interviewer glanced at her notes. 'Now, Fraser's clothes were found on the Tay Bridge on Monday, the twenty-fourth. Have you any idea as to why that was?'

A note of anger entered Edward's voice. 'I know what people are saying. That Fraser took his own life.' He was shaking now. 'It's not true. I know him. He'd never do that.'

'You were the last person to see him. Was he wearing those clothes at the time?'

Edward passed a trembling hand over his forehead. 'Ach, I can't mind now what he was wearing.'

When it was clear that nothing further was forthcoming, the interviewer said: 'You reported your other brother, Watson, missing the following day. Do you think his disappearance is linked to Fraser's?'

'Aye, it would seem that way. But I can't be certain.'

'Do you think your brothers are still alive, Mr Sangster?'

'I know they are,' he said emphatically.

'How can you be so sure?' the interviewer said, leaning forward.

He pressed his fist against his chest. 'I can feel it inside.' He faced the camera. 'I'm appealing to you, the public, to help me find my brothers.' His voice was quivering with emotion. 'I'm offering one hundred thousand pounds to anyone who has information that will help me find them.'

From the look on the interviewer's face, this was the first time she or anyone had heard this offer. 'Thank you for your time, Mr Sangster.' She turned to the camera. 'We'll have details of how Mr Sangster can be contacted at the end of the programme. And I'm sure we'll be coming back to this story in due course.' She moved on to the next segment, a drugs raid in one of Dundee's suburbs.

Hamish stopped the recording. 'I've met that lassie,' he said. 'She's a bit of a nippy sweetie.'

'Edward mentioned a father,' Dania said.

'Logan Sangster. He died in 1990. He was only sixty.'

'What happened?'

'He drank himself to death, according to the medical report. Perhaps he couldn't cope with what had happened.'

'And I suppose no one came forward to claim the reward money?' Honor said.

Hamish scratched his chin. 'There were reports of sightings of one or other of the brothers. They led nowhere. But Edward didn't wait. He engaged a team of private investigators.'

'I'm guessing they were unsuccessful,' Dania said.

'Aye, and he must have spent every penny of the reward money paying their fees, and no mistake.'

'And what did the good people of Dundee think had happened to Fraser and Watson?'

'From what I read in the archives, they reckoned at first that Watson had murdered Fraser, and then done a runner.'

'How did they make that out?' Honor said. 'Did he take Fraser's clothes off after killing him, and leave them on the Tay Bridge?'

'Or maybe he removed Fraser's watch and took a set of clothes from his wardrobe and dumped everything on the bridge,' Dania said. 'That would have been easier.'

'Aye, right enough. Everyone agreed that the abandoned clothing was to make the police think it was suicide. There was plenty of speculation about where Fraser's body was buried. It could have been on the estate itself or in the surrounding woodland.'

'I don't buy it,' Honor said. She counted off on her fingers. 'First, where's the motive for Watson to kill Fraser? Second, if Watson scarpered after killing Fraser, why would he leave his money and credit cards behind? He wouldn't have forgotten a little detail like that. And, thirdly, why didn't anyone consider that it could have been the other way round? *Fraser* could have killed *Watson*.'

'Why do you think that, lass?'

'Fraser could have faked his own death, hidden somewhere, then killed Watson. We had a case like it in London. A man faked his death prior to killing someone so he would be ruled out of the murder investigation because otherwise he'd be the obvious prime suspect.'

'I remember that case,' Dania said. 'It was his bad luck that his DNA cropped up in a case a year later. So what happened with the Sangsters? Did the brouhaha die down?'

'Aye, that it did. But, then, shortly after Logan passed away in 1990, the murder stones appeared.'

'I bet that got the tongues wagging again,' Honor said, with a sneer.

'They wagged all right. But in an entirely different direction. People began to gossip about the estate workers, whether one of them was the murderer. No one was rash enough to actually mention names, mind, but eventually the police got involved.' Hamish rubbed the back of his neck. 'I've been going through the interviews. The problem was that, with no bodies, it was a thankless task for the coppers. As for the stones, none of the workers was a stonemason. Or at least admitted to it. The fact that the murder stones kept reappearing after Edward had them taken down flummoxed everyone.'

'Did the police question the local stonemasons?' Honor said. 'They must have been listed in Yellow Pages.'

'I found only one report about a mason who engraved headstones. He said that headstones are easy enough to come by. As for the style of engraving, there was nothing fancy about it. An apprentice could do it, right enough.'

Dania frowned. 'I wonder why Edward kept removing the stones.'

'Could be that if he believed his brothers were alive, he didn't want people to stop looking for them,' Honor ventured.

'Aye. But the story doesn't end there.'

'What, there's more?'

'In 1994, presumption of death was granted in the courts for Fraser and Watson. With his older brothers declared dead, Edward inherited Sangster Hall.'

'Let me guess,' Dania said. 'The rumour mill began to grind again.'

'Aye, and what it churned out wasn't very tasty.'

'That Edward had arranged the murder of his brothers to get his hands on the family fortune?'

'You've got it, ma'am. The gossip was that those anguished media appearances and engaging investigators was a smokescreen.'

They lapsed into silence. The room was filling as people braved the icy roads and limped into work.

Dania pulled up Marek's map. 'Whoever was erecting those murder stones was trying to draw attention to Sangster Hall.'

'Aye, it chimes with the theory that Edward killed his brothers,' Hamish said. 'And maybe he did, right enough. And this stone-mason, whoever he is, wants everyone to know.'

Honor took the last finger of shortbread. 'And now someone has killed Edward. Although why he's bothered to wait so long is a mystery.'

'Where do we go from here, ma'am?' Hamish said, after a silence.

'We need the results of the post-mortem.'

'And Watson and Fraser? If Edward was murdered, there has to be a connection.'

'Agreed. The problem is that with murders more than thirty years apart, it becomes almost impossible to find one.'

'Where would we start looking?' Honor said gloomily.

Dania gazed from one to the other. 'Are either of you interested in magic?'

CHAPTER 5

'The victim is a white male,' Professor Slaughter said, in his bass voice. 'His appearance is consistent with the stated age of sixty.'

Dania and the procurator fiscal were attending in the dissection room at Ninewells Hospital. Also present was Professor Jean Christie, a hawk-eyed woman with unplucked eyebrows. The rest of her face was hidden under the mask. The fiscal had requested a second pathologist at the post-mortem because there was a question over criminal proceedings leading to the death of the deceased. Dania was curious to see how the two pathologists would interact, but it was clear when everyone was gowning up that they had worked together before. She could only hope they arrived at the same conclusion regarding cause of death.

She gazed at the flabby white body of Edward Sangster. She'd seen people who'd been in car crashes but had worn seat belts, and they'd all suffered abrasions across their chests. Any suspicions she might have harboured that the man reported leaning into the Morris Traveller had unbuckled Edward Sangster's seat belt had vanished. The unmarked torso spoke for itself.

Milo's assistant, the same red-haired young man who'd attended at the identification, was waiting with an expression of concentration. He would divide his time between taking notes and taking close-up photographs.

Dania and the fiscal stood patiently while the pathologists studied every inch of Edward's body, feeling the bones and joints, their faces close to the skin. Dania knew this was a necessary part of an autopsy but what she wanted the professors to move on to were the head wounds. Edward's hair had been shaved, but the body would have to be turned on to its front before she could see the trauma to the back of the skull. From the way the fiscal was fidgeting, he felt the same. He seemed to be shivering more than usual in the cold laboratory, making Dania wonder if his boiler was also on the blink.

Her concentration was starting to drift when she heard Milo say, 'We come now to the facial injuries.'

He nodded to the assistant, who set his notebook aside and lifted the camera. Milo indicated the areas of purplish skin that he wanted recorded.

He felt around the nose and forehead. 'There is trauma to the nasal and frontal bones consistent with a severe impact. Would you agree, Professor Christie?'

They had seen the X-rays revealing the large number of black lines in the white bone. Had it not been for the tissue and skin holding everything together, the skull would have disintegrated.

The fiscal, who was an impatient man at the best of times said, with more than a trace of asperity, 'Did the blow to the forehead kill him?'

Milo glanced up. 'With an impact like this, I expect there to be a significant amount of cranial bleeding. But we'll have a better idea once we open him up.' He straightened, and spoke to the assistant, who helped the pathologists turn the body on to its front.

'There is evidence of major trauma to the head and neck,' Milo said.

Jean stepped forward and felt the bones of the spine. She had fingers almost as long as Milo's. Perhaps this was a requirement for pathologists. Either way, she'd have made a great pianist. 'Agreed,' she said firmly.

'Was his neck broken?' the fiscal asked.

'Not broken,' she said, 'but I can feel various types of misalignment, which are the hallmarks of whiplash.'

'There is evidence of sharp-force trauma to the parietal bone,' Milo continued. 'Three rectangular incisions have been made, seemingly at random.'

Jean fetched a clear ruler from the bench and laid it along one of the wounds. 'The incision nearest the forehead is twenty-five millimetres in length,' she said to the assistant, who scribbled in his notebook.

'Is it a clean wound, Professor?' Dania said.

'It is. The edges are not serrated.'

Milo laid the ruler along each of the two remaining wounds. 'The incisions are identical. The length is twenty-five millimetres.'

'What sort of instrument could have made these wounds?' Dania said, watching the assistant wield the camera.

'I'm not an expert,' Milo said, 'but anything with a sharp edge. A scraper, perhaps? I'm sure there are workmen's tools that fit the bill.'

'How much force would you need?' the fiscal asked.

'With a hammer or heavy object, a woman could have done it.'

'What about the sequence of injuries? Was he already dead when these blows were delivered?'

'There was very little bleeding when I attended at the crime scene. I'm therefore inclined to say, yes, he was already dead.'

'Are you absolutely sure?' the fiscal persisted. 'Just because there wasn't much blood around these wounds, that surely isn't an indicator. I mean the scalp doesn't bleed much, does it?'

'On the contrary,' Milo said, in his best professor's voice. 'There is a large number of tiny arteries and veins in the scalp. Some blood vessels lie deep within the skull, while others are close to the surface of the skin. My point is that the scalp can bleed profusely from even a minor laceration.' He gestured to the victim's head. 'And in this case, it didn't.'

'Professor Slaughter is entirely correct,' Jean added. 'I agree that these incisions are likely to have been made post-mortem.'

Dania glanced at the fiscal, wondering if he knew about blood vessels, but wanted to press the pathologists for absolute confirmation.

They turned the body on to its back.

'Are we ready?' Milo said, looking from Dania to the fiscal.

Dania nodded. The fiscal sighed and said, 'I suppose so.'

They watched the familiar routine – the Y-shaped incision in the chest, the removal of the ribcage, lungs and heart, Milo speaking into the overhead microphone or consulting with Jean, and the assistant taking notes. Then it was the turn of the liver, which was pronounced that of a moderate-to-heavy drinker, followed by the stomach, which was almost empty. Although Dania should have been paying attention, she knew that the main event would come at the end, when Milo sawed off the brain cap. She allowed herself to think through the implications of the pathologists' statements concerning likely cause of death. Because that determined whether Edward Sangster's demise was the result of an accident, or it was murder.

The forensic evidence at the scene, specifically the tracks indicating the deer had been dragged into the road, had led them to suspect that the crash had been engineered. She worked through the possible sequence of events. Someone who wished to kill Edward Sangster for reasons as yet unknown had wanted to make it look like an accident. What had Duncan said about Edward and his drives? *He told me he took a circular route, up to Knapp, then Fowlis, Benvie, and then back here.* Could it be that the killer knew this route, had seen Edward's distinctive blue Morris Traveller on the same deserted roads on several occasions, and always at the same time of day? And decided to create the conditions that would make him crash? And to be certain that Edward was dead, he'd brought a hammer and sharp tool with him. After all, not all car crashes are fatal, even ones where the wearer doesn't have the seat belt fastened.

But he must have hoped that either there wouldn't be an autopsy, or the incisions made to the skull would be seen as having been caused by the crash. In which case he knew little about forensics. But unless Johnty came up with something definitive regarding footprints in the snow, their only hope in getting a handle on the investigation was to establish the motive for Edward Sangster's murder. And that would mean going back more than thirty years to uncover what had happened to Watson and Fraser. And why. Because she was convinced the events were related.

The sound of the Stryker saw dragged Dania from her thoughts. She watched as Milo made a neat cut round the top of the skull. Then, tapping gently, he eased the cap away to reveal not the usual glistening grey organ, but one that was slippery with blood. From where Dania was standing, she could see that the soft tissue attached to the bottom of the skull cap was also bloody. Milo invited Jean to look, and they conversed in low voices. Dania could make out only a few words, but the pathologists seemed to be in complete agreement, each nodding at what the other was saying.

Milo reached in with a scalpel, releasing the brain from the spinal cord and surrounding tissue, then lifted it out. Dania had attended autopsies before and prepared herself for a long wait. A brain examination could take several hours: she knew of a case that had taken days. The fiscal also understood what was in store and took himself off to the chairs at the back of the room. Dania joined him.

'It appears there's been foul play, Inspector,' he said, in a low tone.

The first time Dania had heard the term 'foul play' was when she'd seen a musical by that name in London's West End. It turned out to be about a group of people dressed as chickens and getting up to no good. Then someone had nudged her towards Shakespeare, and possibly the first recorded use of the term.

'But if those incisions at the back of the head were made *after* Edward Sangster had died,' she said, 'that rules out murder.'

'Aye, it does.'

'Let's assume for the sake of argument that they were made after death. What about the deer being dragged into the road, causing an accident leading to death?'

'Scottish law is clear: murder is constituted by any wilful act causing the destruction of life, by which the perpetrator either wickedly intends to kill or displays wicked recklessness as to whether the victim lives or dies.' His eyes smiled over the mask. 'I know that off by heart.'

'I take it that means I have to prove that whoever dragged that deer into the road wickedly intended to kill.'

'Aye, that it does. *Mens rea*, if you know the Latin.'

Dania tried to hide her frustration. 'It's hard to imagine why else he'd do that with the deer. Steal it, kill it and haul it on to the road.'

The fiscal shrugged. 'I can think of one or two reasons. It could have been a prank, right enough, without intent to kill a driver.'

'Or?'

'He was transporting the deer somewhere else and decided it was too much trouble and dumped it. I must admit that wouldn't be my preferred explanation, as he could have left it at the side of the road. Or even in the woodland. There's plenty of that around.' The fiscal threw her a sidelong glance. 'If it weren't for the drag marks, I'd say the deer could have literally fallen off the back of a lorry.'

'And the man seen leaning into the Morris Traveller?'

'Could have been someone who heard the noise of the collision and wanted to check if the driver was okay. Although it doesn't explain why he ran off when your witness approached. But, then, some people don't like to get involved. He could have been innocent, Inspector. The person who rammed something sharp into the victim's skull might have been well away by then.'

They were silent for a while. Dania was about to ask the fiscal if he wanted to stay on for lunch when she noticed renewed activity at the other end of the room. The pathologists were returning to the dissecting table.

Dania and the fiscal got to their feet.

'Have you reached a verdict?' the fiscal said.

'We've examined the pattern of internal cranial bleeding closely,' Milo said. He glanced at Jean. 'We're in agreement on this. The cause of death is massive head trauma consistent with the impact of a car into a tree. The three incisions at the back of the skull were made post-mortem.'

It was mid-afternoon before Dania arrived at West Bell Street. The fiscal had declined her invitation to lunch, so she'd grabbed a sandwich at the Ninewells café and wolfed it down on the way to the car. It hadn't snowed the previous night nor during the day, so the roads were clear, and she'd made good time.

Like many officers, Dania took a shower after an autopsy. But she'd surrendered the single hair dryer in the changing room to Professor Christie. With the mask and cap off, and the pins released, the woman's waist-long grey hair would take time to dry, whereas Dania's bob took only minutes. Her hair was still damp, and she was now regretting having returned the woollen hat to Jackie Ireland.

The duty sergeant collared her as soon as she was through the door. 'Ma'am, the DCI left word that she wants to see you immediately.'

'Has something happened?'

'She didn't say. But it was something that made her lose the heid, no question.'

Dania hurried along the corridor towards Jackie Ireland's office. The door was open, which was a bad sign as it usually meant trouble. Even so, Dania knocked loudly and confidently. The woman didn't think highly of wimps.

'Come in, Dania,' she said, looking up. 'Take a seat.'

'I'm just back from the PM.'

'I gathered that from the state of your hair.' Her voice was brisk. 'I'll get straight to the point. Since mid-morning, we've been inundated with calls.' She swivelled the computer screen towards Dania.

The large headstone was startlingly familiar. But there were two significant differences. This stone wasn't weathered. If anything, it looked pristine. No moss, no lichen, no bird droppings. The second difference was that it wasn't *Watson* Sangster who was purported to have been 'cruelly murdered near here', but *Edward* Sangster. Dania drew in her breath.

'We've had journalists, members of the public, God knows who else, all wanting to know what's happening,' the DCI went on. 'These images aren't in the papers yet, but they're all over social media. As soon as the first one popped up, people piled out to see the stones for themselves.'

'What about Duncan Sangster? Does he know about this?'

'Aye, he rang me at lunchtime. The press have been wanting interviews.' She frowned. 'Honor had filled me in on these murder stones by then. Duncan had never heard of them.'

'He'd have been too young to appreciate what was going on. And it looks as though his father didn't tell him when he was older.'

'I've asked the journos not to bother the family, and let them grieve. And I told Duncan you'd be calling on him.'

'Where was this stone for Edward found?' Dania said, studying it.

'Honor has added the location to your brother's map.' She indicated the bottom of the screen. 'Try one of the icons. Look for today's date.'

Dania pinched and swiped the area around Sangster Hall until she found it. Honor had made the icon larger than Marek's. It didn't take a genius to see that it, too, lay on the rough circle formed by the previous stones' locations. 'Hold on,' she said. 'There's a second one.'

The DCI crossed her arms. 'Tap it and you can admire it in glorious technicolour.'

'*Watson* Sangster?' Dania said, the words barely audible.

'It's not in the same place as before, but it's close by. It looks as though whoever put up Edward's stone decided to replace Watson's into the bargain. A sort of two-for-one deal.' Jackie Ireland resorting to irony was never a good sign.

Dania stared at the ceiling, her thoughts in a whirl. She anticipated the DCI's next question.

'How many people knew that Watson Sangster's murder stone had been smashed?'

'Other than myself and the team, there's Kimmie and the SOCOs, Milo, Lisa. And the fiscal, of course. But Kimmie told me that the pieces of Watson's murder stone were taken to her lab immediately, so no one could have stumbled upon them accidentally.'

'What about Duncan Sangster? Did he know?'

Dania shook her head vehemently. 'We kept Watson's stone and the possibility that Edward might have been murdered to ourselves, pending further enquiries.'

The DCI was silent for a moment. 'The person who erected the murder stones for Edward's two brothers will have known the stones' present locations, because he'd put them there himself. Maybe he heard about the crash.'

'And went to check out the place. And noticed Watson's stone was missing.'

'And decided to replace it, as well as create a new one for Edward. The identical styles suggest it's the same person. He could have erected them under cover of darkness.'

'He must have assumed that, like his two brothers, Edward had been murdered.'

The DCI's eyes narrowed. 'And we know it's murder now, do we?'

Dania went through the findings from Ninewells.

'And both pathologists agree?' the DCI said, frowning.

'They both confirmed that those incisions to the back of the head were made *after* Edward had died.'

'Then our case for murder rests on the deer. What we have to prove is that it was dragged into the middle of the road with the intention of killing Edward Sangster.'

'I've been thinking about that. According to Duncan, Edward always took the same route.' She traced the roads on the screen with her finger. 'Now, if I'd wanted to set up an accident, I'd choose a section of road that isn't used much, especially when the weather's bad.'

'Go on.'

'The crash site is beyond this bend. Leaving the deer there is ideal. You're accelerating out of the curve, with trees on either side rushing into view. You're not going to spot the deer immediately, especially if you've hit a stone.'

'Aye, okay, but how would the killer know that Edward would be there on that particular day? Suppose he dragged the deer out and Edward never arrived. Or someone else did.'

'There would always be the risk that another driver would take that road before Edward came along. But as for knowing Edward would be out for a spin, the killer could have seen him leave the Sangster estate. This road here is the one Edward would have taken to get to Knapp, which is the first place on his usual route. There's plenty of woodland where a van could wait unseen.'

'Aye, and once he'd seen the Morris Traveller leave, he'd have taken this road here, which leads to the crash site, dumped the deer and scarpered.'

Dania ran her hands through her hair, regretting it immediately as it was still damp. 'Perhaps not scarpered. If he had murder on his mind, he'd have stayed behind to see what happened.' She studied the map. 'Waiting here in these trees would have allowed him to see the approaching traffic and given him time to flag down any vehicle that wasn't the Morris. Perhaps say that he'd seen the deer in the road and wanted to prevent an accident.'

'Good of him.'

'But the main reason for hanging back was to deliver those blows to the skull. He needed to make sure Edward was dead.'

'Do you think he was the person Tam Adie saw at the scene?'

'It's possible.'

'To get back to the person who erected the stones – what do you think that's all about?'

'He wants us to know it's murder.' Dania gazed at the map. 'Maybe, to make sure those stones would get into the newspapers, he took the first photos and put them on social media to stir things up.'

'Something to check.'

'It's a long shot but we might get fingerprints off the stones.'

'Aye, well, don't hold your breath,' the DCI said sourly. 'Take a look through the remaining images.'

Dania felt her spirits sag as she saw the large number of selfies taken at the sites. In many of the photos, someone had laid a hand on the stone, and the other was holding the mobile. And, of course, the hands were bare. After all, how easy is it to take a selfie with gloves on? She spotted a few of the same people at both locations. There was no point in dusting or swabbing. When it came to contamination, this was the worst kind.

'While you were at the post-mortem,' the DCI said, 'I issued a press release. It's the usual – we're at the start of our enquiries, we've still to establish the exact circumstances of the deceased's death, we don't know that it's murder, we'll be informing the press of developments et cetera, et cetera. It should satisfy the jackals for a while.' She kept her voice conversational. 'How do you plan to proceed?'

'Whoever has erected the stones is wanting us to connect Edward's death to Watson's and Fraser's. He believes they were murdered and needs us to believe it too, maybe in the hope that we'll catch the killer.'

'I agree. The fact that the wording and the way the stones have been carved is identical, save for the names, leads me to conclude it's the same stonemason. And maybe this mason knows who the killer is.'

Dania rubbed her face. 'He's been around Dundee for a long time, then.'

'I don't like this. It's got a bad smell about it. The public now think all these brothers were murdered, and it's the sort of story that isn't going to go away. We need to get to the bottom of this, and that means finding out once and for all what happened to Fraser and Watson.'

Dania tried to keep the dismay out of her expression.

The DCI raised a finger, the signal that what she was about to say should be viewed as an instruction. 'The clue to solving this lies at Sangster Hall. That must now be your main focus.'

Which was the conclusion Dania had come to herself. 'Did you happen to mention the deer in the press release?' she said slowly.

'I didn't. And none of the journos who called in mentioned it, either.'

'In that case, I think we should keep it that way.'

For the first time, a smile crossed Jackie Ireland's lips. 'Aye, agreed,' she said softly. 'This is a difficult one, Dania. As you say, the case for murder rests on proving that the deer was deliberately left in the road to cause Edward Sangster's accident, and not for any other reason.'

Dania nodded wearily. As with so many cases where the evidence isn't incontestable, they would have to go for a confession. And first, they would have to find the killer.

She was at the door when the DCI said, 'By the way, have you seen today's *Courier*?'

'I haven't. Why?'

'Your brother's article about Euan Leslie is in.'

Dania froze.

The DCI must have seen the anxiety in her eyes because she added, 'The head of the Fraud Squad came to see me. He received Marek's findings earlier in the week. Your brother did a good job, and in normal circumstances, we'd have arrested Leslie.'

'In normal circumstances?'

'Euan Leslie is working for us in another capacity. Which means he has immunity.'

Dania felt her throat tighten.

'I know what you're thinking, Dania, and we've warned Leslie that there's to be no retaliation.'

'And you think he'll heed that warning?'

'He knows what will happen if he doesn't.' The DCI looked at her hands. 'However, it might be an idea for your brother to lie low for a while.'

'I'll speak to him,' Dania said, wondering where Marek was supposed to go to lie low. Euan Leslie's tentacles stretched across most of Scotland.

'You have family in Warsaw, I believe,' the DCI said, lifting her head. 'Maybe he could pay them a visit. A long visit.'

Dania made for the door, her mind churning.

'Hold on,' the DCI called. She reached to where her coat was lying on a chair, and rummaged underneath. 'Take this,' she said, throwing something.

Dania caught the woollen hat.

The woman smiled. 'Your hair's still wet.'

CHAPTER 6

Dania left the DCI's office and pulled out her phone. Her call to Marek went to voicemail. She told herself there was no need for alarm, he was in the middle of something and didn't want to be disturbed; this had happened before and was completely normal. Then again, an investigative journalist didn't switch off his phone. She left a message telling him to call her as a matter of urgency.

The incident room was buzzing with activity. The officers looked up as she entered and immediately started firing questions at her.

'Let me take off my boots first,' she growled.

'I see you've brought your woollen hat, ma'am,' Hamish said, with a grin.

She threw him a look that silenced him. Muttering under her breath, she slipped on her shoes, stood up and marched to the incident board.

'What's the latest, ma'am?' someone at the back said.

'That's what I'd like to know,' she replied irritably. 'Could everyone gather round, please?'

She went through the results of Edward Sangster's post-mortem, specifically the cause of death. The worried looks in the room suggested they understood this would not be a straight-forward case.

'Someone deliberately caused the accident with the intent to kill,' she finished. 'And that makes it murder.'

'And you're thinking that the person who put up the new murder stones also put up the originals?' Honor said, lolling on one leg.

'It's a working hypothesis. And that's what we're going with unless we find evidence to the contrary. We need to track him down, as he may have information that will lead us to the killer.' She paused to get their full attention. 'But as far as the press and public are concerned, we're saying nothing about it being murder.' She glanced round the room. 'That huge red male had been tagged, so it wasn't captured in the wild. I want a list of deer farms and parks in the area. Check if any is missing a deer. But it's imperative you don't say why. No one is to know that there was a deer in the road. I didn't even tell Duncan and Grace.' When she saw the puzzled expressions, she added: 'In the absence of a motive, that may be our best chance of catching the killer. Sorry about the pun but we don't want him covering his tracks.'

'How far do we spread the net?' Hamish said. 'There's a deer farm in Fife.'

'I would go as far afield as Fife and Perthshire. Next on the list are those social media images. I want to know who put up the first photos of the new murder stones, and when. It might be our stonemason.'

'Going back to the killer himself,' Hamish said, 'how many people knew the route Edward took for his wee drives?'

Honor shifted her weight. 'Duncan and Grace knew. They were the ones who told us.'

Dania looked at her with interest. 'Do you think they're involved in this somehow?'

'Maybe we should check their alibis.'

'I'm going over there now, so I'll get the details. Then we can make our discreet enquiries.' She hesitated. 'The problem is motive. Edward was Duncan's father.'

'Aye, but there are plenty of cases where children have killed their parents, right enough,' Hamish said.

'We need to find out everything we can about Edward Sangster,' Honor said.

'Agreed,' Dania said firmly. 'And perhaps more importantly, we need to find out everything we can about Edward's two brothers.'

'Where do we start?'

'The estate workers. There must be some still around who were employed when Watson and Fraser were there.' She studied their expressions. They seemed eager to get on with it. 'Okay, DS Randall will organise the schedules,' she added.

'On it.'

'If anyone wants me, I'll be at Sangster Hall.'

She was in the corridor when she heard someone running behind her.

Honor caught her up. 'Boss, I didn't want to say anything back there, but you need to read this. Your brother's written an article about Euan Leslie.' She handed Dania a copy of the *Courier*.

'Thanks.'

The girl threw her a sympathetic look and left.

Dania decided her visit to the Sangsters could wait.

In the canteen, she took her cappuccino to a free table, then flicked through the pages of the newspaper. Marek's article wasn't difficult to find. The full-colour picture of Euan Leslie was unmistakable. His physique was such that the reader's gaze would be constantly drawn to his gym-toned body.

Dania had met Leslie at a local fundraiser. He was so well dressed that she hardly noticed his superbly tailored suit and tie. At the time, she'd known nothing of his reputation, just that he was a Dundee property developer. She'd been struck by his open, honest face, and they'd started a conversation that had lasted most of the evening. He'd seemed unfazed by the fact that she was a police officer – something that often put a dampener on most first encounters – and expressed interest in her experiences as a Polish national living and working in Scotland. As those experiences had been positive, Dania had had nothing to hide. He'd pressed her on her childhood, life in Poland now that communism was gone, was the Law and Justice Party moving too far to the right et cetera? Another woman might have found this level of attention flattering, yet the fact that he was careful not to reveal too much about himself and his background piqued Dania's curiosity. But she'd had to wait until she was back at West Bell Street before she'd learnt who Euan Leslie was, and *what* he was.

Now, gazing at his smiling face, a chill ran through her. He'd inherited the property business from his father, who'd died of a heroin overdose, and had ruthlessly made a glorious success of it. 'Ruthlessly' meaning he'd eliminated the competition – of which there was plenty in Dundee – in the most direct way possible: he had made his rivals disappear. No forensic evidence was ever found to implicate him, and he always had a cast-iron alibi. The police knew that it was his hidden army of loyal followers that did the 'disappearing' for him, but none was ever brought to justice.

Yet there was another side to Euan Leslie. He gave lavishly to charity, specifically those organisations dealing with drug prevention and rehabilitation. And he donated huge amounts to hospices for the homeless, and to helping the poor and disadvantaged. But Dania had discovered that he could well afford the sums and, as one cynical Fraud Squad officer had pointed out, his charitable work would apply a layer of whitewash to his otherwise murky activities.

Dania read Marek's article as she sipped her cappuccino. It couldn't have been worse. Under an alias, he'd managed to secure a clerical job in Leslie's company. This had enabled him to read correspondence, listen in on and record conversations – something he excelled at – and gather the evidence to prove that, despite Leslie's protests to the contrary, he was working with a local councillor to have several jute warehouses in the Lochee area delisted so he could buy them, demolish them and build on the land.

As far as she could tell, Marek's evidence was solid and should lead to the arrests of Leslie and the councillor. But the Fraud Squad had decided otherwise. Dania wondered what Leslie could be helping them with that was important enough to keep him out of jail.

She ran a hand over her eyes. Then she tried Marek again, with the same result. A call to the *Courier* informed her that he'd been out all day, and no one could say where. Her misgivings were turning to alarm. How long before they turned to panic?

Dania pulled up outside Sangster Hall, wondering when she would see the place in daylight. Even if she arrived first thing, it would still be too grey to view the building properly. That was the trouble with winter in Scotland. The long nights encroached on the day at both ends.

She'd found Sangster Hall online and learnt that the architectural style was Tudor Revival, otherwise known as mock Tudor. Neither of the terms meant anything to her. She had just about got the hang of Scottish Baronial. But it was a Grade A listed building. And that said something.

There was a larger than usual number of cars in the area reserved for vehicles. Perhaps Duncan was holding a commemorative event for his father, in which case it might be wiser to leave it until the following day. Except that she was here now.

She was about to lean against the bell when the door opened. A woman in a thick parka and winter boots nodded at her and left, leaving the door open. Dania peered into the hallway, seeing Duncan speaking to another woman. He was wearing baggy jeans and an Aran sweater.

'Mr Sangster?' she called in. 'Is this a bad time?'

He turned and, seeing her, spoke to the woman, who disappeared into the house.

'Inspector,' he said, hurrying to the door. 'Please come in. DCI Ireland did say you'd be over to see us.'

'If you're busy, I can return another time,' Dania said, trying to sound reassuring.

'I can leave the cleaning ladies to get on. They know fine well what they need to do. Let's go to the office.'

He ushered her down the long corridor. It was only then that she saw that each door was either numbered or had a small nameplate. As they reached the fine oak staircase, he opened a door on the left.

The office was warmer than she'd expected, which she put down to the two ribbed, cast-iron radiators. The furniture consisted of a modern office desk, several chairs and a filing cabinet. On the flocked cream wallpaper, which was discoloured in places suggesting water had seeped in, someone had hung a series of landscapes. The exception was the portrait of a man in uniform, which was bracketed by oil paintings of the River Tay.

Grace was at the desk, hunched over a laptop. She was wearing a coffee-coloured shirt the same shade as her hair, which was hidden under a wide white band. Seeing Dania, she tugged off her reading glasses. 'Inspector,' she said. Her eyes were red, either from staring too long at the screen or from weeping. Given her look of anguish, Dania guessed which it would be.

Duncan indicated the chairs. 'Please have a seat.'

'I've caught you at a bad time,' Dania said, opening her notebook.

'I'm afraid any time from now on will be an even worse time, so we may as well talk now.'

'Of course, Magic Week is starting.'

'We're expecting the international arrivals tomorrow, as well as a few of the residential guests. The event itself doesn't start until the following day, the Saturday.'

'And what is the event? A series of magic shows?'

'Aye, it's a mix of shows and workshops. A number of people have signed up to learn the tricks of the trade, while others will come to watch the entertainments. Not everyone is here for the full ten days.' He waved an apologetic hand. 'I know it's called Magic Week, but so many people wanted to attend that we decided to extend it. The event managers are making it as flexible as possible. Fortunately they're the ones drawing up the timetable.'

'But it must still require an enormous amount of organising for *you*.'

'You have no idea, Inspector.' He managed a tired smile. 'Grace is giving the database a final check.' He peeled a sheet off the pile on the desk and handed it to her. 'This is the programme. As you can see, it's a pretty full timetable. Each day's events go on right through the evening. And this,' he said, taking a larger sheet from another pile, 'is a map of the Hall. We're hoping the room numbers and the signs in the corridors will help.'

She studied the map. Sangster Hall looked like a design by committee.

'The ground-floor layout is on one side of the sheet, and the first floor on the other,' Duncan said. 'The events are on the ground floor, and the bedrooms and suites on the first floor.'

'So you're not using the top floor?'

'Those rooms are mainly empty. You can keep the maps,' he added, as she made to return the sheets. He glanced at his wife. 'We're hoping one of your officers will be at the Hall through-out Magic Week.'

Dania looked at him in surprise. 'Is this because of the press?'

'It's not that. The journalists who called round today were decent enough to leave when they saw the state Grace was in. It didn't stop them taking a few photos, mind.' He rubbed his brow. 'No, we wanted to talk to you about these stones.'

'What's going on, Inspector?' Grace said, her voice a wail. 'Was our Eddie murdered?'

Dania had prepared her script. 'The post-mortem concluded that it was crashing into a tree that killed Edward. He wasn't wearing a seat belt, which didn't help.' She hesitated. 'But in cases like this, if evidence that someone deliberately caused the accident is found, then that would make it murder.'

The colour drained from Grace's face. 'Deliberately caused the accident,' she said, in a whisper. Her hands crept to her throat.

Duncan was gazing at Dania with a vacant expression. It was impossible to tell what he was thinking.

'Mr Sangster, can you think of a reason why anyone would want to kill your father?'

He shook his head slowly, almost automatically.

'Can you tell me about his friends?'

'Aye, well, he didn't have many. The estate was his life. And my mother, of course. They were married for more than thirty years.'

'How did he treat the estate workers? Was he friendly towards them? Or did he keep a distance?'

'I'd say neither. But there was a good deal of respect on both sides, right enough.'

'I'll need a list of their names and addresses.'

A look of alarm crossed his face. 'But why?' he said helplessly.

'It's routine, Mr Sangster. When there is suspicion of murder, we speak to the deceased's associates. I also need to ask for you and your wife's movements on Monday.'

'You're not suggesting we had anything to do with my father's death, are you?'

'Again, it's routine. We need this information for our records.'

After a pause, Grace said, 'Tell her, Duncan. It can't do any harm.'

'Aye, all right. We were up in Aberdeen. Grace and I have been trying for children, with little success. There is a specialist at the Royal Infirmary that we were referred to. We left the hospital late in the afternoon, then stopped off at Stonehaven for a bite to eat. We had a lot of talking to do.' He played with his hands. 'About whether we should try for adoption.' He lifted his head and gazed at Dania, his face slack. 'I'm not sure what time we left the restaurant.'

'Did you pay by credit card?' When he looked puzzled, she added, 'We can check the time of the transaction.'

His face cleared. 'Of course. And I'll give you the name of the consultant we saw in the Infirmary.'

'I'd also like your mobile numbers.'

'Aye, you'll need to stay in touch with us. The place next door doesn't have a landline.'

That was fortuitous, she thought. She'd wanted the numbers so she could determine their locations from the phone masts. Duncan scribbled on a pad, then tore off the sheet and handed it to her. He pulled a wallet out of his jacket and rummaged through it for the credit-card slip. 'I'll need time to compile the list of estate workers,' he said.

'One of my officers will be in touch about that, probably tomorrow.'

'I'll have it ready.'

There was a brief silence, then Dania said: 'You mentioned you wanted to discuss the murder stones. DCI Ireland said you'd never heard of them.'

'I must confess I was stunned when she told me.'

'Shortly after the ones for Watson and Fraser first appeared, your father had them taken down. I wonder why he never talked about them.'

'Aye, well, we've been asking ourselves the same question,' he said, throwing a glance in his wife's direction. She smiled back faintly.

'What did he tell you about his brothers?'

A look of bewilderment crossed Duncan's face. 'It was never a subject of conversation.'

'Surely you must have asked him.'

'The first time I tried, he brushed the questions away, and no mistake. I was a wee lad then, and bairns don't always get answers.' He looked thoughtful. 'But I tried on another occasion when

83

I was older, and he grew angrier than I'd ever seen him. He told me never to ask him about them again. I remember he slammed out of the room, making the pictures on the walls shake.'

'If Watson and Fraser *were* murdered,' Grace blurted, 'then Edward must have been trying to protect Duncan from the truth.'

'That's possible, Mrs Sangster.'

Dania realised she was getting nowhere with this line of questioning. The estate workers looked like their best bet. She had one final question. 'Mr Sangster, can you think of anyone who would profit from your father's death?'

'Profit?' He hesitated. 'Well, *I* would profit. I'm his sole heir.'

'Have you seen your father's will?'

'I haven't. I just assumed . . .'

'Is there a copy here at the Hall?'

'If there is, it will be in the safe. Hold on.'

He lifted the painting of the soldier off the wall. Behind it was a small safe. He punched in a code, opened the door and removed a pile of papers. He set them on the desk and leafed through them.

'Here it is, Inspector. My father's last will and testament.'

A quick look through confirmed Dania's suspicions. Duncan stood to inherit the entire estate. She wondered how much it was worth and, assuming Edward hadn't made appropriate arrangements, what the inheritance tax bill would look like. If the estate was running at a loss, it would hit Duncan hard.

She handed back the papers. 'You're correct, Mr Sangster. You are your father's sole heir.'

He looked unsurprised. He returned everything to the safe and replaced the portrait.

'What happened to Watson and Fraser's effects, clothes and so on?' Dania said.

'My father must have got rid of everything. I assume that items like clothes and books went to charity. Their rooms were left empty. That is until we started the business. They're used as guest bedrooms now.' He drew his brows together. 'But I recently came across a diary in the library. It belonged to Watson. At least, his name's on the front.'

'From when he was a boy?'

'This was more of a work diary. It was from 1985.'

'The year he went missing?' Dania said, feeling her excitement rising.

'Aye. I can let you see it.'

Grace made to stand but he laid a firm hand on her shoulder. 'It's all right. You get on with what you're doing.'

She looked up at him, smiling bravely.

'The library's just here,' Duncan said, as they left the room.

He opened the door on the other side of the staircase. If Dania had expected a large room lined floor to ceiling with shelves, she'd have been disappointed. The library was no bigger than the office. A functional, open-fronted bookcase stood against one wall. If this was the sum total of books in the Hall, the Sangsters were evidently not great readers. Two long, cream sofas, their armrests fraying, were the only other pieces of furniture. Someone had pushed them together to form a right angle.

'We encourage our guests to bring their own paperbacks and swap them with the books here.' He shrugged. 'We know one or two will pinch some, but we don't mind. They're not particularly valuable. Let me find that diary.' He ran his finger along the bottom shelf of the bookcase and pulled out a red-backed book. 'I was looking for a history of Sangster Hall to add to the literature we give our guests when I came across this.' He handed it to Dania.

She opened it at random. It was one of those two-days-to-a-page diary. Someone had written hastily in blue biro: *Jack and Col on wheat. Fencing on south wall needing repaired. Dougie or maybe Gordon? Need to talk to Rabbie about his timekeeping. Could be a drink problem?*

She flicked to June, looking for the last record. There it was – Monday 17 June. A single entry: *Eddie still on at me to get the tractor repaired.*

Dania glanced through the following pages. They were blank.

'If you think that will be of use, please take it, Inspector.'

'Thank you. You'll have it returned in due course.' She glanced at the bookcase. 'Are there work diaries for previous years?'

'Not that I could find. I suspect they were binned.' He took a step closer and lowered his voice. 'I didn't want to say this in front of my wife, but if my father *was* murdered, and so were Watson and Fraser, then I'd very much like to know what's going on.'

'That's what I want, too, Mr Sangster.'

He looked at her pleadingly. 'Inspector, to say that my wife is anxious is a gross understatement. Ever since those images appeared online, she's been unable to function properly. Aye, and it's the word "murder" that is making her panicky. She was very close to my father.'

'You asked earlier for an officer to be on hand. I can arrange that.'

'She would much prefer it – and so would I – if *you* could be on hand.'

Dania was about to make her excuses when Duncan added: 'She said she trusts you. It would make all the difference to her state of mind.'

Dania thought of her other cases, but then remembered the DCI's instruction: *The clue to solving this lies at Sangster Hall.*

'We will give you a pass to the Magic Week events so you can come and go as you please. And there'll be a reserved car-parking space for you. You'll have other cases on your books, right enough, but knowing you'll be here for part of the time will go a long way to helping Grace. Obviously, we won't tell the guests who you are. You'll have the run of the place,' he finished, as if that would be the clincher.

Which it was. Who knows what she might uncover about the Sangster brothers in this vast, sprawling house? 'Very well. I'll try to rearrange my other commitments.'

She could almost feel his relief. 'Perhaps if you could drop by tomorrow,' he said, 'you can pick up your pass. And I should have those names and addresses ready to give you.'

'I'll do that.'

'To get back to the stones, there's one thing that baffles me. Watson's and Fraser's were carved decades ago. Assuming they *were* murdered, why would the killer wait all this time to murder my father? Why not kill him at the same time? Do you think it might have been a different person?'

'At this stage in the investigation, we haven't enough information.'

'Three brothers murdered,' he said, half to himself. 'My question is: why?'

He was gazing at the wall, a baffled expression on his face. It hadn't occurred to him that there were two Sangsters still living. Perhaps the question he should have been asking was: *who's next?*

* * *

87

Dania let herself into Marek's flat. She'd tried his number once more before leaving Sangster Hall. The lack of response was now seriously starting to worry her. It was too late to call his office, but perhaps she could try his friends. There was an outside chance he was out drinking, yet surely he'd have let her know. And it didn't explain why he wasn't answering his phone.

Half an hour later, having rung around, she was no further forward. Only one person had picked up, and informed her that he'd last seen Marek before lunch. He'd left and hadn't returned. And no, he didn't know which assignment Marek was currently on, he wasn't a great one for sharing that kind of information, ken.

Dania loped into the kitchen, wondering if she was being neurotic. Her brother's article had only just appeared in the *Courier*. If Euan Leslie was minded to act, wouldn't he wait until the story had died down? Otherwise, he'd be the obvious suspect if any harm came to Marek. Then again, did Leslie's mind work like that? With immunity from prosecution, he might believe he could do anything.

Marek had left a bowl of his homemade pierogi in the fridge. When had he had the time to make them? She shoved the bowl into the microwave, then opened the freezer and searched for the bottle of Żubrówka Czarna. The temptation to drink heavily was always there but she had a long day in front of her, and it wouldn't do to arrive with alcohol fogging her brain.

She ate the pierogi without really tasting them, and thought through her options. Part of her was tempted to hare round to Euan Leslie's house in Broughty Ferry and demand to know where her brother was. But that would achieve nothing. She imagined Leslie's well-groomed smile as he asked her in for a drink, reassuring her that no, he hadn't seen her brother, why did she think he had, and was there anything he could do to help?

She poured herself a small glass of Żubrówka. Tiredness seeped through her bones and into her marrow, overwhelming her. What she needed was an early night. The following day she would talk to the Fraud Squad, who were in constant touch with Leslie, and ask them for their advice. Having a plan made her feel considerably better. She brushed her teeth, changed into her nightgown and climbed into bed. Her last lucid thought before she plunged into semi-conscious sleep was that perhaps Leslie hadn't yet taken Marek but, having discovered where he lived, was intending to snatch him from the flat.

She woke with a strange sense of foreboding. The illuminated clock on the bedside table told her it was just after 3 a.m. She sat up slowly, wondering what had disturbed her sleep. It could only have been a noise. But from where? She strained to listen, feeling a slight movement of air as though someone was gliding past the bed. It was then that she noticed the room was freezing. Had Marek left a window open? She was about to reach for the light switch when something stopped her. With a growing sense of unease, she became increasingly aware that there was someone else in the flat. Instinct told her that this was an intruder: Marek was never so quiet.

She slipped out of bed and padded towards the door. She'd nearly reached it when she heard the sound. It came from the corridor, footsteps growing louder, then a sliding around the edges of the door, as though something was trying to get in. She sprang back, her heart thudding, and looked around frantically. But it was too dark to make out anything except the outlines of the bed and the dresser. The only thing she could use as a weapon was the metal ornament Marek had been presented with by DC Thomson after winning an award. She ran her fingers over the surface of the dresser until she found it. Then, as quietly as she could, she crept back to the door and listened. But all was silent. It was as if the house were waiting.

She couldn't stay in the room indefinitely. With her heart pounding painfully now, she opened the door a crack and peered into the corridor. The rush of cold air and the faint light from the stairwell told her that the front door was wide open. Had the intruder left? Or was he still in the flat?

She stepped into the corridor and paused to listen. The door to the living room was open. Her habit was to close doors behind her. Yet had she been in the living room the previous evening? She couldn't be certain, but she thought not.

A sudden sound, partway between a knock and a thump, came from the kitchen. Her stomach lurched. She gripped the ornament firmly and inched her way along the corridor. The kitchen door was ajar, and whoever was in there seemed to be happy enough floundering around in the dark. In one decisive movement, she slammed her shoulder against the door and reached for the switch, flooding the kitchen in a cool fluorescent light.

Marek whirled round, his face bleeding white. He clutched at his chest. 'Danka, for God's sake, you nearly gave me a heart attack.' His speech was slurred.

She set the ornament on the table and sank into a chair. When her breathing had approached something like normal, she gazed up at him and said, 'You've left the front door open.'

'Have I?' he said, trying a grin.

He was swaying on his feet, gripping the work surface in an effort to stay upright. There was little point asking him why he'd been groping around in the dark. He'd been unable to find the light switch.

'You'd better sit down,' she said. 'And I'll close the front door before we turn into icicles.'

When she returned, she found him sitting upright with his eyes closed. 'How about I put the kettle on, Marek?'

She made tea and brought the mugs to the table. His head was starting to droop. Gently, she pulled it back, resisting the urge to slap his cheeks to wake him. She took the chair opposite.

He opened his eyes, apparently surprised to see her still there.

'I've been trying to reach you,' she said, keeping her voice level.

He rubbed his eyes. 'I had my phone switched off.'

'I gathered that.'

He seemed to think an explanation was necessary. 'One of my friends, you remember Donny? Well, he had his stag do today. We went to the Hampton, it's nice and central and everyone can more or less walk home from there.' He had several goes at reaching the mug. After he'd succeeded in curling his fingers round it, he brought it to his lips and sipped gingerly. 'Anyway, there was, shall we say, a special kind of entertainment, so we were asked not to take photos. In fact, we had to switch off our phones and leave them at reception.'

'I see.' She leant forward and pulled something red and lacy from the breast pocket of his navy jacket. 'I think I can guess the nature of the special kind of entertainment,' she said, dropping the bra on to the table.

He feigned surprise. 'Good Lord, how did that get there?' His gaze wandered to the DC Thomson ornament. 'And how did *that* get there?' he added, frowning.

'You came very close to having your brains bashed in.'

'Did I make a lot of noise?'

'You know that the slightest sound wakes me up.' She ran her hands over her face. 'I've been worried about you all day. When I couldn't reach you, I began to imagine the worst.'

The tone of her voice seemed to sober him up. 'But why?' he said.

'Euan Leslie.'

'Haven't you arrested him yet?'

'That's just it,' she said, in cold fury. 'He's not going to *be* arrested. He's helping the Fraud Squad, and they've given him immunity.'

She could tell the implication had sunk in. A shadow crossed Marek's face.

'That's why I was trying to reach you,' she went on. 'And that's also why, when I heard someone prowling around, I thought it was one of Leslie's men.'

'I had no idea, Danka,' he murmured.

She gazed steadily at him. 'The DCI said you might want to lie low for while.'

'The DCI said that?' He seemed bewildered. 'Where does she think I should go?'

'She mentioned Warsaw.'

'*Warsaw?*'

Dania finished her tea. 'I did warn you about delaying publication. Can you leave Dundee?'

'I'm booked in for Magic Week.' His expression brightened. 'Out in the country, surrounded by people – what could be a better place to hide in plain sight?'

'You think Leslie's men won't find you there?'

'No one knows I'm covering the event. I've not even told my boss where I'll be. I said I'd got an assignment which would lead to a story.'

She stared at him. *He has no idea,* she thought. *He'll be a statistic. Just another of Leslie's victims.*

And then she remembered that she, too, would be at Magic Week. And now that Marek had got himself into this mess, in addition to trying to find Edward Sangster's killer, which meant piecing together the past with the present, she would have to keep an eye on her brother.

What else was new?

CHAPTER 7

'Isn't he at home, ma'am?' Hamish asked.

'There's no reply on the landline. I've tried his mobile with the same result.'

'Do you think he's still in bed?'

Dania glanced at her watch. 'It's after nine thirty.'

'It's Friday, the last day of his exhibition.'

'He must be at the V&A.'

'Want me to drive you, ma'am?'

'I'll walk. The roads are clear. And it's the only exercise I'm going to get today.'

To everyone's relief, the clouds hadn't shed their snow the night before, although it was forecast for the weekend. Strange weather, Dania thought, as she struggled into her sheepskin. It hardly ever snowed like this in Dundee. Or so she'd been told.

She left West Bell Street and sauntered along the Marketgait, passing the glass-fronted Hampton by Hilton. Through the window, she could see the staff clearing stuff away and vacuuming the crisps trodden into the carpet. Probably cleaning up after the stag do. Her mind strayed inevitably to Marek. After waking him from his alcohol-induced slumber, she'd instructed him to make himself scarce, because she wasn't convinced he'd be safe in the flat.

He reassured her that he'd soon be packing a bag. He was booked in at Sangster Hall from Saturday, but he was sure they'd let him have his room a day early. She informed him that she, too, would be there for much if not all of Magic Week. Her final instruction, delivered over her shoulder, was that under no circumstances was he to switch his phone off again. Ever.

As one thought led to another, she remembered she hadn't called the boiler people. She paused outside Debenhams. Her call went to voicemail. But it was a new message, which informed her that they were solidly booked until the middle of the following week, but if she left her contact details someone would get back to her to arrange a time slot. She ended the call. She'd sort that out later.

She continued along the Marketgait, wondering if seeking out Tam Adie would turn out to be a waste of time. He might have more to say about Edward Sangster's accident, but it could be one of those occasions where she gained information that didn't move her investigation forward. But then she remembered Marek's words: *He's an interesting man. He knew all three Sangster brothers.*

Dundee's museum of design loomed into view. The first time she'd visited the V&A was not long after it had opened, and she'd been intrigued by the layout of the place, lingering long over the wonderfully evocative Ocean Liners exhibition. Since then, she'd made a point of visiting the museum whenever they had anything new, although she had to confess she'd not made time for Tam Adie's artisan pottery display. And today would be her last opportunity.

The museum was opening its doors as she arrived. She showed her warrant card at the desk and asked where she might find Tam Adie. The receptionist, a cheery young man with wild hair and a gold necklace, directed her to the area left of the tall glass lift, apparently unfazed by the fact that a police officer had arrived to speak to one of the artists.

Dania passed the café, which, judging by the hiss of the coffee machine, was open for business, and found the Tam Adie exhibition. The items on display were bird, fish and animal sculptures. The works themselves were highly detailed but what captured Dania's attention were the subtly coloured glazes in muted shades of ochre and aquatint. She wondered idly how much a piece would cost.

A stocky hulk of a man with shaggy grey hair was sitting at the side, reading a book. He was bent over, elbows on knees, frowning at something on the page.

'Mr Adie?' she said.

He nearly fell out of the chair. He dropped the book, then almost toppled over as he leant to pick it up. It was an old book, and hitting the floor had caused the brown cover to shear off. He scooped everything up and held it behind his back, like a naughty schoolboy who's damaged someone else's property and wants to hide the evidence.

'I'm so sorry,' Dania said. 'I didn't mean to startle you.'

He stared at her with a vacant expression.

'I'm DI Gorska from West Bell Street police station,' she added. 'Could I have a word?'

'Aye? And what about?' His tone wasn't unfriendly. It was his unblinking gaze that threw her. She found it disconcerting when people stared at her through their spectacles, their huge eyes swimming behind the lenses.

'It's about Edward Sangster. The man who crashed his car on Monday.'

He didn't answer for a moment. Then he said, 'I've already given my statement. There's not much more I can tell you, eh.'

He had a strong Dundee accent, which fortunately she was now used to.

'We've got a few more questions.' She smiled in what she hoped was a reassuring manner. 'That always happens, I'm afraid.'

The smile must have done the trick because he relaxed visibly. He dropped the damaged book on to the chair. 'I suppose we could get ourselves a brew.' He stroked his chin with a heavy-boned hand, making Dania wonder whether large hands were a prerequisite for an artisan potter.

'Shall we try the café?' she said hopefully. She didn't want to waste time traipsing into the city centre.

'Aye, that'll do fine well.'

At the counter, he ordered a black coffee for himself, and she asked for a cappuccino. She'd intended to pay but the girl shook her head. 'On the house,' she said, smiling at Tam.

Their coffees made, he led the way to a table near the lift. It would be out of earshot, which Dania guessed was his intention.

'I can't place your accent, Inspector,' he said, pouring two sachets of sugar into his coffee.

'I'm Polish.'

He lifted his head. 'Oh, aye? I've met quite a number of Poles here and there. In fact, one came in yesterday. He's commissioned a piece. A mermaid. She's holding a shield and sword. He left me a photograph to work from.' He patted the pockets of his shabby navy jacket. 'Ach, I wore my other suit yesterday. Pity. I could have shown you it.'

'I think I know it. I'm guessing it's the *Syrenka Warszawska*.'

'That's the one,' he said promptly.

'You'll find her everywhere, especially in Warsaw.'

'Is that where you're from?'

'I was born there.'

'And how have you found Scotland?' He grinned, showing uneven teeth. 'I'm betting this snow makes you feel at home.'

'Oh, yes.'

'But I reckon you've not come here for a wee blether, pleasant though it is, right enough.' He blew across his coffee. 'What do you want to ask me?'

'You gave a statement to my colleague, DC Hamish Downie, at the time of the accident.'

'Aye, I mind he was a nice lad. I was in a wee bit of a state, and he did right by me. He let me tell my story without rushing me.'

'He's good that way, Mr Adie.'

'I was on my way back from Abernyte, where I'd dropped off my pottery, when it happened. Do you know the place I mean?'

'I do.'

Dania had visited the Antiques and Arts Centre in Abernyte only once and had been pleasantly surprised by the variety of merchandise on offer. Modern pieces rubbed elbows with antiques in what looked like a large warehouse divided into display areas. She'd bought Marek's Christmas present there: a pair of antique cufflinks in rose gold.

'But if you've come to ask me if I could describe the man I saw leaning into the car,' Tam went on, 'you're wasting your time. It was too dark. And he ran off like the de'il was on his tail.'

'You were travelling in the opposite direction, Mr Adie. Didn't the headlights from your car illuminate this man's face?'

Tam shook his head firmly. 'He was leaning into the car when I arrived. He glanced up when I called out, but it was only for a split second, then he took off. That was when I clocked the man lying with his head half through the windscreen, and my attention was on him, and no mistake.' He took a gulp of coffee.

'And there was that deer in the road. I saw it just in time. Otherwise it might have been me hitting that tree.'

'Did you know there was one of these murder stones nearby? Edward's car hit it before he crashed.'

'The first I knew about that stone was when I heard the lassies here having a confab, and peering into their mobile phones. They showed me the photos.' It was as if he'd anticipated Dania's next question. 'They were exactly like those stones that went up years ago.' His eyes took on a faraway look. 'I mind that time fine well. Everyone was out photographing them. I went out and took a few snaps myself.'

Before Dania had set out from West Bell Street, she'd taken a thorough look at the text of Marek's interview with Tam Adie. She'd hoped it would help her segue smoothly into the next set of questions. However, once again, Tam made things easy for her.

'I knew all those Sangster brothers when I was a young man,' he said. 'I was a labourer then, on a nearby farm. We'd all meet up, you know, have a few bevvies and that. Then I moved away and we lost touch. When I came back, I heard that Watson and Fraser had disappeared under strange circumstances.'

'What were they like, the Sangsters?' she said, trying not to sound too interested.

Tam played with his mug, turning it in his hands. 'You know, Inspector, for three brothers, they couldn't have been more different.' He glanced up, and his expression softened. 'Watson was a bit of a dreamer, and no mistake. I reckon he never took to farm work. He told me once that he was tired of organising the rotas and making sure the labourers arrived on time. There had to be more to life than that. What he had a mind to do was create things. You know, artwork and that.' The way the light gleamed in Tam's eyes, he could have been talking about himself. But then,

99

that was the path he'd chosen to follow. And he'd made a success of it, as far as she could tell.

'And Fraser?' she prompted.

'Fraser did the books. Only because neither Eddie nor Watson had an aptitude for it. He was good with the figures, from what I could see, but he didn't seem to notice that the estate was falling further into the red. Or if he noticed, he didn't care.'

'But *you* noticed it?'

'Everyone noticed it. You can tell when a farm is struggling, Inspector. You don't need to see the spreadsheets. All the labourers there knew all the others, and news soon got around.'

'Didn't their father, Logan, take hold of the reins?'

Tam snorted. 'He couldn't even take hold of himself. He was in his cups most of the time. Nah, he left his sons to shoulder the burden.'

'What about Eddie?'

Tam stared hard at the table. 'He seemed to be the only one of the brothers who had a real interest in the estate. He nearly worked himself to death trying to keep the place going. Aye, and he had a real flair for it, too. Made changes to improve efficiency. Some of the other farmers took notice and made the same improvements.'

'And did the brothers get along?' Dania said, bringing her mug to her lips.

'From what I could see, I'd say they rubbed along.'

'How were they when you went out drinking?'

Tam smiled. 'Fraser was a great one for larking around. He'd do these impersonations of politicians, and such. Had everyone creased up. He got on well with the lads. So did Watson, come to think of it. Edward was more serious. His mind was always on the estate, even when we were having a wee swallie at the pub.'

'Did they have any enemies that you can think of?'

'Everyone has enemies. They were running a huge estate. They'd have had to make deals with suppliers to try and get the best prices. Tempers can run high, and there are those who hold grudges.'

'What sort of estate is it? Cattle?'

He shook his head. 'Arable. Wheat, oil-seed rape. And soft fruit. I think they've got polytunnels now.' He studied her. 'There'll be Polish lads and lassies come in the summer, I reckon. And there's a fair bit of forestry work. The estate is one of the largest in the area.'

'Any shoots?'

'I mind there was a bit of pheasant shooting in summer.'

'Were any of the estate workers unhappy?'

'There was always the odd stooshie, but it never amounted to anything.'

'I meant unhappy about the way they were treated by the Sangsters.'

He looked at her with interest. 'You always get that. Workers who don't like the shift they've been given, or the tasks.' There was a gleam of irony in his eyes. 'That must happen in your line of work too, I reckon.'

She inclined her head, acknowledging the point. 'What I'm trying to find out, Mr Adie, is whether any of the workers had such a grudge against the Sangsters that they'd murder them.'

He drew his thick brows together. 'You're thinking about these stones, eh?'

'The inscriptions state that all three brothers were murdered.'

'Aye, but I can't believe it. Things like that don't happen here.'

'Murder, you mean?' she said, thinking of her recent cases.

'Murdering a whole family. Three brothers.'

'So what do you think happened?'

'How would I know? I reckon Fraser and Watson finally got fed up and did a flit. As for Eddie, he hit that damn deer and went into the tree. It was an accident, pure and simple. I reckon you wouldn't be asking me these questions if it weren't for that stone appearing with his name on it.'

'You don't think the man you saw leaning into the car might have had something to do with the crash?'

'How could he? He was like me. Heard the noise and came over to help.'

Dania finished the coffee. 'Would he be out there without a car?'

'Aye, well, I hadn't thought about that,' Tam said slowly. 'That road is away from habitation, I seem to remember. I reckon the nearest place will be Sangster Hall.'

They fell silent. Then Dania said, 'I believe this is the last day of your exhibition.'

'Aye, right enough. It finishes at midday. I'll be loading up the pickup truck this afternoon. Then I'm meeting a pal and we're going for a cheese toastie.'

The place was starting to fill, and she was conscious that people might be asking for him. She got to her feet. 'I'd better leave you to get on, then.'

He stood up. 'Give my regards to Marek, won't you?'

'Of course. He interviewed you a few months ago.'

'Aye.' Something shifted in his expression. 'With a name like Gorski, I reckon he's your brother.'

'Not my husband?' she said, with a tilt of her head.

'I did wonder.' He gestured to her left hand. 'But you've not got a wedding band.'

She lifted her right hand. 'In Poland, we wear them on this one.' She smiled. 'Thank you for your time, Mr Adie.'

Outside the V&A, Dania tried Marek's mobile.

'Are you checking up on me?' came the breezy reply.

'That's exactly what I'm doing. Where are you?'

'In my room at Sangster Hall. I must say, it's not like anywhere I've stayed before. You need a GPS to find your way around.'

'What's the view like?'

'Mist and fog. It's just come down. Very atmospheric, if you like that sort of thing.'

'Did you see anyone following you?'

'No one.'

'How could you tell, if it was misty?'

'It was clear when I was driving.'

'Right, then, I'll see you later.'

'You're coming to the Hall?'

'I'll be there after lunch.'

'By the way, I'm here as Franek Filarski. As far as the organisers are concerned, I'm just another guest. Although once I start interviewing, they'll realise I'm a journalist.'

'And I'm keeping quiet that I'm a police officer.' She paused. 'Try to stay out of trouble, at least until I arrive.'

A short while later, she'd reached West Bell Street. She was taking the steps up to the door when she heard someone call her name. A serious-looking man with fair hair cut short at the sides was walking purposefully as though he intended to break into a run and rugby-tackle her. It was the walk more than anything that made him instantly recognisable.

'Johnty,' she said, smiling.

'Inspector, I've come to present my report.' Although Johnty Keiller's surname suggested he was from Dundee, his accent was from a different part of Scotland. Dania had yet to discover where.

'Excellent,' she said. 'The entire team should be here.'

The incident room was a hive of activity, but as soon as they saw Johnty, the babble died down and a hush descended. Although he was younger than most of the officers, there was something about him that commanded attention.

'I just need a second to load up my results,' he said, approaching the incident board.

Dania caught the smirk between Honor and Hamish. Johnty never was one for opening with the usual pleasantries. The officers crowded round.

'So, as you know,' Johnty said, as though continuing an ongoing conversation, 'we found footprints leading away from the car.' He brought up a map of the woodland behind the crash site. After giving everyone time to absorb the details, he pressed a button. A tiny set of prints appeared as an overlay.

'The first thing to note,' he continued, 'is that the movement pattern confirms the man was running. He speeds up and slows down to avoid the trees.'

'How did he see them in the dark?' Honor asked. She loved challenging him. Dania couldn't decide if this was because she wanted to catch him out, something she did with all the SOCOs, or whether it was because when he answered, he turned his soft brown eyes on her and gave her his undivided attention. The two of them had such different personalities that Dania often wondered what they'd be like as a couple. Maybe they already were. Honor wasn't always quick to talk about her latest man, especially if he was someone she worked with.

Johnty gazed at Honor. 'With snow on the ground,' he said, 'there's always reflected light. Otherwise he'd have brained himself.'

'And he was definitely running?'

'We can tell from the prints themselves. The impression is deeper in the heel and toe. We were lucky to get there so soon after the event.' He tried a grin. 'The snow was deep and crisp and even.'

No one laughed. They just nodded seriously.

Dania was always amazed at how much technology had moved footwear-impression analysis out of the dark ages. In previous years, a cast would have been taken of a print, and a 3D model constructed. But that was impossible when prints were left in snow.

'Was there only one set?' someone asked.

'From the pattern, I'd say yes, absolutely.' Johnty tapped at a side control and a series of numbered images filled the screen. 'As you can see, the tread is identical. Now, a person's gait also sculpts the footwear in a unique way that can be used to identify the wearer, and that's transferred to the print. In this case, however, we couldn't see anything that would help us with identification.' He scratched his head. 'Nor were there defects in the footwear that would show up in the prints.'

'Does that mean the shoes or boots could have been newly bought?' Dania said.

'We can't tell, Inspector. Because if there's no wear and tear on the tread, it may be because it's from a heavy-duty boot. Those can be worn for a long time before anything shows up on the sole.'

'So what sort of a man was he?' Hamish said. 'Tall? Heavy?'

Johnty cleared his throat. 'As you know, humans have similar body proportions, so there's a reliable correlation between foot length and body height. The footwear was a size ten. That means he's between five foot ten and six foot two in height. The *depth* of the print suggests he weighs between two hundred and two hundred and fifty pounds, depending on how he was running. Some people run more lightly than others, if you see what I mean.'

'What's that in new money?' someone asked.

Johnty grinned. 'Between about ninety and a hundred and fifteen kilogrammes. Give or take.'

'A heavyish lad, then.'

'That tread pattern,' Dania said. 'It looks distinctive. Were you able to identify it?'

'It's Trommer, a well-known German make. Used a lot by construction workers.'

'Or estate workers?'

'Those, too. They also make excellent snow boots. I have a pair myself.'

'And where did the prints lead?'

He brought up the map again and magnified part of it. 'The woodland peters out here at this road.'

'Any tyre tracks?'

'The road leads straight to the A90. It's well used, and there were too many tracks to try to make sense of them. But he must have left his vehicle there.'

'How far away is Sangster Hall?' Dania said, remembering Tam's comment.

Johnty swiped the map. 'There's a way to the Hall from this road here. It doesn't take you directly to the house, but it leads on to the estate. You could easily walk to the Hall from the crash site.'

They were looking at her.

'Are you thinking the killer came from the Hall, boss?' Honor said.

'Just keeping the options open. Anything else, Johnty? Clues found on the road, for example?'

'Alas, no, Inspector.' He pressed a button and the image disappeared. 'My report's online and accessible in the usual way.' He nodded at the officers, his gaze lingering on Honor, then left the room.

Honor was chewing her thumb. 'Not much to go on. A tall man, wearing boots that half of Dundee probably has. And not skinny,' she added, maintaining her genius for understatement.

'A big man could easily drag a deer on to the road,' Dania said, 'although he'd have needed a van to transport it.'

Hamish cleared his throat. 'About that, ma'am, I got the contact details for the Scottish Deer Centre in Fife, as well as ones nearer home. I've asked them whether they're missing a red male. They're going to get back to me.'

'And ask them to examine their CCTV. I can't believe they won't have any.' She looked round the room. 'Anything else?'

The glum looks gave her her answer.

'I'll be at Sangster Hall this afternoon. But I'm back later. Someone on the evening shift can brief me.'

'It can't be Hamish, boss. He's not on shift this evening. He'll be getting ready for the assault course tomorrow.'

'Not possible, lass,' Hamish said primly. 'There's too much to do here.'

'So when are you going to get round to it?'

'When I get round to it.'

'And when's that going to be?'

'I'm not sure.'

'Did I tell you I completed the course in a record-breaking twenty-five minutes?'

'Many, many times.'

The other officers were clearly enjoying the Honor and Hamish Show. Dania left them to it.

CHAPTER 8

Dania set out for the Sangster estate after lunch. Before leaving West Bell Street, she'd collared the head of the Fraud Squad and explained the situation regarding Marek, and his article about Euan Leslie. She could see that the officer, a huge Dundonian with a shaved head, was trying not to show his alarm but the fact that it took him several moments to frame his reply, and even then couldn't look her in the eye, told her everything. The only advice he could offer was for Marek to hide somewhere. And the more remote the better. When Dania repeated what the DCI had said about Warsaw, he ran a hand over his stubble and said that even the moon wouldn't be far enough. With a deepening sense of dread, Dania pulled out of the station's car park and took the road to Sangster Hall.

The fog had wrapped itself round everything with the result that she kept veering off track. She slowed to a crawl, resigning herself to arriving much later than she'd intended. When she finally reached the gates of the estate, her nerves were so finely shredded that she considered stopping for a while to see if the weather improved. But it looked doubtful that the fog would lift – the murky sun was already on its descent – so she changed down a gear and inched her way along the wide avenue to the

Hall. The naked branches of the trees seemed to melt through the curtain of mist, scraping the windows whenever she drifted off course. Every so often, she passed a lamp post. Although the lamps were lit, you could hardly tell through the thick haze.

There were a dozen cars in front of the Hall, Marek's black Audi Avant among them. As Dania drew up in her reserved space, she told herself that not much could happen to her brother while he was here, and there was no reason to be nervous, this was the last time she would worry about him, and anyway he was a big boy and could look after himself.

She locked the car and made her way to the front door, which had been left wide open. A large sign advertised Magic Week in brightly coloured letters.

Inside the hallway, a woman with a sleek blonde bob was bent over a laptop. She glanced up as Dania's shadow fell on her, her hair flopping back to reveal her tiny pearl earrings. She had blue-grey eyes and a longish face, expertly made up. With that hair colour, Dania would have worn red, but the woman had decided on a cream suit, which blended with her blonde hair and pallid complexion.

'Hello,' she said, with what looked like a practised smile. 'I'm Kirstine Welles, one of the event managers. I take it you're here for Magic Week.' She had a hoarse voice, as though there was something wrong with her throat. Before Dania could reply, she added, 'I'll need your name.'

'Dania Gorska.'

'Ah yes, here you are. I see you have unlimited access to the events right through the ten days.' She opened the table drawer and pulled out a long red ribbon attached to a plastic card.

'Your VIP pass.' She studied Dania. 'Gorska. Is that a Polish name?'

'That's right.'

She peered at the screen, biting her lip. 'We have a Polish gentleman here. A Franek Filarski. He's probably in the living room. My husband, Scott, is there greeting the guests.' She drew her finely plucked brows into a frown. 'I see we have a room booked for you.' On the wall behind her were rows of keys on pegs. She handed one to Dania. 'It's on the first floor. I'll have to remember to say "second floor" to our American guests,' she added half to herself. 'Are you okay for maps? Although there are signs everywhere.'

'I'll manage.'

'You can hang your coat up there, if you like,' she said, indicating the rack behind Dania.

Dania shrugged off her sheepskin. 'I'll have to be away this evening. But I'll return with my luggage tomorrow morning.'

'That's fine,' Kirstine said, seemingly no longer interested now that she'd settled everything.

Dania started down the corridor. Voices drifted through the open living-room door. She stopped and peeked in. Two men were standing at the far end, gazing at the portrait above the fireplace. The room was warmer than Dania remembered. Not only would the heating have been switched on, but there was a fire blazing.

The men turned as Dania approached. They looked in their thirties, although the heavyset man had prematurely greying hair. The other man's thick hair was a sandy-blond colour. He was impeccably dressed in a tailored, graphite-grey suit.

'Hello, I'm Scott Balfour, one of the event managers,' the grey-haired man said, extending a hand. He had watery eyes as though he needed glasses and had forgotten them.

'Dania Gorska.'

He smiled at his companion. 'And this is the world-famous illusionist, Hennie Manderfeld. Also known as "the Great Manderfeld". Not everyone is distinguished enough to be known by their last name alone.'

Hennie adjusted the knot in his red silk tie and nodded respectfully. 'Madame,' he said.

'Please, call me Dania.'

'And I'm Hennie.'

'It's Hennie who's booked the Hall for Magic Week,' Scott said. 'Can I leave you two to get acquainted? I need to see to something. Do help yourself to a glass of fizz, Dania,' he added over his shoulder.

'Please allow me,' Hennie said, with a warm smile.

The telephone had been pushed to one side to make room for a bottle and a tray of champagne flutes. Dania studied Hennie's broad shoulders as he poured. He was the kind of man who looked good from all angles.

He returned and handed her a glass. 'Gorska. That's a Polish name, I believe.'

'That's right, I'm Polish.' She sipped carefully. 'Mm, this is superb.'

'What did Lily Bollinger say about champagne? I can't remember exactly, but it was something about drinking it when she was happy or sad. Otherwise she never touched it unless she was thirsty. Do you enjoy champagne?'

'I don't drink it often. I'm a vodka woman myself.' She stopped, her glass halfway to her lips. 'Hold on, your tie is blue! But it was red before.'

His smile widened. 'Your powers of perception do you credit. Not many people would be so quick to notice.'

She could understand that. A woman, especially, would find it difficult to tear her gaze from his face. She couldn't work out if it was his smile, or the expression in his polar-blue eyes. It was as if nothing else mattered to him except being with her.

'How on earth did you do that?' she said, resisting the urge to grab his tie and flip it over. It was a stupid question. The man was an illusionist.

'I'm afraid that would be telling. But I may explain it in one of my workshops.'

'Even if I understood it, I wouldn't believe it.'

He laughed. 'You will see more such illusions. The Hall itself is to become a "stage". We will be trying out our tricks on everyone, and at any time.'

'I'll have to be on my guard, then.'

'And what do you do, Dania?'

'I teach English to the Poles here.' This wasn't a lie. She had on occasion helped her Polish friends with the finer points of English grammar.

'Privately?'

She nodded. 'And you? Is being an illusionist your sole occupation?'

'It is. Stage shows *and* workshops. There seems to be a growing interest in learning about magic.' He tilted his head. 'Are you signed up for any workshops?'

'I haven't decided which ones yet. I've got a pass that lets me attend anything.' She ran a finger over the rim of her glass. 'Scott said it's you who has booked Sangster Hall. What made you choose this place? Wouldn't somewhere near Edinburgh or Glasgow be easier to travel to?'

He seemed to consider this. 'I was looking for a residential building with several large rooms. Scott and Kirstine's website was near the top of the list of choices. When I read the description of Sangster Hall, I knew it would be ideal.'

'And where are you from?'

'I live in Brussels.'

Dania glanced around. 'Do you know anything about the history of this place? Who are these people?' she added, indicating the portraits.

'Scott told me who they are. This one here,' he said, looking at the framed oil painting above the fireplace, 'is Logan Sangster. He's the grandfather of the current owner.'

'Isn't the current owner Edward Sangster?' she said, watching him.

He responded with a faint half-smile. 'That is still the name on Scott's website, but I understand that Edward Sangster sadly died in a car crash a few days ago.'

'Oh?'

'I think Scott was relieved that Edward's son, Duncan, decided not to cancel.'

'And the other paintings?' Dania said, after a pause.

'That's Edward there, above the sideboard.'

The head-and-shoulders portrait showed a young Edward, gazing out serenely. Dania recognised him from the television interview. She wouldn't have recognised him otherwise.

'I believe Edward had two brothers,' Hennie went on. 'They may be those two next to him.'

'Watson and Fraser,' Dania said, reading the inscriptions.

'You can tell they're brothers,' Hennie said, throwing another log on to the fire. 'There's an unmistakable family resemblance. But if you're interested, you'll find a family tree on the other side of the house. Have you got a map?'

'In my bag.'

'The tree is in the music room. It goes back only a few generations.'

Dania had a sudden inexplicable urge to see it. Hennie must have guessed it from her face because he said: 'I'd accompany you, but I should wait here. We are expecting arrivals this evening.' His expression softened. 'Will I see you at dinner?'

'Possibly not. I have to go back to town. But I'll be returning in the morning.' She couldn't resist adding, 'Perhaps when we next meet, you'll be wearing a red tie again.'

He inclined his head. 'Or perhaps I won't be wearing a tie at all.' His gaze lingered on her face. Then he bowed. 'I wish you a pleasant evening.'

He had the same impeccable manners as Marek. Dania set her glass down on the tray and, tamping down the urge to look back, left the room.

In the corridor, she drew out her map and searched the index for the music room. It was in the south wing, the part of the house furthest from the main entrance. She followed a series of passageways, noting the various staircases, particularly the one that would lead to her bedroom, and finally reached the south wing.

The corridors were narrower here and the ceilings lower, making her suspect that this was the oldest part of the house. There were several turn-offs and she needed to be extra vigilant not to take the wrong one. As she walked slowly past the dark walls, many with their panels badly chipped, she became increasingly aware that someone was following her. It was less the sound of footsteps and more a slight disturbance in the air. She stopped and looked over her shoulder, but there was no one. Either she'd imagined it, or whoever it was had disappeared down a side corridor. But it left her with a distinct feeling of unease. This was exactly the sort of house where you could get up to no good and get away with it.

Minutes later, she reached the music room. The two-leaved doors opened into a wide, airy space whose walls were plastered in creamy yellow. The ceiling was decorated with elaborate cornicing, some of which was crumbling. The room was large enough to admit a chamber orchestra and a small audience, but the single item was a black-lacquered Steinway grand. It stood proudly in the centre, advertising itself as open for business. Dania could rarely walk past a piano without at least testing the tone. She lifted the lid and ran her hand lightly over the keys. The piano was in tune. She pulled out the stool and played Chopin's waltz in A minor, one of his many works published posthumously. It had a hauntingly beautiful melody and had been a favourite of her teacher's. He'd made her play it blindfold. She'd been ten. It had been the worst three minutes of her life.

Dania finished the piece, lingering on the final chord. Which one of the Sangsters had been the pianist, she wondered. Maybe they all had. She stared through the wide mullioned window at the wall of fog, which was turning grey in the fading light. Time was slipping away. She closed the lid.

The family tree was on the wall behind her. It was because her attention had been taken by the Steinway that she hadn't noticed it. The fresco was skilfully executed in an old-fashioned style: a thick-trunked tree whose branches dangled names instead of leaves. Disappointingly, there were only four generations. At the top was William Sangster, and his wife, Rhona. Their single child, Logan, had been born the year after their marriage, and he and his wife had had three sons: Watson, Fraser and Edward. Interestingly, no dates of death were given for either Watson or Fraser. Edward and his wife had had a single child, Duncan. There were branches below Duncan's with spaces for names, assuming he and Grace did manage to have children. Above the tree were the words SEMPER PARATUS in large curly capitals.

Dania was taking a step back to study the tree better when she heard the door open. Marek poked his head inside.

'Ah, Danka,' he said. 'I heard Chopin and thought it might be you.'

'Hello, Marek. Or should I say, Franek.' He was dressed for the weather in a heavy tweed suit in shades of dark blue. 'So, where were you when you heard me play?' she said, wondering if he was the mystery person who'd been following her.

'Upstairs. My room isn't directly above here but it's not far off. Mercifully, I'm next to the staircase. You certainly get your exercise tramping through this house.' He looked past her. 'Are you checking out the Sangster family tree? It's a lovely mural, isn't it? The colours haven't faded much. That must be the family motto: Semper Paratus – Always Ready.'

'There's something odd about the tree, don't you think?'

'You mean there are no dates of death for the brothers?'

'The entries seem lopsided. William Sangster had only one child: Logan. You'd therefore expect Logan to be directly below him on the tree. And yet he's off to one side.'

'That's because it's the tree that's lopsided. Maybe there was a tallboy or a grandfather clock against that wall, and the artist realised it too late and had to bunch everything up.'

She studied the fresco. 'I'd have thought they'd go back further than William Sangster.'

'He was in the army, I believe.'

'He must be the one in uniform, then. There are pictures of him and the others everywhere.'

'But you should see the portrait in the ballroom. It's a woman in a full-length dress. Stunning.'

'I'll look out for it. Assuming I ever find the ballroom.' Using her phone, she took several photos of the tree. 'By the way, have you met Hennie Manderfeld?'

'Just an hour ago. He was in the living room with Scott Balfour. I interviewed him.'

'Did he do the trick with the tie? It was red, then a moment later, it was blue.'

'No, it was green,' Marek said, frowning. 'He went to fetch me a drink, and when he returned it was yellow. Unbelievable. He wouldn't let me into the secret, of course.'

She stared at him, trying to work out how anyone could have performed such a skilful illusion.

'Don't waste your time, Danka. He's one of the world's greatest. You'll never figure it out.'

She glanced at her watch. 'Right, I need to find Duncan.'

'There's a back way out. You follow the path that skirts the building and it leads you directly to the house where the Sangsters are bunking. Here, I'll show you on the map. It's like following a maze. Keep one hand on the wall, and you eventually reach your destination.'

It looked straightforward, and since there was little in the way of lighting in the corridor, might be her best bet.

'I have to go,' Marek said. 'More guests are due to arrive and I want to start the interviews. And I'd like another glass of that champagne before it vanishes. What was it Madame Bollinger said about drinking it when she was thirsty?' He made for the door.

'I'll see you tomorrow,' Dania called after him, adding, 'Franek.'

118

Her thoughts drifted to the Edith Piaf Singing Society. She imagined Kimmie and the group crowded round the Steinway. The room couldn't have been better. But what would it cost to hire?

Dania left the music room and followed the map to the south wing's back entrance. As she passed an open door, she heard snoring, although on listening closely she concluded it was more of a wheeze. She peeped in.

An elderly lady was asleep in the armchair by the window. She was tucked under a fraying tartan rug, which twitched whenever a particularly energetic snore sent a shudder through her body. Her wispy white hair was almost gone, and what was left was combed back off her forehead. A blob of drool hung from the lower lip of her shrivelled mouth, threatening to drop each time the woman's body quivered.

A number of ancient, wing-backed chairs were dotted around the room. Had they been removed, a visitor could better admire the fine wooden furniture, particularly the oak bureau. A mahogany bookcase stood just inside the door. It was crammed full of paperbacks by someone Dania had never heard of – an author called Barbara Cartland. Dania doubted she'd ever seen such a cluttered room, and wondered how the lady would get from one end to the other. Then again, if she was wobbly on her feet, there were plenty of handholds. The fact that this was an old person's living room accounted for the greenhouse temperature. But the source of heat didn't come from the dead fireplace with its vase of dried hydrangea heads and brass coal bucket, but from the single monster radiator and the two electric fires, all their bars glowing.

Unlike the other rooms Dania had seen, which were devoid of anything that could be lifted, dusty ornaments lay on every flat surface. There was a door at the side and one at the far end, which Dania supposed must lead to a bedroom and bathroom. There was no indication of who the woman was, but she must have been someone of standing if she had her own self-contained apartment.

Dania left her to her slumbers and continued along the corridor, passing a small mahogany table with a double drawer. On it was a vase of artificial white peonies. Moments later, she found the heavy wooden door, which, according to the map, was one of the ways out of the building.

The contrast in temperature between the woman's room and the outside couldn't have been greater. The smoky fog lay in a suffocating layer, closing in around her. The cold seeped into her lungs whenever she took a breath, making her resort to the childhood trick of taking a huge gulp of air, and holding it in as long as possible. She followed the herringbone-brick path at the side of the house, trying to make a mental map of the building's layout. After several minutes, she reached the tower. It seemed bolted on to the house, and the absence of a door meant that it could only be entered from within the Hall. She was intrigued by the octagonal design and made a note to check it out.

A cluster of spectral trees separated the Hall from the two-storey brick-and-timber building that Grace Sangster had referred to as 'the cottage'. In summer, they would be dense with leaves, shielding the Hall from the building. Or vice versa, depending on your point of view. Dania made her way to the front and pressed the buzzer.

The door opened, and Duncan appeared. He was casually dressed in jeans and a ribbed maroon jumper.

'Are you busy, Mr Sangster?' she said. 'I'm here to collect those names and addresses.'

'Aye, the estate workers. I hadn't forgotten.' He stepped back. 'Please come in.'

She followed him into the small hallway.

'Could I offer you some refreshment?'

'No, thank you. I've already had champagne.'

'I reckon you've met Scott and Kirstine, then.'

'And I've got my pass.'

He smiled, and picked up the USB stick on the hall table. 'This has the spreadsheet with our workers' details. That's names, addresses and mobile numbers. I assume you don't need the details for the seasonal workers.'

'What you've given me here should be fine.'

He thrust his hands into his trouser pockets. 'Some live on the estate in workers' cottages. If you intend to call on them, you'll need a map.' He frowned. 'I do have a few somewhere.'

He disappeared through a doorway and returned with a large sheet. Dania would have copies made for her team. Perhaps the fog would lift long enough for them to find their way around the estate without getting lost.

'I wanted to ask you something,' she said. 'I passed an open door in the south wing. There was an elderly lady sleeping in a chair. Is she a member of the family?'

'The lady you saw was Mavis.' The furrows deepened on his forehead as though he was trying to find the best way of describing her. 'She's a former maid and general factotum, you could say. She's worked at the Hall for longer than anyone can remember.'

'And she continues to live there?' Dania said, in surprise.

'It's a sort of "grace and favour" apartment. She's no trouble. It's the least we can do for her many years of service, right enough.' He hesitated, as though further explanation were necessary. 'She has no pension.'

'I see. Well, I'd better be getting along the road while there's still light left.'

'I'll bid you good evening, then.'

But as Dania made her way to the Hall's front entrance to pick up her sheepskin coat, Duncan's words rang in her head.

She's worked at the Hall for longer than anyone can remember.

Long enough to have known the Sangster brothers. And perhaps long enough to know what had happened to them . . .

CHAPTER 9

It was early evening by the time the Fiat limped into the car park at West Bell Street. Dania had been lucky not to have met anyone on the road but, then, only a fool would be out in this fog. A fool or a police officer.

Hamish was the only one of the team at his desk. He glanced up as she entered, and his round face broke into a smile. Whether it was seeing her, or because he might now be able to go home, she couldn't tell. He looked shattered. Dania felt a twinge of guilt. While she'd been sipping champagne with Hennie Manderfeld, Hamish had been struggling to move the investigation forward.

'How did it go, ma'am?'

She held up the USB stick. 'The Sangster workers' details. And I've also got a map of the estate. The workers' cottages are clearly marked. By the way, I won't be around tomorrow, so when you see Honor, can you ask her to check the workmen's boots? See if they're these Trommers? We may get a lead there.' She sank into her chair. 'So, anything to report from your side?'

'Aye, a couple of things. Tech managed to track down the person who put those social media images up of the new stones.'

'That was quick.'

'Easy enough for Tech, I reckon. Turned out it was a couple of lads. Bikers.'

'Bikers? In this weather?'

'No accounting for taste, ma'am. I had one of the uniforms haul them in for a friendly wee chat. First off, they're too young to have been around when the first stones went up. Anyway, they'd heard rumours that an Arctic fox was in the area and had decided to try and capture it. They even showed me their homemade snare.'

'An Arctic fox? They're not native to Scotland. The clue is in the name, surely.'

'Aye, well, these lads are buttoned up the back, and no mistake. I asked them what they'd intended to do when they'd caught it, and they said they were going to sell it to Edinburgh zoo. They were driving around on their bikes looking for pawprints when they saw the first stone. Then they found the second one. Yesterday morning, they put up the images on social media.'

'So not our stonemason, then. At least we can put that one to bed. You know, Hamish, in a perverse way, I want to find him more than I want to find Edward's killer.'

'The other thing concerns Duncan and Grace's alibi. It checks out. Aberdeen Royal Infirmary confirms they met with the consultant on Monday. And the restaurant in Stonehaven remembered them. They don't have that many customers this time of year, right enough.' Hamish gazed at his screen. 'The transaction on the credit card puts them there at six twenty p.m. As do their phone logs. I reckon they're in the clear.'

'There's still a chance they paid someone to arrange the accident.'

'So they could inherit, you mean?'

'They might not have wanted to wait until Edward passed away. He could have gone on for another thirty years. We need to keep that in mind.'

'To what end though, ma'am? Why take on all that debt?'

'If it were me, I'd sell up, pay the debts and move on.'

'Aye, and there might still be enough for a comfortable retirement.' Hamish put his pen down. 'There's one bit of positive news. One of the deer centres confirmed they're missing a red deer. A big male. The place is somewhere north of the A923.'

'And CCTV?'

'They've installed that everywhere. They're a wildlife enterprise. You know the type – shops, a café, lots of activities, especially for kids. And a huge park for the animals. They're checking the cameras as we speak. We should hear from them tomorrow.' He rubbed his eyes. 'I'm sorry we're not much further forward.'

'What do you mean, we're not much further forward? We can cross off several lines of enquiry. It leaves us time to concentrate on the others.'

It never failed to amaze Dania that even experienced officers like Hamish didn't appreciate the importance of this kind of work. Solving cases always relied on eliminating areas of research as being no longer relevant. And that always moved the case forward.

'When does your shift end?' she said.

'Not for a couple of hours.'

'Okay, I'm ending it now. Go home and get a good night's sleep.' She felt her lips twitch. 'Then you'll be bright and fresh for your assault-course training.'

Dania was conscious of the lateness of the hour as she let herself into Marek's flat. She'd picked up a takeaway from a nearby restaurant before driving to Union Place. It would be her last for a while as the following day she'd be eating at Sangster Hall. She'd have to slip back into the city now and again to check on progress, although she could keep in touch with her colleagues by phone.

She ate quickly. The Żubrówka Czarna was still in the freezer. She took it out, then put it back. A clear head was required for what she had planned for the evening. She returned to the table and opened Watson's work diary.

The first entry was 3 January 1985: *Started inspecting the fencing. Thankless task. But Eddie doesn't trust the workers to do it. And they're still 'recovering' from Hogmanay.*

Interesting. Inspecting fencing was surely not the job of a manager. But if the workers weren't capable . . .

The next entry was 5 January: *Finally finished the fencing. Several sections needing repaired. Will have to be Dougie and Gordon. No one else as competent.*

Nothing for 6 January.

Monday 7 January: *The men have returned. Lots of bickering over who does what. Why can't they just accept the tasks I give them?*

It looked as if Tam was right. Watson wasn't enjoying the job of farm manager. She skimmed the next few entries.

22 January: *Allan mentioned the stone wall in the north field is damaged. I reckon he damaged it himself so he can get the work. Not the first time, either, the wee shite. I'm giving it to Dougie.*

Which wouldn't have made Watson popular with Allan.

Rarely did Watson praise anyone. There was the odd grudging *Col did a fair job painting the sheds. And Rabbie managed to mend the crop sprayer. Didn't expect ever to get any more work out of it. Will talk to Eddie about getting him a wee bonus.* But most of the entries included one or more complaints, either about the quality of the work or the poor timekeeping by the workers.

In the following pages, Watson referred to the men's tasks – slurry spreading, fertilising and crop spraying, but there were still the constant criticisms. Then Dania came to one entry that made her sit up.

27 March: *Heard the argument between Allan and Fraser. Something to do with laying off workers. First I heard of it!*

Then:

28 March: *Eddie called a meeting of the three of us. He's been through the figures. Fraser really got it in the neck, poor bastard. He's the only one who can see how badly things are going. And yet he's never said anything. Follow-up meeting tomorrow.*

The 29 March half-page was empty. But there was an entry for the day after:

30 March: *Eddie presented his plan. Obvious that he and Fraser concocted it between them. Some of the workers will be laid off. No prizes for guessing which ones. The good lads will have to take on more work. Great timing, as the potatoes are about to be planted. And I have to be the one to tell them.*

Dania made a mug of tea and stirred in a spoonful of jam. So far, this was reading like a soap opera set on a farm. She'd expected the next entry to be Monday 1 April, but there was one for the day before.

31 March: *Eddie ran everything past Dad over dinner. The old man didn't take it well. He'd employed some of those lads himself. Demanded to know how it had come to this. We didn't dare tell him. He's been drinking more and more. Not just that, but we hear him up at night. He walks all over the house as though he's searching for something. I'll have to get to the bottom of it, or he'll kill himself.*

Dania was glad Honor wasn't reading this, given her views about creaky old houses. She read on.

1 April: *Called the men together and gave them the news. They were more angry than upset. The ones losing their jobs hurled insults at us, Fraser especially. They blame him. The men we're not laying off weren't too keen on taking on longer hours. Understandable. Some threatened to leave. Ach, I'm so tired of all this.*

The next entries were much the same: disgruntled workers complaining about their longer shifts. And then what Watson had recorded took on a more sinister tone.

21 May: *Allan Mackie back again wanting work. He's been on the dole. At least he's not married with bairns like some of the other men we've laid off. I had to send him away. But he cursed me and my brothers before he slunk off.*

Allan Mackie. He must be the Allan that Watson thought had deliberately damaged the stone wall. Then nothing more about him until:

28 May: *Col told me he'd seen Allan hanging round the estate, the worse for drink. He's been bothering the men, trying to get them to quit the job. Aye, and if I clap eyes on him myself, he'll get a smack in the pus, and no mistake.*

So Allan Mackie was stirring up trouble. The next entries were mostly about farm work, crop irrigation and silaging. Allan Mackie made a couple more appearances.

11 June: *Edward tells me he ran into Allan in town. The man grabbed him by the throat and pushed him against the wall. If this goes on, I'm calling the polis.*

Allan's final mention was Saturday, 15 June, two days before Fraser was last seen.

15 June: *Saw Allan on the estate. For once, he was stone-cold sober. Told me he was giving us Sangster brothers one last chance to see him*

right and give him his job back. I said the job no longer existed, and I didn't want to see him hanging around the estate again. There was a strange look in his eyes. A calm look. As though he had some sort of plan.

Nothing for the 16th. And then the final entry:

17 June: *Eddie still on at me to get the tractor repaired.*

Dania closed the book, her thoughts swirling. The police had interviewed the estate workers after the first murder stones appeared. Hamish had been through the transcripts, but nothing had come to his attention, although that was often the case on first reading. Now that she had a few names, they could go through the records again. She wondered whether any workers from 1985 were still on the estate. If so, Honor would need to question them about Allan Mackie.

Dania had taken photos of the relevant diary entries. She sent them to Honor with instructions to extract everything she could from the workers, particularly about Mackie. The girl's words slipped into her mind.

Are you thinking the killer came from the Hall?

That had been a possibility they'd considered – and were still considering. But maybe Edward's killer hadn't come from the *Hall.* Maybe he'd come from the *estate.*

Dania finished the tea. Allan Mackie had just become a person of interest.

CHAPTER 10

The 10 a.m. news was finishing as Dania reached Sangster Hall. En route, she'd called in at West Bell Street but most of the staff were out. Honor had texted to say that Hamish had uploaded the contents of Duncan's USB, so she and the team could hit the ground running. Dania doubted whether much 'running' would be done on the estate, as the fields were still sheeted with snow. However, now that yesterday's mist had evaporated, the sky was suffused with a brilliant blue.

She pulled up outside the building. Wands of smoke drifted from the chimneys, breaking into long, curling fingers. There were fewer cars than she'd expected but, given the weather and the general state of the nearby roads, she suspected that most attendees, the international arrivals especially, would have taken taxis. She dragged her small wheelie out of the boot and headed for the entrance.

Judging by the number of coats on the rack, and the room keys missing from the pegs, Magic Week was in full swing. Dania had expected to see Kirstine Welles at reception, but a young man with a gold earring in his left lobe was in attendance. She smiled and held up her pass, which was duly inspected. The man returned her smile and hoped she would 'have a nice day'.

She pulled the wheelie along the corridor, hearing the babble of voices swell and recede as she passed the living room. She was scrutinising the map of the Hall, so didn't notice the man stepping out from a room on her right. He had a mocking smile and straight, light-red hair that came down to his shoulders. His navy suit looked creased, making her wonder if he hadn't just taken it out of his suitcase.

He barred her way. 'Madame,' he said, bowing. 'May I show you something?' he added, in a French accent.

'Of course,' she said.

'Is that a map of Sangster Hall?' he said, glancing at the sheet in her hand.

'Yes, it is.'

'May I?'

She handed it to him.

His eyes never leaving her face, he tore it slowly into strips before folding them into a little square. From his jacket pocket, he produced a small black wand. He tapped it against the square three times, then proceeded to unfold it.

'Your map, madame,' he said, handing it back.

She turned it over. There, in blue biro, was the circular mark she'd made next to the staircase leading to her room.

'*Merveilleux*,' she murmured, wondering when he had made the substitution. It must have been when she'd glanced at his face.

'My workshop is on Monday at ten a.m.' He bowed. 'If you would care to attend.'

'I may do,' she said, smiling.

Another bow, and he returned to the room.

Dania followed the corridors, noting the signs, until she reached her staircase. The pictures on the walls were sombre oils in gilt frames and, as far as she could tell, landscapes. That would help if she lost her map. She took the stairs to the first floor and counted off the room numbers.

She was passing a half-open door when she heard Kirstine Welles's throaty voice. She paused to listen.

'No, Scott, I've told you before. We're not having her living with us. And that's final.'

A man's voice. 'Look, love, she's your kin. She'll be no trouble.'

'Aye, maybe no trouble *now*. But in a short while, we'll be having to wait on her hand and foot.'

'Come on, she's sprightly enough.'

'*Now* she is. You're not listening. You never do.'

'She'd be better off with us.'

'You don't get it, you numpty. Let me spell it out, then, seeing you're incapable of understanding. One of us will eventually have to give up work to look after her, and no mistake.' A pause. 'And it's not going to be me,' she added nastily.

'But why not? You're exhausting yourself helping me run my business.'

'Excuse me. *Your* business? It's *our* business – unless I'm very much mistaken.'

'I meant our business,' he said wearily. 'It was a slip of the tongue.'

'More like a slip of the brain.' Another pause. 'I've put too much into the business to give up now. And, anyway, we can't afford it. Arranging and managing these events requires us both to work twenty-four seven. Twenty-five eight is more like it.' There was a note of exasperation in her voice. 'And we're already close to insolvency.'

'It's seasonal, Kirstine. It'll pick up.'

'Aye, right.'

'Anyway, we've had some last-minute bookings. More than we expected.'

'It'll be the ghouls wanting to come because of these murder stones, or whatever they are.'

'You don't think there's anything in that story, do you?'

'That's mince. I read about it in the *Tele*. Edward Sangster's brothers did a flit years ago and tongues started wagging that they'd been murdered. Now that Edward's died in a car accident, someone thinks it's fun to say he's been murdered too. Who cares as long as it's pulling in the punters.'

Yet Scott couldn't let it go. 'Let's get back to what we were discussing, love.' A deep breath, audible even from the corridor. 'We can get someone in to look after her.'

'Och, not this again. Don't talk so wet. Have you any idea how much a carer costs? On top of our bills?'

'It's not right her living alone like that.'

'I'll tell you what's right. *I* decide what to do with her. She's *my* kin, not yours. So shut it.'

Dania had the impression the conversation was coming to an end and, not wanting to be caught eavesdropping, grabbed the wheelie and padded past the door. A few moments later, she reached her room.

The door sighed as she pushed it open. The blended odours of floral polish, wood and new paint greeted her as she stepped on to the beige carpet. She'd expected something grander, like a four-poster, but the room was furnished simply with a double bed, bedside cabinet and mirrored wardrobe. A red phone stood on the cabinet. The single picture on the green-painted wall was a portrait of the man she now recognised as Captain William Sangster. Although he was wearing a severe dark suit, there was no mistaking the soldier in him.

133

Dania parked her wheelie and crossed to the diamond-leaded windows, anxious for a view that wasn't a wall of fog. Fields of snow stretched before her, with dense woodland beyond. The trees were conifers of different heights and various shades of green. A path straggled between them, disappearing into the distance. She made a mental note to explore the wood at the first opportunity, as she'd reached the stage where the endless white landscape was starting to weigh her down.

She shook out her clothes and hung them in the wardrobe. A glance in the bathroom confirmed her suspicions that it had been a recent addition. There was just enough room for one person to move around. Two people? Forget it.

She sat on the bed, thinking through the conversation she'd overheard, and wondered who this unwanted relative of Kirstine's was. Her mother, perhaps? Time was when elderly parents would come to live with their children; women either didn't work or would give up their work to care for them. But in this modern world, that was no longer the case.

Yet she'd learnt something: *We're already close to insolvency*. So would Magic Week turn their fortunes round? Especially since they'd managed to snare the Great Manderfeld? Dania pored over the programme. There were several workshops already under way, although none hosted by Hennie. His show was after dinner, and he was probably deep in his preparations.

Right now, however, she had other plans. She left the room and made for the stairs, pausing to listen as she passed Scott and Kirstine's. But no sound came from the room. After reaching the ground floor, she took the turning towards the back exit. And as she followed the narrowing corridors, she experienced once again the sensation that someone was behind her. Perhaps there was a draught in this part of the house. Yet what she was hearing were faint, pattering footsteps. It was impossible to determine their direction.

Minutes later, she found Mavis's room. The door was ajar. She risked a peek inside and saw that the armchair was empty. She knocked loudly.

'Who's there?' came the thin, reedy voice.

'My name's Dania Gorska.'

There was the sound of footsteps, then the door was pulled wide. Dania gazed into the unnerving, clear blue eyes.

For a second, the woman's expression shifted to one of alarm, but after studying Dania she must have decided she wasn't a threat. She drew her lips back into a smile. 'I don't get many visitors, so you're very welcome. Come in, come in.' She stepped back, still holding the door.

The room was as warm as Dania remembered, but since Mavis was wearing a thick blue cardigan over a thick blue dress, Dania decided to keep her jacket on in a possibly misguided gesture of solidarity.

'Would you like a coffee?' Mavis said. 'I've got a kettle here,' she added, indicating the small table behind the armchair. The kettle stood next to a red telephone.

'Can I give you a hand?'

'No need. Now, it's only instant. The Jaffa cakes are finished and I've no milk, but I take it that's fine with you.' It wasn't a question.

Dania moved one of the wing-backs so it faced the armchair, and lowered herself into it, feeling the seat sink under her weight. The upholstery was completely gone.

'So your name's Dania,' Mavis said, adding coffee powder to two blue mugs.

'That's right.' She felt some explanation was necessary. 'Duncan told me you live here by yourself. And you like a good blether. And so do I,' she added quickly.

'Aye, I live on his charity. He's a good man.'

Mavis returned with the mugs. Dania couldn't help noticing that, although the woman walked slowly, she was perfectly steady and, unlike many old people, lifted her feet rather than shuffled.

'I've not made it too hot, lass.'

'That's fine,' Dania said, sipping. The coffee was lukewarm, and very sweet.

Mavis settled herself in the armchair. 'So what kind of a name is Dania?'

'I'm Polish.'

The woman ran her thin fingers through her wispy hair. Her eyes took on a faraway look. 'I mind well seeing the Polish soldiers when I was a lass. They'd be queuing up outside the Locarno dance hall – it closed after the war – och, and they looked so braw in their uniforms.'

'Did you live in the city at the time?'

'I've always lived on the estate. But my mam took me into the city on occasion.'

'And are you going to take part in Magic Week?'

'Oh, aye,' she said firmly. 'I've been looking forward to it ever since Scott told me.'

'Scott Balfour?'

'He's one of the organisers. Lovely gentleman. He drops in now and again, and we chat about the Hall and what went on in the old days. He's been running his events here for a wee while, now.'

'I've met him. He gave me a glass of champagne when I arrived.'

'Aye? I'll let you into a secret,' Mavis added, with a wink. 'He often brings a bottle of something when he calls. Something stronger than champagne.'

'He introduced me to Hennie Manderfeld, the illusionist. Are you going to his show tonight?'

'What time would it be starting?'

'Eight o'clock.' Dania took the programme out of her bag. 'It's in the ballroom.'

'There'll be plenty of time to get myself over. Someone brings my supper at six,' Mavis said, gesturing with her thumb towards the large table at the back. 'Now and again, I eat with Eddie and the others.'

Dania wondered if Duncan had informed her of Eddie's death. Perhaps not. At least, not yet.

'I only eat twice a day now,' Mavis went on. 'Lunch and supper. For breakfast I just take coffee.' She took a gulp from her mug. 'I mind when the boys were here though, I'd eat like a lion.'

'The boys?' Dania said hopefully.

'Watson and Fraser. But they're long gone.'

'Gone where?' Dania said, trying not to appear too interested.

'To pastures new. I don't ken where, or what they're doing there.'

So the woman didn't believe they'd been murdered. Did she know about the murder stones?

'I've seen their portraits around the house,' Dania said, after a silence.

'I have a pile of old photos if you're interested.' Mavis turned to the bureau. 'In the top drawer, you'll find my album. Perhaps you could fetch it for me.'

'Of course,' Dania said, her heart galloping.

'It shouldn't be locked. I used to lock it, but I've mislaid the key.'

She drew out the black-backed album and laid it on the woman's lap.

'You'll need to come round to my side, lass.'

Dania abandoned the wing-back and brought over a cane chair. Now that she was close to the woman, she recognised that same dry smell of age she associated with her own grandmother.

The album was one of those old-style affairs with heavy paper and adhesive corners holding the photographs in place. The photos in the first few pages were black and white, some old enough to be brown and yellow. The more recent were in colour.

'These are the last ones I have of the boys,' Mavis said, turning to the back. She tapped a photo with a yellowing fingernail, her expression softening. 'They were bonnie lads, right enough.'

Three young men were staring into the camera. They were dressed casually in jeans and sweaters.

'So which is which?' Dania said.

'This one here is Eddie. You can tell. He always had a face like fizz.'

'Why was that, then?'

'He was worried about the estate and that it was no longer profitable. At least, that's what I overheard. I worked as a maid then, so I moved around the house doing my chores and that.' She smiled, the corners of her eyes creasing. 'My mam was a maid before me. She told me that, after a while, maids become invisible. So I'd hear the boys blethering. Shouting would be a better way of describing it. Everyone blamed everyone else for the poor state of the farm. But Watson and Fraser didn't seem to care about it as much as Eddie.'

'And which one is Watson?'

'That's him, in the middle. He was the oldest. You can't see it here, but he had a tattoo. Wait a wee bitty. There's a photo of it somewhere.' She went back through the pages. 'Here it is, lass. He had a close-up taken.'

On the man's right forearm could be seen the inked blue-black words SEMPER PARATUS.

'I haven't a scooby what it means,' Mavis was saying. 'I knew once, but I can't mind now.'

'It means "Always Ready".'

'Aye, that's it.' She rested her gaze on Dania. 'How do you know that?'

'I studied Latin.'

'Are you an RC then?'

'Roman Catholic?' Dania smiled. 'Yes.'

'Me too. You should go and see the wee chapel in the tower. It's Roman Catholic. There's a story about how it came to be there, but my memory isn't what it was.'

'I'll make a point of visiting. But this tattoo, why did Watson have it? Is Semper Paratus the family motto?'

'Aye, now that I *do* remember. The oldest Sangster lad always had it on his right arm. Meant he was ready for anything the world could throw at him. So Logan had it, and his father, William, before him.'

'But only the oldest boy?'

'That was the tradition.' Her expression softened. 'I mind when young Watson had it done. He was greetin' like a bairn.'

'How old was he?'

'Fifteen, I reckon. Or thereabouts. He was my favourite of the Sangster boys. I know you're not supposed to prefer one over the others, but there was something about him that was different. He was a dreamer when he was a lad. Aye, and he never grew out of that.' She smiled. 'We had some grand old times together. Even after he grew to manhood, he'd drop in for a chinwag. We laughed a lot in those days,' she added wistfully.

Dania nodded at the album. 'And who took these photos?'

'My lad, Robbie, took some. But I don't know about the older ones.' She turned the pages, her veined hand shaking slightly. 'This here is William Sangster on his wedding day.'

A serious-looking couple was gazing solemnly at the photographer. The groom was a younger version of the officer whose portrait hung above Dania's bed as well as over most of Sangster Hall. He was wearing a high-collared shirt and one of those suits with ultra-wide lapels that were fashionable before the war. The bride wore a multi-layered silk dress, and a veil that came over her head like a cap, ending halfway down her forehead in a line of tiny flowers. She was holding a bouquet of lilies.

'He married Rhona,' Mavis went on. 'Could you take the photo out? My fingers can't manage it these days.'

Dania lifted the album from the woman's lap. As gently as she could, she detached the photo from the corners, and turned it over. Someone had written in blue ink, in a looped cursive hand.

'Can you tell me what it says, lass? My glasses are in the bedroom.'

'William and Rhona Sangster. Fifth of August, 1929.'

'Aye, 1929. You can't tell from the photo but she had the most gorgeous blonde hair. There's a portrait of her in the ballroom. I remember when she posed for it. I was a lass, then. It took several days before the artist finished. But at that time, women like her didn't have much to do.' She glanced at Dania. 'Not like now, I reckon.'

Dania replaced the photo. 'Are there any of you?'

Mavis cackled with laughter. 'You want to see what I looked like when I was younger, eh? All right.' She took the album and flicked through it, stopping at a page of photos. They were of a younger woman with a boy of about ten, standing outside a stone-built, tiled cottage. There was little difference in the images, only a slight change in stance, or an altered expression, as though the photographer had kept going until he'd got it right, and then had decided to develop all the photos anyway.

'There, that's me and Robbie,' Mavis said.

The boy had wheat-coloured curls that came down over his ears. The woman, whom Dania would never have recognised as Mavis, had shortish dark hair heavily backcombed and flicked out above her shoulders. She was wearing a polo-neck sweater and a flared miniskirt in a red tartan.

'That was taken in the sixties,' Mavis said. 'Aye, I mind that time fine well. It was all Beatles and CND.' She tapped the photo. 'I could do a somersault, and my hair would still stay like that with all the lacquer I sprayed on it.'

'And where is Robbie now?'

'He and his wife died in a plane crash, God rest their souls.'

'I'm so sorry.'

'Ach, well, the grim reaper comes for us all in the end.'

Dania wanted to ask more about Robbie, but the finality with which Mavis shut the album made her wonder whether another time wouldn't be better. She was considering taking her leave, when something through the window caught her attention. It was a circular stone structure, several metres away, in what might be called the south wing's courtyard. Next to it was a large wheel-barrow. 'Is that a well?' she said.

Mavis shifted round, making the armchair creak. 'Aye, it used to have a roof and a handle and all that. But that's long gone.'

'I take it it's no longer in use.'

141

'It wasn't even when I was wee. I was warned to keep away from it. If you fell in, it would be a long time before anyone heard the splash, and no mistake. Mind you, you'd have to climb up, which isn't easy with those smooth stones. And I think there's a wooden lid over it now.'

Dania's gaze strayed again to the album. She wondered idly what secrets it might reveal. The woman must have caught her looking because she gripped the album and held it to her chest. Her face took on a strange expression. It was as though a veil had been drawn over her eyes.

Dania knew when to back off. 'Well, it's nearly lunchtime, so I'd better leave you. Yours will be arriving soon, I expect.'

The woman smiled faintly. 'Aye, that it will.' She relaxed visibly. 'Thank you for looking in, lass. That was a nice wee chinwag we had.'

'Maybe I'll see you tonight at the show. In the ballroom.'

'Eight o'clock.'

'And thank you so much for the coffee.'

She was aware of the woman's lingering stare as she left the room.

In the corridor, Dania took out the map and, deep in thought, studied the route back to the dining room. And what had she learnt about the Sangsters? Not much that she didn't already know. But there was one thought that kept whirring in her head: there was something in that photo album that Mavis didn't want her to see. Something that had happened in the past. And perhaps something that would help her solve her case.

The album was kept in the top drawer of the bureau.

I used to lock it, but I've mislaid the key.

She felt a smile forming.

CHAPTER 11

Dania traipsed back along the corridors, meeting no one. The dining room was in the same wing as the living room and the library, and not far from the office. As she approached, the sound of cutlery and glasses filtered from within but, on entering the high-ceilinged room, she found only a couple of dozen people in a space that could easily hold twice that number. Her guess was that the closer they came to eight o'clock, the more the guests would arrive at the Hall. Curiosity had made her look up Hennie Manderfeld online. She'd been amazed to read about his international standing, some sites even referring to him as the world's number-one illusionist. Definitely a reason not to miss the show. According to one website, his net worth was in the hundreds of millions.

The guests, Marek among them, were helping themselves to food from the long buffet. Marek glanced in her direction, then smiled and nodded to one of the tables. She took a plate from the stack and heaped it with salads and cold meats. After filling a glass with mineral water, she carried everything to where he was sitting.

'I wondered when I'd see you, Danka,' he said, slipping into Polish. 'Where's your pass?' he added. 'Didn't they give you one?'

She put a hand to her chest and noticed only then that the pass was missing. It crossed her mind that it had fallen off at Mavis's. But then a young woman in a floral-print dress in blues and yellows strolled over to their table. She had lively brown eyes and curly hair that wouldn't stay under the old-fashioned straw hat. 'I think this is yours,' she said, handing the pass to Dania.

'Thank you,' Dania said, relieved. 'Where did you find it?'

The woman smirked, then handed the pass she was holding in her other hand to Marek. 'And I believe this is yours, sir,' she said.

'But how . . . ?' Marek began.

She tilted her head, acknowledging their amazement, and backed away respectfully.

'Now *that's* what I call a trick,' Dania said. 'Making our passes disappear.'

'As long as they don't make my food disappear. So, what have you been up to this morning?'

'There's an old lady living in the south wing. She used to be a maid here. I've had a chat with her.'

'And from that look on your face, I'm guessing she knows more than she's letting on. Right?'

'Right.'

'The trick with old ladies,' he said, cutting up a meatball, 'is to charm them.'

'I'll try to remember that. And what about you?'

'I've been interviewing. Not just the illusionists, but the guests.'

'What about the locals? Do you happen to know how many are here?' she asked, remembering Kirstine's comment about the ghouls.

'A fair number.' Marek raised an eyebrow. 'Interesting how they came right out and told me they were here because of the murder stones.'

144

'And did you learn anything that might help my investigation?'

'None of them was old enough to have known the Sangster brothers.' He took a sip of wine. 'Are you staying tonight?'

'I am. Why do you ask?'

He lowered his voice. 'It's that south wing.'

'What about it?'

'I can't put my finger on it. But something woke me in the middle of the night.'

'A lady?'

'Be serious, Danka. No, it was a noise. Not creaking floorboards, I know what they sound like. It was more of a slithering sound, as though someone was running a hand over the door and trying to find a way in.'

She set down her fork. 'Was it coming from inside your room?'

'I don't think so. It could have been from the corridor. Or maybe even from the floor above. I couldn't pin it down.'

'The floor above is unused.' She studied him. Marek wasn't the sort to be easily spooked. If he'd heard something, it wouldn't have been his imagination. 'Are you sure it wasn't a magic trick?'

'Making me believe I was hearing something?' He shook his head. 'I checked the time. It was nearly three in the morning. Even the illusionists have to get their beauty sleep.'

'You know, these old houses can often make strange noises as they start to cool down at night.'

'You may be right.' But he didn't look convinced.

She pushed her chair back. 'I'll get us a couple of coffees.'

'And what are your plans for the afternoon?' he said, after she'd returned.

'I need to check in with Honor. She's interviewing the estate workers.'

'Good luck with that. The ones who live in the workers' cottages are spread out far and wide.'

'Marek, when you researched that article about the murder stones, did you ever interview Allan Mackie?' she said, blowing on her coffee.

'The name's not familiar.'

There was a sudden buzz of excitement. Hennie Manderfeld had entered. He was dressed in a navy suit. And he wore a polka-dot bow tie. Dania would have liked to see him swap that with one in a different colour, assuming it was the type that was knotted properly and wasn't clipped on. He seemed to recognise one or two of the guests, and smiled, exchanging the odd word. On seeing Dania, his smile widened and he bowed respectfully, looking at her longer than was necessary.

'You've got a fan there, Danka,' Marek murmured.

But as she followed Hennie's progress round the room, she became aware that a man at a nearby table was gazing steadily, not in Hennie's direction, but in hers. He had his cup to his mouth and she saw only his thick brows and dark hooded eyes. His hair, which flopped over his forehead, was so black it was almost purple. The man's fixed stare made her suspect he knew who she was. She'd tried to avoid media attention, although it wasn't always possible, and there was a distinct chance he'd caught her photo in the papers. Or maybe he'd heard her give evidence in court. She pretended she hadn't seen him and turned her attention to Marek.

'Are you going to try any of the workshops?' he said, studying the programme. 'There's one on escapology. Learn the secrets of Harry Houdini.'

'Didn't he end badly?'

'No idea. But there's also one on card tricks. I might give that a try. It will help me wow the ladies.'

146

She threw him a look of amused complicity. When it came to wowing a lady, no one did it better than her brother. He didn't need a card trick. He just had to smile. And possibly bow, and kiss her hand.

They finished their coffee and got up to leave.

As they reached the door, the lady with the straw hat was waiting for them. 'Your pass,' she said, handing it to Dania. 'And yours, sir,' she said to Marek.

She was evidently delighted by their reactions, Marek's especially. He was gaping in astonishment.

'Come on,' Dania said, taking his arm. She had the feeling that there would be more of this before Magic Week was over. Maybe she could learn the trick herself, and pass the time at West Bell Street by divesting her colleagues of their warrant cards.

Dania left Marek puzzling over the easiest way to get to the workshop, and made her way to her room, trying a different route this time. But as soon as she entered the south wing, the sound of the footsteps returned. Each time she stopped, so did they. She concluded that what she was hearing was an echo, and must have something to do with the wood panelling on the walls.

In her room, she called the police station. She was surprised to hear Hamish answer.

'I thought you'd be on the assault course,' she said, trying to sound stern, and failing.

'I decided West Bell Street couldn't dispense with my services just now, ma'am,' came the serious reply.

She felt a smile touch her lips. 'I see. Anyway, the reason I'm calling is to check whether the CCTV from the deer centre has come in.'

'We got it an hour ago. Are you able to connect from where you are?'

'The Wi-Fi here is strong so it should be straightforward. Can you stay on the line while I get set up?'

She unlocked the wheelie and lifted out the laptop. Then, sitting cross-legged on the bed, she went through the authentication process to connect to the station's VPN. A moment later, she was online at West Bell Street. 'Right, I've found it,' she said to Hamish.

She played the recording, keeping the phone to her ear. The clip, taken at night, showed a tall wire fence and a double-barrelled wooden gate. After a moment, a figure dressed in black approached, not from the path, but from the woodland beyond. From the camera's angle, it wasn't obvious what he was carrying but it was long and thin. From the way he paused at the gate and positioned the object, Dania guessed he was using a heavy-duty bolt cutter to break the padlock.

'Okay, Hamish, I see what he's doing. He's opened the gate and disappeared.'

'Keep watching, ma'am.'

'Right, he's back in the shot. He's got a rope round the deer's neck and is leading it out of the field.'

'See if you can zoom in.'

'It looks as though he's feeding it.'

'My guess is the deer might not have come willingly otherwise.'

The figure closed the gate, and he and the deer disappeared into the woodland.

'We've had Tech enhance the shots where the face is towards the camera,' Hamish said. 'The man's wearing a balaclava and a black woollen cap. If it weren't for the snow reflecting the light, we'd have had difficulty seeing him at all. Aye, and he's wearing gloves.'

Dania rewound to the start. The timestamp indicated that the theft had occurred on 7 February at 10.38 p.m. 'According to this, it was on Sunday night. That's the day before Edward Sangster's crash.' She played the clip again, stopping as the figure reached the trees. 'Do we know where that woodland leads?'

'Aye, ma'am. It's north of the deer park. There's a road behind those trees. It leads to Lundie.'

'He must have left a truck on the road. Or some other vehicle.'

'My guess is he finished the animal off before driving away.'

'Any cameras on those roads?' she asked, knowing the answer.

'I'm afraid not.'

'That deer was taken on Sunday night. But it's only now we're seeing the CCTV. Didn't they notice the deer was missing? And the padlock on the wooden gate was broken?'

'They said they rarely use that gate. The dirt track behind it is full of potholes. The lass I spoke to was surprised the cameras there are still functioning.'

Dania rubbed her face. 'Not that it's helping us any. There's no way of identifying the person who took the deer. I take it that's the only local centre that's missing one?'

'The only one.'

'In that case, we'll act on the assumption that that's the deer that was dumped on the road. If so, the perp had it for less than twenty-four hours.'

'He could have kept the carcass in his truck. A bit risky, but not if he lives somewhere isolated.'

Dania brought up a map of the area. 'The problem is that almost everywhere round there is somewhere isolated.'

149

'Aye, nothing but farms and cottages, right enough. Is it worth knocking on a few doors?'

'Have we got anyone left? I thought everyone was on Honor's team.'

'There are a few uniforms still here.'

'In that case, we should get on to it. Someone might have seen a man unloading a truck.'

'There's one thing that puzzles me, ma'am. There's a deer sanctuary much closer to the crash site. It has no CCTV and the fencing isn't anywhere near as sturdy. A few clips with a pair of wire cutters and you've got your deer.'

'Any red males?'

'Loads, according to the owner.'

'A sanctuary. Maybe the perp didn't know of its existence.'

'Unlikely, ma'am. It was on the news just the other day for the rescue work it's been doing. So why wouldn't he take a deer from there, eh? He could have killed it shortly before Edward Sangster went on his wee drive, and then transported it straight to that road. Minimum risk. And yet he went all the way up near Lundie for his deer.'

'It can only be because he lives near Lundie and has somewhere he can hide the animal.'

'And if that's the case, we'll definitely be asking a few questions in the Lundie area.'

'But say only that a deer was reported missing. No mention of the Sangster case.'

'Aye, I'll brief the uniforms. And is there anything to report from your end?'

Dania gave an account of what she'd learnt from Mavis.

'A photo album in an unlocked drawer,' Hamish said. She could almost hear him scratching his chin. 'Sounds like an invitation for a thief. One who's a copper, anyway. Although you never heard me say that.'

'The difficult part is finding a time when she's not there.'

'Is her room locked at night?'

'She lives in a private house, in an isolated part of the south wing. It may not occur to her to lock the door, even though the house is full of strangers.'

'There you are. Problem solved.'

Easy for him to say, Dania thought, as she disconnected. He wasn't the one taking the risk.

Dania played the CCTV footage through again, hoping to discover something that might provide a clue to the man's identity. He was well built, but that hardly qualified. There were many well-built Scots who worked the land in these parts. And he walked normally. That was a blow. She'd once solved a case by comparing the limp of someone caught on camera with that of a suspect.

She shut down the clip and powered off the laptop.

At that hour in the afternoon, most people were at workshops, and Dania met no one as she headed to the west wing. She was passing the ballroom when she remembered Mavis's description of Rhona Sangster, and that her portrait was hanging there. Curiosity got the better of her.

The door was open. She looked in, seeing a huge oval room with a wooden floor. Rows of chairs faced a makeshift stage. From where she was standing, she couldn't see Rhona's portrait, so it had to be on the wall behind the door. She crept in, although there should be no reason for stealth: the door wasn't locked and there wasn't a sign telling people to stay out.

She spotted the portrait immediately. It was so tall that it wouldn't have looked out of place in a gallery, but here it took up almost the entire height of the wall, dwarfing the pictures on either side. She gazed at it, then stepped back to take it in properly. The woman had the sort of looks she'd seen in actresses from Hollywood's Golden Age. Her waved blonde hair was parted at the side and fell thickly to her shoulders in a style reminiscent of Lauren Bacall's. She wore long white gloves and a strapless evening dress in a colour best described as ashes of roses. Round her neck was a silver chain from which hung a pale pink gemstone in the shape of a heart. The artist had positioned her so that the light fell on the stone and was reflected from its many facets. Her eyes wore a dreamy expression, as though the interaction between herself and the painter was the only thing that mattered.

Dania was so engrossed that she jumped when she heard the voice.

'What do you think, Dania?'

Hennie was standing behind her. 'I believe this is Rhona Sangster,' he said. He gazed at the portrait, his expression softening. 'Rarely have I seen such a beautiful woman.'

'It's the dress I can't get over. And that colour.'

'Ah yes, a man sees only beauty, and a woman notices the clothes.'

'That's a little unfair.'

'Does she remind you of anyone?'

Dania studied the painting. 'The hair says Lauren Bacall, but the face says Grace Kelly.'

'That would be my diagnosis, too. I believe it is the only image of her in the Hall.'

'With looks like that, you only need one.'

He laughed. 'How true.'

'And are you here to prepare for your show this evening?'

'Indeed I am.'

'In that case, I'd better leave you to it.'

He gave a little bow. 'I hope to see you later. I would come early if you wish to find a seat in the front row.' His lips twitched. 'That will give you the best chance of working out how I create my illusions,' he added, his voice a challenge.

He'd seen right through her. 'What sort of time should I arrive?' she said, trying to keep her face straight.

'I would say about seven thirty.'

'I'll try to be there.' She smiled, and made for the door.

As she loitered in the corridor, wondering whether there was enough light in the sky for a walk, her phone rang. It was the boiler man informing her that due to a sudden cancellation they had a free slot on Monday morning, and he could fit her in provided she dropped her front-door key off at his place before six o'clock, as he'd be going out then, it was Saturday night and he had a life, ken. She glanced at her watch. She'd need to get to her flat to pick up the spare key, then zip out to his place in Hilltown. No worries, she told him. She'd make it easily.

CHAPTER 12

By the time Dania reached Sangster Hall, it was close to eight o'clock. A traffic accident on the A90 had necessitated a detour, but she'd made it to the boiler man's in time. On the way back, she'd stopped off at McDonald's to gobble a burger, finally understanding what was meant by the expression 'fast food'. She'd decided against returning the same way and played with her sat-nav to see if there was a better route. But the road she chose south of the A90 was a disaster – a tree had fallen on to one of the lesser-used B-roads and she'd had no choice but to turn round. She arrived at the Hall frazzled and exasperated. What was wrong with this bloody place that they couldn't keep the roads clear?

Scott Balfour was at the reception desk. He handed her the key. 'I wouldn't bother trekking to your room, Dania,' he said kindly. 'Hennie's show is about to start. You should be able to make it, although I think we're at the standing-room-only stage.'

'Thanks,' Dania said, leaving her coat on a hanger.

She hurried along the corridor and joined the latecomers outside the ballroom. As she entered, she heard Hennie's voice.

'Dania, there you are.' He was at the door, greeting the guests.

'I'm sorry I'm late. Something came up.'

'I've reserved a seat for you in the front row.'

'That's kind of you, but you didn't have to go to such trouble.'

He smiled. 'It was no trouble.' He laid a gentle hand on her back and gestured along the aisle. 'As you can see, we have a full house.'

'From what I've been hearing, this isn't a show to miss.'

'I do hope so. Your seat is there on the left-hand side. There should be a ticket on the chair.' With a slight bow, he returned to the guests milling at the door.

As she reached her seat, the spectators in the front row smiled and nodded. There was no one she recognised. She looked around, hoping to find Marek, but before she could scan the audience, the lights dimmed. To huge applause, Hennie walked up the aisle and on to the stage.

'Ladies and gentlemen, welcome to my magic show. For the next hour, I hope to entertain you. And when you leave, I trust you will not leave disappointed.'

A wave of excitement rippled through the audience.

For the first illusion, Hennie asked for two volunteers. Several guests raised their arms. He chose a man in the row behind Dania. 'I think you had your arm up first, sir,' he said courteously. 'And you, madame,' he said to someone near the back.

As the guests left their seats, Hennie's assistants wheeled in what looked like two wardrobes, and parked them at opposite ends of the stage. Hennie opened the doors to show the audience that the wardrobes were empty. He then invited the lady to enter one, and the gentleman the other. To the strains of lively music, the wardrobes were then moved backwards, forwards and towards each other, but they never crossed. When the music stopped, Hennie opened the doors. The audience gasped. The two volunteers had swapped places. Dania had to admit that this was a different calibre of illusion from those she'd seen on television.

Similar illusions followed, including levitating objects and passing them in front of and behind the open-mouthed volunteers. The act that impressed Dania the most was when Hennie draped a red sheet over a seated guest, removed the sheet with a flourish to reveal an empty chair, and then looked expectantly along the aisle towards the door. The audience turned to see the guest pushing his way through the crowd at the back. It was the speed with which Hennie pulled off this illusion that stunned Dania.

He smiled disarmingly. 'Now, for my final act, I need one more volunteer.' He stepped off the stage and scrutinised the rows left and right, searching for a suitable guest.

Dania glanced over her shoulder. Hennie had stopped halfway down the aisle and was extending a hand to someone sitting at the end of a row. 'Madame,' he said, 'would you join me on the stage?'

Mavis got to her feet. 'Aye, gladly. I've always wanted to be part of a magic show.' She took his arm and they walked slowly up the aisle, an unlikely bride and groom, Mavis beaming and acknowledging the applause.

As they passed Dania, the woman's eyebrows shot up, and she grinned broadly. 'You're here too, lass,' she said.

Dania nodded, smiling.

Hennie helped Mavis on to the stage. She was wearing thick brown stockings, and an old-fashioned flowery dress in pinks and reds, which buttoned up to the neck.

'May I ask your name?' Hennie said politely.

'You may ask, son, but I'm not sure I'll give it to you.' This was greeted with roars of laughter. 'Ach, I'm joking,' she added. She was clearly enjoying the attention. 'My name's Mavis.'

'Delighted to meet you, Mavis.'

'And what should I call you?'

156

'Hennie.'

'Aye, all right.'

He picked up the pack of cards. 'Do you play cards, Mavis?'

'I used to when I was younger.'

'And which games did you play?'

'When I was a wee lass, it was snap. But in my teenage years, I played poker.' More laughter. 'And I was good at it, too. Beat all the boys in my class, and no mistake.'

'And what type of poker was it?'

'Every type. I can't mind the names now. But there was one with seven cards and two of them were dealt face up.'

'Seven-card stud, I think it's called.'

'Aye, that's the one. You present your five best cards.'

Hennie shuffled the pack. 'Can you remember your best hand, Mavis?'

'I never got higher than a flush.'

'That's pretty good. Maybe you and I could have a game afterwards.'

'Provided you buy the drinks, laddie.' More laughter.

'So, let me put together a poker hand with a flush.' He glanced up. 'For the non-poker players in the audience, a flush is any five cards of the same suit.'

'There's also a straight flush and a royal flush,' Mavis said, with an air of importance.

'That's right.' He picked out five cards and showed them to Mavis. 'Would you agree that that's a flush?'

'Aye, it is.'

'And would you tell the audience what they are?'

'They're all hearts. There's a four, six, nine, ten and a jack.'

'Thank you.' He set the cards on the table and picked up a small white envelope. 'Now, I'd like you to check that there's nothing inside,' he said, handing it to Mavis.

She pushed back the flap, then made a show of emptying the contents on to the floor. 'Right enough, it's empty,' she said, handing back the envelope.

He picked up the poker hand and shuffled the cards, then held them out, face down, in a fan. 'I'd like you to take a card and show it to the audience. Perhaps you could say which it is for the benefit of those at the back. And then put it inside the envelope and seal it.'

Mavis held up the card, calling out, 'Ten of hearts.' She placed the card in the envelope, licked the flap with relish and pressed it down.

'Would you please place the envelope in this glass bowl? Thank you. I'm going to cover the bowl with a red cloth.'

She watched with interest. 'That's a bonnie colour, and no mistake.'

'And now would you be so good as to remove the cloth?'

With a flourish, she pulled off the cloth. There were gasps from the audience. The bowl was empty.

'Aye, well, that's a trick and a half,' she said. 'I wish I could have done that with my electricity bills.' She studied him. 'So where's the envelope, eh?'

'We'll have to find it. Perhaps someone in the audience could help us. Would you choose someone and point them out to me?'

Mavis scanned the rows, finally letting her gaze rest on Dania. 'That lady, there,' she said, lifting her arm and extending a bony finger.

Hennie smiled at Dania. 'Madame, would you tell the audience your name, please?'

'It's Dania.' She got to her feet.

'I notice your bag is on the floor. Would you mind opening it?'

'Not at all.' She lifted the flap. Inside the bag was a white envelope. It looked identical to the one he had made disappear. She took it out and held it up.

'Would you open it, please? And can you tell us what is inside?'

She removed the playing card. 'It's the ten of hearts.' Without prompting, she held it up for the audience.

As everyone applauded wildly, she handed the card to Hennie, who had stepped down off the stage.

'Thank you,' he said, inclining his head.

He returned to the stage and, after acknowledging Mavis's assistance, helped her to her seat. The way she was grinning suggested it was she who'd performed the trick. He returned to the stage, took several bows, then parted the curtains at the back and disappeared.

That was impressive, Dania thought. She remembered the layout from earlier and knew there were no doors there, only wood panelling.

The guests were leaving the room, chattering excitedly. She waited until most had left, then started to make her way out. As she approached the door, she caught sight of someone familiar. It was only a fleeting glimpse, and he'd turned his head away, but for an instant she thought she'd recognised Euan Leslie. That expertly cut brown hair and tailor-made suit were unmistakable. She grew cold with fear.

She tried to push through, but the crowd in the corridor was moving too slowly and, by the time she'd left the room, Leslie had disappeared. She leant against the wall, her mind in turmoil.

'Dania? Are you all right?'

Scott Balfour was gazing at her with an expression of concern.

'I'm fine,' she said. 'It was a little hot in there, that's all.'

159

'It was good of you to take part.'

'How could I refuse?' Her mind was still churning. 'I couldn't help noticing that many of the attendees seem to have come just to see Hennie Manderfeld,' she said, directing her gaze towards the front entrance.

'His show was sold out almost as soon as Magic Week was advertised.'

'I've got a friend who was unable to get a ticket.' She injected a note of hope into her voice. 'I don't suppose there are any vacant slots for Mr Manderfeld's workshops?'

'I'm afraid not,' Scott said, smoothing his hair. 'Those tickets were sold out almost as quickly as the ones for tonight's show.'

Dania tried to look disappointed. 'Are there *any* tickets left for *anything*?'

'Aye, we have a fair few. Some of the lesser-known magicians aren't sold out.' He looked at her enquiringly. 'Would you like to come to the office and we'll see what we can do?'

'I'd be so grateful,' she said, smiling dreamily.

She followed Scott across the corridor, dodging the people making their way to the dining room. He opened the door to the office. It had been left unlocked.

She was surprised to see that no password was required to get into the bookings database. Or even into the system. Wasn't this the machine Grace had sat at when she'd visited a few days before? Perhaps not. Scott and Kirstine might have brought their own.

He pulled up a spreadsheet. 'Now, is your friend interested in anything in particular? Card tricks? Making things vanish? Pickpocket tricks?' He scrolled down the events column.

'You know, I might be wrong, but I have a feeling she's already got one ticket for something, although I can't remember what.'

'Mm, yes, it wouldn't do to buy another ticket for the same event. What is your friend's name, and I'll check?'

'Bonnie Leslie. Although she might not have used that name. She sometimes uses her middle name, Fiona.'

'I'll search on surname, then.' He entered the name 'Leslie' in the search field and hit return. A second later, a single record appeared. Euan Leslie had bought a ticket for Hennie's 8 p.m. show.

'Looks as if we're okay,' Scott said, returning to the previous screen. 'Now, let me see what we can do for you. Aye, there's a vacant slot for the Children's Magic session on Wednesday afternoon. You learn how to perform tricks at children's events, like birthday parties, and so on.'

'She'd like that,' Dania said enthusiastically. 'She's a primary school teacher. May I buy the ticket?'

Scott smiled indulgently. 'I think we can let your friend have a complimentary ticket, seeing as Magic Week's already started.'

'That's very generous of you,' Dania said, surprised. If this was how Scott conducted business, no wonder he and Kirstine were almost on the rocks.

'Your friend can pick it up at the door. Shall I put Bonnie or Fiona?'

'Bonnie,' she said, already thinking up a reason to explain why 'Bonnie' would be a no-show for the event.

He tapped at the keyboard. 'All done,' he said, with a smile. 'And to seal the deal, could I buy you a drink in the bar?'

'I rather think I should be the one buying.'

'Wouldn't hear of it,' he said, pushing back his chair.

As they left the office, Dania watched Scott close the door but leave it unlocked. She wondered whether this was how he and Kirstine always operated. Perhaps one or the other was either in

161

the room or not far away, and constantly locking and unlocking would be too much of an inconvenience. But it struck her that residential guests' names and room numbers would also be on the computer. And that included Franek Filarski's.

'So what did you think of Hennie's show?' Scott said, as they took a table in the dining room.

The area had been converted into a makeshift bar. An assortment of spirits and beer bottles stood on the buffet table, but unfortunately Dania's brand of vodka was not among them. She settled for a glass of Scotch while Scott helped himself to a beer. From the corner of her eye, she glimpsed Marek sitting with a man, demonstrating a card trick, doubtless one he'd learnt at the workshop. At least he was where she could keep an eye on him. Yet the more she thought about Euan Leslie the more her anxiety grew. She forced herself to look at Scott.

'The show?' she replied. 'It was brilliant. I've never seen anything as professional.'

'How do you think he did that final trick? With Mavis and the cards?'

Dania turned the glass in her hand. 'He obviously decided on the ten of hearts in advance of the show. When he removed the five cards from the pack to make the flush, he made sure that the ten was one of them. It was probably right at the top.'

'What if Mavis hadn't said it was a flush? Wouldn't that have ruined it?'

'You can have a ten in any hand. Even a royal flush. In fact, especially a royal flush.'

'Aye, go on,' Scott said eagerly.

'He put the poker hand down on the table and asked her to check the envelope. It's at that stage that he must have made the substitution.'

'For what?'

'For five cards, all of which were the ten of hearts.'

'That way, whichever Mavis chose would be the ten of hearts, right enough,' Scott said, his voice drifting. 'And that's what she put in the envelope.'

'Exactly. And before the show, he put another sealed envelope with a ten of hearts into my bag.'

Scott slapped his forehead. 'Of course. He must have.' He gazed at her in admiration. 'Any idea when?'

'He greeted me at the door and spoke to me for a minute or two. I remember he diverted my attention away from him and towards the room.' She smiled self-consciously. 'I'm guessing that's when he slipped the envelope into my bag.'

Scott brought the bottle to his lips. 'What if Mavis had said she'd never played cards?'

'It's hard to find anyone of her age who hasn't. But Hennie would have come up with another way to perform the trick using the ten of hearts. I'm sure illusionists know how to think on their feet.'

'And the reason she chose you must be because you were sitting directly under one of the ceiling lights. The room lights were dimmed except for the ones above the stage and the front row.'

The flaw in that argument was that everyone else in the front row was also either sitting directly under a light or was well illuminated. Hennie was unlikely to have secreted similar envelopes on them all. Dania swirled the whisky, wondering how he had pulled this off. And then it came to her that he had walked Mavis slowly up the aisle and, given where Dania was seated, the

163

woman couldn't have failed to see her. Given a choice, she was more likely to have selected someone she knew rather than a complete stranger. Dania lifted her head and stared into the distance. And that meant that Hennie must have known that the two women were acquainted. Yet how? Mavis's behaviour towards him, although entertaining, wasn't that of someone who had already met him. It could only be because he'd seen her either enter Mavis's rooms or leave them. Which meant he'd been in the south wing. But then, it was he who'd told her about the family tree in the music room, so he'd been there at least on one other occasion.

'And I suppose that trick with the glass bowl was sleight of hand,' Scott was saying.

'He removed the envelope as he was placing the cloth over the bowl,' she said, almost mechanically.

'Sounds like you should be running our workshops.'

But she was no longer listening. Her mind was on Hennie. What had he been doing in that deserted south wing? Searching for the back door? Or for something else?

'You look as though you're dreaming up a trick of your own, Dania.'

'Sorry.' She forced a smile. 'So, tell me, how long have you been an events organiser?'

'About ten years. Kirstine and I were librarians before that. That's how we met.'

'And what made you change career?'

'Oh, you know, we wanted something different, more exciting.'

'And has it been exciting?'

He threw her a grin. 'Aye, well, it's certainly been different. But it's harder work than either of us anticipated.' He smoothed his hair. 'It's made me go prematurely grey,' he added, with a laugh.

'And is it always Sangster Hall that you book for events?' she said, lifting her glass to her lips.

'Mostly. There's a place up in Perthshire we use sometimes. But Sangster Hall was ideal for what Hennie wanted, right enough.'

'Why February, though? Wouldn't summer have been better?'

'Trying to marry up Hennie's availability with that of the Hall proved to be near impossible. Summer was a write-off. In the end, this was the best time, although he had to do a bit of rearranging of his other commitments. We hadn't expected this snow, though. When it came down, we thought it would deter the locals. Mind you, they'd heard about these murder stones. Aye, I think it was more that than Hennie's reputation that made them plough through the drifts to get here.'

'Do you know anything about these murder stones?'

'It was before my time. It's been interesting reading about them, though. I had no idea this place has such a rich history. Two brothers murdered, and now possibly a third.'

The voice came from behind Dania. 'Scott! I've been looking everywhere for you!'

Kirstine was marching towards their table. From the expression on her face, it was clear she was only just keeping the lid on her simmering anger.

'You were supposed to relieve me on the front desk,' she said, ignoring the glances from the room.

'Sorry,' he said, in a timid voice. 'I forgot.'

'Will you excuse us, Tanya?'

Scott scraped back the chair. Dania was about to thank him for the drink, then thought better of it. 'I really appreciate your sorting out that ticket for me,' she said, looking at him gratefully, and hoping this would reinstate him in his wife's good books.

He beamed. 'My pleasure.'

He followed Kirstine out of the room. If he'd had a tail, Dania thought, it would have been between his legs. She felt sorry for him.

She finished the whisky. The man at Marek's table was taking his leave. Dania seized her chance.

'Franek,' she said, approaching his table, 'how was the workshop?'

Before he could reply, she slipped into Polish. 'I need to talk to you as a matter of urgency. Were you at Hennie Manderfeld's event?'

'I was held up.'

'You missed a great show,' she said. She dropped her voice. 'You also missed Euan Leslie.'

Marek paused in the act of bringing his beer to his lips. He set down the glass. 'Here? At Sangster Hall? Are you sure it was him?'

'I had Scott Balfour check the database. Leslie bought a ticket for Hennie's show.'

Marek ran a hand over his mouth. 'But he won't have seen me. I was in another part of the building.'

'But he might know you're booked into the Hall. Scott and his wife seem to be lax about locking the door to the office. Not only that, their laptop isn't password-protected. Anyone who's determined enough could slip in and see which sessions you're booked into. And, more seriously, which room you're in.'

'I keep the door locked at night, Danka.'

'As if that would deter Leslie,' she said, with a sneer. 'Look, it's perfectly possible he doesn't know you're here. He might have wanted to see Hennie's show. As far as I could tell, he left the Hall straight after. On the other hand, he could have found your room number and has now passed it on to one of his goons.'

Marek considered this. 'What would you suggest? I return home?'

'That's the last place you should go. If things get sticky here, you can bunk at mine. Hold on, though. Leslie will know by now that we're related. So avoid my flat.' She glared at him. 'Just be careful, Marek. Don't do anything stupid.'

He tried a grin. 'What could happen to me here? I'm surrounded by people. No one can make me disappear. Even in a magic trick.'

But Dania was less sure. If anyone could make people disappear, it was Euan Leslie.

CHAPTER 13

It was nearly midnight by the time Dania reached her room. She'd insisted on seeing Marek to his, and was relieved to find that it was not far from her own. Not that it would help if one of Leslie's men found his way in there at night. An experienced assassin was more than capable of dealing with a locked door and silently dispatching a sleeping victim. Marek had assured her that his phone would be on his bedside cabinet, and he'd call her if he felt he was in danger.

Dania lay on her bed, thinking not about Marek, but about Mavis. Most of the guests were still boozing in the bar, and she'd met no one on her way to the first floor. And, more likely than not, the south wing would be completely deserted. More to the point, however, Mavis would be fast asleep and snoring away. Now was the time.

Dania slipped off the bed and rummaged in her wheelie for the pair of shoes she'd packed especially for such an eventuality. She'd had them made by a London shoemaker, who'd assured her that, on almost any surface, unless the wearer had the tread of an elephant, their footsteps wouldn't be heard. She tugged them on and left the room.

The stairs were well lit so she didn't need to use her phone's torch. She'd not brought her map, but she had a good memory for places she'd visited and knew how to get to Mavis's room in the dark. But as she stole along the corridors, she again heard the faint pattering that she'd attributed to the echo of her own footsteps. Except that her footsteps no longer made a sound. There was now no doubt: someone else was in the south wing.

She considered giving up, but why waste an opportunity? And whoever it was might not be near enough to catch her in the act. Moments later, she was in Mavis's corridor. There were no lights, but the only door was the one to the woman's apartment. Dania ran a hand along the panelling until she found it. After pausing to listen, she gripped the doorknob and turned it first one way, then the other. But the door wouldn't budge. She swore softly in Polish. She would have to bide her time and wait for another chance. And the chance would present itself, of that she was certain. She retraced her steps.

She was passing the music room when she heard the piano. Someone was playing Mozart, the third movement of his Piano Sonata K. 284. The pianist was highly proficient and she was tempted to creep in and see who it was, but disturbing a pianist in the middle of a performance was not something she was inclined to do. Strangely, there was no light from under the door, suggesting that the mystery person was playing in the dark. Not many could tackle the lively third movement with its rapid variations even in daylight. She listened for a minute or two longer, then crept away.

Back in her room, she heard the faint dying notes of the piano sonata. Then silence. So who was this midnight player? She was now regretting not waiting for the piece to finish and seeing who left the room. But that would mean coming up with an explanation for loitering in Mavis's corridor. It irked her that the woman had locked her door. Did she do that every night? If so, it left Dania with few options. She wondered if she could enlist Marek's help, perhaps have him distract Mavis or, better still, offer to take her for a short walk and somehow arrange for her to leave the door unlocked. But before trying this, it would be worth another attempt. She prepared for bed, remembering to leave her phone where she could grab it. As she drifted off to sleep, she thought she heard a bumping noise from the floor above. But that was impossible. The rooms there were empty.

Dania rose early, and managed a shower, despite banging her elbows on the walls. At least the water was hot and not lukewarm, as she'd expected at this hour. After a quick breakfast, she would head out to West Bell Street.

As she entered the dining room, the rich smell of roasted coffee beans reached her nostrils. The only person there was Kirstine Welles. She was staring at something on the wall, her hands cupped round a mug. Seeing Dania, she frowned. 'Good morning. If you're after a cooked breakfast, I'm afraid you're too early. There are only croissants.'

'Croissants will be fine,' Dania said cheerfully.

The almond croissants were dusted with icing sugar, and the closest thing she'd been able to find to the *chrust* her grandmother made. This pastry delight was hard to come by in today's Poland, which served up the sort of confectioner's cake found in the rest of Europe. It was mostly in certain areas of rural Poland that *chrust* was sold. Dania helped herself to two pastries, then poured coffee from the urn.

'Have you eaten?' she said to Kirstine.

'Ages ago.' She continued to study the wall.

Dania set her breakfast down on the nearest table and joined her. Kirstine was gazing at a large photograph.

'These must be the Sangster brothers,' Dania said, recognising them from an identical photo in Mavis's album.

Kirstine shot her a glance. 'Aye, their names have been in the papers for days. It's these murder stones. You must have read about them.'

'I think everyone has by now. So do *you* think these brothers were murdered?'

'The polis did a thorough investigation for the two who disappeared. If they'd been murdered, they'd have found their bodies.'

Dania was surprised by the comment, given the large number of ways in which bodies could be disposed of. 'If you had to hide a body, couldn't you do it on the estate?' she said, keeping her gaze steady.

'But that would have been the first place the polis would have looked. And they didn't find a scooby.'

'There was talk that one brother, Fraser, had committed suicide.'

'That's all clishmaclaver,' Kirstine said, in a superior tone. 'Idle gossip,' she added, seeing Dania's blank look. 'I can understand someone murdering Edward Sangster, mind. He was worth a bob or two.'

'The estate, you mean?'

'I heard a rumour he'd taken out life insurance. For an obscene amount of money . . . and it will go to his next of kin, right enough,' she added meaningfully.

'Duncan?'

'There's no one else.'

'This rumour. Can you remember where you heard it?'

'Scott and I went out for a wee swallie on Thursday night. The bar was packed, and everyone was nattering about Edward's death,

171

and these murder stones. Someone said he happened to know that Edward had this life-insurance policy.' She gestured with her mug to where bits of cornicing were missing from the ceiling. 'I reckon the amount Duncan will rake in will restore this place to its former glory. Aye, and there'll still be a packet left over.' She finished her coffee. 'I have to run, Tanya. Lots to do today.' She dumped her mug on the table and hurried out of the room.

Dania pulled out her phone and, selecting the highest resolution, took several photos of the Sangster brothers. They were wearing severe black suits, as though they'd returned from church, which they probably had, given the bible in Edward's hand. She took close-ups of the faces. Then, after bolting her breakfast, she left the room, not looking where she was going. She collided with someone.

She gazed into Hennie's alert blue eyes. 'I'm so sorry,' she said, stepping back.

'Dania.' He looked surprised to see her. 'Someone else who's up early, I see.'

'I'm a light sleeper. And the first night in a strange place is never brilliant.'

He smiled. 'I'm the exact opposite. As soon as my head hits the pillow.'

'I wanted to tell you how much I enjoyed your event last night.'

'Thank you,' he said, with a slight bow.

She was tempted to ask if he'd met Mavis before the show, but decided against it. He would suspect she might have cracked his card trick. But how he'd managed the others was beyond her.

He peered into the dining room. 'Have you had breakfast?' he said hopefully.

'I have.'

'Maybe I'll see you at lunch, then.'

'I'll look forward to it,' she said, in the full knowledge that she'd be having lunch at West Bell Street.

He nodded, smiling, and then disappeared into the room.

She watched him go, unable to get the conversation about Edward's life-insurance policy out of her mind. Another chat with Duncan was high on the agenda.

Dania arrived at the police station later than she'd intended. She'd checked the traffic and discovered that the A90 was still blocked. Acting on the assumption that the tree on the B-road wouldn't yet have been lifted, she'd tried another route. But the sat-nav had refused to acknowledge it and kept trying to direct her to the road she suspected would still be impassable. After stopping and studying Google Maps, she'd switched off the sat-nav and found the city centre the old-fashioned way.

'Boss,' Honor said, as Dania entered the incident room. 'We didn't think you'd make it. The roads are hopeless.'

A few officers were at their desks, entering their reports. 'So, where's Hamish?' Dania said, struggling out of her sheepskin.

'His turn to fetch the coffees.' The girl stared at Dania's jacket. 'Where did you get the flower?'

'Flower?' she said, glancing down. In her lapel was a red rose. 'How on earth . . . ? That wasn't there when I put it on this morning.' The only person she'd seen was Kirstine, but there'd been no opportunity for the woman to place the rose there, and why would she? Then she remembered bumping into Hennie. That had to be it. Another one of his illusions. While she was extricating herself and gazing into his eyes, he must have slipped the rose into her lapel.

173

'Well, it *is* February the fourteenth,' Honor was saying. A smile flickered on her lips. 'Looks as if you've got an admirer.'

Dania was removing the flower when Honor said, 'Better leave it in, boss. You don't want to hurt his feelings. You know how frail the male ego is.'

Hamish arrived with the coffees. He set the tray down on Dania's desk. 'I saw you come in, ma'am, so I've got you your usual cappuccino.'

'Thanks,' she said, smiling at him.

Honor peeled the wrapper off a Tunnock's teacake. 'Shall I go first, then?'

'Before you do, let me bring you up to speed on a couple of developments. There's a rumour that Edward Sangster not only made a will, but also took out life insurance. And the sum to be paid out is huge.'

'Who told you this?' Honor said.

'Kirstine Welles, one of the event managers, mentioned it at breakfast. She'd overheard it in a pub.'

'Could be speculation, ma'am.'

'But we can't afford to ignore it.'

'Why would Edward Sangster take out life insurance?' Honor said. 'Wouldn't the premiums be better spent fixing up Sangster Hall? Or putting it into the estate? Buying new equipment, perhaps?'

Dania cradled her mug. 'Maybe he wasn't the one taking out the policy. It could have been Duncan.'

'Can you do that? Take out insurance for someone else?'

'I believe so. But there are conditions, otherwise there's a risk the beneficiary could murder the person insured and stand to pocket a huge payout. I'll make enquiries at the Hall. If there's any truth to it, I'd like to know who would benefit.' She paused. 'The other thing involves Euan Leslie.'

'The gangster property developer?' Hamish said.

'I saw him at a magic show last night.'

'Did *he* see *you*?' Honor said, frowning.

'I was part of the show.'

'Whoa! Really? What happened, then? Did you levitate? Or disappear?'

'It was a card trick. But Marek's at Sangster Hall for Magic Week.'

'Is that a problem, ma'am?'

For Hamish's benefit, she explained the situation with Marek's undercover work, his article in the *Courier* and the Fraud Squad's deal granting Leslie immunity. And her fear that Leslie might have seen Marek and discovered which room he was in.

'You need to get him out of there,' Hamish said firmly. 'Euan Leslie's not the type to play nice.'

'I'll try to make him leave, but it won't be easy.' She understood then that she'd made a mistake in not being more insistent, something she'd have to rectify on her return. Suddenly she wanted the meeting to be over, so she could get back to the Hall. 'It's not just pulling him out. It's finding somewhere he can hide.'

'He can bunk with me,' Honor said. The corners of her mouth lifted. 'I understand he's a great cook.'

'That's not a bad idea,' Dania said slowly. 'So now that's sorted, tell me what you've got.'

'Okay, boss, we've interviewed all the workers, the ones living on the estate and the ones in town. We quizzed them first about the route Edward was in the habit of taking.' Honor unwrapped another teacake. 'They all knew about it. One even traced it on a map. Up to Knapp, then Fowlis, Benvie and back home.'

'How did they know?'

'That old banger of his had broken down more than once. Edward didn't have a phone. The first time, he was lucky enough to flag down a passing car, and there aren't many of those out there. The second time, he wasn't far from a cottage, and they rang the Hall. In both cases, Duncan arranged for an estate worker to fetch Edward while a farm vehicle towed the Morris Traveller back. One of the estate mechanics fixed it.'

'I take it the car didn't have breakdown insurance.'

'Apparently not. Anyway, word soon got round the estate that Edward took these little drives.'

'What did the workers say about him? Did they like him? Was there anyone who didn't?'

Honor screwed up her face. 'It wasn't dislike exactly. But they didn't speak particularly warmly about him. Although he liked to think he ran the estate, the men would often double-check his instructions with Duncan.'

'And what about the footwear?' Dania said, pulling up Johnty's report.

'Everyone we spoke to has the same German Trommers the mystery man wore. They swear by them. Even the workers who've been there for years wear them. Most take a size ten. It's a common size for men.'

'We're not getting very far, are we?' Dania said, running her hands through her hair.

'Not only that, boss. The men are between five foot ten and six foot two in height. And weight-wise they fall into the range Johnty gave us. They're big guys. They have to be for the kind of work they do. And, before you ask, we took a pair of bathroom scales with us.' Honor grinned. 'We made them take their boots off before we weighed them.'

176

'How did they feel about that?'

'They were okay with it, on the whole. We peddled the usual stuff about eliminating them from our enquiries.'

'Except it looks as though we haven't eliminated anyone.'

'Those are the breaks,' Honor said sympathetically.

'What about alibis for the night of the seventh? When the red male was stolen from the deer place?'

'Some had alibis. Some didn't.'

'How many are left from the old days?'

'A fair number. And they helped me track down one or two who are retired. We asked them all about Watson and Fraser, and what they thought had happened to them. They remembered those early murder stones, how they kept popping up again and again. But as for who the stonemason was, or the killer, they weren't prepared to speculate ... which brings me to Allan Mackie.'

'Go on.'

'The men who remembered him didn't have a good word to say about him. One even spat on the floor when I brought his name up.'

'That's nice. What did the carpet have to say?'

'We were in a shed at the time.' Honor took a gulp of coffee. 'They pretty much corroborated what was in Watson's diary. That Mackie drank, threatened people if he didn't get his own way, and his behaviour worsened after he was laid off. He was a quick learner, though. His manager didn't have to explain anything more than four times.'

Dania brought up the photos she'd taken of the work diary. 'Let me remind you of what Watson wrote about Mackie on the fifteenth of June. "Saw Allan on the estate. For once, he was stone-cold sober. Told me he was giving us Sangster brothers one last chance to see him right and give him his job back. I said the job no longer existed, and I didn't want to see him hanging around the estate again. There was a strange look in his eyes. A calm look. As though he had some sort of plan." The fifteenth of June was two days before Fraser was last seen.'

Hamish made a grab for the last teacake. 'You think this plan might have involved killing Fraser and Watson, ma'am?'

'Although it begs the question why he didn't finish Edward off at the same time.'

'Maybe he needed Edward alive to keep the estate running so he could get his job back. Duncan was a wee bairn, wasn't he? He couldn't run the place. And wasn't Logan blootered the whole time?'

Dania gazed at Hamish. 'That's a good point. Did either of you find out whether Mackie ever did get his job back?'

'I'm one hundred per cent confident he didn't, boss.' Honor worked the controls on the computer. 'It's not a pretty story. He was arrested on June the twenty-sixth. That's a few days after Fraser and Watson went missing. Here's his charge sheet.'

'He murdered an entire family?' Dania said, in disbelief.

'According to the records, he claimed he'd been possessed by the devil, and so couldn't be held responsible for his actions.' Honor snorted. 'You can imagine how *that* went down in court.'

'I take it the evidence was irrefutable?'

'He'd been seen entering the house with a butcher's cleaver. When they tracked him down to his place, not only was he still wearing the bloodstained clothes he'd had on earlier, but the cleaver was on the kitchen table.'

'And he didn't deny the charges?'

'He continued to claim he didn't know what he'd done. It was the devil inside him made him do it, he kept on saying. But he was examined by two psychiatrists. They both testified that he was perfectly sane and was probably pointing the finger at the devil in a feeble attempt to get a more lenient sentence.'

Dania read through the reports until she came to the SOCOs' photographs. '*Boże mój*,' she murmured. 'Two teenage children, along with their parents.'

'The kids were well known in the community. And much loved, by all accounts.'

'I hope the bastard's still in prison,' Hamish muttered, running a hand over his eyes.

'He got life with a minimum sentence of thirty-five years,' Honor said. 'He's been released on licence under supervision of a criminal justice social worker.' She must have seen the looks on their faces, because she added: 'The parole board concluded he was no longer a risk to society. He'd been a model prisoner, who'd co-operated with the system, taken part in various anger management programmes and so on. And he had no previous convictions.'

'When was he released?' Dania said.

'A fortnight ago . . . February the first. Exactly one week before Edward Sangster's crash.'

They stared at one another.

'Let me get this straight,' Dania said. 'He's imprisoned shortly after the two older Sangster brothers – for whom he had no love – go missing. He serves thirty-five years. And then a week after he's released, Edward – for whom he also had no love – dies in suspicious circumstances.'

'That's about the size of it, boss.'

'Where is he now?'

'He lives in the Lundie area. We've got the address.'

'Lundie? Near the farm where the deer was stolen?'

Hamish glanced up. 'Aye, ma'am.' He straightened. 'And I heard from Tech today. They've analysed the CCTV footage from the deer farm. Their conclusion is that the man in the balaclava matches the physical profile, regarding height and weight, of the mystery man Tam Adie saw leaning into Edward's car.'

'We'll need to check out Mackie's height and build. Which prison was he in?'

'Shotts,' Honor said.

HMP Shotts, a maximum-security prison for long-term adult males, was exactly the kind of prison the man would have been sent to.

Hamish stroked his chin. 'I wonder how he fared inside.'

'After being convicted for butchering kids?' Honor sneered. 'It's a miracle he survived thirty-five hours, let alone thirty-five years.'

Dania scrolled down the screen until she found Allan Mackie's image.

'That's the photo taken shortly after his arrest,' Honor said. 'He was twenty-three when he was sent down. I'd have to say he doesn't melt my butter,' she added scornfully.

Allan Mackie gazed at them with insolence in his cold metallic eyes. His thick hair was badly cut, as though he'd done it himself without using a mirror. He had a tight mouth, and a flattish nose, suggesting it had been broken. But it was his weathered complexion that identified him as someone who laboured outdoors.

'I wonder what he looks like now,' Dania said.

'And what he's been doing with himself, ma'am.'

'He's been out for exactly two weeks.' She glanced at Hamish. 'I think we need to pay him a visit.'

CHAPTER 14

'We'd better check which roads are clear,' Hamish said, as he started the engine.

'Okay, sweet cheeks, where d'ya wanna go?' the sat-nav's voice purred.

'What the——?'

Dania laughed. 'Blame Honor, not me. She switched it.'

'I'm not having this,' Hamish muttered. He played with the settings and got the female voice back.

'Honor won't like that, you know.'

'Tough. If she wants a Yank, she can change it back.'

'Oh, I'm sure she will.'

He found the channel that informed drivers of the road conditions. 'Looks as if our best bet is to take the Coupar Angus, ma'am, and then follow the Newtyle Road.'

'Let's hope Mackie's at home.'

'Where would he be in this weather, eh?' Hamish said, pulling out on to the Marketgait. 'I doubt he'll have found a job yet. And, anyway, it's nearly lunchtime.'

'Would you harbour a grudge after thirty-five years, Hamish?' Dania said, after a while.

'Depends on what caused the grudge.'

'I could understand it if someone had killed your wife. Even after such a length of time, you might want to take your revenge. But is losing your job that big in the grand scheme of things?'

'Aye, well, for some it might be. The 1980s saw rising unemployment, and no mistake. Having work wasn't just a means of staving off hunger. It gave you status. You could hold your head up.'

'I've been thinking about the modus operandi. If Mackie killed Fraser, and made it look like suicide, he must have gone to all that trouble because he thought the finger would be pointed at him.'

'I reckon so. According to the police records, he was in prison when he was interviewed. But he was never charged.'

They were passing through Lochee. The old snow lay piled up on the pavements in greasy-looking grey mounds, and people walking the streets had to pick their way round. Not everyone was equipped for the weather. A woman with a pram was trying to negotiate the ice while holding a young child by the hand. She wasn't even wearing snow boots.

'What I can't understand,' Dania said, 'is that if Mackie did murder the Sangster brothers and was careful not to leave traces of himself, a few days later he walks into a house with a meat cleaver and slaughters four people. No attempt to hide what he's done, or even deny he's done it, except for that excuse about the devil possessing him.'

'I read one of the psychiatrist's reports, ma'am. She concluded that something had made him lose the plot big time.' He shrugged. 'Maybe killing the Sangsters tipped him over the edge.'

'Did he show any remorse at the trial?'

'None. But the prison counsellor's reports show that he quickly accepted responsibility and was a model inmate.'

They were now on the Coupar Angus Road, approaching the

Camperdown circle. Dania peered through the windscreen at the heavy sky. This was Dundee in winter – grey ice, grey buildings, grey sky. Grey people. And the weather was forecast to deteriorate. She would have to get back to Sangster Hall, or she might be snowed out.

She glanced at Hamish. 'Is Honor still giving you flak over your no-show at the assault course?'

'Aye, well, she seems to have forgotten about it.'

'That won't last long.'

He grinned. 'No, I reckon not. Right, ma'am, here we are. Newtyle Road.'

Newtyle Road, also known as the B954, took them out of the village of Muirhead and into farmland. The ground sloped gently upwards to the left but, once they'd taken the bend, it was unbroken flat fields on either side. The land was furred with snow, and the road ahead wound its way through the fields, like a dark snake.

'Do you think Mackie will tell us anything useful about Fraser and Watson?' Dania said.

'Assuming he remembers. And if he does, assuming he wants to talk about it.'

'I feel like I'm chasing shadows. Yet someone must know something.'

Hamish said nothing, the sign that he agreed but didn't want to make the usual confirmatory noises just for the sake of it.

They'd reached a line of trees, beyond which was the turn-off to a single-track road. A bunch of wilting flowers lay next to a pylon, marking the place where someone had died in an accident. As if conscious of this, Hamish changed down a gear and kept his speed low. The landscape grew more varied, and they passed the odd farmhouse with its attendant cottages. A dog ran out after them, barking like a maniac.

A short while later, they passed a signpost to Lundie.

'Mackie's cottage is somewhere here, according to the sat-nav, ma'am. If we reach the church, we've gone too far.'

'There's the church,' she said, indicating the redstone building on the right. 'Just as well it's winter. With all these trees, we'd never have seen it.'

'Then where's the cottage?' Hamish backed into the lane and turned the car round. 'I'm going to crawl back. Perhaps you could tell me when you see it pop up on the sat-nav.'

'This is it,' she said suddenly.

The building, set well back from the road, was made of rough-hewn stone. The door had been carpentered together with different-sized planks, the newer ones nailed over the old. The wood was neither painted nor treated, and there was evidence of rotting, which would grow worse if not given attention. The same was true of the seals round the windows. To say that the roof was tiled was a gross overstatement. There were more slates missing than present, and all it needed was one good gust of wind for them to clatter to the ground. There was no gate or fence, or foliage of any kind. Patches of gravel were visible through the snow.

'Someone's at home,' Hamish said, nodding at the blue farm lorry half hidden behind the building. It was the type with a tipper that discharged its load. Next to it was what passed for a garden shed, except that there was no garden.

'See those trees on that ridge?' Dania said, squinting through the windscreen. 'Beyond is the deer centre, according to Google Maps. And there's a straight road from here to there,' she added meaningfully.

They left the car.

'Hold on a minute, Hamish.' Dania crunched across the gravel and peered through the lorry's window.

'How come Mackie has the money for something like this after only two weeks out of prison, ma'am?'

'We're about to find out.'

There was no bell, so she rapped loudly, feeling the door shake.

'Who's there?' came a voice from inside.

'Dania Gorska. I'm looking for Allan Mackie.'

There was a brief silence, suggesting the occupant was weighing up his options. Then they heard footsteps shuffling across the floor. A bolt was drawn back and the door creaked open slowly.

A huge bear of a man in a shabby black suit stood at the entrance. He was holding a bible in one hand.

Dania held up her warrant card. 'Allan Mackie?' When there was neither confirmation nor denial, she added, 'I'm DI Gorska, and this is DC Downie.' She glanced at the bible. 'I hope we're not disturbing you. Could we have a word?'

For a second, she thought he was going to slam the door in her face, but he turned and walked into the cottage, leaving the door open. She took this as a sign of invitation.

The door opened directly into the living room. The peeling grey wallpaper was from a bygone age and splotched with mould. There was little in the room other than the shabby armchair and sofa. No carpet or rug over the scuffed wooden floor, and no lampshade over the bare bulb hanging from the ceiling. A rickety chair had been pulled back from the rickety table. A storage heater stood under the window but, given the temperature, Dania doubted it was fully functioning. Through the partly open door at the far end, she glimpsed an ancient washing machine.

The man lowered himself into the armchair. He stared up at the officers without asking them to sit down. His suit was too tight for him, Dania noticed then. He'd put on weight in prison, something which was almost impossible, given the regimen. Studying his physique, she concluded he must have worked out regularly, and what she'd thought at first was fat must have been muscle. That wasn't the only feature that made him unrecognisable from his pre-prison appearance. He'd lost most of his hair and there was a deep scar across his cheek. His skin was no longer weathered but was the colour of putty. Only the flat nose and slit of a mouth identified him as the man in the photo.

'Are you Allan Mackie?' Dania said.

'Aye, that I am.' He had a thick voice as though there was something in his mouth that he hadn't completely swallowed.

She glanced at Hamish. They lowered themselves on to the battered sofa.

Mackie folded his hands over his bible. 'I didn't expect the polis. It's usually the supervisor who comes.'

'We're not checking up on you, Mr Mackie,' Dania said.

'No? What are you here for, then?'

'Did you live here before you were sent down?'

He drew his lips back into a sneer. 'If you're polis, you'll know I didn't.'

'And have you found work yet?'

'I'm on benefits. I'm still looking,' he added.

'I did wonder if you'd landed on your feet. I couldn't help noticing your tipper lorry.'

He bristled. 'If you're suggesting I lifted that, you're havering. It belongs to the farm up the hill. They've let me rent this place.'

'Why does the farmer keep the vehicle outside your cottage?' Hamish said.

'It's easier to park it on low ground when there's snow. So he told me, anyway.' He shrugged. 'No skin off my nose where he keeps it.'

'I see the key is still in the ignition,' Dania said, watching him.

What passed for a grin crossed Mackie's face. 'Aye, well, he mislaid it once, and his bidey-in gave him a row for it. He keeps the key in the vehicle so he can't lose it.'

'But he could lose the vehicle. Anyone could come along and drive it away.'

'That old thing?' He snorted. 'I doubt it.'

She opened her notebook. 'I'd like to ask you where you were last Sunday, Mr Mackie. That's the seventh.'

'I was here.'

'Alone?'

'Aye.'

'All day?'

'I went to church in the morning. I go every Sunday.' He clutched the bible. 'I'm not long back. As you can see, I'm in my Sunday clothes.'

'The church here in Lundie?'

'It's closed for renovations. I took the bus into town.'

She glanced at his shoes. 'You surely didn't wear those shoes in the snow.'

'Are you calling me a liar?' he growled.

'Not at all.' She gestured to her boots. 'But I couldn't walk in the snow without these.'

Her reply seemed to calm him. 'Mine are over there by the door.'

A worn pair of heavy-duty boots stood against the wall. She was too far away to determine the make.

'Did the farmer lend you those boots?'

'They're from the old days.' He seemed to think an explanation was necessary. 'A mate kept my belongings while I was in prison.'

'I see. And where were you last Monday round about six o'clock?'

'I was here. Alone.'

'Can anyone vouch for that? Did anyone talk to you? The farmer, perhaps?'

'Farmers haven't the time to blether,' he said, throwing her a withering look. 'He was away at his work. Why are you asking me these questions?'

'We're investigating the death of Edward Sangster. He crashed his car on Monday evening.'

Mackie stroked his chin. 'I mind now that I read something about that,' he said slowly.

'Were you surprised he'd met with an accident?'

'In this weather, people have accidents all the time.'

'There was no love lost between you and Edward, I understand.'

His voice was hard. 'What are you suggesting?'

'He laid you off, didn't he? When you were working at Sangster Hall back in the eighties.'

Mackie seemed to be weighing up his response. 'What if he did? He laid a number of us off.'

'And his two brothers, Watson and Fraser. What happened to them?'

'How should I know? They went away off somewhere.'

'You didn't get on with the Sangsters, did you?'

He froze then, like a rabbit in headlights, something that was not lost on Dania. He couldn't have been more different from the defiant young man of his arrest photos.

She decided to push him. 'There were rumours that Watson

and Fraser had been murdered. You wouldn't know anything about that, would you?'

He dropped the bible on to his lap and gripped the arms of the chair. His knuckles were white. 'If you're accusing me, you've forgotten one wee detail. I was in prison then.'

Dania glanced through her notes. 'You were arrested on June the twenty-sixth. Watson was reported missing the day before, and Fraser was last seen on June the seventeenth.' She looked up. 'So, no, you weren't in prison when they disappeared.'

'You're wasting your time if you're trying to pin their murders on me.'

'And you know they were murdered, do you?'

'I didn't say that. *You* did.'

'You were in prison, so you wouldn't have seen the original murder stones. But did you see the ones that have been erected recently?'

'Murder stones? I don't know anything about that.'

'Didn't you read about them in the papers? There were photos in the *Courier*.'

He shrugged, saying nothing. He picked up the bible and flicked through the pages, as though unaware of their presence.

'You mentioned you were looking for work, Mr Mackie. What sort of work would that be?'

He lifted his head. 'The land. That's all I know how to do.'

She was tempted to reply that farm work was a young man's job, but a glance at his body told her he'd easily be able to hold his own.

'Did you wear those old boots when you worked for the Sangsters?' she said, trying to make it sound like a throwaway comment. 'It's a German make, isn't it? Trommer, I think they're called.'

189

'Aye,' he said, in a bored tone, his attention back on the bible. 'I believe that's the make.'

'I think you can't get them now. What size do you take?'

'I take a size ten. Why do you want to know?'

'No particular reason.'

He closed the bible and stared at her.

'Are you glad Edward Sangster is dead, Mr Mackie?'

He seemed taken aback by the question. 'I don't much care either way.'

'What about Fraser and Watson? You had more to do with them, I understand.'

'Aye. And?'

'Are you glad *they're* dead?'

There was a strange light in his eyes. 'They're not dead.'

'How do you know?'

'Because I saw them a couple of days ago. Friday, early afternoon.'

Now it was her turn to stare. 'Where did you see them?' she said, feeling shock surge through her.

'I'd been to the Jobcentre at the Wellgate and was going into town. I saw Watson. Clear as I'm seeing you. He was walking in front of me in that particular way he does. Fraser was with him, although I didn't see his face, mind. But I saw Watson's. He turned round, like he was looking for someone.'

'Did he see you?'

'If he did, he didn't recognise me.'

'You're sure it was him?'

He lifted the bible. 'As God is my witness.'

Dania's mind was racing. 'What did he look like?'

'Like an older version of himself. He'll be what? In his sixties.'

190

He hauled himself to his feet. 'And now, if you've finished with your questions, I have lunch to prepare.'

'What do you make of that, ma'am?' Hamish said, when they were back on the road.

'I don't know what to think. Is it possible that, after all these years, Watson and Fraser have returned to Dundee?'

'And are alive, which is more to the point.'

'Could they have heard about Edward's death and decided that now is the time?'

Hamish threw her a sidelong glance. 'If Watson's alive, doesn't that make him the rightful heir to the Sangster estate? Although I don't know what the law says once presumption of death has been granted, right enough. Maybe Duncan still gets to keep everything.'

'Of course, it could be a fabrication by Mackie. He thinks we've reopened an old murder case and are about to accuse him, so he gets in first with some nonsense about seeing the brothers.'

'Except it may not be nonsense, ma'am.'

'Suppose it's true. Why would Watson and Fraser be walking around Dundee in full view of everyone?'

'I don't understand it, either. But could Mackie have been mistaken? Those brothers might be well-nigh unrecognisable now. I mean, look at Mackie himself.'

'True. Let's park that one for the moment. What else have we learnt?'

'He has no alibi for the time the deer was stolen. He had the means to transport it in that lorry. The key's always kept in the ignition. And the deer place is just over the ridge.'

'He could have hidden the animal's carcass in the garden shed.'

Dania massaged her temples, feeling a headache coming. 'And he also has no alibi for the time of Edward's death. And then there's that pair of Trommer boots. His shoe size is right. What about his weight?'

'Aye, well, he's a bit on the heavy side but I reckon he's in the range.'

'I bet he'd know about Edward's drives from the old days.'

'He'd also know those roads around Sangster Hall like the back of his hand, ma'am. And which ones to take with the least chance of being spotted. It all fits.'

'And it's all circumstantial.'

'What did you make of the bible, and the church-going? Do you think he's a reformed character?'

'Hard to say. I'm not a psychologist, but I've always thought that festering in prison for the best years of your life isn't likely to reform anyone.'

Hamish changed down a gear as they approached the inter-section with the A90. The blue in the sky seemed to have dissolved, and thickening clouds were gathering ominously as the sun started its decline. Dania checked her watch. There was still time to make it to Sangster Hall. She had a list of tasks she would assign the team once she returned to West Bell Street, and then she'd be on her way.

They were nearing the entrance to Dudhope Park when she caught sight of the men on the pavement. It was the red muscle car on double yellow lines that she spotted first. Hamish had slowed to a crawl to accommodate a couple of cyclists, although why anyone would be cycling in this cold was beyond her, so she was able to get a good look at the men. They were deep in conversation and paid no notice to the unmarked police car. Euan Leslie was wearing a navy coat in what could have been cashmere, and a Russian-style hat with the flaps up. His companion was bareheaded, otherwise Dania wouldn't have identified him. But as he moved his head, she recognised the thick brows and dark hooded eyes of the black-haired man who'd been observing her closely in the Hall's dining room. Except that, she now realised with something approaching terror, it must have been Marek he'd been studying.

As Hamish braked sharply to avoid the weaving cyclists, Dania grabbed her phone and took several quick shots.

She didn't wait until they'd reached the police station before calling her brother. 'Marek?' she said.

'Danka, this is a surprise. I've been looking all over for you.'

'Never mind that. I've just seen Euan Leslie with one of his hard men.'

'Where?'

'Here in Dundee. This man was at the Hall yesterday lunchtime. I saw him in the dining room. I thought he was staring at me but he must have been staring at you.'

Marek took so long to reply that she was afraid the line had gone dead. 'Hello? Are you there?'

'Still here.'

'Right, this is what you're going to do. No ifs or buts. Pack your bag and get over to Honor's. You know where she lives on the Lochee Road?'

'I can't, I'm afraid.'

'What the hell do you mean, you can't?'

'We're snowed in. It started to come down heavily around midday, and it's now impossible to drive. All the roads around here are blocked. Isn't it snowing where you are?'

Hamish was pulling into the station car park. Dania stared through the window. The first snow was sifting down, covering the ground like a baby's shawl. The weather would have come from the west. First Sangster Hall, and now Dundee. Although it could have been worse. If Marek was snowed in, that meant Euan Leslie's man was snowed out. But, then, so was she.

'All right,' she said. 'But be on your guard. And try not to be alone. And I want you to call or text me at least once an hour.'

'Leslie's hardly likely to parachute someone in, is he?' A pause. 'I've got to go, Danka. I'm booked in at a workshop.'

As they left the car, Marek's remark rang in her ears. No, Leslie was unlikely to parachute anyone in. But she happened to know that he owned a helicopter. And once it stopped snowing, all bets were off.

CHAPTER 15

'I'm guessing from the Polish that it's your brother you called, ma'am,' Hamish said, as they hurried inside.

'Did you see Euan Leslie just now before we reached the Dudhope circle? He was with the same man I saw at Sangster Hall. This man is one of his thugs, no question. I rang Marek to warn him to get out of there, but they're snowed in.'

'Aye, the forecast is for a huge downfall, but I thought we wouldn't get it until evening. Mind you, if Leslie's man is here in town, he won't be able to get out to the Hall.'

'The problem is that Leslie might have installed someone else there.' Seeing Hamish's glance, Dania added, 'Maybe I'm being paranoid.'

'Perhaps not, ma'am,' he said gently. 'The man has a large number of heavies he can call on, right enough. But Marek's been warned now. Even Leslie won't try anything in front of a crowd.'

'Marek's there for the rest of Magic Week. Leslie could easily find his room.' She stopped suddenly. 'That's given me an idea. I'll meet you in the incident room.'

She rang Marek again.

'Danka, for heaven's sake, I'm about to go into the library.'

'Then I'll make this quick. On the floor above your bedroom, there should be loads of unused rooms. But some will have furniture, possibly even beds. Find one and take your things up there.'

'I think you're overreacting.'

'Listen to me. I've attended the autopsies of Leslie's victims. There's no limit to what he's capable of. Promise me you'll do this.' When he didn't reply, she shouted, 'Promise me!'

Marek must have heard the panic in her voice, because he said, 'All right. I promise.'

'You'll have to make sure no one sees you coming and going to that floor.'

'I understand,' he said firmly. 'But I have to go now.'

She stood cradling the phone, wondering why the duty sergeant was looking at her strangely. Perhaps he'd never seen a near-hysterical woman screaming into a mobile in a foreign language. She signed in, avoiding his gaze, and hurried to the incident room.

The officers were standing gazing through the window and speaking in low tones. They turned as she entered. The wind had started up and was whipping the snow into puffs. By the time she'd crossed the room, all that could be seen was a white wall of swirling snow.

'Those of you who have far to travel had better leave,' she said, noticing that some had already disappeared.

All except Honor and Hamish picked up their jackets and nearly ran towards the door.

'What about you two?' Dania said. 'It's a bit of a trek to your respective flats.'

'I reckon we can walk, ma'am,' Hamish said, glancing at Honor.

'Hamish is right, boss. And if we get stuck, we'll limp back and spend a night in the cells. That'll look great on my CV.'

'Better still, why don't you both come back to Marek's with me?' Dania said. 'There's plenty of room.'

Honor grinned. 'Is there voddie in the freezer?'

'What kind of a question is that?' Dania said, trying to look scandalised. 'He's a Pole.'

'Aye, sounds good to me,' Hamish chipped in.

'So, how did you get on with Allan Mackie?' Honor said.

Dania pulled off her jacket. 'He's in the frame for setting up Edward's crash. He's the right height and weight, takes a size-ten shoe, owns Trommers. What else? Ah, yes, there's a lorry outside his cottage with the key kept in the ignition. And a shed where he could have stashed the deer's carcass.'

'And not forgetting that the deer place where the red male was stolen is just along the road,' Hamish added.

'But the most interesting thing is that he claims to have seen Watson and Fraser in Dundee. On Friday, in the early afternoon.'

'Get away,' Honor said, her eyes wide.

'He was insistent it was them. Even took an oath on his bible.'

'Then Watson and Fraser aren't dead?'

'Mind you, after so much time, he could have been mistaken. But we have to act on the information, and that means we assume they're alive.'

'They've not been back to Sangster Hall.'

'Which means either they're staying with friends from the old days, or they're renting.'

'Or one or other has bought a place, ma'am.'

'How many properties are there to rent?'

'Hundreds. And that's only in the city itself.'

Dania gazed out at the whirling flakes. 'They'll be in their sixties. Possibly still working. We'll start by supposing they're here under their own names.'

'It's Sunday,' Honor said. 'We're not going to get very far contacting the letting agents.'

'We'll make a start first thing tomorrow. That's if the agents can get in to open their doors.'

'If they're here under their own names,' Hamish said, 'people are going to notice, especially with them appearing on those murder stones. And if Mackie recognised them, there'll be others in Dundee who will, too.'

Honor chewed her thumbnail. 'They must be incognito, then.'

'Aye, and that will make finding them almost impossible.'

'There's something I don't get, boss. If Watson and Fraser were here on Friday, they'll know about Edward and his crash from the papers. You'd think they'd have been in touch with the Hall by now.' She tilted back in the chair. 'And if they had, wouldn't Duncan Sangster have told us?'

'He might have had a good reason for keeping quiet. If Watson rises from the dead, Duncan could lose the Sangster estate.' Dania glanced at her watch. 'Which reminds me. I have to make a call.'

Duncan answered at the first ring. 'Duncan Sangster,' came the weary voice.

'DI Gorska.'

'Inspector,' he said, in surprise. 'How can I help you?'

'There's something I need to check with you. Do you happen to know if your father took out life insurance?'

'If he did, that's news to me.'

'Mr Sangster, I have to ask. Did *you* take out a policy in his name?'

'I certainly didn't. Why would I?'

'If your father had taken out insurance, would he have told you?'

'It depends on when. If it was when I was a bairn, then, no, I'm sure he wouldn't. But if he'd done it more recently . . .' She

198

could almost hear the cogs whirring in his brain. 'He was a wee bit forgetful, especially after my mother died. Ach, if he had, I can't understand why he'd take out a policy so late in life.'

'Where would a policy be kept?'

'In the safe in the office, I expect.'

'Not in his room?'

'I suppose it could be. But he wasn't in the habit of keeping documents there. I'm willing to come over to the Hall now, if you like. We could check it together.'

'I'm in Dundee. I'd hoped to be back at the Hall this evening, but the roads are closed.'

'Aye, I see.' She detected the disappointment in his voice. 'When do you think you'll be back?' he said.

'As soon as the snow stops and the roads are cleared. I've no idea when that will be.'

'Tell you what, Inspector, I'll get myself over shortly, check the office safe and get back to you.'

'Could you also give me the name of your solicitor? And the name of your father's bank?'

'In case the policy isn't in the safe?'

'There's a chance it's been mislaid. Your father's solicitor would have a copy.'

'And you think the bank might have a copy, too?'

'If they don't, they could at least tell us if your father was still making payments.'

'Aye, I understand. I'll text you the information.'

'And how are things at the Hall?'

'I've not been over today, but I saw fewer cars in the car park. I reckon the only people here just now are the residential guests.'

'And how is your wife managing?'

'She's not too bad. She gets a wee bit teary when we talk about my dad.'

It was on the tip of Dania's tongue to mention what she'd heard about Watson and Fraser, but she stopped herself. They could be going down a blind alley, and she didn't want to get anyone's hopes up. Or perhaps, in Duncan's case, dash them altogether.

'I'd better leave you to get on, Inspector. I hope it won't be too long before we see you back here.'

'I hope so, too.'

Honor was frowning. 'From that, I'm guessing he's never heard of this life-insurance policy.'

'That's not to say there isn't one. And I expect Duncan will move heaven and earth to find it if he thinks he'll be the beneficiary.'

'Since when did you become so cynical, boss?'

'Since I became an adult.' She listened to the howling of the blizzard. 'There's not much more we can do today. We'll wait for that to die down, then trek out to Marek's.'

On Tuesday morning came the news that the roads had been cleared, which meant that Dania could finally make the trip to Sangster Hall. The previous day, she and those members of her team who had trickled back to work had started the seemingly endless quest to discover whether Watson and Fraser had either rented a property in or around Dundee or bought one. Duncan had come through with contact details for both Edward's bank and the family solicitor. And he'd checked the office and his father's room but had found nothing resembling a life-insurance policy. Dania was sure he'd have put his efforts into this, given what was at stake. There'd been no reply from the Sangster solicitor when she'd phoned, although Edward's bank had confirmed that no payments had been made into an insurance policy by Edward Sangster in recent years. And no, they didn't have a copy of a policy taken out by him.

Dania had left her team to it and, after brushing the snow off her Fiat 500, had started the ignition, pleasantly surprised to find the engine still turned. She kept to the main roads, hoping against hope that the B-roads had also been cleared. And they had. She arrived at the Hall a little after eleven.

Kirstine Welles was sitting in the hallway examining her nails. She looked up reluctantly as Dania entered, an expression of boredom in her blue-grey eyes.

'Ah, Tanya, you're back.' She straightened. 'I'm afraid we can't give you a refund for the nights you've missed.'

'That's all right. I'm just glad I made it. The roads seem to have been cleared.'

'That's something, at least. We should be getting more arrivals shortly.' She returned to studying her nails. 'There's coffee in the dining room, if you're interested.'

Dania hung up her coat and walked briskly along the corridor. She was hoping to catch Marek, but as she passed the ballroom she almost collided with Hennie. It had been only three days since his magic show but she'd forgotten that melting smile. And the look in his eyes, which gave the impression he was about to do something completely unexpected. He glanced at the rose in her buttonhole. The flower would be wilting now, and she hoped he wouldn't attach any significance to the fact that it was still in her lapel.

'Good morning,' he said, with a slight bow. 'Have you time to join me for a quick coffee?'

'Of course,' she said warmly.

There was a large number of guests in the dining room,

swarming round someone out of view. But then she heard the oohs and aahs, and the crowd dispersed to reveal Marek holding a pack of cards. His gaze wandered around the room, as though he was looking for another audience, and then he spotted her and his face broke into a grin.

'I'll get the coffees,' Hennie said. 'What do you take, Dania?'

'Milk, and no sugar. Thank you.'

As Hennie made his way to the back of the queue, she caught Marek's attention and jerked her head to indicate he should join her.

He crossed the room. 'Danka, do you want to see my latest trick? It's called Twisting the Aces.'

'Not now,' she said quietly, although they were speaking in Polish. 'Did you find a room on the top floor?'

'I eventually found one with a bed.'

'Where is it, exactly?'

'More or less above the room I was allocated. Near the stairs. That makes it easy to come and go.'

'How do you mean?'

'I left my stuff in my bedroom. Otherwise it would attract attention. The lady who does the room would wonder where I'd got to, and might report it. It would look suspicious if I was then seen around the Hall.'

'Good point. What about sheets and towels?'

'I managed to sneak into the linen cupboard.'

'And is there a lock on the door of your new room?'

'I made sure to find one that had a key.' He lowered his voice. 'There is one thing I need to tell you, though. I'm now firmly of the opinion that there's something in what you say. This morning, I went to my old room to pick up some clothes and have a shower and shave. I noticed that the door was unlocked. That wasn't me.'

'Could the cleaning lady have forgotten to relock the door?'

'She hadn't started her shift. The cleaners usually come around eleven, and this was just after nine.' His expression changed. 'There's something else. My things had been disturbed. The cleaning staff don't do that. Someone had been in there searching.'

Dania felt herself grow cold. She scanned the room, which was filling as more guests arrived.

'Whoever it was must have picked the lock,' Marek went on. 'But don't worry. Nothing was taken.'

'Your belongings should be the least of your worries,' she said acidly. 'When were you last in your room? Before this morning, I mean.'

'Yesterday morning at about the same time. I went down for a shower. And I definitely locked the door behind me.'

'Then whoever the intruder is has been here at the Hall the whole time,' she said half to herself. 'The roads were blocked all yesterday. The other possibility is that he arrived at dawn. The farmers start clearing the roads even before it's light. Although it's hard to see how he could have got into the Hall. They don't open the doors until eight a.m., I believe.' She made a sudden decision. 'Right, this is what you're going to do.' After a glance round the room, she slipped her car keys into Marek's jacket pocket. With luck, anyone spotting this would assume it was part of a magic trick. 'Take my Fiat and get yourself to West Bell Street. Find Honor. If she's not there, wait for her. She's going to look after you from now on.'

'Is that necessary?' he said, with a trace of irritation. 'What about my workshops?'

'You've surely got enough for your article.'

He conceded the point with a shrug.

'And leave your stuff here. Leslie's man may try to get into your room again. I need him to think you're still around.'

203

'Why do you want me to use your car?'

'Because yours might have a tracker on it.'

The expression in his eyes told her he was starting to take this seriously.

'And slip out the back way,' she said.

'The door near the music room?'

'Make sure no one follows you there.'

Hennie was returning with the coffees.

'Now show me Twisting the Aces,' she said. 'Quickly.'

Marek pulled four cards out of his pocket. 'These are four aces,' he said, lifting them to show her. He shuffled them, then brought each card face up, one at a time, as he shuffled and twisted them. Dania had to admit that his sleight of hand was superb, and wondered how much time he'd had to practise the technique.

'I can show you how it's done if you like,' he said. 'It uses something called the Elmsley Count.'

'Another time, perhaps, Franek.'

'Franek,' Hennie said, smiling. 'Are you staying for coffee?'

'I'm afraid I need to get to my workshop. It's due to start in a few minutes.'

'Another card manipulation technique?'

'It's called Out of This World. Are you familiar with it?'

'All card magicians are. Did you know that this trick was performed for Winston Churchill?'

'And did he work out how it was done?'

'I believe not. He had other things on his mind at the time. Like waging a war. He was quite a man.'

Marek raised an eyebrow. 'Yes, you should ask the Poles what they think of Churchill.' He glanced at his watch. 'I'd better run.' With a nod to Dania, he hurried out of the room.

'I'm afraid I will have to gulp this and run too,' Hennie said.

'I'm holding a workshop on levitation and the room is some distance away. What's that wonderful English expression? There's no rest for the wicked.' He held her gaze. 'I must confess that I sometimes feel a bit wicked.'

'I feel wicked all the time.' She was about to add, 'Maybe we should be wicked together,' but stopped herself. She doubted he was as plagued by desire as she was.

'And what do you do to prevent yourself actually *being* wicked, Dania?'

'That's easy. I drink vodka. It usually cures most ailments, physical and mental.'

He laughed. 'With me, it's playing the piano.' He tilted his head conspiratorially. 'You must have seen the Steinway grand in the music room. I sneak in when I have a moment. The instrument's tone is magnificent.'

His face was so close that she could make out the different shades of blue in his irises. So, he was the mystery pianist who'd been playing Mozart in the small hours. She had a sudden urge to ask him to play for her so she could see his long fingers move over the keys.

For a moment, neither of them spoke. Then he said, 'Will I see you at lunch?'

'I should think so. I'm not going anywhere.'

She wanted a second longer but he set down his mug and, with a quick smile, left the room. It was only after he'd disappeared that she realised it must have been on one of his piano-playing excursions that he'd seen her either entering or leaving Mavis's room. Yet something in her waters told her it wasn't only the Steinway grand that had lured him to the south wing.

CHAPTER 16

Dania was considering following Hennie to his workshop on the pretext that she wanted to learn about levitation when she became aware that someone was watching her. It was that prickling feeling on the back of her neck that did it every time.

She turned to see Tam Adie studying her. His hair was swept up into a man bun, which did him few favours as it only served to draw attention to his pallid, drawn face. He was smartly dressed, or what passed for it for a man who spent much of his time working with clay. The brown suit looked newly bought, or newly pressed. Either way, it gave him a certain unpolished charm. Seeing her acknowledge his presence with a tilt of her head, he smiled self-consciously and started to weave his way through the crowd, apologising to everyone for pushing through. As he reached her, she put a finger to her lips. The gesture startled him into silence.

'I'm here incognito, Mr Adie,' she murmured. 'So, please don't address me as Inspector.'

He peered at her through his glasses. 'Aye, I get that. How should I address you, then?'

'Everyone seems to go by first names here, so call me Dania.'

'I reckon that makes me Tam,' he said, in the tone of an undertaker.

'I didn't know you were interested in magic.'

'It was more the lure of Sangster Hall.' He looked round the room, seeming not to notice the fraying carpet and plaster crumbling off the walls, but appreciating instead what it had once been. 'I had a notion to see the place again after all these years.' A smile touched the corners of his mouth. 'We had grand old times, and no mistake. We'd be asked round at Hogmanay, for the festivities. The brothers would organise a ceilidh in that fine ball-room yonder. The one with the portrait of Rhona Sangster.' He stroked his chin. 'I've not been in yet, but I wonder if it's still there on the wall.'

'It's still there.'

'She was a great beauty, right enough.'

'Do you remember someone called Allan Mackie?' Dania said, seizing the opportunity. 'He was employed by the Sangsters at one time.'

Tam's expression hardened. 'Aye, I mind him fine well,' he said, almost in a growl. 'Always causing grief of one kind or another.'

'Did you ever hear him threaten anyone?'

'All the time,' he said dismissively.

'Did he threaten the Sangsters?'

'I never heard it myself, but the other lads mentioned it. Mackie had a temper on him. The wrong word or look, and he'd go from simmering to boiling in a couple of seconds.' Tam sneered knowingly. 'And when that happened, anyone with sense would get out of his way.'

Dania chose her words carefully. 'Do you think he could have murdered Watson and Fraser?'

'Who knows? But didn't he end up in prison for something similar? I was in Orkney at the time, but I read about it in the newspapers. Killed some bairns, I believe.'

'He left prison about a fortnight ago. I called on him on Sunday, and he told me something interesting. He claims to have seen Watson.'

The colour leached from Tam's face. Fear registered in his eyes, and for a moment Dania thought he was going to keel over.

'Are you all right?' she said.

It was a few seconds before he spoke. 'You're sure that's what he said?' His voice was full of tension.

'I'm positive. And so was Mackie. He swore on the bible it was Watson.'

'When was this?'

'Friday. He was walking into town from the Wellgate and he saw him in the street. Fraser was with him.'

'Fraser?' Tam gripped his mug, his hands trembling. His eyes darted around the room as though searching for something he didn't want to see.

Marek's words filtered into her brain. *He knew all three Sangster brothers.*

If so, then what was it about this information that was having such an effect on him? Why had the suggestion that Watson Sangster was alive shocked him to such an extent that his breathing was becoming shallow? Wouldn't he have been pleased to hear the news?

A fine sheen of perspiration had appeared on his cheekbones. 'I think I need to go outside for a wee bit, and get some fresh air,' he said, in a hoarse voice. He loosened his tie. 'Will you take a walk with me, Dania?'

'Of course.' She'd been about to suggest it herself. 'I've wanted to have a look around the grounds ever since I came here,' she added brightly.

'We could take the path through the woodland. My coat and

208

boots are in the pickup. Perhaps I could meet you in the car park.'
He straightened, and left the room.

Deep in thought, Dania followed the corridor to the main
entrance.

Kirstine was at the desk, frowning into the computer. She
looked up. 'Tanya, are you off for a walk before lunch?'

'A quick one.'

'That's a lovely rose in your jacket, by the way. Where did you
get it?'

Dania glanced at her lapel. Instead of the wilting flower, there
was a fresh red rose. She tried to remember when Hennie had
been close enough for long enough to remove the old flower and
insert a new one.

Kirstine's smile was without warmth. 'Well, don't get lost.'

'I've got a map of the estate. And I'm accompanying Mr Adie.'

The woman looked at her as if to say, 'That's two of you who'll
get lost, then.'

Dania lifted her coat from the rack. The DCI's stripy hat with
cat's ears was still in the pocket. She pulled it on, ignoring
Kirstine's open-mouthed stare, and left the building.

Tam was in the driver's seat of the red pickup, lacing his
military-style black boots. He was wearing a peaked beanie hat
and a thick parka that came down to his knees.

He glanced up as she approached, then stared openly. 'That's a
fine wee piece of headgear, and no mistake,' he said, grinning.

'It belongs to the chief inspector. She let me borrow it.'

'Aye?'

'She's good like that. So, lead the way, Tam.'

They trudged towards the back of the building, their footsteps
squeaking against the snow. As they passed the tower, Tam said:
'There's a wee chapel in that wing. Did you know?'

'Mavis mentioned it.'

'Mavis? She's still alive?' he said, his voice trailing away.

'The Sangsters have given her a set of rooms.'

'Have they, now?'

'What was she like back in the day?'

He paused before speaking. 'Feisty. Commanded respect. She was older than the rest of us, mind. That went some way towards it. In those days, you respected your elders.'

'Did you have much to do with her, seeing you worked on another estate?'

'She helped organise the wee get-togethers the Sangsters held for the adjacent farms. And she attended them, too. Aye, you could say she was a member of the family.' A smile flickered on his lips. 'She and Watson got on like a house on fire.'

'In what way?'

'Watson's mother died while he was in his teens. He took it badly, worse than the other two. Mavis stepped in quietly. She couldn't take the place of his mam, but she was the next best thing. As he grew up, he relied on her more and more. I mind they were always laughing and joking.'

'She must have seen a few things in her time,' Dania said, setting the bait.

'All servants have.' He gazed into the distance. 'If you want to know a family's secrets, ask the help.'

Which was the conclusion Dania had come to. The problem was that not all servants were prepared to open up. It reminded her that she still hadn't devised a way of getting her hands on Mavis's photo album. 'And did she ever reveal the family's secrets?'

'Not her,' he said enigmatically. 'She knew how to button it, and no mistake. But one time, though, it was around Christmas, we were in town at the Covenanter. She'd had more than her usual wee dram, and began to ramble on about Logan Sangster.'

'Watson's father?'

'Aye, that's him. Logan was still alive at the time.'

'What did she say?' Dania prompted, when Tam fell silent.

'Only that he knew something. A secret so tremendous that it could bring down the Sangster family. Perhaps that's putting it a wee bit strongly. I can't mind her exact words, now. But it was something he couldn't cope with, and that's why he'd taken to the drink.'

'And you think Mavis knows this secret?'

'I don't doubt it for a second. The instant she realised she'd let this information slip, a change came over her. You can tell when the fear's taken someone, ken.'

'Did Logan start drinking before Watson and Fraser disappeared, or after?'

'I can't mind now. It was too long ago.' Tam put his head down and marched on.

Logan had died five years after Watson and Fraser had vanished. Maybe he'd felt responsible, and it was that that had driven him to drink. Or maybe *he* had been instrumental in their disappearance. And Mavis had stumbled across the secret.

Maybe, maybe, maybe. The possibilities were endless.

Dania was thinking through the implications and didn't notice the large stone structure until they were almost on top of it.

Tam stopped so suddenly that she crashed into him. 'That's a deep well, and no mistake,' he said. 'It was Logan who had the lid made after one of the boys nearly fell in.' He glanced at her. 'I heard tell that if you wanted to make people disappear, that's where you'd drop them.'

'People like Watson and Fraser?'

211

'Are you thinking those brothers might be down that well?'

'It's possible.'

'If they *have* been murdered, and they're down there, you'll never find them. It's so deep it comes out on the other side of the planet.'

Dania remembered a case in Warsaw. Rumour had it that during the occupation a *Volksdeutscher*, an ethnic German who held Polish citizenship, had been instrumental in identifying members of the resistance to the SS. He'd continued to live in Warsaw when hostilities ended, believing there was no one left who could identify him. But fifty years later, an elderly lady had pointed him out to her grandchildren as the man who was behind the arrest and execution of her companions. It was only the widespread use of pseudonyms in the Polish underground that had saved her, as those arrested never knew her real name and were therefore unable to reveal it under what was known as 'enhanced interrogation'. The grandchildren had kidnapped the man and taken him out of Warsaw to a nearby farm, said to have one of the deepest wells in Poland. The rumours soon trickled back to the city.

When Dania had asked her father why this *Volksdeutscher* hadn't been handed over to the authorities, he'd looked at her strangely, saying nothing. It was years before she came to appreciate the large number of wartime crimes that went unpunished through lack of evidence. Little wonder that the population took the law into their own hands and meted out rough justice, with the communist authorities looking the other way. But the story didn't end there. The grandson of the *Volksdeutscher* paid handsomely for a caver to search for the body. However, halfway down the well, the cable snapped. No one dared try it again.

'Anyway, they can't be down there,' Tam was saying. 'Didn't Allan Mackie claim to have seen them?'

'He could have been mistaken. Or lying. Correct me if I'm wrong, Tam, but you seemed a bit shaken when I gave you the news. Actually, shaken is the wrong word. Shocked would be a better description.' She was conscious she might be going too far too quickly, but she added, 'I'd even say you looked frightened.' She searched his face. 'Did those brothers do something to make you afraid of them?'

He seemed anxious to move off the subject. 'It wasn't that. I was surprised to hear they might be back in Dundee, that's all.'

Dania had interviewed too many people not to recognise when someone was lying. So what was Tam hiding? Perhaps Mavis wasn't the only one harbouring secrets . . .

She followed him past the windows of Mavis's apartment. A glance inside told her that the living room was empty. Maybe the woman was at a workshop. And had left her door unlocked.

They rounded the corner. 'There's a path between those trees,' Tam said, gesturing to the distant woodland. 'You can't see it now, what with all the white and that, but it's a fine walk.'

'Sounds good.' She gazed at the snow shrouding the land. 'I'm guessing there's grass under that.'

'Aye, it used to be a meadow. Not sure what it is now, mind.' He seemed in better spirits. 'There's something in those trees I want to show you.' He took a step and sank to his shins in the soft snow.

Dania followed more cautiously, placing her feet in the imprints made by his boots. Although her own had a good tread, like many tall people she was afraid of losing her balance. A while later, they reached the edge of the woodland.

The thick snow covered the path, and the absence of footprints suggested they were the first to come this way since the blizzard had cloaked the land. They trudged on, the only sound the creaking of the branches in the snow-covered conifers.

Tam was scanning the area with a puzzled expression. 'I can't understand it. I thought it was there in that clearing. But there's nothing, just those cypress trees.'

'What are you looking for?'

'The old shepherd's hut. See that tree stump? It should be beyond that.'

'Are you sure?'

'Sure I'm sure.'

'Didn't you say you've been in Orkney all these years?'

'Aye, I have.'

'Then the only explanation is that those cypresses have been planted since. There's only one way to find out.' She ploughed through the snow.

As she approached the trees, she glimpsed a stone structure behind them.

'It's back here,' she called over her shoulder, her breath fogging the air.

He joined her. 'Aye, that's it. I was beginning to think I was havering.'

The walls of the derelict building, constructed from rough-hewn stone, had stood the test of time, but whether the same could be said for the roof was impossible, as it was hidden under a thick sheet of snow. What was left of the wooden door was hanging off its hinges.

'Did you say this was a shepherd's hut?' Dania said. 'But isn't the estate arable?'

'It is now. But I reckon at one time they had sheep.' He shrugged. 'We called this the shepherd's hut but it was probably used for something else.'

Dania peered inside. Snow had blown in and accumulated against the opposite wall. Through the far window, she caught sight of what she thought was an igloo, but on closer inspection was a snow-covered brick building. The sturdy wooden door was secured with a rusty padlock.

'What's that behind it?' she said.

'It'll be the ice house.'

'I don't suppose you've been inside?'

There was a gleam in his eyes. 'When I was a wee lad, we reckoned there was treasure hidden there. We were fair disappointed.' He shot her a glance. 'I used to work the neighbouring estate. The path curves round, and you reach the boundary wall. I understand they've installed wind turbines now.' He gripped the collar of his parka more tightly. 'Maybe we should be getting back. Talk of turbines reminds me that I can feel the wind rising.'

Dania couldn't, but then, she'd not worked close to the land the way he had.

They clumped back along the path. As Dania gazed at distant Sangster Hall, it struck her that this was the path she could see from her bedroom window. She could leave Tam to retrace his steps to the pickup, and she could enter by the back door on the pretext that her room was nearby. It would give her the opportunity to try Mavis's again.

But as they approached the building, she heard the sounds of scuffling, followed by grunting, then a shout. She rushed past Tam, trying not to lose her footing, and rounded the corner.

Marek had just been dealt a punch in the stomach that had caused his legs to buckle. He fell against the wheelbarrow, then slid in slow motion to the ground. Leslie's hard man, the dark-haired thug who'd been watching them in the dining room, had managed to prise the lid off the well. In one fluid movement, he crouched and hoisted the semi-conscious Marek over his shoulder. Then he straightened, and sat him on the rim of the well.

He was bending down to grab Marek's legs with the clear intention of toppling him over the side when Dania shouted, 'Stop! Police!'

He released Marek, who fell forward, and then the man swung round. There was no mistaking the intent in his eyes. He took a step towards her but, before she could react, Marek hauled himself to his feet and gripped the man's shoulders. He wheeled him round and brought his knee up while simultaneously yanking his head down. The man staggered backwards, his mouth full of blood.

Dania pulled the handcuffs out of her jacket pocket, spun him round and cuffed him.

'I am arresting you under Section One of the Criminal Justice Scotland Act twenty sixteen for the intent to commit murder.' She continued with the words of arrest, but it was clear he wasn't taking anything in. He tottered around, then sank to his knees. Dania gripped one arm, and Marek, who seemed to have recovered, grabbed the other. Marek's face was devoid of colour. Whether it was his brush with death or the fact that he had almost certainly knocked the man's teeth out, Dania couldn't tell.

Tam had joined them. 'Aye, and where did those cuffs come from?' he said to Dania.

'I never leave home without them.'

'Hi, Marek. Long time no see.'

Marek smiled weakly, saying nothing.

'I'm afraid we'll have to leave you,' she said to Tam. 'Due to circumstances beyond our control.'

'Right enough.' He glanced at the blood on the ground, then ran his boot over the snow, piling it over the stain. 'I'd better put that lid back on before anyone else falls in.'

'Please keep this to yourself,' Dania murmured. 'I don't want the guests getting spooked.'

'Aye,' he said, rolling the lid along the ground.

'We may need to call you as a witness. Are you all right with that?'

He lifted the lid and pressed it back on to the well. 'I understand that might happen.'

As she turned to her brother, she saw the curtain twitch in Mavis's window. She wondered how long the woman had been there, and how much she'd seen. 'Can you help me take him to my car?' she said to Marek.

He indicated the wheelie by the door. 'What about my suitcase?'

'I'll bring it,' Tam said.

He gripped the handle and followed them to the front. Fortunately, no one was around to see them bundle the man into the back seat of the Fiat.

'Well, I reckon I'll be on my way,' Tam said.

Dania squeezed his arm. 'Thanks for your help.'

'I take it you won't be back for lunch, then.'

'I'm afraid not,' she said, realising she wouldn't be seeing Hennie, either.

Tam smiled, then lumbered towards the entrance.

'Do I need to come back with you?' Marek said, slipping into Polish. 'You've got Leslie's man.'

'And once Leslie finds out he's failed, he'll be sending someone else.'

Marek seemed to appreciate the force of the argument. 'All right, but I can drive into town in my own car,' he said, handing her the keys to the Fiat. 'It's in the overflow car park.'

'Actually, would you mind coming to the station with me? Although he's cuffed, he may try something.'

'From the back seat?' Marek said doubtfully.

'It happened to a colleague of mine. He was head-butted while driving.'

'What a dangerous world you live in,' he muttered, apparently unaware of the irony of the statement. 'All right, then, I'm sure Honor will drive me out later to fetch the Audi.'

He squeezed into the back and fastened the man's seat belt before doing up his. 'You're going to behave yourself now, aren't you?' he crooned.

'Go bile your heid, you dumb Polak,' the man snapped.

Which was a mistake as it earned him a smack in the face.

Dania glanced into the rear-view mirror. 'Marek, I need to get him to the station in one piece,' she said, starting the ignition.

But as she pulled away, it wasn't the men's glowers that were uppermost in her mind. It was the sight of Mavis's face pressed against the window. She hadn't been looking at Dania and Marek, or the semi-comatose man they were about to drag away. She'd been gazing at Tam, a blissful expression on her face, no doubt remembering her youth and those Hogmanay parties and ceilidhs she'd helped organise. Dania made a mental note to suggest to Tam that he drop in on the woman and reminisce about old times. Provided he didn't mind oversweet, lukewarm coffee.

CHAPTER 17

The custody sergeant had taken the man's name – Bruce Heriot – and his address and date of birth, and was recording his effects and putting them into a bag.

'Hold it,' Dania said sharply.

She pulled on her gloves and picked up the green metal box. It had a switch, a safety mechanism and a short aerial.

She looked at Bruce Heriot. He returned her gaze without flinching, but something had passed across his eyes that told her what she wanted to know.

'Book him under the Terrorism Act,' she said to the sergeant. 'We can keep him for up to fourteen days.'

'Listen, lass,' Bruce said, making his voice reasonable. 'I've no idea how that wee gizmo got to be in my pocket. It must have been that Polak who attacked me. He slipped it into my coat.'

'Can you take his dabs as a matter of priority?' Dania said to the sergeant.

'Aye, ma'am.'

Bruce was glaring at her. 'I want to register a complaint. I haven't been seen by a doctor, and I'm bleeding to death here.'

'We'll get you checked out by a healthcare professional,' the sergeant said. He was one of those unflappable officers who had seen and heard it all and was never riled by anyone or anything.

'And have him and his clothes, including his gloves, swabbed,' Dania said. She turned to Heriot. 'Is there a solicitor you want to call?'

She could see him hesitate. She was hoping against hope that he'd give her the name of Leslie's. But he was too smart.

He surprised them. 'I don't need a solicitor,' he said. 'I've done nothing wrong.'

She glanced at the sergeant. He rolled his eyes.

Marek was in the canteen, speaking to Honor, who was making notes.

He looked up as Dania approached. 'DS Randall is taking my statement,' he said, flashing Honor one of his smiles. The smile faded as he saw the expression on Dania's face. 'So, is he locked up, Danka?'

'I need your car keys.'

'Are you going back already?' he said, in a puzzled voice.

'Not me. The bomb-disposal squad. They need to check your car. One of the items we found in the man's pocket is a remote detonator.'

Marek ran a hand over his face. '*Jezus Maria!*'

'Tell me what happened. The short version.'

He took a huge breath. 'The workshop was over, and I went up to pack my case—'

'I told you to leave your stuff behind,' she said sternly.

'I had to fetch my laptop, Danka. And a couple of other things.'

'And I told you not to go to any more workshops.'

'I know, but Out of This World was going to be the last one.'

'And you were supposed to go out the back way.'

'That's just it. I did. I'd left the building and was passing that wretched well when I heard him in the snow behind me. He must have followed me out.'

Dania's gaze sharpened. 'I wonder if he's the man I've been hearing walking over the south wing.'

'He must be. But I don't get it. Why was he trying to push me into the well if he'd wired my car for explosives?'

'Detonating explosives would cause a huge commotion and bring the police and all sorts of units in. But pushing you into the well would be quick and clean, allowing him to make an easy getaway. He must have seen you with your wheelie and tailed you to the back door. He'd have seen that well. And seized his chance.'

'Even though he might have been spotted?'

'He probably thought it was worth the risk. I have it on good authority that that well goes on for ever. No one would know what had happened to you.'

Marek's shock had turned to anger. He was clenching his fists.

'Anyway, are you okay?' she said. 'I mean physically. I saw him punch you in the stomach.'

'It's a bit tender, but there's no lasting harm done.'

'It's all right, boss,' Honor said. 'I'm taking him to get checked out. We'll need a doctor's report.'

'So?' Dania said to him. 'The keys?'

He fished in his trousers pocket and passed them over.

'Honor, from now on—'

The girl lifted her hand. 'I know, boss. I don't let him out of my sight.'

Dania nodded wearily and left the room.

In the incident room, Dania rang the Explosive Ordnance Disposal Unit and explained the situation. She sent them an electronic copy of the estate map, with the road to the overflow car park clearly marked. The officer she spoke with confirmed that it was sufficiently far from habitation that Sangster Hall need not be evacuated. Dania would meet them there.

Half an hour later, she and Hamish were supervising the uniforms who were erecting a cordon round the overflow. Other officers were stationed at the exits to the main roads.

'What do you reckon, ma'am?' Hamish said, indicating the parked cars. 'They're not going to detonate it here, are they?'

'They take it somewhere remote, like a beach. But I hope we'll get the chance to examine the device. If we can find a fingerprint match, we might get our suspect to talk.'

She wasn't holding out much hope. Euan Leslie's hard men had a tendency to keep their mouths zipped, partly because of fear of what Leslie would do to their families if they implicated him, and partly because they knew that Leslie would look after those same families if they were sent down.

'So, Sangster Hall is over that ridge, eh?' Hamish said, his breath condensing in the cold air. 'The estate is a right maze, and no mistake. Roads in and out all over the shop.'

Dania pulled her sheepskin more tightly round herself. 'Did you spot the murder stones on that B-road?'

'Aye. And people are leaving flowers, now. And they've set up a Facebook page.'

Dania said nothing. What was there to say? They or, rather, she was getting nowhere with the Sangster case. She didn't even have a prime suspect.

As she scanned the horizon, a huge white van appeared along one of the estate roads. It had the sort of tyres that would enable it to traverse every kind of terrain easily, even one that was rutted and full of potholes. It pulled up not far from where they were standing. The back doors opened and several figures in army uniforms sprang out, and immediately started pulling on dark blast suits.

A woman in army fatigues jumped down from the passenger seat. She had a slight build, and an intelligent face, which would reassure the more nervous members of the public. Her sleek brown hair was tied back in a ponytail. The markings on her uniform told Dania she held the rank of sergeant.

'Inspector Gorska?' she said to Dania. Her accent was English.

Dania made the introductions. 'This is the key to the Audi Avant,' she added. 'It's that black car there. What I'm not sure of is whether there actually is an improvised explosive device fitted. But our suspect had a remote detonator in his pocket, and he was apprehended in the act of trying to kill the owner of the Audi.'

'Good enough.' The woman gazed at the landscape. 'Okay, I need you to stand at least a hundred metres away, so over there by those trees would be fine. We'll take it from here.'

'Sergeant, if there's a chance we could examine the device, it would help our investigation enormously. We badly need the forensic evidence.'

'Understood.' She waited until Dania and Hamish had set off before calling her team over.

'You ever seen this sort of thing before, ma'am?' Hamish said, as they reached the woodland. He leant against a sapling, which started to bend under his weight.

'In London. It was so big they evacuated the entire street. In the end, they couldn't defuse it or even move it because it was booby-trapped. They had to blow up the building.'

'Successful, then.'

'Not entirely. They'd missed the cleaning lady, who was having a quick smoke in the basement.'

Dania had been new at the Met and wasn't involved in the case. The officer in charge was held responsible for the woman's death.

She lifted an arm to shade her eyes from the sun. 'Can you see what they're doing?'

'They've opened all the Audi's doors, including the one to the boot. Hold on, they're sliding something under the car.'

'They're scanning the vehicle. My hope is that, since Heriot intended to detonate the device remotely, it won't be wired to the ignition or anything fancy like that.'

Minutes passed. Standing around wasn't ideal for maintaining one's temperature. Hamish beat his hands against his upper arms. 'I think we should get ourselves a wee hot chocolate after this.'

'With something alcoholic in it.'

'Aye, and no mistake.' He stiffened. 'Ma'am, I think they've got it.'

Two members of the bomb-disposal squad were slowly pulling something out from under the Audi. They bent over, blocking it from view. Time crawled by. Then one of them straightened and gave a thumbs up.

'We might be in luck, Hamish.'

A few minutes later, the sergeant marched towards them, looking like a deep-sea diver in her suit. She removed the helmet. 'You were right, Inspector. We found an IED under the car. We've taken several photographs of it and the surroundings. Although I should say that the snow around the car is pretty well mashed, so footprints are out.'

'Was it a professional job?'

'Professional enough, but nothing my team haven't seen before. We've made the device safe by detaching the explosive itself. It'll be taken away, analysed and disposed of in a controlled manner. There's a metal shell that was intended to add to fragmentation when the device went off. The shell and the electronics have been put into an evidence bag, which we'll drop off at your forensics lab.' She must have seen the look of surprise on Dania's face because she added, 'I used to be a SOCO before I joined bomb disposal.'

'How was the IED attached, ma'am?' Hamish said.

'Whoever did it would have jacked the vehicle up, then screwed the shell casing under the car.' She frowned. 'He might have worn gloves up to that point, but it would have been almost impossible – and dangerous – to try and fix the casing except with bare fingers. Which means you have an excellent chance of getting his dabs.' She glanced around. 'This place couldn't have been better. No cameras, the perp could hide in the woodland, he could watch the mark arrive and climb into the Audi. Then he'd have used the detonator.'

'My guess is he came here first thing,' Dania said. 'As soon as the roads were cleared, but before the guests arrived.'

'If you can find his car, Inspector, his tools might still be there. But it's unlikely to be parked here.' She scanned the area. 'The blast would have taken these cars out.' Her colleagues were waving at her, signalling they'd finished. 'We'll be on our way, then,' she said.

It was after the bomb squad had left that the sergeant's words flew into Dania's head. *The blast would have taken these cars out.*

She felt a sudden constriction in her chest as she realised how close Marek had come to death. She closed her eyes, hoping to shut out the image of bits of him scattered across the car park. But it was impossible. She turned away so that Hamish wouldn't see her shaking.

★　★　★

Dania and Hamish arrived at West Bell Street well after five. Before leaving the Sangster estate, Dania had obtained the registration number of Bruce Heriot's car from the DVLA and arranged for the uniforms to search the grounds nearby, even if it meant erecting arc lights. She couldn't take the risk that Euan Leslie would get wind of Heriot's arrest and would have the car disposed of. Marek's Audi would be taken to Forensics in case Bruce had left his dabs or DNA, although it was looking increasingly likely that it was the shell casing that would deliver the goods. En route to the station, she and Hamish had called in at Kimmie's to brief her on developments, particularly that officers from the Explosive Ordnance Disposal Unit would soon be arriving. Kimmie's cheerful expression had changed to one of shock on learning that the Audi had belonged to Marek. She'd straightened her shoulders and reassured them that she'd rearrange her schedule and make this a priority. Until the forensics were complete, there was no point in questioning Heriot. Fortunately, time was on their side.

Now, in the incident room, Dania studied the reports that had arrived in her absence. The Sangster family solicitor had finally responded to their calls and confirmed that he knew of no life-insurance policy taken out by Edward Sangster. So much for information overheard in a packed bar. Speculation at best, tittle-tattle at worst. But everything had to be checked. Duncan would doubtless be disappointed. It was still at the back of Dania's mind that, as the sole surviving heir, he stood to inherit on his father's death. His motive for killing Edward was the strongest so far. And in this game, motive was everything. It was a pity that the same couldn't be said for the evidence. With Duncan and Grace's solid alibi, he was untouchable. What they needed was the evidence that he had paid someone to steal and dump the red deer on the road Edward frequented.

As for the deer, the uniforms had finished their enquiries in the Lundie area and established that no one had seen any suspicious behaviour involving a stolen deer. The final report confirmed that no Watson or Fraser Sangster were registered as staying in a Dundee hotel, leasing a Dundee property or having recently bought one. That investigation wasn't over, however, and reports were still to come in.

Dania motioned to Hamish to bring his chair round.

'We're going to shift direction now,' she said. 'Allan Mackie claims he was walking into town from the Wellgate last Friday afternoon, and saw Watson and Fraser. I want to examine the CCTV from that area. He'd been to the Jobcentre. That narrows it down.'

'Aye, he's likely to be walking down Panmure Street. And then what? Murrygate would be my guess.'

'Let's go with that.'

Several clicks later, they were scrolling through the camera feeds.

'Pity Mackie didn't give much of a description,' Hamish said. 'An older version of Watson is all we've got to go on.'

'But two sixty-year-old men walking together. How common is that? Better still, we should find Mackie himself. At least we know what he looks like.'

An hour later, they were no further forward.

'I reckon Mackie would be heavily disguised, ma'am. After all, there was that piece in the *Tele* that he'd been released. He's hardly going to get a hero's welcome in this city.'

'True.' Dania pulled up the feed from another camera. 'I'm seeing a few couples, but they're much younger than Watson and Fraser. Wait!' She froze the image, then magnified it.

A man in a heavy dark coat and close-fitting red cap was

walking past Specsavers. What had caused Dania to pause the footage was that he was turning round. The magnified image showed the pale, lined face of a man who looked in his sixties, but the camera angle made identification almost impossible. Nothing of his hair could be seen, suggesting that either he'd lost most of it, or it was pushed under the cap. Next to him was a man in a navy pea jacket. He was without a cap, and his white-streaked hair put him in the right age group. The men walked on out of sight. Behind them was a figure in a black coat and baseball cap.

'Is that Mackie?' Dania said.

'Aye, ma'am, I think it might be. He's keeping his head down, though.'

'The timestamp is fourteen thirty-three, which is roughly when Mackie said he saw them. Now that we've got their images, let's go through the footage again.'

'If we can find better mug-shots, we could get them into the media.'

They checked the feed again, more rapidly now that they knew what they were looking for. The first sight of the men was as they were leaving the Greggs opposite the main entrance to the Wellgate. Both men, particularly the one in the red cap, walked with their heads down.

They split up at the end of Murrygate, each taking a different direction along Commercial Street.

'Follow the one in the red cap,' Dania said.

The man headed south towards the A991. And that was where they lost him.

'Damn it,' she muttered. 'Where's he gone? I can't see a red cap anywhere.'

'Could be he's taken it off. Or he might have gone into a flat.'

'None of the images is good enough to go into the media. The men kept their heads away from the camera, except for when they parted company. But the camera angle was wrong.'

'We can hardly ask the public to look out for men in red caps. I saw more than one, right enough.'

Dania twirled a lock of hair round her finger. 'The first thing we need to do is get Mackie in here to identify them. And himself.'

'Now?'

'No time like the present.'

'He won't be happy missing his supper.'

'We'll tell him he can eat as much as he wants in the police canteen.'

Hamish looked unconvinced.

'And someone will drive him home afterwards.'

'Aye, well. Maybe that'll do it.'

'You'd better take a uniform with you in case he gets ideas.'

Hamish said nothing. A smile crossed his lips.

But as Dania watched him leave the room, she asked herself again whether chasing two men who might or might not be Watson and Fraser wasn't a complete waste of time. On the other hand, if the men on the CCTV footage were indeed the brothers, they might be able to shed light on the strange things that had happened – and were still happening – at Sangster Hall. Because she was sure of one thing: Sangster Hall and the people in it had their share of secrets, which seemed to be mounting on a daily basis. And it was high time she found a way to unlock them.

CHAPTER 18

'Thanks for agreeing to come in and speak to us, Mr Mackie,' Dania said. 'Please take a seat.'

Allan Mackie lowered himself gingerly into the chair next to hers. 'Mind if I take my coat off?' he said. 'It's a wee bit on the warm side.'

'Of course. Would you like a coffee?'

He glared at her. 'I was told I could get my supper here,' he said, suspicion in his voice.

'Yes, our offer still stands.'

'In that case, I'll have it then.' He got to his feet and shook off his black coat. He was wearing faded jeans and a thick blue jumper, which was fraying at the hem and cuffs. As he took his seat again, she caught the sour smell of body odour, and was reminded of a favourite phrase of Honor's – deodorantly challenged.

Dania had wondered about starting with small talk to put him at his ease, but he seemed undaunted by the prospect of contact with the police. He glanced around the incident room with interest.

'Not many coppers at work, eh,' he said. 'I though the polis were always busy, busy.'

'Aye, and so they are,' Hamish said stiffly. 'They're out in the city busy, busy catching criminals.'

Dania swivelled the screen towards Mackie. 'We'd like you to look at this footage and tell us if you can identify Watson and Fraser. This is CCTV from the area around the Wellgate, taken on Friday afternoon,' she added.

He frowned, turning the black baseball cap in his hands.

'I'm going to run it slowly, and I want you to stop me when you see Watson and Fraser,' she said, working the controls.

He squinted into the screen. After the footage had run for a few minutes, he suddenly called out, 'Stop!'

Dania paused the film.

'There,' he said, with satisfaction. He was pointing to the two men leaving Greggs.

'I'll run it along a bit. Perhaps you can show me where Watson turns round.'

Mackie licked his lips, a look of excitement in his eyes. 'Aye, all right.'

She pressed a button.

'There!' Mackie shouted, making her jump. He was pointing at the two men passing Specsavers. The one in the red cap was turning round. 'And that's me,' he said, indicating the man in the black coat. 'I'm wearing the same coat I've got on today.'

'How far did you follow them, Mr Mackie?'

'I went into Costa, the one on the corner of Commercial Street.'

'Why didn't you call out and try and speak to them? You look as though you're a stalker.'

'Why would I want to talk to those wee shites?' he said, with a sneer. 'It was thanks to them I lost my livelihood.'

'What would you say to them if they walked through the door?'

231

'Say to them? I'd give them a smack in the pus.'

'I see.'

'By the way, I had a keek at those murder stones you told me about. The farmer knew where they were. He gave me a lift as he wanted to see them for himself.'

'And what did you think when you saw them?'

'My first thought was that someone will have to have them taken down. Watson and Fraser weren't murdered.'

'Why do you think they haven't gone back to Sangster Hall?'

'Haven't they? I'd have thought that's the first place they'd run to.' He drew his brows together. 'Maybe it's because it's full of people. The farmer told me about this event that's taking place at the Hall. Magic and stuff.'

'Are you thinking of going yourself?'

'Aye, I might at that. Maybe I could magic up a job,' he added, with bitter sarcasm.

'How are you getting on with finding work?'

A wounded expression appeared in his eyes. 'It's harder than I thought. Everyone knows my name. That piece in the *Tele* didn't help.' He gripped the baseball cap. 'But no one's recognised me, mind. I keep my head down.'

'And it's farm work you're after?'

'I'll take any type of work where they'll have me.' His mouth quivered. 'I've done my time. Paid for what I did.' His voice broke. 'I deserve another chance.'

Dania almost felt sorry for him. 'Thank you for coming in, Mr Mackie. DC Downie will take you to the canteen.'

He gave a brief nod. 'I'm grateful to you.'

'And if you want to take some food home with you as well, we can arrange that.'

He stared wide-eyed.

'This way, Mr Mackie,' Hamish said, getting to his feet.

Mackie clutched the baseball cap. 'I don't suppose you're in need of a cleaner here,' he said hopefully. 'I can work any shifts you like.'

'We've no vacancies at the moment,' Dania said gently.

He lowered his head. 'Aye, well, no harm in asking.'

She watched the men leave. Hamish would do the right thing, making sure Mackie ate his fill and took a fair-sized doggy bag home with him. And at least the identification of Watson and Fraser had been made, even though none of the images was good enough to display in the media. But if the brothers were here under assumed names, how would she go about finding them? She doubted that an appeal in the papers would help, because something told her that they wanted to remain incognito. After all, they could have made contact with Sangster Hall. And yet they hadn't. The question was: why?

Wednesday morning saw Dania driving back to Sangster Hall. Before setting off, she'd given Kimmie a quick call and learnt that it would be Thursday at the earliest before her forensic examination would be over. But she could confirm that she'd been able to extract an excellent set of fingerprints from the IED's shell casing. The uniforms had spotted Heriot's blue Ford Puma on a secluded farm track and arranged for it and Marek's Audi to be transported to Kimmie's. She would keep Dania updated. Honor had called to confirm that Marek was safely ensconced at hers, he'd promised not to leave the flat, and could she come back to work as there was too much to be done?

Now, as Dania cruised along the avenue of bare trees towards

Sangster Hall, she was anxious to get to her destination, as she had one task to accomplish before all others.

The young man with the earring was on duty. 'Miss Gorska,' he said, checking her pass. 'We thought you'd left for good. The Polish gentleman, Mr Filarski, checked out earlier than expected, too.'

She threw him a dazzling smile. 'You know how it is. I had things I needed to do in the city.'

'Aye,' he said, the word heavy with meaning. 'Real life rears its ugly head. By the way, I'd recommend the levitation workshop. It's in the ballroom, so there are plenty of seats.'

She nodded, then hurried along the corridor until she reached the south wing. There were sounds of movement from Mavis's room. She knocked loudly.

Moments later, the door opened and Mavis appeared. She was wearing black woollen trousers and a thick beige jumper. On her feet were those sheepskin bootees with a zip up the front, but Dania doubted she was going out. Unless the boots were specially treated, water would seep through.

'It's you, lass. Come in.'

'Do you have time for a chat?'

'Aye, I do. I was about to go and say a wee prayer for my Robbie. Today is the anniversary of his death.'

'I can come back another time.'

'No, no, park yourself on that chair. I've a few questions for you, too.' She settled herself in the armchair. 'I saw what happened by the well,' she said, her gaze fixed on Dania. 'And I saw what you did with those handcuffs. I take it they weren't a sex toy.' She must have seen the astonishment on Dania's face because she added: 'No, I didn't think so. That means you must be polis.'

There was no point in beating about the bush. The woman was too smart. 'I'm a detective,' Dania said.

'I reckoned so. I won't ask why you're here. I ken polis can't reveal things like that. What I want to know is what that stramash between those two men was about.'

'The man I arrested was trying to kill the other.'

'And who was that fair-haired laddie who nearly went down the well?'

'He's a journalist who's written something that has put him in danger. I happened to know he was covering Magic Week so I came here incognito to keep an eye on him.' It wasn't the entire truth, but it wasn't a lie, either.

'Looks as if you saved his life.' Mavis angled her head. 'And now you've arrested that other man, will you be leaving us?'

'There are some loose ends I need to tie up.'

'And is that journalist all right? He took a few punches. Aye, and in the stomach, too.'

Dania smiled grimly. 'He's fine.' She looked at her hands. 'Mavis, I need you to keep this to yourself. No one is to know that I'm a detective, or that someone was nearly pushed into that well. Can you do that for me?'

Mavis nodded respectfully. 'Aye, lass. You can count on my silence.'

'I'd be enormously grateful.'

The woman hauled herself out of the armchair. 'And now, I'm away to the chapel.' Her expression brightened. 'Why don't you come with me? You've probably not seen the place.'

'Actually, if you wouldn't mind, I'd very much like to.'

'I need to fetch my coat. It's chilly in there even in summer. But you know what churches are like, you're a Catholic yourself.'

She studied Dania's clothes. 'That's a bonnie tartan jacket, right enough, but you'll want something warmer.'

'I'm a Pole, Mavis. We have iced vodka flowing through our veins.'

The woman cackled so much that she nearly fell over. 'I'll be back in a tick.'

She left the room and returned with a moth-eaten fur coat. 'This belonged to my mam,' she said, struggling into it. 'Now, give me your arm and we'll be on our way.'

They left the apartment. Mavis didn't bother to lock the door – something Dania didn't fail to notice. The corridors were beginning to fill as people queued for workshops or piled out of rooms wanting their coffee.

'Do you remember much of your Catholic education, Dania?' Mavis said.

'Pretty well. I can even remember the Latin Mass.'

'I've forgotten most of what I learnt. Although I can still remember how the different saints were martyred. That kept us awake in class, and no mistake.'

They approached the main entrance. The man with the earring had gone, and Scott Balfour was in his place. He glanced up and, seeing the women, his face broke into a smile. 'Morning, ladies. Are you away for a walk? It's a good time for it. The sun has put his hat on.'

'We're going to the chapel,' Mavis said. 'I want to say a few prayers.'

He grew serious. 'I understand. Do you know the way?' He rolled his eyes. 'Silly question. Of course you do.'

'And then I'll take myself off to the dining room for morning coffee.' She tugged Dania's arm. 'It's this way, lass.'

To the right of the entrance was a corridor, which Dania had missed on her visits to the Hall.

'There used to be a light here,' Mavis was saying, 'but the bulb's gone.'

Dania peered along the gloomy passageway. 'How do you see your way?'

'I keep one hand on the wall. And the carpet's sound enough, so I don't trip.'

They moved slowly down the corridor towards the door at the end. Dania tried the handle, but the door wouldn't budge.

'I've got it here,' Mavis said, rummaging through her coat pocket. She inserted the key.

'Why is the chapel kept locked?'

'It's been like that since I was a lass. I'm not sure why. But I was given several rings of keys when I was old enough for cleaning duties. I worked out which was the one to this place easily enough.' She pushed against the door, which opened with a pained creak.

No attempt had been made to accommodate the octagonal shape, and the chapel was like others, with two sets of pews and a small marble altar facing the door. The musty smell suggested that the windows in the white-plastered walls were rarely opened.

A crucifix was positioned above the tiny gilt tabernacle, which had two glass doors with handles. Light suddenly streamed into the room, hitting the side of the tabernacle and making it gleam like a small sunrise.

On the right-hand wall, next to the carved holy-water stoup, there was a sheet with information about the tower's architecture.

'Is Mass ever said here?' Dania said, scanning the notice.

'I've never known a Mass here in my lifetime. I'm the only one who ever came to the chapel.' A note of sadness crept into Mavis's voice. 'I've been doing that more often since Robbie died.'

She made her way to the front pew. After genuflecting and crossing herself, she slipped in and knelt down.

Dania sat a few rows behind, studying the woman's bent head. A draught blew in from somewhere, disturbing her wispy hair. Dania closed her eyes, imagining herself back in Warsaw at St John's Archcathedral on Świętojańska, blown up in 1944 as part of the planned destruction of the city, and rebuilt after the war. As a child, she would sit in the pews and close her eyes, as she was doing now, in the hope that Ignacy Paderewski, whose remains were interred in the building's crypt, would intercede on her behalf so that God would give her the inspiration – and manual dexterity – to pass her piano exam. It was years before she learnt that the pianist, who ranked second only to Chopin in her estimation, had been laid to rest in the Archcathedral as recently as 1992. His remains had been temporarily housed in a vault at the USA's Arlington National Cemetery since his death in 1941. His wish to be buried in a free Poland could only be fulfilled after the end of the Cold War.

A movement made her open her eyes. Mavis had left the pew and was genuflecting before the altar. Dania did the same, then took the woman's arm and guided her out of the chapel.

'Will you do the honours for me, lass?' Mavis said, handing her the key.

Dania locked the door and slipped the key into the pocket of the fur coat.

'Ready for coffee and cake?' the woman said, her eyes shining.

'Always.'

They eased their way through the groups standing around waiting for the eleven o'clock events.

There were fewer people in the dining room than Dania had expected, and they found a table without difficulty.

'Milk and three sugars for me, lass.'

Dania brought the coffees and lemon sponges to the table.

'Aye, that's what I call real coffee,' Mavis said, slurping. 'Better than the powdered stuff I use myself.'

'Have you thought of getting a coffee maker?'

'I used to have one, but it went bang, and smoke came out.' She rested her gaze on Dania. 'I meant to ask, who was the other gentleman at the well?'

'The one I arrested?'

'Nah, there were three. The fair-haired lad who was about to be tipped in, the one you slapped the cuffs on, and the other one.'

'Yes, that was Tam Adie.'

The woman screwed up her face. 'Tam Adie?'

'Don't you remember him? He told me about the ceilidhs you used to organise for the workers in the neighbouring estates.'

A look of understanding appeared in Mavis's eyes. 'I did a lot of that, right enough. There were so many workers, I can't remember all the names.' She took a bite of cake. 'So, has this Tam been working around these parts all this time?' she said, with her mouth full.

'I believe he moved to Orkney for a while. He makes pottery now. There was an exhibition of his work at the V&A.'

'Aye?' She looked wistfully into the distance. 'If you see him again, ask him to call on me. It would be nice to blether about the old days.'

'I thought I'd find you two here,' came Scott's voice.

'Come and join us, lad,' Mavis said, smiling. 'Are you on your break?'

'Kirstine's taken over at the desk. I'll just grab a coffee.'

239

He returned quickly.

'Where's the nearest loo, Scott?' Dania said.

'It's along the corridor, on the left. It's well signposted.'

'Will you excuse me?' she said to Mavis.

'Aye, of course.' The woman extended a bony hand and gripped Dania's sleeve. 'But you'll be back, eh?'

'I will. I intend to have another slice of cake, so don't eat it all.'

She left the room and hurried towards the south wing. On reaching Mavis's room, she paused to listen. So far, so good. She opened the door and slipped inside, pulling on the latex gloves she kept in the pockets of her jackets. From the bureau's top drawer, she removed the photo album, only then remembering that her bag was still in the dining room. She swore softly. It was too far to her bedroom. And she was likely to run into someone on the way to her staircase.

Then she remembered that not far from Mavis's there was a small mahogany table with a double drawer. She left the room and ran down the corridor. Inside the left-hand drawer, there was a shoehorn and a pair of leather gloves. The other drawer was empty. She slid the album inside. Pity there was no key.

She retraced her steps to the dining room, skirting the people thronging the corridors.

Mavis and Scott were as she'd left them, except that Scott was demolishing a piece of chocolate cake as though he hadn't eaten in years, and Mavis was laughing at something he was saying. Neither seemed to have noticed Dania's absence, which suggested they probably hadn't much idea of how long she'd been away. She fetched another coffee and joined them.

'Scott has been telling me about one of the workshops,' Mavis said, wiping her eyes.

'You should have been there, Dania. It was a total disaster. The magician was demonstrating how to change a jack of hearts into a five of diamonds. The trick is called a snap change.'

'Is that the one David Blaine does?'

'I believe so. Anyway, you need a lot of practice so it looks as if it's an instantaneous morph. You can do it one- or two-handed but you've got to get the fingers positioned correctly.'

'So what happened?'

'Well, the guy couldn't get it to work. I mean, he explained what to do, right enough, but he either dropped the cards or made one of them fly out of his hand. The audience was beginning to get restless, and I could see them coming to the office and demanding a refund. In the end, a wee lass, who couldn't have been more than ten, went up on to the stage. She picked up the cards and did the trick perfectly. Everyone fell about laughing. You should have seen the look on the magician's face.' Scott finished the cake. 'And now, ladies, I need to go. Work calls.' He grinned and pushed his chair back.

Dania watched him head for the door, smiling at the guests. He seemed popular, certainly more popular than his wife.

'Aye, and I think it's time for a wee nap before my lunch arrives,' Mavis said.

'I can take you back to your room,' Dania said quickly.

'There's no need, lass. I know the way.'

'I'm a bit worried about the corridors. There's quite a crush outside.'

'Ach, well, if you don't mind.'

Dania lifted her bag off the floor, and they left the room, Mavis clutching at Dania's arm.

Negotiating the clusters of people in the corridors was easier, as there were fewer now that the next set of workshops had started. And, unsurprisingly, the south wing was empty.

Mavis opened the door to her rooms.

'I'll be leaving you, then,' Dania said.

'Aye, lass. And drop in again before you finish here, won't you?'

'If I can. I may be called back to the station at short notice.'

'Well, we'll see how it goes.' She closed the door.

Dania waited until she'd heard the footsteps recede, then almost ran down the corridor. The shoehorn and leather gloves were still inside the left-hand drawer of the mahogany table.

The other drawer was empty.

CHAPTER 19

Dania leant against the wall, her heart sinking. The photo album was missing. She thought through the implications. Someone must have seen her place it in the drawer. But who? She'd heard no one in the south wing, although she had to admit she'd hardly been quiet as she'd rushed along the corridors. Had someone been lurking in one of the side passages? And had seen her hurry past, and poked his head round in time to catch her entering and leaving Mavis's apartment? And then watched as she hid something in the drawer?

But perhaps this was mere curiosity on the part of whoever had taken the album. Or perhaps there was another guest at Sangster Hall who wanted to know what secrets were hidden there. Then again, maybe this was part of a magic trick.

She made her way to the music room. What she needed was something rousing that would take her mind off her predicament. But Scott Joplin's lively 'Gladiolus Rag' didn't boost her mood. If anything, it dampened it as she concluded from the number of mistakes that she was out of practice. Playing the piano often helped her work through her more difficult cases, because the shift in her brain to analysing the music acted as a dry-cleaning mechanism. But as she finished the piece, she realised she was no further forward. She didn't know which bothered her more: the fact that there was another person interested in the album, or that someone knew she had taken it and hidden it.

As she sat staring into space, her phone rang.

'Danka,' came Marek's voice. 'Are you at Sangster Hall?'

'I'm in the music room playing the piano.'

'I wondered how things are going with Bruce Heriot.'

'There's nothing I can tell you. I'm hoping Kimmie will have enough forensics by tomorrow for us to grill him hard.'

'Is my car still at the Hall?'

'We brought it in in case we can find more evidence. In this game, nothing is too much.' She thought she could detect his frustration. 'Anyway, you don't need the car now you're at Honor's. And what's it like there?'

'The place is a bit of a mess. But I can't complain. She went to the Polski Sklep and bought the ingredients I asked for. And she wouldn't take payment.'

'Well, you can thank her by tidying the flat. By the way, you haven't told anyone at work where you are, have you?'

'I haven't. But why would that be a problem?'

'Where Euan Leslie is concerned, you can't be too careful. With luck, everyone will think you're still at Sangster Hall.'

'And what progress is there with your own case?'

In a few words, she told him about Mavis's photo album.

'Strange things are going on in that place, Danka. Are you still hearing footsteps in the south wing?'

'Not since we arrested Heriot.'

'Okay, I'd better go. Honor is coming back after her shift. She said it's to check up on me.' He laughed softly. 'But I happen to know she's a fan of Polish cuisine.'

'And I happen to know that's only because you're doing the cooking. I'll be in touch later.'

She lowered the piano lid and left the room. As she was closing the door, her gaze travelled to the mural of the Sangster family tree. But the wall had been screened off. No doubt part of an illusion, as the music room was booked heavily for workshops.

Lunch was a rowdy affair, with guests laughing, and trying out magic tricks on each other and on the catering staff. Dania scanned the room, but either Hennie had already eaten or he was delayed. The latter was more likely, given the number of women who thronged round him whenever they had the chance. She ate slowly, hoping he might appear. She gave him one last chance by lingering over her coffee, but the queue for tables was growing, so she gulped the last mouthful and shouldered her way out.

In the corridor, she spotted Grace Sangster. The woman's light-brown hair was hidden under a bobble hat, and she nearly didn't recognise her.

'Mrs Sangster?' she said, as Grace made to pass her. Then, knowing that the woman might make the same mistake she'd warned Tam against, she added, 'It's me, Dania.'

Grace stopped, and her look of surprise changed to one of recognition.

'Remember I'm here incognito, Mrs Sangster,' Dania murmured.

'Of course.' Her gaze drifted to the dining room. 'So, how are you getting on, eh?'

Dania wasn't sure if this was light conversation or whether the woman was fishing. She came straight to the point. 'I wanted to ask you about Logan Sangster. What do you know about him?'

'Logan? I don't know very much. He died before I met Duncan.'

'I understand that, but I wondered if Duncan had ever mentioned him. Or if Edward had.'

'Edward . . .' She pulled off her gloves. 'Aye, the few conversations I had about the family were with Eddie. It was when Duncan and I were first engaged, and he'd brought me to Sangster Hall.' Her face grew slack. 'Eddie was very kind to me. I think he saw that I was a wee bit overwhelmed by everything. The Hall, and the estate. I'd come from a fishing village, where we lived in a small cottage.' She waved a hand. 'Anyway, Duncan and his mother were out somewhere, and Eddie – he told me to call him by his first name – took me round the rooms and showed me the portraits.' She smiled apologetically. 'There's a large number of them.'

Dania returned the smile. 'I've noticed.'

'His grandparents, Captain William Sangster and his wife Rhona, had died relatively young. They were children in 1918 and, although they survived, they were weakened by the Spanish flu. The captain was unable to run the estate during his last years and left it more or less up to Logan.'

Dania nodded encouragingly. She didn't want to push the woman. Sometimes it was better to let people take things at their own pace.

'Captain Sangster was a big shot in intelligence during the war,' Grace went on, 'but Eddie didn't know what exactly. He thought he was in F Section, in SOE. The agents who worked in France. Something like that.'

'Was Logan good at sharing the family history with his sons?'

'Aye, but I had the impression from something Eddie said that Logan would only blether away after he'd had a few whiskies inside him. And so Eddie didn't know how much of it was true.'

Dania's experience of listening to drunks was that it was

precisely when they were under the influence that they told the truth.

'Did Edward ever mention a family secret, Mrs Sangster?'

The lines on her forehead deepened. 'A secret?'

'Something he might not have referred to as such. Maybe an important event that had happened in the past?'

'When the Captain and Rhona were alive, do you mean?'

'Or more recently, when Logan was running the estate.'

Grace shifted her gaze. 'Eddie did let slip once that something had troubled Logan so much that he'd taken to drink.'

'Something he'd seen?'

'Something he'd done. And deeply regretted. He said he wished he could turn the clock back, but he couldn't.' She smiled sadly. 'I think we all have feelings like that.'

'And Eddie didn't know what it was?'

'He never found out.'

'Would Duncan know?'

'Duncan was only three when Logan passed away.' She glanced around. 'I have to go, Dania. I need to track down Scott and Kirstine. Someone wants to book an event, and they've contacted us and not them.'

Dania was about to reply that Grace should find the office unlocked and the computer system wide open, but perhaps the woman already knew that.

Grace took her leave with a nervous smile, and hurried away.

Dania watched her go, her words ringing in her head.

Something he'd done. And deeply regretted. He said he wished he could turn the clock back, but he couldn't.

So, what had Logan done that had driven him to drink? And could it have anything to do with Watson's and Fraser's disappearance?

There was one person who knew the secret. She would have finished her nap by now and be tucking into her lunch. But Dania doubted anything would be gained by knocking on Mavis's door and challenging her. Nevertheless, she found herself wandering along the emptying passageways towards the south wing.

As she approached Mavis's corridor, she heard it – the patter of footsteps. She stopped. And so did the sound. She peered into one of the dark side passages. For an instant, she caught a glimpse of something in the shadows, and thought she saw movement, although she might have been mistaken. But there was no doubt about the footsteps. Yet Bruce Heriot was under lock and key. It must have been one of the kitchen staff, bringing Mavis her lunch.

Dania reached Mavis's, and decided it was worth a try. She was about to knock when she remembered the table. Without knowing why, she hurried along the corridor and opened the right-hand drawer. A shiver raced up her spine. She lifted out the photo album and slipped it into her bag. After a furtive glance around, she ran to the staircase, and took the steps to her room two at a time.

She sat on the bed and tugged out the album. Whoever had taken it hadn't kept it long. What had they been after? Or was it idle curiosity? They'd seen her enter Mavis's room and leave holding the album, then hide it in the hall table. Wouldn't most people want to know why?

She opened the album at the colour pictures of the Sangster brothers. With great care, she went through the prints systematically, easing them out from the corners and taking high-res photos with her tablet. Where something was written on the back, she made a record of that also. Slowly, she worked her way towards the older prints.

She reached the ones of Mavis and her son, Robbie, taken in

the sixties. She removed the first photo and turned it over. The scrawled writing was in blue biro, but perfectly legible: Mavis Welles and Robbie Welles. April 1963.

Mavis Welles.

Dania stared at the name. Welles – the same surname as Kirstine's. Was it a coincidence? Or were the women related? Her mind strayed to the conversation between Kirstine and her husband.

No, Scott, I've told you before. We're not having her living with us. And that's final.

Look, love, she's your kin. She'll be no trouble.

Your kin. Could it have been Mavis they were talking about? They'd gone on to discuss how she would soon need more care than Kirstine at least was prepared to provide. The woman had flung into Scott's face that they were close to insolvency and needed to keep working.

Dania called the police station.

Honor answered after one ring. 'Boss. What do you need?'

'Can you do a quick background on Kirstine Welles? She's married to Scott Balfour. I need to know who her father was. And once you've got that, who *his* mother was. I'll stay on the line.'

'On it.'

Dania waited while Honor checked the databases. She herself could have connected to the station's server, but Honor knew her way around the records better than anyone. And her fingers ran over the keyboard faster than Dania played the piano.

A minute later, she heard the girl's voice again. 'Boss?'

'Yes?'

'Kirstine Welles's father was Robert Welles, born in 1953. He died in 1995, if that's helpful. Robert's mother was Mavis Welles, born in 1933.'

So, Mavis was indeed Kirstine's grandmother. Dania recalled Kirstine's final words.

I'll tell you what's right. I decide what to do with her. She's my kin, not yours. So shut it.

Honor's voice cut through her thoughts. 'Anything else?'

'Not at the moment. And thanks.'

Dania walked across to the window and stared out at the snow-dusted fields and the conifers in the distance, trying to make out the path she and Tam Adie had taken to the shepherd's hut. The sun was on its descent, lengthening the shadows of the trees, and already the blue of the sky was deepening.

She returned to the album and continued to photograph the remaining prints. There were several of Logan Sangster taken after the war. In one, he was wearing a smart suit with a handkerchief in the breast pocket. His dark hair was Brylcreemed back off his forehead and, had he bothered to grow a thin moustache, he'd have been the spitting image of Clark Gable.

In a few of the photos, he was with a young blonde woman. As there was nothing on the back to say who she was, Dania assumed she must be his wife. In one picture, he had his arm round her waist and was saying something into her ear that was making her laugh. In another, she was smiling into the camera, but he was looking at her with an expression that could only be described as lustful. Strangely, there were no wedding photos. The last few prints were of William and Rhona Sangster.

Dania connected to West Bell Street's server and transferred the images. Then she closed the album and shoved it into her bag. What she kept coming back to was that Mavis was Kirstine's grandmother. Interesting that Duncan hadn't mentioned the fact when she'd quizzed him about the old lady asleep in the south wing. She'd assumed the woman was a member of the family, but he'd put her straight by informing her that her name was Mavis, and she was a 'former maid and general factotum' who had worked at the Hall. Why, then, hadn't he mentioned that she was Mavis Welles, the grandmother of Kirstine Welles, one of the organisers of the forthcoming Magic Week? It would have been easy enough to slip into the conversation. And yet he hadn't. Should she read anything into it? Of course, it could be that Kirstine, Scott and Mavis were so well known to him that their relationship rarely figured in his thinking. Dania picked up the mobile, noticing only then that it needed charging. After hunting unsuccessfully through her things, she realised she'd have to get the spare charger from the Fiat.

She slid off the bed and left the room.

Dania made her way to the front entrance. Before leaving the south wing, she'd replaced the album in the hall-table drawer. She would have to come up with a way of returning it to Mavis's without her discovering she'd taken it. But that was for another day.

She pulled her coat off the rack and struggled into it under Kirstine Welles's watchful gaze.

'Off for a wee walk, Tanya? It'll be dark soon.'

'I need to fetch something from the car.'

Kirstine nodded in the way people do when they're not interested in the reply.

Dania left the building and sauntered across the car park. She retrieved the charger from the glove compartment and was straightening when she caught sight of a vehicle bouncing along the avenue in the direction of the Hall. The lamps were on, and she recognised the blue tipper lorry that she'd seen parked outside Allan Mackie's cottage. Instinct made her duck behind the Fiat.

The lorry edged into the disabled spot. The door opened and a figure jumped down. Although she couldn't see his face, the black coat and baseball cap identified him as Allan Mackie. He trudged over the snow towards Duncan and Grace's cottage.

Dania moved away from the car but, instead of retracing her steps to the entrance, she inched towards the trees that shielded the cottage, reaching them in time to hear the buzzer. A quick peek showed her Mackie scanning the landscape. At one point, he turned his head in her direction but evidently didn't see her.

The door opened, and she heard Duncan say: 'So, it's you. What do you want this time?' He spoke calmly, but his voice carried the sharp edge of authority.

'You know what I want,' Mackie said, in a thick growl. 'Just what I'm owed.'

'I told you not to come back here.'

'I ken that but, like I said, I reckon I'm owed.'

'Listen, Mackie,' Duncan said, in a tone Dania hadn't heard before, 'you've had what you're owed. I gave you more than enough cash.'

'Aye, but cash has a habit of running out.'

'You're not getting a penny more.'

'Is that right, now?' Mackie said, folding his arms. 'And what would your good lady have to say about it? You *have* told her about me, haven't you?'

He'd hit a nerve. Duncan took a step forward. But he must have understood that, if it came to a fight, he'd be no match for the other man.

As if to press home the point, Mackie said: 'I see Grace around the estate sometimes, going on her wee perambulations. Lovely lady.'

That did it. 'Are you threatening me, Mackie?' Duncan said, balling his hands into fists.

'Aye, if you want to call it that.'

'Wait here.' He disappeared.

Mackie entertained himself by kicking the snow into dusty white arcs. Moments later, Duncan reappeared with a shotgun, cradling it in his arms.

'Get off my estate, and don't come back.'

Dania couldn't see the men's faces, but the way Mackie's chest was heaving gave her an idea of what was going through his mind.

'All right,' Mackie said, with a bitter laugh. 'You win this time. I'm going. But don't think this is the end of it.'

'No?' Duncan lifted the shotgun and pointed it at Mackie's head.

Before Dania could react, Mackie took a step back and said, in a thick voice, 'You're going to regret this, Sangster . . . aye, and do give my best regards to your lady.' Without waiting for a response, he loped off towards the car park.

He reversed out of the space and eased the lorry on to the tree-lined avenue. As the vehicle dwindled to a blue speck in the gathering twilight, Dania heard the door to the cottage close quietly.

She leant against the tree. So, Duncan had given Mackie money, a considerable amount, by all accounts. The fact that he kept a quantity of banknotes on the premises didn't surprise her. Even in this age of digital financial transactions, there were still workers who preferred to be paid in cash. No, what interested her more was that Mackie claimed to have been *owed* the money. But why?

Payment for doing something illegal, perhaps? Like stealing a deer and leaving the carcass on a remote country road? The tipper truck would have been ideal for transporting a large animal. Although the vehicle belonged to the farmer, Mackie was obviously not averse to 'borrowing' it when it suited him. Whatever the reason for the initial payment, he was prepared to return and extort even more from Duncan. He must have hoped that his thinly veiled threat to involve Grace would ensure that Duncan was the gift that kept on giving. A threat like that suggested that either he didn't have the evidence to implicate the man, or by doing so he would implicate himself. Having spent decades in jail, he wouldn't be in a hurry to revisit the place.

Dania was tempted to confront Duncan, but if he'd arranged for Mackie to set up Edward's accident, he would have made sure there'd be no trail that led back to him. Everything done verbally, and cash transactions only. Mackie, on the other hand, might well cave under the pressure of a police interrogation.

But as she trekked back through the snow, it was his words that rang in her head.

You're going to regret this, Sangster.

CHAPTER 20

Dinner was over. At least, it was over for Dania. She'd gone for the earlier sitting as she wanted to write her report. She lay on the bed and called the station.

It was Hamish who answered. 'Ma'am, are you at the Hall?'

'Still here. Anything to report?'

'No joy tracking down Watson and Fraser, I'm afraid. The team has now contacted every property developer and letting agent. If those brothers are back in Dundee, they're not here under their own names.'

'I was afraid of that.'

'The more I think about it, the more I reckon Mackie is lying about recognising Watson.'

'To divert attention away from himself, you mean?' She chewed her thumb. 'Do you think he killed those brothers?'

'Aye, that's where I'd put my money. And now he's out of prison, he's targeted Edward, too.'

'Here's something else to throw into the mix. Mackie was at the Hall earlier. I overheard him ask Duncan for more money.'

'*More* money?'

'That's right. Duncan said he'd already given him enough, but Mackie seemed not to agree. He said it was owed him.'

'Do you reckon Duncan paid him to arrange Edward's accident?'

'He has the best motive. He'd inherit the Sangster estate without having to wait for his father to die.'

'But a son arranging his father's death?'

'The history books are full of cases where family members kill each other, Hamish. Just read about the Plantagenets.'

'We'll pull Mackie in, then, first thing tomorrow.'

'I'll be over straight after breakfast.' She ended the call.

Dania finished her report and filed it at the station. She would have an early night and be up in time to avoid the commuters. Assuming it didn't snow. A quick check of the forecast told her she was in luck. Tomorrow, the skies should be clear. She slid off the bed and ambled over to the window. The night sky was sprayed with stars. As she gazed at the winking lights, her thoughts drifted to Marek. He'd have finished supper, no doubt having rustled up one of his magnificent Polish dishes. Although the chicken stew she'd had this evening was excellent, it was nothing compared to the strong-flavoured soups she was used to. And Marek usually started with soup. Would he have made *szczawiowa*, the wild sorrel soup with hard-boiled egg? Or had he gone for red beetroot soup, *barszcz czerwony*? Either way, the attention to detail he put into cooking would have ensured that whatever he set in front of Honor would be demolished in record time. Lucky Honor.

Thinking about Polish food invariably drew her towards music. There was time for a brief session at the piano, assuming there wasn't a workshop on. But no sooner had she crossed the room than the sound of the Steinway reached her from the floor below. As if reading her thoughts, someone had decided to play Chopin. It could only be Hennie. It was one of her favourites, the sparkling

'Grande Valse Brillante', with its mad dash towards the end and the final, decisive chords. It was marvellous hearing Chopin played proficiently without having to play it herself. Hennie polished off a couple more waltzes, and then the music stopped. Was this part of his magic show? A brief interlude before he continued to dazzle his audience?

She prepared for bed. Tomorrow would be particularly busy. They would try to wring from Allan Mackie the circumstances behind his conversation with Duncan Sangster. And, with luck, the forensic evidence that would nail Bruce Heriot would be in. What she was less certain of was whether, when presented with Kimmie's report, the man would give up Euan Leslie. Because without that, they had nothing. Pulling in Leslie would be a massive feather in her cap. And, judging by the way her case here was going, might be the only one.

Dania woke with the sense that something was wrong. There was a fuzziness behind her eyes, something she always felt when her sleep was disturbed. She groped around the bedside cabinet for her phone. It was nearly 2 a.m. The dining-room bar would have shut long since, and the late-night revellers would be tucked up in bed. At least they should be. So what had caused her to wake? She sat up and listened, but the house was silent.

Yet something niggled, and she couldn't think what it was. Then suddenly she had it. The curtains had been left open, and a strange light was casting its glow into the room. She pushed back the sheets and swung her legs out of bed. Instinct made her tiptoe to the window. But as she reached it, the light disappeared. Was it a motion sensor that someone had tripped? Or had there been a guest outside with a lamp, and he or she was now back in the

Hall? She strained to listen but could hear no movement from the corridor below. She pressed her face against the diamond-leaded window and peered out, seeing glittering stars in the velvet darkness. The impenetrable woodland hung over the white fields, causing her gaze to drift to the path. It was then that she noticed the dark silhouette. At first, she thought she must be mistaken, but the longer she stared the more she became convinced that something was moving out there. It was unrecognisable, an amorphous shape in the distance, creeping into the wood. Had this been Poland, she'd have sworn it was a wolf, except that it was advancing too slowly and methodically and, given the distance from the Hall, it was too large to be a wolf. Could it be a cow? But there was no livestock on the Sangster estate.

She watched it dwindle until it was swallowed up by the trees. Then she returned to the bed. But instead of slipping in between the sheets, she sat with her knees under her chin, staring into space and trying to make sense of what she'd seen. A part of her was tempted to get dressed, rush out and try to pick up the trail. And challenge whoever was out there. But that would be foolish. The more she considered it, the more she came round to thinking that it must be an estate worker. Perhaps he'd had one too many wee swallies and was taking a short cut to his cottage. He'd found the path by following the outline of Sangster Hall, as she and Tam Adie had done. Yes, that would be it.

She lay down and drew the sheets over herself. It wasn't long before she felt her eyelids grow heavy.

Dania sat up, instantly awake this time. Her heart was pounding. For a second, she couldn't remember where she was. Then the room's floral, woody smell reached her nostrils, and memory

258

flooded back. She checked her phone. It was after four. What had woken her? A nightmare? But she'd slept without dreaming. She should try to catch a few more hours' sleep, but her level of anxiety was such that she was unlikely to drift off again.

She was struggling to a sitting position when she heard a noise. It was partway between a knock and a thump. After a moment's silence, it was followed by footsteps from the floor above. Someone was moving around, trying not to make a sound, and failing. Now that she had identified what had woken her, her anxiety vanished, to be replaced by an intense curiosity.

Conscious that sound travels in all directions, she slipped out of bed and padded silently to the chair where she'd dropped her clothes. She tugged on her jeans and sweater, but abandoned her boots in favour of the ultra-silent shoes that would give her the best chance of walking around undetected. Then she unlocked the door and stepped into the corridor.

She paused to listen. The footsteps, which had stopped briefly, started again further along. Who was up there, and what were they doing on an unused floor in the oldest part of the house? She was visited by a sudden feeling that what she'd witnessed earlier that night – the dark shape inching towards the distant trees – might have had something to do with it. Perhaps even something to do with her case. And, as the footsteps grew fainter, she knew there was no time to lose.

Like most pianists, Dania had an excellent memory, not only for retaining a perfect mental image of the piece she was playing, but of the placement of her hands on the keys. And this ability translated to a spatial awareness that helped her remember the outline of a map or floor plan. Or the route she had taken in the dark.

She made her way to the staircase and climbed stealthily to the second floor. Perhaps she should use the phone's torch. But she decided against it for the simple reason that whoever was here had switched on theirs. All she had to do was follow the weaving shadows on the walls.

Strangely, the oil paintings on this corridor hadn't been removed. Their gilt frames threw back the faint light from the torch. When it vanished, signalling that the figure had turned into another corridor, she hurried on, anxious not to fall behind. Something about the figure's build and the way he held himself convinced her that this was a man. He seemed to be moving purposefully, as though he knew what he was looking for. After several minutes, he stopped in front of a door and held something to his face, lifting his phone to illuminate it. From where she was standing, Dania couldn't see what it was. But then he opened the door and disappeared.

It was tempting to follow him in. Yet at this hour, and in this abandoned corridor, it wouldn't be prudent. If this was Edward's murderer, she was determined to bring him in, but not over her dead body. She tiptoed along the corridor and slipped into the adjacent room, shuffling through the raw dark until she reached the adjoining wall. More bangs and thuds, and the sound of something heavy being dragged across the carpet. Then a slithering noise, like a hand running over the wall. It stopped, and for a second she thought her presence had been discovered. She half expected the walls to come crashing down on her, but after a tense pause, the sounds started up again.

Whoever was there was searching for something. Or possibly looking for a hiding place. After several minutes of the same, whatever was happening came to a startling end with something slamming against the wall, accompanied by what could have been a growl of frustration. She sprang back, her heart pumping furiously.

Something made her suspect that the man's exploration was coming to an end. Anxious to get a clue as to his identity, she hurried to the door, and slid it open just enough to see into the corridor.

A second later, she heard the adjoining door open. A faint draught fanned her face as a large shape moved past. She peered out, catching the man loping away. He was dressed in black and wearing what could have been a balaclava. He was holding a phone in his gloved left hand and using its torch to light his way. In his right hand was a sheet of paper. He turned into a corridor, and the light vanished.

Dania sneaked out. She glanced along the corridor, then opened the door to the next room.

She felt around for the switch, half expecting it not to work but, to her surprise, the light came on. There was that stale smell and vague air of neglect she recognised from rooms that haven't been used for decades. This one was situated in the eaves, so you could stand up in only part of it. But that wouldn't have been a problem for the occupant because this was a child's room. Everything from the furniture to the carpet and curtains was in wax-crayon colours. The shelves on the walls were loaded with toys, which on close inspection were those a boy would play with: cars, a train set, tiny soldiers. Even a toy pistol. A blue bookcase had been dragged away from the wall, and strewn across the floor were books that had toppled out of it.

Dania picked one up at random. *Chitty Chitty Bang Bang: The Magical Car* by Ian Fleming. The book had been signed by the author, who had wished Edward Sangster much enjoyment in reading it.

Edward Sangster. This had been his room.

There was evidence that someone had rummaged around inside the wardrobe and chest of drawers, although from the scattered items, there'd been little there – a small woollen sweater and a few odd socks. But this had been the room of a man who'd recently been murdered, the significance of which hadn't escaped her. Yet what had the black-clad figure been after? What secrets could Edward Sangster possibly have had as a child?

In that instant tiredness descended with such force that she knew she had to sit down. She staggered over to the single bed in the corner and lay down on the mattress. She curled into the foetal position, intending to shut her eyes for only a few minutes. Her breathing grew steady, her thoughts drifted and, as her limbs became heavy, she felt darkness wrap itself round her.

CHAPTER 21

It was the sun streaming through the windows that woke Dania. For a second, she tried to hang on to sleep, and with it her dream. Hennie had slipped into her room and sat on the bed with an expression of hopeless tenderness on his face. He'd cupped her cheek with his hand and bent to kiss her, his mouth soft against hers. But at that point she'd known it was a dream, and her subconscious had gently lifted her out of it.

She hauled herself off the bed and ran her hands through her hair. She was still in Edward's room. She must have been exhausted to sleep with the light on, something she would have found impossible otherwise. The phone had slipped from her hand and lay on the floor. Good God, it was nearly eleven! She was supposed to be at West Bell Street.

The door to the corridor was ajar. Had she left it like that? She couldn't remember. Her stomach felt hollow as it occurred to her that someone could have walked in. And perhaps someone had. A sudden noise from below made her heart leap. But it was only the sound of the vacuum cleaner. They would be starting on the guests' bedrooms. It was time to leave but, before she did, she took several photos of the room in case they might prove useful. Then she switched off the light and slipped out, taking care to shut the door behind her.

Dania made for the stairs, meeting no one there or on the floor below. In the distance, a cleaner had left one room and was entering the next. It would be a while before the woman reached hers, and she might manage a shower, but she'd told Hamish she'd be at the station early. She splashed water over her face, changed her clothes and dragged a brush through her hair. It would have to do.

As she was passing the dining room, she heard something that stopped her in her tracks. Two women were walking towards the door, gossiping excitedly in clipped English accents.

'It's the third night in a row that I've heard it. The noise from upstairs.'

Dania leant against the wall, pretending to play with her phone.

'But that floor is supposed to be empty,' the other woman said.

'How do you know?'

'I asked my cleaner. She said they never go up there now. In fact, *no one* ever goes up there. What did the noise sound like, then?'

'Footsteps. Unmistakable. Must have been someone heavy because the floorboards were creaking. But the first night, there were other sounds. Thumping and the odd crash. Haven't you heard anything?'

'Nothing.' The woman lowered her voice. 'But there are other strange things happening here.'

'Like what?'

'You know the area they call the south wing?'

'Where the music room is?'

'Well, things have been moved. It's as though some of the paintings have been lifted and not put back properly.'

'Could it be the cleaners disturbing them while dusting?'

There was doubt in the voice. 'Could be. But that doesn't happen in our bedrooms, does it? You'd never know the cleaners were in. Everything is put back exactly as it was. And the cleaners only work in the mornings. But here's the thing. You know those wax flowers under glass, the ones on that stand near the music room? Well, I passed them twice one afternoon, once going to the music room and once leaving it. The second time, the lid had definitely been prised off.'

'How do you know?'

'Because it hadn't been like that the first time. It had obviously been removed and not put back properly. Not only that, but the flowers had been disturbed, as though someone had run their fingers through them. And that won't have been the cleaners.'

The women were in the corridor now.

'Do you think these are part of a magic trick?'

'Maybe, but I can't think what sort of a trick it could be. Unless you can make paintings fly off the wall and then return to their original places all wonky. Even the Great Manderfeld can't do that. Although I'd like to see him try.'

The voices drifted away as the women disappeared into the ballroom.

Dania headed for the front door, her thoughts swirling. The sounds the women had described could only have been made by the black-clad man she'd seen on the top floor. She couldn't think about this now. But of one thing she was certain: it wasn't Bruce Heriot. The man was safely behind bars.

She was pulling on her coat when she noticed Scott Balfour approaching. He exchanged a few words with the young man with the earring and took his place at the desk.

'Are you away to town, Dania?' Scott said. He sounded tired, and there were scratches on his cheek where he'd cut himself shaving.

'There's something I need to do. But I'll be back later.'

'Just as well the snow's stopped. The downside is that at this time of year, when the sun's out, it's usually in your eyes. So take care on the road.'

Scott's prediction was correct. The clear sky was that shade of blue that is almost white. Dania made good time on the roads and arrived at the station at midday.

'Boss,' Honor said, looking up in surprise. 'We expected you earlier.'

'And I expected to be here earlier. Has Mackie been pulled in?'

'Hamish went over, but the place is empty. He's posted a couple of uniforms. They'll call in when Mackie gets back.'

'Maybe he's out looking for work.'

'Maybe.' Her expression brightened. 'But the forensics are in on Bruce Heriot. And it's looking positive. Everything's online, if you want to check.'

Dania read the reports through twice, the second time formulating the questions she would ask, and the order in which she would ask them.

'From that look on your face, boss, I'm guessing you're thinking what I'm thinking.'

'Which is?'

'That Bruce Heriot is well and truly screwed.'

'I wouldn't have put it quite so subtly.'

'He'll have to confess.'

'Will he? He'll play the politician and deny everything, even when the evidence is irrefutable. What are those new expressions? Fake news? Alternative facts?'

'The question is: will he give up Euan Leslie?'

Dania rubbed her face. 'I doubt it.' She studied Honor. 'I have a more important question. Do we interview him before lunch? Or after?'

In the end, they decided to wait until after lunch before questioning Bruce Heriot because, as Dania had pointed out, he would only complain he'd been mistreated if he didn't get his mince and tatties. Especially if the meeting overran.

Bruce Heriot was sitting in the interview room, his arms folded and a defiant look on his face.

The women took seats opposite, and Dania went through the usual preliminary spiel for the tape.

'Do you wish to be represented by a solicitor, Mr Heriot?' she finished.

'I've told you before, I don't need one. I've done nothing wrong.' As his lips moved, Dania could see that his upper front teeth were chipped. It was to his credit that he made no mention of his treatment at Marek's hands. Whether this was bravado, or whether he didn't want to draw attention to the incident, was unclear.

'For the record, Mr Heriot has waived his right to a solicitor.' Dania opened her folder. 'Can you tell me when you first arrived at Sangster Hall?'

'It would have been last Saturday morning. I was signed up for Magic Week.'

This tallied with Dania's observations. She'd seen him at lunch in the dining room.

'Are you interested in magic, Mr Heriot?'

He pushed the hair off his forehead. 'Isn't everyone?'

'And which events have you attended so far?'

From the expression of surprise, followed by one of unease, he hadn't expected the question. It told Dania what she wanted to know: he'd booked himself into only one or two shows, intending to spend the rest of the time looking for an opportunity to kill Marek quickly, silently and in a way that couldn't lead back to him.

'We're waiting, Mr Heriot.'

'I can't mind now which events,' he said dismissively. 'What does it matter?'

'It matters because I don't believe you attended any.'

'That's not true. I was signed up for a pile of them.'

'And we can establish which ones by checking the bookings database.'

Love fifteen, she could almost hear Honor say.

Dania removed a photograph from the folder and placed it in front of him. 'The suspect is being shown the first in a series of photographs. Is that your car, Mr Heriot?'

He gazed at the blue Ford Puma. 'I doubt it. It's not my car's registration.'

'We've checked with the DVLA. It's registered in your name.'

He wiped his face.

Dania glanced at Honor. She knew what the girl was thinking from the scorn in her eyes. Heriot was a bit of a dim bulb. They were about to find out exactly how dim.

'This toolbox was found in the Puma's boot,' Dania said, removing another photo.

'Aye, and?'

'Can you confirm that these are your tools?'

He paused, suggesting he suspected a trap. He opened his mouth and then closed it.

'Our forensics team checked the toolbox for fingerprints,' Dania said. 'We found yours. Only yours.'

'That doesn't prove anything,' he said, with a sneer.

'What do you think it doesn't prove?' Honor chipped in. It was her favourite response to the remark, and often tripped up the suspect.

For an instant, Dania thought he was going to claim that it didn't prove he'd used the tools to jack up Marek's car and attach an IED to the underside, but if he'd been about to say it, he stopped himself.

He kept his voice level. 'Like I said, lassie, it doesn't prove anything.'

'This is a map of the Sangster estate,' Dania said, pushing the sheet across. 'Your car was found here,' she added, tapping the paper. 'It wasn't in either the main car park or the overflow. In fact, it was on an unused farm track a fair distance away. Why would that be, Mr Heriot?'

He shrugged. 'The car parks were full. I had to find somewhere to leave it.'

'We have several photos of the car parks. There were plenty of spaces in the overflow.'

'Not when I arrived.'

'And what time was that?'

'I can't remember.'

'And did you leave Sangster Hall at any time during Magic Week?'

'I went for the odd walk outside. When it wasn't snowing, mind.'

'I meant by car. Did you return to Dundee?'

He drew his thick brows together. 'Why would I? Like I said, I paid for those magic shows and workshops.'

Dania pulled out a copy of the photo she'd taken of him and Leslie near Dudhope Park. 'Can you identify these men, Mr Heriot?'

'I've no idea who they are.'

'Then the man without a hat isn't you?'

'Aye, he isn't.'

'A jury might not agree.'

'They can agree or not. But I swear on my mother's life that isn't me.'

'Your mother's no longer alive, Mr Heriot,' Honor said, examining her nails. 'We've done a background check.'

He stared at her, his eyes glittering. 'And who gave you permission to do that, eh?'

She looked at the ceiling, then at him. 'The law.'

'If you examine the date and time at the bottom of the photograph,' Dania said, 'you'll see that this puts you in Dundee on Sunday, February the fourteenth. Who's the man with you?'

'What does it take to get through to you lassies? That's not me.'

'Were you on a Valentine's date with him, then?' Honor said provocatively.

She'd touched a nerve. Heriot clenched his fists. 'You'd better watch that mouth of yours,' he muttered.

'The other man in the photo is Euan Leslie,' Dania said, studying his reaction.

He said nothing. But the flicker at the corner of his eyes suggested he was preparing himself for what was coming.

'What were you two talking about, Mr Heriot? Were you plotting the best way of killing Marek Gorski?'

'Why would we be doing that?'

'Don't you read the papers? Don't you know that Mr Gorski

wrote an article exposing corruption in Euan Leslie's property development business?'

His sneer widened into a smile. 'If Mr Leslie has been doing anything he shouldn't, then the Fraud Squad would have picked him up. And they haven't.'

Fifteen all.

Dania could have gone straight for the jugular and presented the evidence that Kimmie's team had painstakingly uncovered, but she wanted information from the man. And the longer she took, the more rattled he'd become.

'Why did you try to kill Marek Gorski?' she said.

He rubbed his throat. 'You're havering, Inspector.'

'I was there. At the well outside the south wing. I saw what you were doing.'

'Aye, everyone knows how the polis like to lie and stitch up innocent bystanders.'

'There was an independent witness. He saw what I saw. And he'll testify to that.'

'I don't deny I was there. But it's not how it looked.'

'No? How was it then, Mr Heriot?'

She could almost see the cogs moving in his brain. 'I was out for a wee walk, and that Polish man attacked me. It was self-defence. All I did was push him against the wheelbarrow.' He sat back and folded his arms. 'I ken it'll be my word against his.'

'You punched him in the stomach. And you removed the lid from the well.'

'Did I? I can't remember.'

'You tried to push him over the rim. That's going above and beyond self-defence.'

'You're lying. He must have clambered up intending to jump down on top of me.'

Dania had interviewed many suspects who had tried to twist the truth to save their skins, but none who did it as blatantly – and clumsily – as this one. Did he not realise that his actions had been witnessed?

'That wasn't the first time you targeted Marek Gorski,' she said. She riffled through the file. 'Mr Gorski claims that someone entered his room at Sangster Hall in the early hours of Tuesday morning. Was that you?'

'Prove it.'

'What was your intention? To kill him while he slept?' When there was no response, she went on, 'And when you found the room empty, you looked through his things for clues as to where he might be.'

'Listen, Inspector, how would I even know where Gorski's room is?'

'Euan Leslie found out and told you.'

'Ach, Leslie's been nowhere near Sangster Hall.'

'He was booked in for Hennie Manderfeld's show on Saturday evening. I saw him there with my own eyes. Which means other guests will have as well. You recognised Marek Gorski at the Hall on Saturday morning, and tipped off Leslie, who decided to come and assess the situation. He knew the name Franek Filarski, which Marek Gorski uses undercover.' She watched the emotions come and go on Heriot's face. 'I put it to you that Leslie went into the office and found Marek's room number on the computer's database. And then told you.' She locked her fingers together. 'Did he call you on the burner phone we found in your pocket?'

'How many of those phones have you even got?' Honor said, when Heriot refused to answer.

He scowled at her. She smiled back sweetly.

It wasn't the first time Dania had interviewed suspects like

Heriot, who denied everything, or refused to answer. She had no choice but to press on. 'Later that Tuesday morning, you spotted Marek, and followed him to his room. You saw him take his suitcase and leave by the back. When you realised how isolated the area round that old well was, you made a snap decision. Pushing him into the well would have solved the problem in one go. With no one around to witness it, it's unlikely his body would ever have been found.'

Heriot sneered, shaking his head slowly.

'Let's come now to the more serious charges against you.' She pushed across another photo. 'As I'm sure you're aware, this is a remote detonator. We found it in your coat.'

He licked his lips. 'It's not a detonator.'

So, he'd abandoned his earlier story that Marek had slipped it into his pocket. 'What is it, then?' she said.

It was a few moments before he spoke. 'It operates another type of device. Understand what I'm saying?'

'I'm sure we will if you carry on with your account.'

He seemed to be searching his repository of lies. His expression cleared. 'It works with a drone. That's why it has that short aerial.' Ignoring the open-mouthed looks of disbelief, he went on: 'It's a hobby of mine. I belong to a drone club.'

Honor ran a hand over her mouth, something she did when she was trying not to laugh.

'We've had the detonator tested, Mr Heriot,' Dania said. 'It has your fingerprints on it. The same fingerprints we lifted from the device we found under Marek Gorski's car. What have you to say to that?'

Sweat had broken out on Heriot's forehead. He was struggling, unable to formulate a suitable reply. 'No comment,' he said finally.

'The device is an IED, or improvised explosive device in case you're not familiar with the acronym. Your fingerprints were lifted from the shell casing. You'd taken your gloves off to screw it to the underside of the car.' She inclined her head. 'After all, once the bomb had detonated, your fingerprints would have been blown away along with everything else.'

'No comment.'

'Our forensics team checked the circuit attached to the IED. It was tuned to the exact same frequency as the detonator.'

'No comment.'

'The explosive was tested and found to be TATP. We found traces of it on your gloves and coat. When did you pick up the device, Mr Heriot? I can't believe you kept it in the Puma since your arrival on Saturday, given how dangerous it is. Did you slip out of Sangster Hall on Tuesday as soon as you got the call from Leslie? We know from your burner phone that someone called you just before five a.m.'

'If Leslie called me, you'll find the record on his phone.'

'He'll have used a burner like yours,' Dania said patiently, 'which I'm sure he's destroyed by now. Five a.m. would have given you plenty of time to reach Dundee, pick up the IED and detonator, return to Sangster Hall and attach the device to the underside of Marek Gorski's car. You knew which was his car and where it was. You parked your car on that farm track so you could make a quick getaway after the detonation.'

'No comment.'

'The bomb squad told us there was enough explosive in the charge to take out the nearby cars.' Dania folded her arms. 'What did you intend to do? Wait in the trees until you saw Marek get into his car? And detonate the charge then? Or follow him out of the estate and detonate it on the road? Either way, there was a risk you'd injure or even kill others. That's something to add to the charge sheet.'

He wiped his mouth. His body language told her his anxiety was mounting.

'Do you have anything to say?'

'Just this,' he blurted. 'You're wrong about everything.'

'DNA places you at the scene of the crime, Mr Heriot. You can deny it all, but eventually the weight of evidence takes on a gravitational force of its own. A jury will come to only one conclusion.' She gathered up the photos and replaced them in the folder. 'But there is a way you can help yourself. If you tell us who paid you to kill Marek Gorski, it will play well in court and help mitigate your sentence. Which will be a long one, believe me.'

'No comment.'

'I expect you'll want to get in touch with Euan Leslie. When you do, you can tell him that Marek Gorski is currently on his way to Kraków. He took a flight this morning.'

Heriot frowned. 'What the hell does Euan Leslie have to do with anything?'

'We know that Leslie looks after his own. You have a wife and four children, I understand.'

A look of bewilderment crept into his eyes. 'How did you know that?' he said, anxiety edging his voice.

'We have access to various records.'

He swallowed hard. 'Whatever you think I have or haven't done, my family had nothing to do with it.' When there was no response, he added, 'I'm begging you to leave them out of this.'

'They may be able to corroborate your story.'

His face suddenly grew dark with anger. 'I said leave them out of this, you wee hoor.'

The remark earned him a slap on the head from the uniform standing behind him.

'Perhaps your wife can shed light on your activities.' Dania glanced at Honor. 'We have her address, don't we?'

Heriot's face contorted with rage. Ignoring the uniform, he lunged at Dania. She pushed her chair back in time to avoid his swinging fist. The uniform leapt forward and immobilised Heriot, gripping his neck and yanking his arm behind his back.

'I'll be requesting bail denied, Mr Heriot,' Dania said, getting to her feet.

The muscles of his face tightened. With his free hand, he drew a finger across his throat. 'If you ever get lost in this big city of ours, lassie,' he said, in a strangled voice, 'I'll know where to look for you.'

The women watched the uniform bundle Heriot out of the interview room.

'What do you think, boss?'

Dania picked up the folder. 'He'll be put away for a long time, even if Leslie gets him the best lawyer his tainted money can buy.'

'What I can't understand is whether those idiotic replies were deliberate, and the guy is playing the long game, or whether he's thick as mince.'

'He can't be as thick as all that if he was entrusted with the IED. He could have blown himself up attaching it to Marek's car.' She glanced at the girl. 'What did the background check reveal?'

'He's new in town. Comes from Edinburgh. He's had the odd spell in prison for GBH.'

'So, not one of Leslie's tried and trusted?'

'Nope. Which makes me suspect Leslie had no intention of letting him live after the detonation. Kimmie could tell us how close you'd need to be to use that remote device. Maybe it wasn't as remote as we think. The metal shell was intended to add to fragmentation, remember.'

Dania checked her watch. 'I need to look in on the DCI.'

Honor nodded and took the corridor to the incident room.

Dania reached Jackie Ireland's office. She knocked loudly.

'Come in.' The woman looked up as Dania entered.

'I thought I'd brief you on where I am with everything, ma'am.'

As succinctly as she could, she filled Jackie Ireland in on her interview with Bruce Heriot, including the falsehood about Marek being on his way to Poland. Her hope was that Heriot would pass that snippet on to Leslie. And Leslie would believe it. But she couldn't keep Marek hidden at Honor's for ever. He would have to resurface and, as soon as he did, Leslie would learn of it.

On the Sangster case, she described her success – or lack of it – with Mavis's album. 'The photos in that family album didn't shed much light, I'm afraid,' she finished.

The DCI smoothed back her hair. 'Family albums rarely do. But there's one thing you could try. DC Thomson has an archive of old photographs going back centuries. And documents, too.'

'What sort of documents?'

'Obituaries, electoral register records. That kind of thing. And photographs of Dundee itself. There might be something there that'll help us.' She must have caught Dania's look of scepticism because she added, 'We could get our resident historian on to it.'

But as Dania left the office, she questioned whether anything would come of it. The archive would hold records from the nineteenth century, and what she wanted would be from the century after. And, even then, she doubted there'd be anything useful. Logan Sangster had taken whatever secret he had to the grave. And, unless Mackie confessed to colluding with Duncan to kill Edward, with it went possibly her last chance of uncovering what had happened to the three Sangster brothers.

CHAPTER 22

'You mean there's no sight of him or the blue lorry?' Dania said.

Hamish was looking the way he did when he had to deliver bad news. 'We had the vehicle registration number from the farmer, and ran it through ANPR, but nothing so far.'

'Given the lack of traffic cameras on those country roads, I'm not holding out much hope. Does the farmer have any idea where Mackie could have taken the tipper?'

'He doesn't have a scooby. Not only that but he gave me an earful, and no mistake. As if this is somehow our fault.'

'And the uniforms confirmed he's not been back all day?'

'Aye, that's what they said. It's after six. If he's been in the city, he'll be heading back now, right enough.'

'Or maybe he's going to make good on his threat to Duncan Sangster.' She picked up her bag. 'I'll head over there now. If I see his tipper, I'll call you and you can send the uniforms home.'

'Shall I come with you?' Hamish straightened. 'He might get nasty.'

'If he does, I'll get nastier. No, you'd better stay in case the uniforms bring him in. If they do, phone me immediately.'

Dania left the station and took the now well-used road to Sangster Hall. She arrived to find the car park only half full. There was no sign of the blue tipper. She followed the arrows to the overflow and checked that too, then returned to the main area and eased the car into her reserved spot. There were lights on in the cottage, suggesting Duncan and Grace were at home.

Scott Balfour was on duty. 'You're back, Dania.' He smiled. 'Just in time for dinner.'

'You look tired,' she said, unbuttoning her coat. 'You're working too hard.'

'Tell me about it.'

'I noticed fewer cars in the car park.'

'It's Thursday and the events are petering out. We still have some fully booked, right enough. Hennie's, for example.'

'Are people leaving Magic Week early?'

'Not that so much. They didn't book as many shows at the tail end.'

He sounded dispirited. Dania remembered the conversation between him and Kirstine about how close they were to insolvency. Money worries must have been uppermost in his mind.

'Have you got anything on next week?' she said.

'A conference.' He rolled his eyes. 'Accountants.'

'The place is surely a bit large for that.'

'It's an international conference.'

'I see.' She pulled off her hat. 'I'd better make my way to the dining room before the food goes.'

'Lamb cutlets,' he called after her. 'In red wine.'

A queue was forming at the buffet. She stood holding her plate, her gaze roaming the room. Hennie was already seated. Two tables had been pushed together to accommodate all the women who wanted to sit with him. He was trying to eat his supper, but the ladies were constantly challenging him to show them yet another trick. Dania smiled to herself. Poor Hennie. The price of fame was not being able to eat your lamb cutlets in peace.

She took her plate to the nearest table with a free seat. 'Do you mind if I sit here?' she said to the elderly man. He was tucking into dessert – apple pie and ice cream – with such enthusiasm that blobs of it had decorated his tie.

'Of course not, my dear,' he said enthusiastically. He had rheumy eyes, and a bald crown, which was glistening in the heat. 'That is, provided you don't try anything.'

'Excuse me?'

'I've noticed that whenever I'm not on my guard, someone – usually a lovely lady like yourself – tries to play a trick on me.'

'Well, you can rest assured that I'm here to eat my dinner.'

'Have you got the hang of these tricks?'

'I'm afraid not. I'm a slow learner when it comes to magic. You?'

'I'm much the same. I'm here for the shows, actually. I've sat in on a few workshops but, to be frank, I'd rather not know how the illusions are done.' He smiled. 'I suspect that puts me in the minority.'

'I'm the complete opposite. I can't rest until I've worked everything out.'

He glanced at his watch. 'Oh dear, I'd better get going. The Shock Magic show is about to start.'

'Shock Magic?'

'You know, eating razor blades, needle through the tongue. That sort of thing. Will you excuse me?'

He got to his feet, only then noticing the food on his tie. He ran a hand over it, then wiped the hand on his jacket. It was a yellow-green tweed in a style that had once been fashionable. Apple pie and ice-cream would blend in wonderfully.

281

The room was emptying as the early sitters bolted their food so they could make the next event. Dania's mind slipped back to the confrontation between Mackie and Duncan. The more she thought about it, the more she was forced to the conclusion that the two men had conspired to kill Edward. But, Duncan's guilt aside, she couldn't take the risk that Mackie wouldn't follow through on his threat. She made the sudden decision to call Hamish and arrange for round-the-clock protection for Duncan and Grace.

Abandoning her coffee, she hurried from the room.

Strangely, the reception area was deserted, making her wonder if Scott had been called away on an emergency. Without knowing why, she felt the first stirrings of unease. She pulled on her sheepskin and stepped outside, scanning the car park. Still no sign of the tipper.

The long avenue of distant trees was illuminated by the light from the lamp posts. Her gaze drifted up to the tar-black sky, its stars like tiny, winking ice crystals.

She was tugging out her phone when she heard a voice behind her. 'Beautiful, isn't it?'

Hennie was lighting a cigar. He drew on it slowly and fanned away the cloud of smoke.

'I'm relieved it's no longer snowing,' she said, leaving the phone in her pocket. 'The weather must have been a nightmare for the guests.'

'I'd offer you a cigar but I believe ladies here don't smoke them.'

'I heard you playing the piano the other night. Chopin's "Grande Valse Brillante".'

'One of my favourites.' He studied her through the smoke. 'Were you listening from the corridor?'

'My room is directly above the music room.'

'Then I hope I didn't wake you.'

'If you had, I wouldn't have minded. Not the way you play Chopin.'

'My favourite piece is his nocturne, opus twenty-seven, number one in C sharp minor. It's enchantingly beautiful to begin with, then very dramatic.'

'And then brooding again.'

'Before it tails off to perfection.' He examined the lit end of the cigar. 'I've often wondered what other masterpieces Chopin would have created had he not died at the age of thirty-nine.'

'It's a tantalising thought, isn't it?' The lights in the cottage reminded her why she'd braved the cold. 'Will you excuse me, Hennie? I need to make a phone call.'

'Perhaps we can meet later in the bar?'

But Dania's concentration had been thrown by a sudden movement at the far end of the avenue. Whoever was in the blue vehicle must have turned on to it from another road on the estate, or she would have seen it leave the car park.

A second later, she heard a terrifying whoomph behind her. She wheeled round and stared through the curtain of trees shielding the cottage. Flames seemed to appear from nowhere, flickering, growing, spreading frighteningly quickly.

Hennie threw his cigar on to the ground, muttering something she didn't catch.

Instinct made her run towards the burning cottage, but strong hands gripped her arms and pulled her back.

'No, Dania, it's too dangerous!'

'But Duncan and Grace are inside,' she cried out.

The yellow flames were licking the walls. In a matter of seconds, they reached the roof. White smoke poured out of the building. Moments later, the upper windows blew out with an enormous crash, and the stink of smoke and burning wood caught in her throat. She struggled to free herself, but Hennie dragged her away. Without warning, the front door collapsed. Although she'd seen it before, she was always amazed at the speed with which a fire took hold.

She let her body go limp. Hennie was right. She couldn't help them now. 'I need to call the emergency services,' she shouted over the noise.

She pulled out her phone, moving far enough away that her voice could be heard, and dialled 999, urging the operator to put her through to the fire control room. 'This is DI Dania Gorska,' she said, in a hoarse voice. 'There's a fire in the building adjacent to Sangster Hall. Yes, west of Dundee. You need to hurry! We think people may be inside.' She disconnected, then called West Bell Street. 'Hamish? Dania here. Listen carefully, and don't say anything until I finish. I think Allan Mackie has started a fire in the Sangsters' cottage. I've called the emergency services, but what I want you to do is find Mackie. He's just left the estate in the blue tipper. I'm guessing he'll be returning to his cottage, but maybe not, so you'll need to get uniforms out on the roads. If he causes a fuss, arrest him. The charge is arson to endanger life. Is Honor there?'

'Aye.'

'Send her out here with the uniforms. I need her to liaise with the fire investigators and hold down the scene. I've got to go.'

People were spilling out of the Hall, no doubt alerted by the roaring of the flames. Dania's main worry was that the screen of trees between the cottage and the Hall would catch fire, but fortunately the wind was blowing the sparks in the opposite direction.

'Could everyone please go back inside?' Hennie said, lifting his arms. 'The fire services have been called, but it's not safe to stay out here.'

Reluctantly, people drifted back. It said something about Hennie's standing that they were prepared to listen to him. Dania had the impression she would have fared worse if she'd tried to take control.

Someone was pushing through the crowd. It was Scott Balfour.

'What's happening?' he mouthed, looking from Hennie to Dania.

A sudden crash from the burning cottage made him whirl round. His lips moved. 'My God,' he seemed to say. He tugged at his hair. 'Duncan and Grace,' he shouted, gripping Dania's arm.

'There's nothing we can do,' she shouted back.

Already, the roof timbers had burnt through, and the tiles were falling, smashing as they hit the ground. 'Go inside, Scott,' she said, leaning into him so he could hear, 'and keep everyone in the Hall.'

'What about you?'

'I'll wait here for the fire services.'

He nodded miserably, and left.

She became aware of Hennie beside her. He removed another cigar from his jacket, glanced in the direction of the destroyed cottage, then seemed to think better of it. 'I'll stay and keep you company, Dania.' He put the cigar away. 'Or should I address you as Detective Inspector Gorska?'

She looked at him, wondering what was going through his mind. What was going through hers was that whoever had erected those murder stones would need to make a start on carving two more, one for Duncan and one for Grace. But that thought was immediately superseded by another – Duncan and Grace had requested her presence at the Hall specifically because they were worried for their safety and wanted protection. And in that, she had failed spectacularly. She turned away so that Hennie wouldn't see the remorse in her eyes.

By the time the fire engines arrived, it was nearly over. The cottage was a burnt-out shell with much of the first floor caved in. Smoke stained what was left of the façade, although the fire was by no means spent. Every so often, something burst into flame, reminding Dania how treacherous fire can be. It was like a wild beast, sometimes attacking, other times lying low, ready to pounce when its prey least expected.

'What happens now?' Hennie said, watching the fire engines crowding the car park.

'When the fire is out, a structural engineer enters the building to check it's safe to enter.'

Firemen were unloading the equipment. Once they got the hoses working, it wouldn't take them long to get the situation under control.

'I'm assuming a search will be made for the bodies,' Hennie said. 'Or what's left of them.'

'That's the first thing they do. But they'll then hand over to the fire-scene investigators.'

'These are forensics specialists?'

'And they'll be looking for clues as to what caused the fire, and where the seat of the fire is. In other words, is there a single point of origin? Or is there evidence of several instances of fires starting at same time?'

'Which would indicate foul play, wouldn't it?'

Dania gazed at the ruin, knowing that all too often the cause of the fire was destroyed along with everything else. She was well acquainted with the effects of fire on the body, how heat causes muscles to lock, drawing legs and arms into the well-known pugilistic pose. But badly charred bodies were surprisingly well preserved internally, and forensic investigators could distinguish between normal effects of fire on the body, and evidence of something more sinister. An arsonist who set a fire to destroy evidence of murder didn't always succeed. If Duncan and Grace had been murdered, the investigators would soon know.

'So, how do they go about it?' Hennie said.

'They look for smoke patterns on walls, which windows are broken, that sort of thing. The problem here is that the ceilings and walls are down. And hundreds of gallons of water will make interpretation harder.'

'I wonder why we didn't hear the smoke alarms.'

'Perhaps there weren't any.' She laid a hand on his arm. 'Look, Hennie, would you mind going inside? You did such a great job with the guests. Perhaps you could get people into the living room and keep them entertained until the police arrive. We'll have to interview everyone, yourself included.'

He gave a small bow. 'Of course, I understand. I will do whatever I can to help.' He disappeared into the Hall.

The sound of vehicles on the avenue signalled the arrival of Honor and the uniforms, closely followed by the fire-scene investigators.

'Boss,' Honor called, not waiting until the car had stopped before opening the door. She hurried over. 'Crikey,' she muttered, staring at what was left of the cottage.

'I think Allan Mackie is behind this. And I don't think he'll have been particularly sophisticated about how he did it. What we need is the evidence.'

'Did you see it start?'

'It would be more accurate to say that I *heard* it start.' Two fire-scene investigators were setting up a cordon round the area. Others were erecting large arc lamps. 'There wasn't a single point of origin,' she continued. 'The flames were yellow to begin with. And there was white smoke.'

'He used an accelerant, then.'

Dania beckoned to the uniforms, who crowded round her. 'Right, no one is to leave the Hall. I want you to start taking statements. Most people will be in the living room, but there'll be some in workshops scattered around the place. The organisers, Scott Balfour and Kirstine Welles, will be able to tell you where those are, and give you maps. There's more than one way out, so you'll need to cover the exits.'

The uniforms pulled out their notebooks and headed for the entrance.

'I take it Duncan and Grace are still in there,' Honor was saying.

'We'll know soon enough,' Dania said grimly, watching the investigators getting kitted up. They picked their way through the gap that had once been the front door.

'Is there a way out the back? Could they have escaped in time?'

'Then where are they? They'd have raised the alarm, surely. I was out here with Hennie when it started, and I saw no one. My guess is that Mackie set the fire from the back, where he couldn't be seen. If they'd tried to escape that way, he'd have stopped them.'

'If they were on the first floor, they won't have made it,' Honor said, echoing Dania's thoughts.

A noise from behind made them turn. A van was coming up the avenue.

'I called Milo, boss. He was about to begin an autopsy, but he's

288

sent the mortuary van.' She puffed out her cheeks. 'Burnt to a crisp. That's one post-mortem I'd hate to attend.'

The van pulled up behind the fire engines.

'I'll go and brief them,' Honor said. She hurried away.

'Dania?' Scott was holding a mug. 'I thought you might like a coffee.'

'Thanks,' she said, taking it gratefully. Now that the fire had been extinguished, the wind had dropped, as had the temperature, and the cold had closed round her.

'Did you give your statement?' she said, sipping.

'Aye, the polis are working the living room at the moment.' He thrust his hands into his trouser pockets and gazed at what was left of the cottage. 'What the fuck happened?'

'That's what the investigators are hoping to find out.'

'What about Magic Week? . . . I mean, do you think we'll have to close?'

'I'm afraid so. There's evidence the fire was started deliberately, so this is now a crime scene.'

'And the guests? Can they leave?'

'Until we're satisfied that no one at the Hall was involved, everyone will have to stay where they are.'

'The ones who've come from abroad will be relieved, and no mistake. Most aren't expecting to fly back until Tuesday.' He stared at her. 'Hold on. You said, "until *we're* satisfied".'

'I'm a detective. DI Gorska.'

His mouth gaped open.

'And this is DS Randall,' she added, as Honor approached. 'Honor, this is Scott Balfour, one of the event organisers.'

He gazed from one to the other, his surprise slowly turning to suspicion. Dania could see he wanted to ask what her business was at the Hall, but seemed to decide against it.

She handed back the mug. 'Thanks, Scott. I'm hoping you'll keep everyone fed and watered for the next day or two.'

He straightened. 'You can rely on me and Kirstine to step up.' He disappeared, almost running.

'It'll be a while before we hear from the fire investigators, Honor. We may as well help the uniforms.'

It was nearly ten before the first report came in. Dania's phone rang.

'DI Gorska,' she said, leaning against the living-room door. She was conscious everyone in the room was listening. Kirstine's face could best be described as a 'wet weekend', to use a favourite expression of Honor's. She clearly felt she'd been duped by 'Tanya', and she didn't like it.

Dania recognised the chief fire investigator's voice. 'Can you hold on a minute?' she said. 'I'll meet you outside.'

The man was waiting for her at the door. He'd removed his breathing equipment and looked pale in the light from the arc lamps.

'What can you tell me?' she said.

'We've been incredibly lucky. We found a number of spent matches outside, at the back of the cottage. Forensics should be able to identify the brand.'

'And possibly get dabs off them. Were the matches in one place?'

'They were under all the windows. Pretty conclusive evidence there wasn't a single seat of fire.' The man glanced towards the cottage. 'There's also a strong smell of petrol. My guess is the arsonist poured petrol into bottles or jam jars, stuffed in some rags and lit them. He broke the ground-floor windows and chucked

290

them in. It'll be a while before we can be sure of that, but that's where my thinking is taking me so far. It's a common way of setting a fire.'

Dania took a deep breath. 'And the bodies?'

'There are none, Inspector.' He must have been conscious of her stare. 'It's the first thing we look for. And, believe me, if they were there, we'd have found them.' He lifted a plastic bag. 'You may not recognise these, but they're mobile phones. Or, rather, they were.'

She gazed at the two molten lumps, wondering how he could possibly identify them. Stupid thought. These people were experts.

'Did you find a shotgun?' she said. 'Or what had once been a shotgun?'

'We didn't. We're always on the lookout for firearms, and particularly ammunition. It usually combusts quickly, although not always. But there was nothing.'

So Duncan's shotgun was missing. If Mackie had taken it, he'd still have it. And the ammunition.

'We can keep working for another hour or more,' the man said, 'but then we'll call it a day. We'll be back first thing tomorrow.'

'Phone me immediately if you find anything I should know about. Any time of day or night.'

Dania watched him hurry away, her thoughts tumbling over one another. If Allan Mackie had intended to kill Duncan and Grace by burning down their cottage, he'd failed. Assuming it *had* been Mackie. She sent Hamish a text informing him of the investigator's findings and instructing him to have Mackie's house searched. And warning him that the man might be armed.

But the question her mind kept straying to was: if Duncan and Grace weren't in that cottage, then where the hell were they?

CHAPTER 23

'I've checked with Duncan and Grace's service provider, ma'am, and the last time Duncan used his mobile was Tuesday, the sixteenth of February. With Grace, it was the Saturday before.'

Dania frowned at Hamish. 'I saw Duncan on Wednesday, so that doesn't help us.'

'And the connection with their mobiles was lost at six forty-eight p.m. yesterday, Thursday.'

'Which is roughly when I was outside with Hennie.'

'Do you think Mackie's kidnapped them?'

The man's words slipped into her mind. *You're going to regret this, Sangster.* 'Why would he, though?' she said. 'Unless he planned to kill them somewhere miles away and hide the bodies. But then why bother torching their dwelling place? He could have been caught in the act.'

'Aye, it doesn't make much sense.' Hamish studied her. 'You look tired, ma'am,' he added.

'Five hours sleep – the kind where you toss and turn – has that effect on me.'

She'd left Sangster Hall at midnight and returned to her flat, dreading what she might find. But to her relief, not only was the boiler working, but the men had left it on a low setting to keep the chill off the room. She'd set the alarm, which was loud enough to wake the dead, and risen early. After gulping the extra-strong coffee that was breakfast these days, she'd driven to West Bell Street.

The door opened, and Honor loped in. She looked as tired as Dania was feeling. 'What are your orders, boss?' she said, collapsing at her desk.

'We continue the search for Duncan and Grace. They may still be alive. It overrides everything.'

'Where do we start?' Honor said, glancing at Hamish. 'Mackie's place?'

'Kimmie's staff are in there now,' he said. 'He's not been back.'

'What about the tipper?' Dania asked.

'Nothing on the cameras.'

Honor was chewing her thumb. 'There's something not right about this.'

'That's what we were saying, lass.'

'I'd discount a kidnap, for the simple reason there's no one around to pay a ransom, is there? Edward's dead, and they had no kids. So, if his plan was to kill them, my money is on him doing it quickly. Burning the building would be risky, as they might escape. So, he goes in, forces them out, and kills them somewhere on the estate. Except why not kill them there and then?' she added, with a puzzled expression. 'And torch the cottage to get rid of the evidence.'

'We'll get our answers once we find them. Or their bodies.'

'Yep.' She seemed unconvinced. 'Anyway, when the report came in that there were no charred corpses, we reinterviewed everyone about the last time they'd seen Duncan and Grace. Most of the guests had no idea who they were. Those that did couldn't remember.'

'We were only going through the motions with those inter-views,' Dania said wearily. 'From the uniforms' reports, everyone was inside the Hall. And when the fire was set, they were in full view of people in the dining room or at workshops. That includes Scott and Kirstine, and the catering staff. The only exception was Mavis. She was alone in her rooms.' She rubbed her face. 'Okay, you know what to do. Coordinate the search for Duncan and Grace. And I want Allan Mackie.'

They left the room. Dania was tempted to close her eyes briefly, but this wasn't the time for a snooze. Mentally, she went through where they were, and what they still needed to do. The fire investigators would be at work for days, if not weeks, system-atically sifting and checking. But finding those spent matches had been an astonishing stroke of luck. If Kimmie could deliver the goods at Mackie's place, they'd solve this one quickly. Yet the disappearance of Duncan and Grace was the mystery here, not who had set the fire. Maybe they were wrong about Mackie. Maybe the fact that the two remaining Sangsters had vanished was unconnected to the fire and had more to do with the mystery surrounding Watson and Fraser. The other thought that was uppermost in her mind was that, whatever the reason for their disappearance, Duncan and Grace were already dead. So where were their bodies? If she were the murderer, where would she hide them?

Tam's words crept into her mind: *If they have been murdered, and they're down there, you'll never find them. It's so deep it comes out on the other side of the planet.*

He'd been talking about the old well, and referring to Watson and Fraser. But he could equally have been referring to Duncan and Grace.

★　★　★

The news came in at lunchtime. A worker on the neighbouring estate had been clearing snow from a field, ready to spread slurry, when he'd spotted something in the distance. Something he knew was out of place. Once he'd picked his way over the field and seen what it was, he hadn't hesitated. He contacted the police.

Everyone was out, so Dania picked up the call. She listened to the details, grabbed her bag and rushed to the car park. Before she started the engine, she called Milo.

'Milo Slaughter,' came the deep voice.

'Milo? Are you busy?'

A soft chuckle. 'What kind of question is that? I could ask you the same.'

'Point taken. Can you spare the time to accompany me to a crime scene?'

'I'm assuming you wouldn't be inviting me unless we were talking corpses. In which case, I'd better come with the van. Shall I meet you there?'

She thought rapidly. 'Where we're going will be difficult to find, and I'm not sure I can give you sensible instructions. I suggest I call for you at Ninewells, and you and the van can follow me there.'

'Or I can ride with you, and my assistants can follow us in the van,' he said, in a cheeky voice.

'And it might be wise to wear thick boots. We may have to trek over open country. Okay, I'm leaving the station now.'

Dania reached the Ninewells car park to find the mortuary van with its engine running. Milo had wasted no time. He was standing talking to the mortuary assistant and the photographer, Lisa. They were wearing thick parkas, warm hats and snow boots.

'Good to see you, Dania,' Milo said, as she reached across and opened the passenger door. He signalled to the others, then clambered in, struggling to lift his long legs inside. He reminded Dania of an enormous spider she'd seen in the forests outside Warsaw. It, too, had had legs so disproportionately large that it didn't know what to do with them.

Milo peered through the windscreen. 'Amazing how the weather's changing. It's feeling positively mild today.' He threw her a smile. 'Mind you, the term "mild" has an altogether different meaning in Scotland.'

They were halfway down the Perth Road when he said: 'So where are we going? The Sangster estate?'

'The estate adjoining it. I've programmed the sat-nav, but I've no idea if the roads there will be clear.'

In the event, they reached the area without major mishap, although they had to stop to lift a fallen branch off the road. The snow had almost melted, and what remained had been cleared away by farm vehicles and was piled up at the verge.

'It's round that curve, according to this,' Dania said, slowing to a crawl.

The road narrowed to a single track. They bounced over the ruts.

'Best if we stop here,' Milo said grimly. He squinted through the rear window, as if to check that the van was still in one piece. 'It's the potholes I'm worried about. I wouldn't like to be stranded in a vehicle with blown-out tyres.'

Dania slowed to a halt and cut the engine. Through the rear-view mirror, she saw the van pulling up behind her.

'There's someone coming,' Milo said.

A stocky man was hurrying towards them. He was dressed warmly in heavy-duty labourer's clothes. As he approached, she glimpsed the weathered features of someone whose working life was spent outdoors.

She and Milo scrambled out of the car.

'Are you polis?' the man gasped, looking from one to the other anxiously. It was unlikely that an estate worker would be panting from exertion. The expression in his eyes suggested it was more likely to be from fear.

'DI Gorska, and this is Professor Slaughter.'

'I'm the one who phoned it in, eh. They're at the other end of the field. I can take you there.'

Lisa and the mortuary assistant had left their vehicle, and together they tramped after the man. As they neared the low boundary wall, a turbine came into view. Since the wind had long since spent itself, the blades were stationary. Next to the turbine was a small crane.

'I wouldn't normally have noticed it, right enough,' the man was saying. 'It's been there for ages. But then I saw that,' he added. He looked up, then away again.

Two figures were dangling from the crane's long arm. It was Duncan's black hair and Grace's mousy brown curls that identified them. Duncan was in sweater and jeans, and had been wearing slippers, one of which was missing. But Grace was barefoot. The patterned pyjamas suggested she'd either been in bed, or getting ready, when she was taken. Without being prompted, Lisa lifted her camera and took several shots, first carefully photographing the ground under and around the crane, then lifting the camera to record the couple from every angle.

'Okay, Prof,' she said to Milo. 'I'm done from down here.'

'Do you know how to operate the crane?' Dania said, glancing at the estate worker.

'Aye, that I do.'

She moved closer to him. 'Are you okay to go up?' she murmured.

'What about fingerprints?' he said, rubbing his chin thought-fully. 'I might wipe them. I have to grip the rails.'

'That's a risk we'll have to take. But my guess is that whoever did this will have brought gloves. As we all have.'

He threw her a crooked smile. 'I reckon he would at that. It's just that I've been watching these CSI programmes on the telly.'

The crane stood on a wide concrete base, which was overlaid with frozen mud. He ran his hands down the sides of his trousers and started to climb the vertical ladder.

At the top of the tower, he clambered into the operator's cab. A moment later, the faint sound of the controls reached Dania's ears. The crane's long arm tilted and the bodies began their descent, swaying slightly. As they drew closer, it was the staring eyes and open mouths that she noticed first, and then the colour of the skin. Had she not known better, she'd have said they were blushing, but the redness was the signature of bleeding from the capillaries.

Milo and the assistant had spread a sheet on the ground. As Duncan's feet touched it, she signalled to the worker to stop the crane.

Round Duncan's neck was a thick black cable. Lisa stepped forward and took more photos. The assistant cut the cable and he and Milo lifted Duncan on to the ground. Then they did the same with Grace.

'What can you tell me, Milo?' Dania said.

He was feeling Duncan's limbs. 'There's still plenty of rigor. Onset is delayed and the duration lengthened when the temperature is low. Hard to say how long they've been dead. We need to wait for the results of the potassium eye test.'

Which, as Dania knew, was not affected by temperature.

'As for cause of death,' Milo went on, 'the petechial haemorrhaging in the upper face and eyes is consistent with death by asphyxiation.' He slipped his gloved fingers under the cable and lifted it slightly. 'However, there is no ligature mark up by the ears. See this line here? It's horizontal across the victim's throat. My guess is that the killer approached from behind and threw a rope or cable over the head, then pulled hard. No, I'm afraid this is a posed hanging.' He clambered over the sheet to where Grace was lying. 'It's the same with this one.' He glanced at Dania. 'Maybe a clumsy attempt to make us think this is a double suicide?'

'But surely no one would seriously consider that.'

'You think not?'

'For one thing, how on earth would they get up there? Grace is barefoot.'

'Indeed, but have you forgotten the recent case of the man who hanged himself this way? He climbed up, walked along the crane's arm, fixed a rope to it and jumped. All his mates saw it.'

'Now you mention it, I do recall the case. He was drugged up to the eyeballs.' She stared at the corpse. 'But this is murder, from what you say.'

'And here's another indicator.' Milo lifted Grace's hands. The nails were unvarnished. But under the index and third fingers, there was a reddish-brown discolouration. 'My guess is she fought back. If this is what I think it is, then you'll have the murderer's DNA.' He shook his head. 'Two more Sangsters. Looks as if someone has it in for that family. We'll get the bodies back to Ninewells and I'll make a start on the autopsies once rigor has left. In the meantime, we'll work on the DNA.'

'And I'll get SOCO over.' She made the call, describing how to get to the area, and confirming that she'd wait for them near the road.

Milo waved to the assistant, and together they set about transporting the bodies to the mortuary van.

The estate worker had climbed down and was standing a respectful distance away, staring at the ground.

'I'll need your contact details,' Dania said to him.

'I reckoned you would.' He pulled out his phone.

'Did you know Duncan and Grace Sangster?'

'Aye,' he said promptly. 'We all did. We'd occasionally borrow their farm equipment. They were good like that.'

'Is there anything else you can tell me?' she said, copying his details.

He looked uncertain. 'Like what?'

'Were you here yesterday, for example? You see, I'm trying to get an idea of when the bodies were hoisted.'

'I haven't been in this field for weeks. No one has. We've been working elsewhere on the estate.'

'What's on the other side of that wall?'

'That's the Sangster estate. Sangster Hall is in that direction,' he said, waving a hand.

And then she remembered the walk she and Tam Adie had taken to the shepherd's hut. And his words: *I used to work the neighbouring estate. The path curves round, and you reach the boundary wall. I understand they've installed wind turbines now.*

Could it be that whoever had killed Duncan and Grace had followed the same route she and Tam had taken? Had Allan Mackie used Duncan's shotgun to force him and Grace into the woodland, past the hut and over the boundary wall? And then murdered them and strung them up before returning to torch the cottage?

It seemed a strange thing to do. But then she'd seen things that were stranger. Yet, the thought that was uppermost in her mind was that, with the deaths of Duncan and Grace following on so soon after Edward's, the Sangster dynasty had died out.

CHAPTER 24

Dania reached West Bell Street well after 2 p.m. The estate worker, still visibly shaken, had taken himself off to clear a field elsewhere, despite her advice he go home and rest. The SOCOs had arrived. The chief officer had taken one look at the crane and groaned theatrically.

'I know it's a tough one,' Dania had said, 'but do what you can. The cables on that sheet might be your best bet. It's possible the perp took his gloves off to string them up.'

Before she'd left, she'd called Honor and Hamish and brought them up to speed, directing them to call off the search for Duncan and Grace and concentrate on finding Allan Mackie. And to keep her posted.

Now, as she entered the almost deserted incident room, her mind strayed again to the early hours of Thursday morning, when she'd woken suddenly and crept over to the window. And seen something on the path that meandered towards the woodland – a dark shape advancing slowly and methodically into the trees. She'd concluded it was an estate worker picking his drunken way to his lodgings. But perhaps it was something else. Perhaps it was Allan Mackie forcing Duncan and Grace into the woods and over the boundary wall to where they'd met their death.

She sat at her desk, staring straight ahead.

'Inspector?' came a voice from the left.

A man with cloudy blue eyes and a thatch of silver hair was standing smiling at her. He was wearing his usual brown woollen jacket and beige corduroy trousers. She recognised him as the station's resident historian, formerly of the University of St Andrews where he had been professor of history until his early retirement. After a year of twiddling his thumbs, he'd applied for the part-time post at West Bell Street and been snapped up in record time. Around the station, he was treated with enormous respect, and referred to always as 'the professor'. Dania had worked with him before and found his exquisite manners – and his academic rigour – delightful.

'Professor,' she said, returning the smile.

'DCI Ireland asked me to research the Sangster family. I thought you might like to see what I've uncovered. Is now a good time?' He had a rich, deep voice, which would have kept his students on their toes. She'd discovered he'd been a lecturer in Cambridge before coming north to settle in St Andrews, where, he'd told her over a couple of lattes, the staff at the university had welcomed him with great affection and awarded him a personal chair.

Honor and Hamish were still out, the SOCOs were combing the area around the wind turbine, and it would be some time before the preliminary reports reached her.

'Now is an excellent time, Professor.'

He beamed. 'I've got it up online. I've had only twenty-four hours,' he said, in his usual self-deprecating manner, 'but I've found a number of photographs that might be relevant. They're part of this digitisation initiative that was started over a year ago. DC Thomson is one of the partners. The library at the University of St Andrews is another.'

'How far back do the archives go?'

'Nearly five centuries. There are scanned documents too, all indexed by name.' He operated the controls, and a number of images flooded the screen. 'I started with the current generation and worked back. This is Duncan Sangster and his bride on their wedding day. They make a lovely couple, don't they?'

She threw him a glance. But the report of Duncan and Grace's demise wouldn't have reached him.

'And here we have Edward and his wife,' the professor was saying.

It was the same wedding photo Dania had seen in the newspapers. Honor had made a comment about the lace dress.

He worked through the family images, pausing at the obituaries. Perhaps sensing that Dania was becoming restless, he touched one of the side controls, and an image of Sangster Hall appeared. The black-and-white photograph had been taken by someone standing in the avenue of trees. A dusting of snow lay on the ground and roof and, had Dania not seen the date – 31 December 1930 – she would have sworn the photo was from a few days before.

'There was a Hogmanay party, and the great and the good were invited.' He ran through the photos slowly. She recognised the rooms. The furniture was different, but the curtains and rugs were remarkably the same. It was a shame that what she was seeing were still images. A video would have captured the party spirit marvellously. She imagined the laughter, the clinking of glasses, the band tuning up for Strip the Willow, a dance she'd tried but which had left her dizzy. Or maybe it was the champagne.

The professor tapped the screen and brought up another set of photos. One was of the music room. The elaborate cornicing hadn't yet started to crumble.

'The piano's not there,' she said suddenly.

'The piano?'

'There's a Steinway in that room now.'

'And have you played it?' he said, with a dreamy expression on his face.

'I have, but one of the guests played it better.'

'I find that hard to believe. I've heard you perform at the Caird Hall.'

'There's a family tree on the wall. But you can't see much of it with the guests milling about.'

'I think there's at least one more shot of that room, with a close-up.'

He fiddled with the controls until he found what he was looking for.

'Is that mural still there?' he said.

'It is.'

He squinted at the screen. 'Semper Paratus. Always Ready. I've seen that before, having a real tree with names instead of leaves. It's quite cute, isn't it? But it's a pity it doesn't go back further than William Sangster.'

'Just a minute,' she said, her voice faltering. She pulled out her mobile. 'These are the photos I took of the family tree earlier in the week. Let me cast them on to the screen.'

The professor enlarged them, moving one so it lay side by side with the photo from the archive.

'Good heavens,' he said. 'There's an entire branch missing.'

'Amelia Sangster,' Dania said, feeling her heart thumping. 'According to the tree from the archive, she's Logan Sangster's sister. But she's not on the tree in the Hall.'

'You took the photos this week, you say?'

'I'd wondered why the tree looked lopsided.' She recalled her conversation with Marek, how if William Sangster had had only one child – Logan – then he should be directly below him on the tree. But he was away to the side. Marek's theory was that there must have been furniture against the wall, and the artist realised it too late. Thinking about it now, the explanation seemed far-fetched. An artist would have moved everything before starting. There was only one explanation.

The professor said it before she did. 'William Sangster had another child, Amelia. But she was deliberately painted out of the mural.'

Dania stared at him, her thoughts tumbling over one other.

'I've got the birth records going back to William,' he said, with a historian's enthusiasm. 'Here's Logan's.' He tapped again. 'And this is Amelia's.'

'They were *both* born in 1930, on July the tenth. That makes them twins. Let me see the family tree again. Can you enlarge it?' She studied Amelia's dates. 'She died in 1953.'

'Poor girl. They married young then, but she never did, according to this.'

'Have you found any photos of her?' Dania said, her excitement growing.

'There are some of her as a child.'

An image of a blonde girl in a school uniform appeared on the board. Her hair was partly hidden under a straw hat.

'Any of her older?' Dania said.

'Just the one. She looks to be in her late teens. Here it is.'

Dania gazed at the photo, immediately seeing the resemblance.

The professor had spotted it too. 'You know, she's a dead ringer for the lady who's been in the *Courier* this week. The one organising Magic Week.'

'Kirstine Welles,' Dania said, feeling a rush of blood to her ears.

'That's the one. Let me find that photo in the papers, and I'll put them up side by side.'

A minute later, they were gazing at the images.

'They're uncannily similar,' he said. 'They must be related, don't you think?' he added, throwing Dania a quizzical look.

'I can't see how. Kirstine's grandmother is Mavis Welles. She was a servant at Sangster Hall.'

'Have you any photos of Mavis?'

'None that are recent. But in her album there are some when she was younger.'

'Pity we haven't got the album.'

'Actually, we do. I managed to sneak it out of her room and took photos with my phone.'

'Inspector!' the professor said, trying to look shocked. But the merriment in his eyes betrayed him.

'I sent the images to our server.'

It took a while, but she found the snaps of Mavis and Robbie outside their cottage.

'That's her son,' Dania said.

'I'd never have thought it.'

'Why?'

'Well, look at the hair colour, for one thing. Hers is jet black and his is blond.'

'Her husband might have had blond hair.'

'True, but she and the boy don't look at all related. Their faces are too different.'

'Just a minute, just a minute,' Dania said half to herself. She walked round the room, running her hands through her hair. Suddenly, she marched back to the screen. 'All right, according to the family tree, Amelia never married. But did she have any children?'

The professor's enthusiasm was infectious. 'A good question, Inspector. But there's nothing in the archive.' He studied her. 'What are you thinking?'

'That Robbie wasn't Mavis's son. He was *Amelia's*.'

'And if she had a child out of wedlock, which was something of a scandal in those days, it would explain why she was painted out of the mural.'

'According to the family tree, she died in 1953. Honor did a background check on Kirstine Welles. Her father, Robert Welles, was born in 1953. What we need to establish is the day and the month.'

'I'm sure we can do that,' the professor said, turning to the screen.

'It'll be faster from my desk.'

Sometime later, the information was on Dania's computer.

He sat back, folding his arms. 'And there we have it. Robert Welles, born on the exact same day that Amelia died. I know Mavis Welles's name is on the birth record, but it's too much of a coincidence, don't you think?'

'Amelia must have died giving birth to him. And Mavis brought him up as her own.'

He was looking at her expectantly.

'You're right,' Dania said. 'There's only one person who can shed light on this mystery.' She picked up her bag. 'And it's time I paid her a visit.'

'Looks as if most folk are leaving,' Mavis said, gazing around the near-empty dining room. 'I reckon what with the fire, and now Duncan and Grace gone missing, no one wants to hang about.'

The news hadn't yet reached the general population that

Duncan and Grace's bodies had been found suspended from a crane. On arriving at the Hall, Dania had taken Scott and Kirstine to one side. They'd agreed to keep the information to themselves and accelerate winding up Magic Week. Scott looked more shaken than his wife. There was a look of despair in his moist eyes, but whether it was the revelation about Duncan and Grace's murder or the realisation that he might have to give refunds to those guests who were leaving early, Dania couldn't tell.

'Afternoon tea was such a nice idea.' Mavis lifted her cup to her lips. 'So what did you want to talk to me about, lass?'

Dania had thought long and hard about the best way to approach the woman, and decided in the end just to come out with it. 'Tell me about Amelia. What was she like?'

Mavis stiffened. 'Aye, well, it's a long time since I heard anyone utter that name.' She looked hard at Dania. 'Where did you come across it?'

'Our historian found an old photo of the family tree. Like the one in the music room. Except that it had an extra branch for Amelia, Logan's twin sister. And then we discovered she'd had a child.'

Mavis ran her fingers over her cracked lips. 'Ach, well, they're in their graves, so what does it matter now?'

'Tell me what happened,' Dania said softly.

It was some time before Mavis spoke, leaving Dania wondering if the woman was fabricating her narrative. But the ache-filled eyes suggested otherwise.

'Logan was away for much of the time, and didn't know that Amelia was with child. Some women carry babies for many months before it shows. I knew, but I held my wheesht.'

'But eventually he realised?'

'Aye, and then everything started to go down the pan. He

insisted she get rid of the wain.' Mavis's expression hardened. 'Said he knew a woman on the estate who would do it. He'd pay her well to keep her trap shut.'

'So was this the secret Logan thought could bring the family down?'

'You have to understand how things were in those days. A child born out of wedlock was a stain on a family's honour. The Sangsters were big in this area. Aye, and in the city, too. I heard Logan telling his wife – who was still only his fiancée at the time – that they'd never be able to hold their heads up in society.' She snorted. 'What did that matter compared to the life of a child?'

'But Amelia refused the abortion.'

'Aye, that she did. Logan said he didn't intend to be around when the baby was born. He was about to get married. When Amelia was near her time, he took his new bride away for a long honeymoon.'

'Did Amelia have the baby at the Hall?'

Mavis played with her hands. 'In her bedroom. I assisted at the birth. I was hardly twenty. She begged me to help her. I should have got one of the older women to do it, but she said no, there'd be too much tittle tattle. She'd spent the last months of her confinement in her room, and no one knew about her condition. I'd waited on her hand and foot, and I was glad to do it. She was such a gentle wee soul. A bit soft in the head, I reckon. Always singing nursery rhymes. But her heart was in the right place.'

'And she gave birth to a boy, Robbie.'

Mavis gazed at Dania for a long moment. 'Aye. And then she had such a bleed from down there that she died not long after.' She let her head droop. 'I've always blamed myself. I thought I knew what to do, I'd seen lambs born and that, but what did I know about birthing babies?'

'Did you get in touch with Logan and his wife?'

'They came back in time for the interment. Amelia's buried in the family cemetery at the back of the estate.'

'And Robbie?' Dania said gently.

'I reckoned Logan would send him away to an orphanage – they weren't the nice cosy places they are now – and I couldn't bear that. I'd taken one look at the bairn and knew I had to keep him. When the bleed started, I called the family doctor. He couldn't help the lass, he arrived too late. He was stunned. He'd known nothing about her being with child.'

'I think I can guess the rest. You persuaded him to record on the birth certificate that you were Robbie's mother.'

'Aye, he was a good man that way. He knew I'd do right by the bairn. I cradled him in my arms, and carried him to the wee cottage I shared with my mam. She looked after him while I was on my duties.'

'And Logan never found out?'

'I told him the bairn had been stillborn and, knowing how he'd felt, I'd buried him deep in the woods in an unmarked grave.'

'And he was okay with that?'

'He paid me well enough to keep my mouth shut. Which I did. With Amelia passed away – he put it about that she'd had a sudden illness – you'd think he'd leave it at that.' Her mouth twisted. 'But no, he had to go and paint out her name on the family tree.'

Dania's tea had grown cold. 'And did you ever find out who Robbie's father was?'

A guarded look crossed Mavis's face, the same look Dania had seen when the woman had clutched the album to her chest.

'Was it one of the estate workers?' Dania said. She lowered her voice. 'You can tell me. He's unlikely to be alive now.'

Mavis shifted in her seat. 'It wasn't one of the workers.'

'Surely not your husband?'

'I never married, lass.'

'Who then?'

She dropped her voice to a whisper. 'It's only a hunch, mind. I mean I never saw them at it, but I think it was her own brother.'

'Logan!'

'Aye. I saw the way he looked at her, right enough. The help becomes invisible after a while. And there's not much that gets past me.' Her eyes filled with disgust. 'There was one time when I saw her running out of her room, her clothes all in disarray. And a moment later, Logan came out, doing up his flies.'

'Did Amelia ever say anything to you?'

'I asked her once, when she was near her time, but she started greetin' and pulling at her blouse. I left it. And I never asked her again.'

Dania could well imagine how easy it would be for Logan in this rambling house with its many rooms. He could have had sex with his sister many times, and no one in the building would ever have suspected. And didn't Mavis say that Amelia had had learning difficulties? She might not even have understood what was happening. Maybe after his sister's death, Logan had had a crisis of conscience that had driven him to drink. Hadn't Grace said he'd done something he'd deeply regretted? And wished he could turn the clock back? But those intimate photos of him with a young blonde woman now took on a greater significance. Dania had assumed the woman was his wife, but perhaps not.

'What colour hair did his wife have?' she said.

'Dark brown, almost black. Why do you ask, lass?'

'Curiosity, that's all.'

'Now that you know the secret, what are you going to do, eh?'

'Do? Nothing.'

'So you'll keep this to yourself?'

'I can't see that it's relevant to my case.'

'Aye, some secrets are best left buried.'

'By the way, does Kirstine know this history?'

'I never breathed a word. Not to her, not to Robbie. And neither did the doctor whose name is on the birth certificate.'

'Because if Kirstine is a direct descendant of Logan's sister, that makes her a Sangster.' Dania pushed her cup away. Forgetting that Mavis hadn't yet been informed of Duncan and Grace's demise, she added, 'The last living Sangster, in fact.'

Then, as the realisation of what she'd said hit her, the events of the past few days rushed into her head. And, in one blinding second, everything clicked into place.

CHAPTER 25

'Thanks for walking me back to my room, lass,' Mavis said, disentangling her arm from Dania's. 'I'm not so steady on my pins, these days.'

'It was no trouble,' Dania said, trying to keep the impatience from her voice.

'Aye, there's nothing like a good blether. And if we don't meet again, good luck with everything.'

'You too, Mavis. I'm glad we met.'

Dania left the corridor and almost ran to the office, passing no one on the way. Apart from faint voices from the ballroom, the Hall seemed deserted.

Kirstine was at the desk. She lifted her head in surprise. 'Inspector. What can I do for you?'

'I'm looking for Scott. Do you know where he is?'

'You've just missed him. He's gone up to our room.' She frowned. 'Is there something I can help you with?'

'It's your husband I need to speak to.'

'I can call him and ask him to come down,' she said, reaching for her mobile.

'No, that won't be necessary. I'll catch him up.'

Without waiting for a reply, Dania hurried out.

She was partway up the stairs when her phone rang.

'Boss,' came Honor's voice. 'It's Mackie. We haven't found him. His place looks abandoned. And his clothes are gone.'

'And the blue tipper?'

'No sign of it. We'll keep looking.' A pause. 'Any progress from your end?'

'I now know who killed Duncan and Grace. And possibly Edward,' she said, staring at the carpet. 'I'll explain everything when I get back but it's to do with another Sangster line. It turns out that Logan had a sister, Amelia. Hello? Honor? Can you hear me?' The line had faded and all she could hear was a faint hiss. 'Damn it,' she muttered, staring at the phone. It was fully charged. The problem must be at the mast. She tapped at the controls, trying to reach Honor.

She was gazing at the screen when the wall lights went out. A shadow moved, startling her. She looked up, seeing a figure silhouetted at the top of the stairs, but in the faint glow from the corridor she couldn't make out the features.

Before she understood what was happening, the figure gripped her arm, dragged her into the corridor and bounced her head off the wall. The rush of pain at the back of her head was followed by nausea, and for a second she thought she was going to throw up. She tried to take control of her movements but the red fog behind her eyes grew thicker and darker. The last thing she remembered before slipping into unconsciousness was hearing the thud as her body hit the floor.

Dania awoke to find herself lying on her side in a snowdrift. She tried to recall how she'd got there, but her scalp was a hot throbbing mass, chasing all thought from her mind. There was a

314

dull pain in her neck, which flared when she tried to move her head. The temptation to slip into unconsciousness was overwhelming. But she had to stay alert. She'd been in similar situations before and knew that if she didn't fight this, she wouldn't stand a chance. She clenched her teeth and lifted her head slowly.

A hurricane paraffin lamp stood in the snow, its light not strong enough for her to make out the features of the figure sitting against the wall. He was wearing a thick parka and gloves, but no hat.

'I'm sorry I had to do that to you, Dania,' Scott said. There was a tremor in his voice. 'But you left me no choice. Another second, and you'd have given your officer my name.'

As he shifted his weight, the amber light from the lamp tinted his grey hair blond, and gave her a better view of his face with its watery eyes. And it also illuminated what he had in his hands. She felt a spasm of fear ripple through her body. Unless he owned a shotgun, which she doubted, it could only be Duncan's. Yet he hadn't finished her off. He wanted something, information perhaps. That could work for her.

'Where are we?' she muttered.

'This is what used to be known as the shepherd's hut. Did you come across it on one of your walks?'

'With Tam Adie. Look, I have to sit up. I'm freezing to death in this snow.'

He said nothing, which she took for assent. She pushed herself up carefully, trying not to make any sudden movements. Not because she didn't want to spook him, but because lifting her head brought on a wave of agony. Slowly, she hauled herself into a sitting position and drew her knees up, pressing her hands against the ground, palms down. It would give her the best possible chance of scrambling to her feet. Provided she didn't lose her footing in the snow. Or pass out from the pain.

There was a faint buzzing noise. Scott pulled out his phone, gazed at it, frowning, then returned it to his pocket.

'Who else knows about Amelia?' he said nervously.

'My team at West Bell Street. Our resident historian briefed us on the research he'd done on the Sangsters.'

His expression suggested he didn't believe her. 'I heard you say you'd explain when you got back to the station. So who was that you were talking to on the phone?'

'One of my officers. She was away at the time.'

'She'll know you're at Sangster Hall, won't she?'

'The whole station knows,' Dania said irritably. 'I told them I was coming to arrest you.'

'But they don't know where you are right now, do they? Your phone's still in the corridor.' He shifted his weight, nearly dropping the shotgun. 'I don't believe anyone knows you were looking for me.'

'Kirstine knows.'

'I'll tell her you didn't find me.'

'What time is it?'

'Half past seven, give or take.'

'Won't you be missed at dinner?'

He hauled himself to his feet. In the strange light from the lamp, she saw that he was trembling. 'You need to get up, Dania. We're taking a wee walk.'

'You mean you're not going to murder me here?'

He lifted the shotgun and gestured towards the door.

Dania struggled to her feet, her head swimming. But she was determined not to cry out. As she lumbered past Scott, he stepped away in case she was rash enough to make a grab for the shotgun, something she wouldn't attempt given how jittery he was. Through the window, she glimpsed the ice house with its wooden door and rusty padlock.

She reached the door, and briefly considered making a run for it through the cypress trees, but he was already behind her. He must have lifted the lamp high, because her shadow spread like ink over the snow. The light fell on the wheelbarrow, and she wondered why he hadn't pushed her into the well. But then Mavis might have seen everything through the window.

Something hard was pressed into her back. 'Carry on,' Scott said. 'We've some distance to go yet.'

She lurched forward, wondering if she had the strength. The cold air scouring her lungs was starting to revive her, although if she tried anything now she'd come off badly. She would have to bide her time and pray for an opportunity.

Beyond the trees was the path, with woodland further on. She felt the shotgun in the small of her back again. 'Straight on, Dania.'

'In there?'

'You'll have to watch your footing, right enough.'

She gazed into the dense wood. 'I can't see a thing. You'll need to give me the lamp.'

He seemed to consider this. 'Aye, okay.' He passed it to her. 'But remember, I'm right behind you.' He tapped her arm gently with the shotgun. 'And I'll use this if I have to.'

She lifted the hurricane, casting its eerie light over the snow. It was enough to stop her crashing into the trees, although the uneven ground made walking difficult. But with each step she felt her strength returning. She moved slowly, Scott trailing close behind.

Before long, they'd left the wood. 'Where now?' Dania said, gazing around in the vain hope of sighting a worker's cottage. But there was only the pristine carpet of snow stretching endlessly in all directions.

'Turn right and keep to the line of trees.'

After a time, the land fell away. Below were several old stone buildings. They looked deserted. No lights in the windows. No smoke from the chimneys.

'See that wall on your left?' Scott said. 'In there is the Sangster family cemetery. The ground slopes down to the graveyard.'

'And that's where we're going?' Dania said, her stomach lurching.

He said nothing. Despite the cold, she felt the sweat run down her spine.

'What are those buildings?' she blurted, desperately wanting to keep him talking.

'They're workers' cottages. Or at least they used to be. But the workers abandoned them. Too near the graves. People can be remarkably superstitious. No one goes near the cottages now.'

So that was the plan. Murder her out here in this godforsaken place.

He steered her behind the last building. 'Stop here,' he said. 'Put the lamp down, please.'

She stared at the circular stone structure.

He must have guessed her thoughts. 'Aye, it's like the one outside the south wing, and every bit as deep from what I've heard. It's missing its roof. But that will make it easier,' he added, in a voice that suggested he was trying to find his courage.

So Scott intended her to go over the side, and take that last long drop to oblivion. She stared into the sky. It was peppered with stars. Was this the last thing she would see? She felt strangely detached. But she'd read that that was what the raw knowledge of certain death felt like.

'I want you to sit on the rim, Dania.'

She turned to face him.

He took a step back and lifted the shotgun. His hands were shaking. 'Don't come any closer.'

'You won't get away with it,' she said, her breath coming in ragged bursts. 'My colleagues will come looking for me.'

'But they won't come looking here, will they? Now, please climb up and sit on the rim.'

'I won't. Go ahead and shoot me. It's better than falling in and drowning.'

'I doubt there's water at the bottom. Anyway, I'm *going* to shoot you, but you need to sit on the rim first. Now, for the last time, climb up,' he added, in a voice edging towards hysteria.

She stood paralysed. 'I can't. I won't.'

'Then close your eyes.' He aimed the shotgun at her head.

'If you're going to shoot me, you'll have to look into my eyes while you do it.'

'Oh, God,' he murmured, lowering the weapon.

For the barest instant, she thought he wouldn't do it. But then he straightened and drew the stock firmly into his shoulder.

Before he could pull the trigger, there was a loud metallic thud that made her heart clench. He let go of the shotgun and dropped like a stone.

'Inspector! Are you all right?'

Kirstine was shaking uncontrollably. She was holding a heavy-duty spade. 'I heard him say he was going to shoot you,' she said, in a voice trembling with emotion. She stared at Scott, who was lying on the ground, groaning.

Dania picked up the lamp. 'Can you hold this?' she said, handing it to Kirstine. She lifted the shotgun and opened the action. In other circumstances, she would have laughed. But it was the knowledge that she'd endured this hell for nothing that made the anger swell inside her.

'*Kurwa*,' she muttered, through clenched teeth. It was a Polish swear word she rarely used, but it seemed appropriate on this occasion. 'It's not loaded,' she added, gazing at Kirstine.

'I had no idea Scott owned a shotgun.'

'It belongs to Duncan Sangster.'

'You mean—'

'That's right.'

Kirstine's eyes widened. 'Oh, no,' she whispered. 'Please tell me it's not true.'

'How did you know where we were?' Dania said, glancing at the spade in the woman's hand.

'Something came up with one of Scott's bookings. I called him but he didn't answer. He's always losing his phone, so I installed a tracker a while ago. When I saw where he was, I panicked. After what had happened to Duncan and Grace, I thought he'd been kidnapped. I mean, the wind turbine isn't far from here.'

'Why didn't you phone the police?'

'Och, it would have taken them an age to get from the city centre. I did phone *you*, though, but there was no reply.'

'I'm afraid my phone is back at the Hall.'

Kirstine's face was in shadow, but there was no mistaking the anguish in her voice. 'Why was he going to shoot you? And throw your body down that well?'

'I'll explain everything when we get back to the Hall,' Dania said gently. 'But now, could I borrow your phone? I need to call this in.'

Kirstine handed over her mobile without a word.

As Dania rang West Bell Street, and the adrenalin left her body, the pain at the back of her head returned. She gazed at the whining figure sprawled in the snow. She wasn't the only one with a raging headache. The thought gave her little satisfaction.

CHAPTER 26

It was Sunday before Dania and Hamish finally interviewed Scott Balfour. The delay allowed him to contact his solicitor, something which worked to their advantage because it gave Forensics time to process his DNA. In the event, the woman had been unable to attend. Scott had been offered the duty solicitor but had declined.

He was slumped in the chair, picking at his cuticles. His greying hair, which he normally kept neat, was a mess. Every so often, he ran his fingers through it, messing it even more. The look of resignation on his face suggested he wouldn't be putting up much resistance.

Dania had concluded her opening statement. She spread out the contents of her folder.

'How did you come to suspect me?' Scott said, before she could begin her questioning. He lifted his head. 'And why didn't you suspect Kirstine?

'I did, briefly. Because all this revolves around her. But the way you two behaved towards each other made me believe you were unlikely to be in cahoots. I had intended to interview you both separately, to make sure. Although when she whacked you over the head with that spade, and I saw the state she was in, I realised she had nothing to do with what's been going on.'

'No, she doesn't.' He shifted in his chair. 'So, how did you put it all together? You mentioned your historian found out that Logan had a sister.'

'That led me to the discovery that Kirstine is a Sangster. With no other Sangsters alive, she would therefore be heir to the estate. Your events business is close to insolvency, so it didn't take me long to fit the pieces together.' Her eyes were fixed on his. 'But when did *you* discover the truth about Amelia? Was it during one of your many chats with Mavis? She told me you and she often talked about the history of the Hall. And you sometimes brought a bottle.'

'She was partial to a wee dram. It went straight to her head because she rarely drank.'

'She mentioned she'd lost the key to the drawer where she keeps her album. Was it you who took it?'

'Aye. It was at one of our events last year. I sneaked the album away when she was out of the room.'

'And how did you join the dots?'

'Mavis slipped up and mentioned a sister of Logan's. I was interested in the Sangsters because we trace out their history in our advertising. People are always curious about mansions and dynasties.' He ran a hand over his face. 'So I plied Mavis with Scotch, and she began to ramble. When she came to the bit about the baby and how she'd passed it off as her own, I realised – and it came as a huge shock, and no mistake – that Kirstine was a member of the Sangster clan. I reckoned there might be pictures of this Amelia in the album.'

'And did you find these pictures?'

'There were some of her with Logan.'

Dania pushed two photos across. They were the ones of Amelia with her brother.

323

'Aye, I saw those. When I clocked the resemblance between Amelia and Kirstine, any doubts I might have had about Mavis's story melted away.'

'Why didn't you tell Kirstine?'

'I ken what she's like. She'd make a huge fuss. The first thing she'd do would be to find out if Amelia was born before Logan or after. If before, she'd be the rightful heir, and not Duncan. But even if Amelia was born after her brother, Kirstine would lay claim to part of the estate. I could see endless wrangles between solicitors, and our savings going down the drain in fees, and the lost revenues from a business we'd no longer have the energy to run.'

'Is that when you decided to get rid of the Sangsters?' Hamish chipped in.

Scott played with his fingers. 'I couldn't think what to do with the information, to be honest. But as things got steadily worse with the business, it became clear that with all the Sangsters gone, Kirstine would inherit everything, right enough, and our problems would disappear.' He took a deep breath. 'And then something happened that made me decide once and for all.'

'You caused an accident that killed Edward Sangster,' Dania said, watching the play of emotions on his face.

He nearly jumped out of the chair. 'I did not.' He was pale with anger. 'That's one thing I'm *not* admitting to. I never did that.' He rubbed his eyes wearily. 'When Edward died,' he continued more calmly, 'I knew there was only Duncan standing in the way. And Grace.'

It was a while before he spoke. Dania had seen this before – perps who had difficulty when it came to details, as though they didn't want to relive it.

'I went to their cottage late on Wednesday night,' he said.

324

'Can you remember the time?'

'It was around eleven. The light was still on. I rang the front doorbell. It was Duncan who answered.'

'What excuse did you come up with to call on him at that late hour?'

'Aye, I'd thought that one through. I said there'd been a problem with one of the guests. With the room. And could I come in and discuss it? Of course, he said yes.'

'And he didn't think it odd that it couldn't wait till morning?' Hamish asked.

'He said any complaints from the guests, and I was to come straight to him, no matter the time.'

Hamish nodded, apparently satisfied.

'I had the cable in the pocket of my parka,' Scott went on. 'His back was to me. He was fixing the drinks.' He lowered his head. 'It didn't take long for him to hit the floor. But I kept going for a bit, to be certain.' He looked directly at Dania, a wounded expression in his eyes. 'You see, I've never killed anyone before.'

'And Grace?'

'She was upstairs in the bathroom. In her pyjamas, getting ready for bed. She saw me in the mirror, but she didn't move. Frozen with fear, I guess. But as I tightened the cable, something must have clicked inside her because she reached up behind her and clawed at my face.' He stroked one of the scratches on his cheek. 'I jerked my head back but she could see me in the mirror. It took longer with her. Or it seemed to.'

'It didn't occur to you we'd find your DNA under her fingernails? We received the report this morning.'

'So that was why you took a saliva sample ... and my fingerprints.' He smiled faintly. 'I'm guessing you didn't get a match on those. I wore gloves the whole time.'

'The DNA – and your confession – will be enough for the courts.'

Which was just as well, Dania thought, as the SOCOs had found nothing that could be used in evidence on or around the crane.

She had a sudden image of the shape moving towards the trees in the early hours of Thursday morning. It hadn't been a drunken worker heading home, nor had it been Allan Mackie urging Duncan and Grace on with the shotgun. It had been Scott pushing a heavy wheelbarrow.

'So you fetched the wheelbarrow from the back of the Hall,' she said, 'and loaded Duncan and Grace's bodies into it.'

'I must have.'

'You mean you can't remember?'

'Everything went hazy from then on.'

'Why didn't you throw the bodies down the well?' Hamish said.

'If they disappeared, what good would that do me? You have to wait years for presumption of death to be granted. Like it was for Watson and Fraser. And we didn't have years. No, I needed them to be found. I just can't remember the details of what happened next, or why I did what you say I did.'

Dania stared at him. Needing the bodies to be found would explain why he'd hung them from a crane, in full view of the estate workers. But did he really not remember doing that? Could it be that the enormity of his crime had caused his subconscious to erase from his memory the details of what had followed? She'd seen this before: reluctant killers whose brains couldn't cope with what they'd done. Or was he lying in the hope that a psychologist would speak in his favour? Yet he'd willingly confessed to the murders themselves, which would be enough to convict him.

'Why did you take Duncan's shotgun?' she said. 'Were you expecting to run into someone?'

'I spotted it in the hallway when I arrived. I must have lifted it on the way out.' There was a tremor around his mouth. 'I'm so glad it wasn't loaded.'

'It wasn't even a shotgun,' she said. 'It's a replica. The barrels are blocked through with metal.'

He gaped at her. After a moment, he said, 'Why aren't you asking me whether I torched the cottage?'

'Because we know you didn't.'

Hamish folded his arms. 'I daresay you'll be reading about it from your prison cell.'

Kimmie's report had satisfied them that the arsonist was Allan Mackie. A packet of the same brand of match used to set the fire had been found in his lodgings, and fingerprints lifted from it were identical to those on the spent matches under the cottage's windows. Kimmie, knowing there was a chance this could be viewed as circumstantial, had lifted prints from several more items in Mackie's place, including the chain pull in the outside cludgie.

Another piece of evidence, which would surely clinch it, stamping Mackie's guilt firmly on to his forehead, was that the fire investigators had found an abandoned petrol can in the trees behind Duncan's cottage. When dusted for prints, they matched those in Mackie's lodgings. But there was still no sign of him, or the blue tipper. The DCI had ordered the team to redouble their efforts.

Scott was staring at his hands. 'So it's only murder you'll be charging me with.'

'Among other things,' Dania said.

He glanced up. 'Aye, I did try to kill you, too,' he said sadly.

'Lucky for me your wife came along.'

327

His eyes misted over as though he were about to cry, and a look of regret crept on to his face. But was it regret that he'd failed to kill Dania, or regret that his wife had found out what sort of a man he was?

'I'll give you one last chance, Scott. Did you cause Edward's accident?'

He looked at her searchingly. 'I did not. And that's the God's honest.'

She was inclined to believe him. The modus operandi for Edward's murder was completely different – and more sophisticated – than the one for Duncan and Grace.

As she read out the charges, the question she asked herself was: why did this success in bringing Duncan and Grace's killer to justice not fill her with elation? Could it be that it paled into insignificance compared with the crushing disappointment of failing to uncover what had happened to the three Sangster brothers? And, unfortunately, with other cases piling up on her desk, she would have to close that chapter of her investigation.

CHAPTER 27

The last guests were wheeling their luggage out of Sangster Hall. Some were exchanging contact details, but most looked straight ahead as they made for the car park.

Dania strolled into the living room. Hennie was standing where he'd stood that first day, gazing at the portrait above the fireplace. But the fire was no longer lit, and the chill in the room made her suspect that the heating had been turned off.

'Hennie?' she said.

He turned. He was wearing the same grey suit and red silk tie. His face broke into a smile. 'Dania, I was wondering if I'd see you again.'

'You're leaving Scotland today, I understand.'

'My flight to London is this afternoon.'

'Another Magic Week?'

'A little sightseeing. Then I head home to Brussels.'

'I'm glad I caught you. Not just because I wanted to say goodbye and tell you how much I've enjoyed meeting you, but because I was hoping you could clear up a few things for me.'

He gave a slight bow. 'I'll do my best.'

'I've been wondering these past few days what your real interest in Sangster Hall is.'

'My real interest?'

'When we first met, you said you'd been searching for a residential building with several large rooms, which is why you chose Dundee rather than Edinburgh or Glasgow.' She kept her gaze steady. 'I happen to know that there are such large houses near those two cities. They're also bookable for events, and much easier to get to than Sangster Hall.'

He said nothing, but the change in his expression told her he was now on his guard.

'I've had reason to visit the south wing,' she went on, 'and I've been hearing strange sounds.'

He tilted his head. 'But don't all old houses suffer from those?'

'I'm not talking about creaking floorboards, or the wind whistling through cracks. What I've been hearing are footsteps.'

'And you think that's strange?' He smiled enigmatically. 'Some shows were held in that south wing.'

'But not always at the times I heard the footsteps. In many cases, when I stopped, the footsteps stopped also.'

'An echo, perhaps?'

'Perhaps,' she said, acknowledging the point with a nod. 'I concluded it must have been the man we later arrested. But then the footsteps started up again. And that was after the man had been detained.'

Hennie's smile was becoming forced. She paused to give him the opportunity to say something, but he remained silent.

'On Wednesday night,' she continued, 'I was woken in the small hours by someone walking around on the top floor. The floor that's unoccupied,' she added meaningfully. 'When I went to investigate, I saw someone go into the room Edward Sangster used as a child. Whoever it was did a thorough search, pulling things away from the wall and emptying cupboards. I caught a glimpse of him as he was leaving. He was dressed in black and wore a balaclava. And he was carrying a map.'

She could see from Hennie's face that he knew the game was up. 'I found that old map of the south wing in the library,' he said.

'And it's only the south wing that interests you?'

'It's the oldest part of the house.'

'So when I told you I'm a light sleeper and you said you're the exact opposite, that's not strictly true, is it?'

'Fortunately, I need very little sleep.' He looked at her appreciatively. 'And when did you realise I've been roaming around?'

'I think it was when you chose Mavis for the card trick, the one with the ten of hearts. You made sure I was sitting in the front row. You'd even reserved me a seat. You knew Mavis would choose me because you knew she and I were acquainted. And that can only be because you'd seen me visit her. Her rooms are in the south wing.'

He bowed slightly. 'That's perceptive of you.'

'And the album I took from Mavis's bureau. Did you see me hide it in the drawer?'

'I visited the music room often to play the Steinway. I was curious when I saw you go into Mavis's room empty-handed and come out with the album. I wanted to know what was in it that interested you so much. After a quick look, I replaced it in the drawer.'

'And did you find what you were looking for in the south wing?'

'I didn't. And I still haven't.'

She smiled faintly. 'And can you tell me what you're looking for?'

It was several moments before he spoke. 'I'm looking for diamonds.'

'Diamonds!' she said, astonished. 'Here? In Sangster Hall?'

He gazed at the floor, then at her. 'You won't know the story of the missing Manderfeld diamonds.' When she said nothing, he went on: 'I live in Brussels, but my family hail from Amsterdam, which before the war was known as the City of Diamonds, although it was well on the way to losing that title to Antwerp. My grandfather was a diamond merchant with premises on Tolstraat.' Hennie reached into his jacket. 'This is our family coat of arms.'

The wallet was stamped 'with a gold crest. It was a shield with a saltire and crossed swords, and a feathered helmet above the shield.

'Do you know anything about the fate of the Amsterdam diamonds?' he said, returning the wallet to his pocket.

'Didn't the Germans get their hands on most of them?'

'What they got their hands on were the diamond *workers*, over a thousand of whom were Jewish. The Germans needed their expertise, but eventually they deported them. Some survived the war and returned, but the pre-war diamond glory days never did. As for the diamonds themselves, the British mounted a daring mission in May 1940 to bring them to Britain. The men left Harwich in an old World War One destroyer on the evening of Whitsunday. Late the following day, the diamonds had arrived in England. Many of the merchants had handed them over for safe-keeping.'

'This included your grandfather?'

'The operation had to take place with great speed, so there was little time for him to make up his mind, but thankfully he did.' Hennie smiled. 'That was a famous day for the British. The prime minister said he had nothing to offer but blood, toil, tears and sweat. But I digress. Twenty-four hours later, Holland was crushed and the main Dutch forces surrendered. A statement to that effect was issued from the Royal Netherlands Legation in London.'

'And what happened to your grandfather?'

'This is where it gets interesting,' he said, as though the story so far hadn't been. 'Before he disappeared, he left behind evidence that the diamonds had been sent to France. It was a ruse intended to set hares running in the wrong direction. He then went into hiding because he didn't want the Germans to find him and extract from him the truth that they'd been taken to London.'

'I'm guessing the Germans found out eventually.'

'I'm afraid they did. Most of the merchants had refused receipts out of fear that the enemy would discover exactly how many diamonds they had prevented the Third Reich from getting their hands on. But the speed with which the rescue operation was conducted meant that many didn't have time to count their diamonds before handing them over. It was left up to the British to make an inventory once they were safely in London. They were then kept at the premises of the Diamond Trading Company on Charterhouse Street for the duration.'

Dania was starting to suspect where this was going.

'One of the officers counting the stones was a Captain William Sangster,' Hennie continued. 'It took me a long time to track him down in your archives. The Manderfeld diamonds, which my grandfather handed over, numbered one hundred and thirty-nine. But the diamonds returned after the war numbered only one hundred and twenty. And that was the number Captain Sangster had recorded in the inventory.'

'So, somewhere between Amsterdam and London, nineteen stones went missing.'

Hennie kept his voice level. 'It's possible they were lost in transit, but I doubt it. There is no record of the stones from the other merchants suffering the same fate.'

'Then what do you think happened?'

'My guess is that Captain Sangster kept nineteen stones for himself. It would have been so easy. No one had seen the contents of the bag until it had landed on his desk.'

'And that's why you booked Sangster Hall for Magic Week? You thought they were here somewhere, and you intended to find them?'

'Or for evidence that he had once had them. I couldn't be absolutely sure I had the right man, of course. That is until I saw the portrait of his wife Rhona in the ballroom.'

'The lady in the pink evening dress?'

'Perhaps you didn't notice what was round her neck.'

Dania cast her mind back. 'There was something on a silver chain.'

'The Manderfeld diamonds are distinctive. They are pale pink and heart-shaped. And that was what Rhona was wearing. As soon as I saw the portrait, I knew my hunch about Captain Sangster was correct. He'd had one of the diamonds mounted for his wife.'

'And you've been looking for the others all this time.'

'I tried to put myself in his shoes. Where would you hide diamonds in this house? My first thought was that they might be somewhere in the office. But when I saw Scott and Kirstine opening the office safe, I discounted that, although I did slip into the room when it was empty and have a hunt around. I concluded the hiding place must be somewhere in the oldest part of the building, where William Sangster and his wife had lived, and where there are many unoccupied rooms.'

'How do you know the captain didn't sell the diamonds?'

'Because they've not come on the market anywhere. I'm well

connected in the diamond industry, and I've checked the lists going right back to the end of the war.' Hennie glanced round the room. 'Besides, if he'd sold them, this house would be in better condition than it is, don't you think? No, Dania, the diamonds are here somewhere. But I've failed to find them. And now, I've run out of time.'

'So what will you do?'

'There's nothing I *can* do. I can't return to Sangster Hall, year on year, and continue snooping round the rooms in the dead of night. I will have to accept that my quest has come to an end.'

She gazed at him. 'I'm so sorry, Hennie. I can't imagine your frustration.'

'My grandfather was not the only diamond merchant who lost something during the war. Many lost their lives.'

She hesitated before asking. 'Was your grandfather able to continue his business when he returned?'

'He was. But when my father took over, it was clear he had little aptitude for the trade. And the workers who knew how to cut and polish those heart-shaped diamonds never returned from Bergen-Belsen. The business lost money over the years, and eventually went into liquidation. My brother has started up a new company, but in Antwerp.'

Dania thought of Hennie's net worth and wondered why the diamonds were so important to him.

As if guessing her thoughts, he said: 'It's not the value of the diamonds themselves that is the issue here. It's the fact that they were stolen from the Manderfelds. They belong to our family. We should have them back. And then decide what to do with them. It's a matter of principle, nothing else. Do you understand?'

'I think so. But you've not joined your brother in his diamond venture. What made you become an illusionist instead?'

Before he could reply, a man poked his head round the door and called, 'Taxi for Mr Hennie Manderfeld.'

'I'll be right there,' Hennie called back. 'Perhaps you could take those cases by the door.'

The cabbie picked up the luggage and disappeared.

'And now, I must leave you,' Hennie said, smiling warmly. 'Could I ask a favour?'

'Of course.'

'I would very much like to kiss you goodbye.'

Dania was at a loss how to reply. He must have taken this as a signal to continue, because he took her in his arms, his eyes lingering on her face. Then, slowly, he leant forward, and she felt his mouth on hers. When he released her, she half expected his tie to have changed colour, but it hadn't. Her hand crept up to her lapel but, no, there was no flower there, either. He laid his cheek against her hair, and murmured, 'If you are ever in Brussels, Dania, look me up.'

And, with a final smile, he left the room.

'Ma'am, there's someone to see you,' the duty officer said. 'She seemed happy to wait. I've put her in the visitors' room.'

Dania pulled off her gloves. 'Did she leave a name?' She peered at the visitors' register. It wasn't someone she knew.

She headed along the corridor. The instant she opened the door, she recognised the slender woman with the soft grey hair. Seeing Dania, the woman started to struggle to her feet.

'Please don't get up,' Dania said, glancing at the empty coffee mug on the table. 'I hope you haven't been waiting long.'

'Not at all, Inspector.' She smoothed her skirt. 'I'll get to the point as I know you're busy. I'm a super recogniser. At least I was until I retired. I worked in the Greater Glasgow Division.'

Dania had worked with super recognisers at the Met and was greatly impressed by their patience in trawling through grainy CCTV images. Their rare skill in memorising and identifying faces put them a cut above computer-recognition software in those cases where the images were neither clear nor in close-up. The secret, so she'd been told, was to look at, for example, eyes, mouth and ears. In other words, features that don't change with time.

'Go on,' she said, her pulse quickening.

'Aye, well, you probably won't remember me but I dropped in at Sangster Hall for some of the Magic Week shows.'

'No, I did see you. You were at Hennie Manderfeld's opening night.'

The woman seemed pleased that Dania remembered. 'I was sitting along from you in the front row.' She smiled self-consciously. 'Anyway, there's been this stuff in the media about the murder stones and the missing Sangster brothers.' She pulled a tablet out of her bag. 'This photo of the three Sangster boys was hanging in the dining room.'

Dania remembered the image. The brothers were in black suits, and Edward was holding a bible.

'You're probably wondering why I took the photo,' the woman said, in a slightly embarrassed voice. 'I reckon it's force of habit. There was something about one of the faces.'

Dania held her breath. She didn't dare interrupt.

'And I remembered where I'd seen it before.' She drew out an old copy of the *Courier*. 'This man,' she said, tapping the photo in the paper, 'is this Sangster brother here,' she said, pointing to the tablet.

Dania felt her blood tingle as she gazed from one image to the other. 'Are you absolutely sure?'

'Sure enough that I would swear to it in court, right enough.'

Dania stared at the wall.

'Are you all right, Inspector? Your face looks strange.'

'That's my thinking face.' She switched her attention to the woman. 'You've been incredibly helpful.'

'It's my job.' The woman smiled wryly. 'Aye, well, at least it used to be.' She returned the tablet and newspaper to the bag and got to her feet.

'I'll walk you to the door,' Dania said.

At the front entrance, she was about to take her leave of her visitor when the woman said, 'That's a bonnie wee bauble you've got round your neck, and no mistake. Goodbye, Inspector. If you need me again, I've left my details with the duty sergeant.' She disappeared down the steps.

Dania's hand flew to her throat. Under the watchful gaze of the officer, she unclasped the chain. The air left her lungs. Threaded through her fingers was the silver chain with the heart-shaped, pale-pink diamond that Rhona Sangster had worn when she'd sat for her portrait.

So Hennie hadn't been entirely truthful when he'd said he hadn't found the Manderfeld diamonds.

He'd found one, at least.

CHAPTER 28

Dania pulled up outside the small stone cottage and cut the engine. She'd had a strange sense of déjà vu as she'd followed the Coupar Angus and Newtyle roads, and then taken the turn-off on to the single track. The flowers still lay next to the pylon, their wilted blooms scattered now. She'd passed the sign to Lundie but instead of continuing on as she and Hamish had done when they'd visited Allan Mackie, she'd turned sharp right, heading north. The snow of the previous week had all but vanished, leaving a web of icy lace fanning out over the fields. The narrow road was well maintained and would lead eventually to Long Loch and Thriepley House. And then the sat-nav told her she had reached her destination.

A large garage stood next to the cottage and, from the sounds that came from within, Dania guessed this was where Tam Adie had installed his potter's wheel.

She left the car and sauntered across the gravel forecourt past the red pickup truck and black Volkswagen. The door to the garage was ajar.

'Tam? Is that you?' she called, after knocking loudly. 'It's me, Dania Gorska.'

The humming of the wheel stopped and she heard footsteps

approach. Tam appeared, his straggly hair tied back. He was wearing jeans and a grey-white shirt that had gone yellow under the arms. He'd rolled it up above the elbows, obviously not expecting visitors. Otherwise, he would have kept the blue-black tattoo on his right forearm hidden. Seeing Dania's fixed gaze, he started to pull the sleeve down.

'Don't bother, Tam.' She looked squarely at him. 'Or should I call you Watson?'

He opened his mouth to speak, and then closed it again.

'Semper Paratus,' she went on. 'Always Ready. The family motto, which the oldest Sangster boy had tattooed on his arm.'

He gazed at her, saying nothing.

'May I come in for a chat?'

'Aye, I reckon you'd better.'

The garage was spacious and airy. Electricity had been installed, and several modern radiators fitted, otherwise it would have been impossible to work for any length of time. Shelves had been fixed to the walls and were sagging under the weight of books. Dania caught a couple of titles: *The Mysterious Affair at Styles*; *The Man in the Brown Suit*. He was an Agatha Christie fan. One end of the room was reserved for the potter's wheel, but at the other were a small table and chairs, and a moth-eaten sofa. A kettle and microwave sat next to the sink. The place struck her as more of an open-plan bachelor pad than a garage. All that was missing was the bed. Then she spotted it in the corner.

Watson gestured to the chairs. 'How did you know who I was?'

'A lady came to see me. She's a super recogniser. Do you know what that is?'

He shook his head.

'They have a special skill. They can recognise people, even ones who've aged, by looking at particular features that don't really change.'

He scratched his chin. 'But I look nothing like my younger self. In fact, I've gone to some trouble to change my appearance.' He lifted the spectacles off the table. 'That's plain glass.'

'Super recognisers take account of things like that.' Dania studied his reaction. 'This lady had been to Magic Week. She'd seen that photo of you and your brothers in the dining room. And the article in the *Courier* about the V&A exhibition. Once she pointed out the likeness, it got me thinking. And then everything fell into place.'

'Aye? Like what?' he said stiffly.

'When I told you that Allan Mackie claimed to have seen you and Fraser in town, you went white as a ghost.' She folded her arms. 'Allan saw you the Friday your exhibition ended. Was that Fraser on the street with you?'

'It was a friend. He helped me load up the pickup with my pottery. We went into town and had a bite at Greggs.'

'Yes, I remember you told me you were going for a cheese toastie. Do you know you were caught on CCTV?'

'I knew about the cameras. It's why I kept my head down. Still do.'

'And you wore that red cap,' Dania said, glancing at the pegs on the wall. Underneath were the military-style black boots he'd worn when they'd taken the walk to the shepherd's hut.

He grinned. 'I have a blue one in the coat pocket. In a different design. I've got into the habit of switching caps when I'm out. And I have a jacket that's reversible.'

'Didn't you realise that if Mackie had recognised you others might, too?'

'Aye, that was always a possibility.'

341

'You've been lucky. Although I think Mavis knows who you are.'

He frowned. 'How do you make that out?'

'That scene at the well, where Marek was nearly killed. Her rooms are in the south wing. She was at the window, and I saw the expression on her face. After your stories about the Hogmanay parties and ceilidhs, I thought she must have recognised you as Tam Adie. You did say that you and she got on brilliantly.'

He ran a hand over his face. 'That we did, right enough.' He looked hard at her. 'You haven't told her who I am, have you?'

'I've told no one. But maybe you should drop in on her. I think she'd like that.'

He continued to gaze at her. It was impossible to tell what he was thinking.

'So, what happened, Watson? Why did you leave Dundee in 1985? I read your work diary,' she added, pulling it out of her bag. 'The last entry was Monday, June the seventeenth. *Eddie still on at me to get the tractor repaired.*' She looked up. 'That was also the last time Fraser was seen alive.'

'According to the papers, he drowned himself.'

'You don't believe that any more than I do.'

It was a while before Watson spoke. He stared fixedly at the diary. 'Eddie was in a terrible mood so I reckoned I'd better go and find someone who could fix the axle.' He smoothed his hair back. 'I was returning to the house when I heard a commotion through the open window. It was Eddie's voice, and no mistake. He was shouting and making all sorts of threats. I didn't ken at first who he was railing at. And then I heard Fraser shouting back. It sounded like a right rammy. But what stopped me in my tracks was hearing Eddie say that if his brothers were dead, he could run the place properly.'

'Go on,' Dania urged, when he seemed reluctant to continue.

'I was debating with myself as to what to do when I heard the shot. I ran to the side window where I couldn't be seen.' His breathing was becoming laboured. 'Eddie was holding a gun. I reckoned it must have been the captain's Enfield revolver. It was always kept in a cupboard, and the key had long since disappeared.'

'And Fraser?' Dania said, her heart pumping.

'He was lying on the floor,' Watson said, in a whisper. 'He was dead, no question. And I knew then that Eddie had meant what he'd said, and he'd be coming for me. I didn't wait to pick up my things. I ran.'

Dania cast her mind back to what she'd read in the police files. Eddie had reported Watson missing a few days later. He must have spent some time looking for him.

'What conclusion do you think he came to when he couldn't find you?' she said.

'He knew I was on the point of jacking everything in. Maybe he thought the earful he'd given me about the tractor was the final straw.'

'Why didn't you go to the police?'

'I wish now that I had. But I panicked. And each day that went by, it became more difficult. Your mind goes into overdrive when you've seen something like that, your brother dead on the floor.' He gazed into the distance. 'Eddie might have found a way to pin the blame on me. For all I know, he could have wiped that revolver down and hidden it in my room. Something like that, anyway.' He shrugged. 'I'd just been to the bank, and I had a load of money in my pocket. Enough to get me started. When I got to Stromness, I managed to get work as a labourer. Cash in hand. Then I apprenticed as a stonemason.' He glanced at the statue of the deer in the corner. 'That's one of my works. But I soon moved on to making pottery.'

'What do you think happened to Fraser's body?'

'Ach, how would I know? There are plenty of places on the estate where Eddie could have buried it. He might even have thrown it down that old well, right enough. But with Eddie dead now, I reckon we'll never find it.' He snorted. 'I followed the story in the papers, how Fraser's clothes had been found on the bridge. And how Eddie had offered this huge reward for information, how he'd hired a private investigator. I wonder what he'd have done if this investigator had tracked me down.'

'It was a good ploy. It threw everyone off the scent. For a long time, people thought you and Fraser were still alive.' She played with the diary. 'What made you return to Dundee?'

'I read in the obituaries that my father had died. I wanted to visit his grave and pay my respects.'

'Yes, you mention Logan in the diary,' Dania said, turning the pages. '*Not just that, but we hear him up at night. He walks all over the house as though he's searching for something. I'll have to get to the bottom of it, or he'll kill himself.*' She looked up. 'Did you ever find out what he was searching for?'

Watson drew his brows together. 'There was one time when he was in his cups, he started to ramble on about diamonds the captain had brought back from the war. Fraser and Eddie were out of the house, so it was only me he told. But I didn't pay him any heed.'

'You didn't think there was any truth to the story?' she said, watching him closely.

'And I still don't. If the captain had brought back diamonds, the estate wouldn't have got into the mess it did.'

'But your father believed it.'

'Aye, and those diamonds are what he must have been after.'

344

There was a strange light in his eyes. 'But there was something else, nothing to do with diamonds. He had a secret of his own.'

'You mentioned it before. And that Mavis knew it.'

'And if she hasn't told anyone by now, she never will.'

It was on the tip of Dania's tongue to detail her last conversation with Mavis, how the woman had suspected a liaison between Logan and his sister, Amelia. Yet something stopped her. Mavis was right. Some secrets are best left buried.

She left the diary on the table. 'Shortly after Logan's death, those murder stones for Fraser and Watson appeared. Was it you who's been carving them? You mentioned you'd apprenticed as a stonemason.'

'Aye. It was me.' He nodded to one of the bookshelves. 'Those leather-bound volumes are all Dickens. Do you know *The Life and Adventures of Nicholas Nickleby*? It's where I got the inspiration.'

'The only Dickens I've read is *A Tale of Two Cities*.' She threw him a crooked smile. 'The best of times. The worst of times. But I do know about the reference to the murder stone in *Nicholas Nickleby*.'

'It made me want to see that stone.'

'And did you?'

'Aye, I went on a wee trip to Surrey. And I found it.'

'So, you carved those original murder stones. But Eddie kept you busy. Each time he had them removed, they sprang up again, didn't they? Why did you erect a murder stone for yourself?'

'I wanted everyone to think I was dead. And, in a way, I was. I'd been reborn as Tam Adie.'

'But you also wanted to lead us to Eddie. That was why you erected the stones round Sangster Hall, wasn't it?'

He threw her an appreciative look. 'I sometimes forget that the polis have these powers of deduction.'

345

'It was actually Marek who drew my attention to it. He'd created a map.'

'Aye, well, he struck me as a bright lad.'

'But Eddie never came under suspicion.'

'And when I concluded he never would, I gave up and went back to Orkney. I was making a name for myself there, and my artisan pottery business was growing. But I needed to expand if I wanted to enjoy a comfortable old age. I heard about this new V&A museum and the exhibitions it puts on, and decided it was the place for me.'

'There are other museums in other cities where Watson Sangster wouldn't be recognised,' Dania said softly. 'It would have been much less risky to move there.'

His eyes flicked towards her, but he said nothing.

The silence lengthened. 'Tell me, Watson, who do you think killed Eddie?'

He frowned. 'It wasn't an accident, then?'

'It wasn't.'

He gazed at the floor. 'And you don't know who this man was that I saw at the scene?'

'Do *you* know?'

He lifted his head. 'My guess is it was Allan Mackie. He had the best motive of anyone. Eddie laid him off. He couldn't get work anywhere after that.'

'Wasn't it Fraser who sacked him?'

'I can't mind now whether Fraser gave the men their marching orders, but everyone knew it was Eddie's decision.' The words came tumbling out, as though he'd rehearsed them. 'As soon as Mackie was out of prison, he went after Eddie. He must have killed that deer and left it in the road to cause the crash. Ask him how he did it.'

'Mackie has disappeared.'

Watson's face clouded. 'Do you think you'll find him?'

'We're looking. He's wanted for arson. You must have seen it on the news.' She gazed at him. 'I take it it was you who erected those murder stones for Duncan and Grace.'

Once the news of Duncan and Grace's deaths had been covered in the press, it hadn't taken long for two more stones to appear. They had been placed side by side, and lay on the same rough circle round the Hall where the stones for the Sangster brothers had been erected. It was obvious from the shape and size, and the inscriptions and style of lettering, that whoever had carved the originals had carved these.

He nodded. 'I reckon they were owed that at least.'

'There's one thing I don't understand. Why don't you claim your birthright? You're Logan's sole surviving heir. DNA will prove that. Your claim is stronger than that of Kirstine Welles.'

'Kirstine Welles?' he said, in a puzzled voice. 'But she's Mavis's granddaughter. She has no claim to the estate.'

'Do you know that your father had a twin sister? Who lived at Sangster Hall?'

He gaped in astonishment.

'Her name was Amelia. She had a child out of wedlock, and died giving birth. It was in 1953.'

'Before I and my brothers were born, then.' He scratched his head. 'And what happened to the bairn?'

'He survived, and Mavis brought him up as her own. She called him Robbie.'

'You're saying *Robbie* was *Amelia's* son?'

Dania could see this had come as a shock. 'It means Kirstine is *Amelia's* granddaughter, not Mavis's. Kirstine is a Sangster. She's already started the ball rolling by laying claim to the estate.'

Something passed across Watson's face, a look of com-
prehension. 'Good luck to her,' he said firmly. 'I don't want the
responsibility of running the place. She's welcome to it.'

'Does that mean you want to remain as Tam Adie?'

'Aye, and for the rest of my life.' He ran a hand over his eyes.
'And I'd be eternally grateful if you kept my secret.'

'You could declare that you're Watson and renounce your claim
to the Sangster estate.'

'And why would I make such a declaration, eh?'

'Publicity, for one thing.' She smiled. 'I know of one investigative journalist who'd love to do a feature on you. Think of the
sales of your ceramics.'

'That's not going to happen.'

Her smile faded. She'd hoped to persuade him to do this of his
own accord. On her return to West Bell Street, she would have
to compile a report on what had happened to Fraser, and Edward's
role in his death. And that meant exposing Tam Adie as Watson
Sangster. But it was unlikely charges would be brought. If he'd
been in fear of his life, his decision not to denounce Edward was
understandable. He would need to sign the document, but it could
be done with the minimum of fuss and publicity.

'Don't you want to be buried alongside your ancestors?' Dania
said, trying once more.

There was great sadness in Watson's eyes. 'When my time
comes, lass, I'll be cremated and my ashes thrown into the Tay.'

'I see.' She got to her feet. 'I'll let you get back to your pottery,
then.'

They looked at each other for a long moment, Dania aware
from his expression that he understood with perfect clarity
everything that was going through her mind.

'Goodbye, Watson. I'll let myself out.'

348

As she climbed into the car, her glance fell upon the red pickup. It was easily large enough to transport a deer. She remembered Hamish wondering why the deer hadn't been stolen from the sanctuary much closer to the site of Edward's crash. They'd concluded the reason the man in the balaclava had taken the animal from the more distant deer park was that he lived near it. The road behind the trees had led to Lundie. And Allan Mackie. And yet Watson lived in the same area.

The red male had been stolen on the night of 7 February. Watson could have left the animal's body under a tarp in the pickup, and the following day lain in wait on one of the roads on the estate and seen Edward leave in the Morris Traveller. He'd have reached the crash site and dumped the deer well before Edward came anywhere near the road. And then, in the time it would have taken Edward to make his round trip, Watson could easily have driven to his cottage, exchanged the pickup for his Volkswagen and returned to the site of the crash.

Was it Watson who had leant into the Traveller and, to make sure his brother Edward was indeed dead, used his stonemason's chisel to make those three incisions? That statue of the deer in the garage had caused her gaze to wander round the room looking for, but failing to find, his stone-cutting tools. And, to deflect attention from himself, he'd made up a story about a man leaning into the Traveller, and then running through the trees. They'd assumed it was to a vehicle parked on the other side of the woodland, but Watson could have returned to his Volkswagen via the road, leaving little trace of himself. And had he been wearing the German Trommers she'd seen next to the military-style black boots? Had he rushed through the trees to leave the footprints that Johnty had recorded, knowing that most of the estate workers wore the same make of boot?

Watson would have given this plan careful consideration. And he must have concluded it was worth the risk of returning to Dundee to put it into effect. The question was: why hadn't he done it sooner? His words drifted into her head: *As soon as Mackie was out of prison, he went after Eddie.*

Allan Mackie had been released on 1 February. Watson would have seen it in the papers. Had he spotted an opportunity and taken it, knowing that the man would become the prime suspect in his brother's murder? And had he decided to kill Edward near that murder stone in an attempt to reawaken police interest in Edward and his missing brothers? Or had that been a coincidence?

Dania started the engine. Perhaps she was wrong, and it had indeed been Allan Mackie who'd caused Edward's crash. But they had no chance of establishing it until they found him. And even then, the man would deny everything. She imagined the scene: Mackie defiant in the incident room, knowing they had nothing on him, blurting out obvious answers to obvious questions. She pulled away and followed the road to Dundee. Yes, with no hard evidence to convict either Allan Mackie or Watson Sangster, the murder of Edward Sangster would join the growing list of unsolved cases. The question she asked herself was: how many times had she seen that?

The question she *should* have asked herself was: in Edward's case, why did it not bother her?

CHAPTER 29

'Ah, Franek,' Euan Leslie said cheerfully. 'Or should I call you Marek?' He spoke in a rasp, as though he had a bad throat. Marek remembered that distinctive voice from his time undercover.

'Hello, Euan.'

'Euan, is it? You're taking a lot for granted.'

'Would you prefer me to call you Mr Leslie?'

'Aye, I would. But let's not stand on ceremony.'

They were in the café bar of the Dundee Contemporary Arts centre. It had been Marek's choice of venue, and he hadn't been sure if Leslie would turn up. But the man had accepted the invitation with alacrity, and even arrived on time, for which Marek was grateful. The longer he sat there, the more he wasn't sure if his nerves would hold out. As it was lunchtime, the place was full. Even the rain sweeping in from the west hadn't prevented the customers from making the trip. They were mainly couples, although there was the odd solitary diner, gobbling his food, or eating slowly while reading the paper. A thirty-something woman in a houndstooth coat was constantly checking her watch. She'd obviously been stood up. Marek caught snatches of conversation from two men in smartly tailored suits. They were arguing about football, specifically whether Dundee United were in danger of being relegated again. If they'd bothered to ask, Marek could have told them.

Leslie glanced around the room. With his film-star good looks and carefully groomed brown hair with not a strand out of place, few people would have guessed what he really was. He seemed so convinced that he was beyond the reach of the law that he hadn't even bothered to ask Marek if he was wearing a wire. But then he unbuttoned his navy tweed coat, leaving it on, and removed something from his jacket pocket. It was no bigger than a cigarette packet. He laid it on the table next to the menu holder.

'This little device will ensure that our conversation is kept strictly between ourselves,' he said, pulling out a chair.

'How does it work?'

'I've no idea,' he said carelessly. 'I think it emits a signal that interferes with nearby electronic devices. But don't ask me to go into the physics. I'm a humble property developer.'

Already the couple at the next table were frowning at their mobiles. The fair-haired woman was leaning into her companion and peering at his screen. He shrugged and put his phone away.

'Shall we order?' Leslie said.

'Why not?' Marek gestured to the waiter, who hurried over.

Leslie smiled up at him. 'What would you recommend, lad?'

'The fish cakes with chilli sauce for the starter is always a popular choice, sir.'

'We'll go straight to the mains, I reckon.'

'In that case, how about the grilled sea bass?'

'Aye, sounds braw. I'll have that.'

'And I'll have the pasta with sticky shredded beef,' Marek said, scanning the menu.

'And to drink, sir?'

'Get us a bottle of mineral water,' Leslie said. 'And I mean mineral water, and not that carbonated stuff.' He watched the waiter disappear into the kitchen. 'You know, Marek, I didn't expect to see you again. I heard a rumour you'd gone back to Poland.'

'Your attempts at making me disappear went nowhere. That's not like you. You usually succeed.'

'I could say I haven't a scooby what you're talking about, but we both know that's not true.' When he continued, there was regret in his voice. 'I had great plans for you. You were one of the few people I thought I could trust. We worked well together.' His eyes filled with disgust. 'What made you write that article?'

'It's my job. I'm an investigative journalist.'

'I know that. At least I did when your piece came out.'

'Were you surprised?'

'More than you can imagine.' He inclined his head respectfully. 'You fooled me. Not many do.'

Marek returned the nod, one professional acknowledging recognition from another.

'It takes balls to do what you did,' Leslie went on.

'Hardly. I thought you'd be arrested before the piece came out.'

Leslie laughed then, although it was more of a cackle. He ran a hand over his hair.

Marek had seen the gesture before and recognised it as one of supreme confidence. He was finding his own evaporating. 'I didn't know the Fraud Squad were offering you protection,' he said.

'Are you saying that, if you had, you wouldn't have been an eejit and published your findings, eh?'

'Something like that.'

'Ach, well, no harm's been done.'

'What do you mean?' Marek said suspiciously.

'Well, I'm still here, for one thing, and not in prison. And for another, the sale of those jute warehouses has gone through. They'll be pulled down in a few weeks, ready for the builders.' He played with his fork. 'My reputation's had a knock, though, thanks to your piece.' He glanced up. 'But the public will soon forget what you wrote about me once those new affordable flats come on the market.' His eyes were gleaming. 'Have you any idea how hard it is to get decent accommodation in the city centre?'

Before Marek could reply, the food arrived. Leslie tucked into the fish. He himself found that his appetite had vanished.

'Not eating?' Leslie said. 'I mind how you used to put food away.'

'Shall we get down to business, Euan?'

'Och, let's wait till we've had our food. It's a wee while since I've had sea bass like this.'

Marek played with the pasta, then tried a few mouthfuls. To his surprise, he was suddenly ravenous.

'Now, that's more like it,' Leslie said, watching him with amusement. He drank down the mineral water. 'I've always liked this place. Not just the café, but the cinema. They show some unusual films here. Did you know I've got an MA in Film Studies?'

Marek was starting to sweat inside his suit. But it would be counter-productive to bottle it now. For what he had in mind, he had to remain cool. Or at least appear to. 'Bruce Heriot,' he said, looking steadily at Leslie. 'The man you sent to kill me. He's not from around here, is he?'

'I've never heard of him.'

'Cut the bullshit,' he said, with a bravado he didn't feel. He gestured to the device. 'You've assured me no one can listen in.

So, it's safe to let your guard down. But it's force of habit with you, isn't it? Denying everything that's an inconvenient truth.'

Leslie said nothing. The remote coldness in his eyes said it for him.

Marek finished the pasta. Leslie was eating more slowly, either because he was savouring the taste or because he was buying himself time. Time for what? Were his heavies about to burst through the door? That wasn't the man's style. Marek was as safe as he was going to be. And, with luck, after today, he'd be untouchable.

Leslie dabbed at the corners of his mouth with his napkin, his pinkie extended. It was a strange gesture for a man whose capital was built on his image as a hard man. He glanced towards the bar. That was enough to cause the waiter to hurry over.

'A double espresso for me,' Leslie said. He looked questioningly at Marek.

'I'll have a cappuccino.'

After the coffees had arrived, Leslie sat back, a look of satisfaction on his face. 'So, lad, what do you want?'

'To cut a deal.'

He laughed softly. 'As they say across the Pond, it ain't gonna happen.'

Marek brought the cup to his lips. 'You remember how you sent me to your office that time so I could fetch a folder you needed for a meeting?'

'Aye.' There was a trace of suspicion in Leslie's voice.

'Well, it gave me enough time to instal a recording device. And it's still there.' He paused to let this sink in. 'And it's still recording.'

That part wasn't true. Before he'd left, Marek had found an opportunity to sneak back into the office and retrieve it. But

Leslie wasn't to know that. The statement had the desired effect. The man sat up slowly.

'It was how I stumbled upon your little arrangement with the councillor,' Marek went on, enjoying the expression on the other man's face.

'I have immunity from prosecution.'

'For that, yes. But I somehow doubt that even the Fraud Squad will be able to save you when the police hear this.' From his jacket pocket he drew out a device of his own. 'This is a copy record-ing of a conversation between you and one of your men.' He smiled, his confidence returning. 'As I'm sure you'll appreciate, the original is in a safe place. A *very* safe place.' He pushed the device across, then handed Leslie a pair of cordless earphones. 'You'll have to switch your own gadget off,' he added. 'Hold on, let me do that for you.'

Without shifting his malevolent gaze from Marek's face, Leslie inserted the earphones, and switched on the recorder. This was the part Marek had been looking forward to – watching the expressions come and go on the man's face as he heard himself issue instructions to have two people killed, how it was to be done, and how the bodies were to be disposed of. By the time Marek had retrieved the recording, it had been too late to save the victims. The bodies were discovered by a young couple hiking in the woodland north of Tealing. Having heard voices, they'd crept towards the sound, arriving in time to see two men with shovels over their shoulders strolling into the wood. Behind them was a mound of fresh earth.

Marek had listened to the recording for the first time only the day before, as the device had been mislaid at DC Thomson's. The instant he'd heard it, he'd understood the connection between what Leslie was ordering and the bodies buried in the woods. Leslie's detailed description of how the men were to die and the mutilations found on the corpses would leave a jury in no doubt that it was he who had ordered their execution. Marek's initial reaction had been to contact Danka. But he'd remembered how easily Leslie had been granted immunity from prosecution, and he couldn't be sure this wouldn't happen again. And then, as he'd downed one vodka after another, it had dawned on him that he could use the recording to his advantage. After making a few phone calls, he'd finally contacted Leslie. And set up today's meeting.

The recording finished, Leslie removed the earphones. His face was taut with tension, and there was a tremor in his hands. For an instant, a look of pleading appeared in his eyes, which made Marek almost feel sorry for him. But he took control of himself immediately.

He switched the jamming device back on. 'What do you want, Gorski?' he said, without emotion. 'Money?'

'I want something more valuable than money, Euan.'

Leslie tilted his head questioningly.

'My solicitor has strict instructions that, on my death, the original recording is to be sent to the police along with my signed affidavit that it was recorded in your office.' Marek finished his cappuccino. 'The affidavit may not be necessary, because a forensics expert will demonstrate that it's you issuing those orders. It's amazing what they can do with voice recognition these days. And before you get any ideas about cutting a deal with my solicitor, let me assure you that further authenticated copies of the recording have been made and left with others.'

Leslie stared at him unblinking.

'So, you see,' Marek continued, 'not only is it greatly in your interest not to – how shall I put it? – *disappear* me, but you'll also have to ensure that I don't die accidentally.'

Leslie's lips hardly moved. 'You're mad.'

'Maybe.'

'Anyway, that's the most idiotic bluff I've heard in my life. I don't believe you've contacted a solicitor. In a second, you'll be asking me for an exclusive.' He seemed to rally. 'What's to stop me ordering my men to kill you once I've left this place?' His gaze swept the room. 'Do you know how many people I have here?'

Marek laughed. 'Do you know how many people *I* have here?' He turned to the customers and, raising his voice, said, in Polish, 'Ladies and gentlemen, say hello to Mr Euan Leslie.'

The men in the tailored suits called out a greeting and waved merrily. The woman in the houndstooth coat smiled at Leslie and lifted a hand in greeting. The blonde woman blew a kiss, although it wasn't clear if it was intended for Leslie or Marek. Even the waiter, who was chatting to the barman, waved, as did most of the other customers.

'Very clever, Gorski,' Leslie said, getting to his feet and buttoning his coat. 'The first round is to you.'

'*First* round?' Marek said, making a show of looking puzzled. 'I rather think it's game, set and match.'

Leslie signalled to the waiter to fetch the bill.

The man hurried over. 'There's nothing to pay, sir. Compliments of the house.'

Leslie's gaze drilled into Marek's. Then, without another word, he snatched up the jamming device and stormed out.

'Another coffee, Marek?' the waiter said, in Polish.

'I'll have a glass of vodka.' He wiped his face. 'Actually, no, bring the bottle.'

★ ★ ★

'Have you seen this, boss?'

Dania had been working on her report while listening to the patter between Hamish and Honor. The girl had been trying to get her colleague to call Sergeant Fairbairn and make an appointment for the assault course because, as she revelled in pointing out, the sooner he got it over with, the sooner she would stop pestering him. It was Saturday morning, and she happened to know there were vacant slots on the afternoon's course. Hamish did what he did best – he fielded the barbs expertly, even sending some Honor's way.

Dania glanced up. Honor was holding a copy of the *Courier*, folded in such a way that Dania couldn't fail to catch the title: Kirstine Sangster Bravely Continues Her Events Business.

'Kirstine *Sangster*?'

'That's the name she gave the reporter,' Honor said.

'She's wasted no time, then.'

According to the text, Kirstine, having moved in to Sangster Hall, was running events single-handedly.

'Good heavens, she's holding murder mystery tours!'

Honor grinned. 'You've got to hand it to her. That place is tailor-made for them. All those creaky corridors and rooms tucked out of the way, to say nothing of that abandoned top floor.'

'You'd think, given that real murders took place on the estate, the public would give it a miss. But it seems that Sangster Hall's notoriety is working to Kirstine's advantage.'

'And you know what people are like when it comes to murder. They can't get enough of it. Not round here, anyway. And that stuff about the murder stones is still fresh in people's memories.'

Dania handed the paper back. 'I wonder who'll be running the estate now that Duncan's gone. Kirstine will have to get a manager in.'

'About that, I heard a rumour that she's gradually making the labourers redundant.'

'Then who'll work the land?'

'That's just it. There soon won't be any land to work.'

'What do you mean?'

'She's selling it off piecemeal. The neighbouring estates are snapping it up.'

Dania recalled the vast expanse surrounding the Hall. Somewhere in the soil lay the body of Fraser Sangster. What would it look like after more than thirty years? Mummified, no doubt. Perhaps the new owner of that plot of land had plans that would eventually unearth it. But maybe Edward had thought of that and had buried it deep in an outlying field. Or in part of the woodland that was rarely visited. But, either way, he must have lived the years following the murder in fear that Watson might return, even though he couldn't have known that his last horrific scene with Fraser had been witnessed.

'So Kirstine plans just to keep the Hall and run events there,' Dania said.

'Looks like it, boss.'

In the way that one thought follows another, Dania's mind slipped to her forthcoming meeting with Jackie Ireland. The woman was not long back from Glasgow, and had requested a briefing.

'I have to speak to the DCI,' Dania said, getting to her feet.

Honor caught her up in the corridor. 'Boss, I've been meaning to ask. Where's Marek?'

'He's in Poland for a few weeks. I think he'll be staying with our parents.'

'And Euan Leslie?' the girl asked, chewing her thumb. 'Won't he send someone after him?'

'I talked to Marek before he flew out. He seemed in excellent spirits, and reassured me that where Leslie is concerned, he's no longer in danger.'

'And *are* you reassured?'

Dania thought back to the conversation at Edinburgh Airport. Marek had taken her hands and looked into her eyes and told her she was not to worry. He'd put wheels in motion that would ensure Leslie would never touch him, and no, he couldn't tell her what those wheels were, but she was to trust that he knew what he was talking about. And, yes, when he returned, he would host Kimmie's Edith Piaf Singing Society. He might even join in. Dania didn't know what to make of it. Her brother was capable of many things, but cutting a deal with someone like Euan Leslie wasn't one of them. She would have to do what she always did: keep an eye on him and hope for the best.

'To be frank, Honor, I don't know what to think.' She smiled faintly. 'I need to go.'

She left the girl looking unhappy.

Dania reached Jackie Ireland's corridor and tapped at the open door.

'Come in, Dania.' The DCI had on one of the power suits she wore when she met with the brass. It was expertly tailored in a soft grey wool. 'What have you got?' she said, without preamble.

As briefly as she could, but leaving nothing out, Dania relayed what she'd learnt from Watson: who Tam Adie was, and his account of what had happened to Fraser. The DCI listened, frowning. After Dania had finished, the women looked at one another, each trying to guess the other's thoughts.

Finally, the DCI sighed, and massaged her temples. 'We'd never make it stick. The evidence is circumstantial.'

'That Watson murdered Edward, you mean? It's equally likely

it was Allan Mackie. We've no hard evidence there, either. And Mackie has disappeared.'

'Watson wants to remain incognito, right enough. I reckon we should grant him that, at least.' She looked steadily at Dania. 'After you've written your account of Edward's role in Fraser's death, and Watson has signed it, then you might file it in the wrong place. Accidentally. Aye, so it won't be found for a long, long time.'

Dania held the other woman's gaze. 'Understood.'

She left the office, deep in thought.

So why had the DCI instructed her to bury Watson's testimony? Was it the cost of running a case that would lead nowhere? More likely it was compassion for the man. She'd seen that in the woman's eyes.

She was still pondering the question when she reached the incident room.

'Gorska!' came the familiar voice.

He was wearing army fatigues and twirling the beret in one hand.

She stared into the blue eyes. 'Sergeant Fairbairn,' she said faintly. She was aware that the conversations in the room had stopped.

'I believe we have unfinished business,' he said, a smile touching his lips.

'I'm sure DC Downie is ready for the assault course,' she said, glancing around. But Hamish had vanished.

'Aye, well, it's not DC Downie I've come for,' the sergeant said, drawing himself up as though expecting to be challenged. 'It's you.'

'Me?'

'You never finished the course.'

'Didn't I?' she said, thinking rapidly.

362

'I had to pull you off, remember? You were wanted at the station.' He glanced at Honor, who threw him her prettiest smile. 'But DS Randall here has assured me that the case is now done and dusted.'

Dania stared at Honor, who seemed to be deliberately avoiding her gaze.

The sergeant pulled on the beret, adjusting the angle. 'So, you see, Gorska, there's no reason you can't come along now.' His lips twitched. 'Ready, then?'

CHAPTER 30

Allan Mackie shivered as he lifted the bottle of Scotch to his lips. The problem with living in an old campervan was the heating, and no mistake. Except he could hardly call this a campervan. For one thing, it was missing its wheels. And for another, it was missing its doors. The vehicle had been abandoned behind the woodland near Balkello and was now almost solid rust. But, provided he was careful about how he came and went, no one would know he was there. Hiding the tipper had been a wee bit more problematic. In the end, he'd driven it deeper into the wood. He'd have to find a better place, because anyone strolling in this area could stumble across it, right enough. And he couldn't ditch it because he needed it to get into the city.

After setting the fire with the intention of killing that wee shite, Duncan Sangster, and his cow of a wife, he'd scarpered to Balkello. But he couldn't stop there: he had to make plans that were more long term. And it would mean leaving Dundee. Although he wouldn't be sorry to see the back of the city with its growing number of druggies. How had that happened? Dundee wasn't like that before he was sent down. But now you could hardly walk down a street without catching sight of people trying to buy the stuff. Or stumbling across them lying in the alleys with needles in their arms.

First thing in the morning, he'd make a decision as to his next port of call. He took another gulp of Scotch. As the alcohol seeped into his bloodstream, his mind strayed to the night he'd sneaked on to the Sangster estate and torched the cottage. It had been a piece of piss to smash the ground-floor windows and toss in petrol and a few lit cigarettes. Aye, and the building had gone up like a Roman candle, and no mistake. He'd driven away, watching the flames in the rear-view mirror, imagining Duncan's flesh charring in the heat. Had he felt remorse for what he'd done? Not a bit of it. If the man had done right by him and given him what he was owed for having been fired years ago, he and his woman would still be alive. He felt his lips twist into a smile. They were all gone, now. All the Sangsters. And God rot them.

He finished the whisky. His head was starting to swim, but he wasn't so groggy that he didn't catch the stealthy sound of someone moving about outside. He sat up slowly, feeling a tightness in his chest. Were those voices? For a week or so now, he'd become convinced that, despite his efforts at concealment, someone in the city had recognised him. And, what was worse, knew where he was stopping. It was nothing he could put his finger on, right enough, just a look across the aisle in Aldi's that lingered longer than it should have, or footsteps in a deserted street that stopped whenever he did. He'd tried to take different routes back to Balkello, but he'd heard about these wee devices you can put under vehicles that broadcast your location. Those years he'd spent in prison, technology had passed him by. He hadn't recognised the world on his release.

It had been a mistake to return to Dundee, he knew that now. Especially since there were still folk in the city who remembered those times. Aye, and remembered what he'd done. Some nights in prison he would dream about it, how in cold fury he'd taken the cleaver from the kitchen drawer and burst into the first house he'd come to, butchering everyone inside, those two lads included. But the dream he'd been having recently was strikingly different. He rampaged through the house, but when the slaughter was over, and he gazed down at his victims, the faces that stared back were his own. With a trembling hand, he reached for the bottle, forgetting it was empty. Ach, fuck it! He snatched it up and hurled it against the wall. As the sound of shattering glass faded, he heard the voices. They stopped suddenly. There was a moment's silence, and then they started up again.

He turned down the paraffin lamp and sprang to his feet. He peered through the window. But at that time of night, he could see nothing. No, wait, was that movement in the trees? For an instant, he thought he'd glimpsed something. As his eyes adapted to the dark, he made out the figure of a man. It was joined by another, then by a third. But it wasn't until they were a few feet away that he saw what they had in their hands.

He felt as though his blood had stopped flowing. For a second, he was too paralysed to move. Then the will to live rose in him, and he bolted through the doorway and into the trees. He hadn't gone far when something landed on his back, bringing him crashing to the ground. Rough hands seized his shoulders and turned him over. He stared into the ghostly faces, seeing no compassion there.

'Aye, Mackie, the grim reaper's come for you, and no mistake,' one of the men growled. He glanced at his companions. 'Ready, lads?'

The men raised their cleavers.

He tried to scream for mercy, but his throat closed in on the words. In silent terror, he crossed his arms in front of his face, and waited for darkness to take him.

Mavis Welles was curled up in her favourite armchair in the sitting room of the grand-looking building. It was July, and the sun, beating out of a cloudless sky, was burnishing the river and making it shine like gold. If she listened carefully – and her hearing had always been good – she could hear seals barking.

She'd been at the care home now for nearly five months. Given the choice, she'd have preferred to stay in her wee apartment at Sangster Hall. But that besom, Kirstine, who thought of no one but herself, would have none of it. Once she'd discovered that she was a direct descendant of Amelia Sangster, she'd wasted no time in moving into the Hall and turfing her grandmother out. And then registering her name as Kirstine Sangster. And why not, she'd told Mavis? With Duncan gone, she was the last Sangster left alive. And, anyway, Mavis wasn't her real grandmother and had no right to stop at the Hall.

She felt her lips curve into a sour smile. The woman was havering. The last Sangster, indeed. Aye, except for one. Mavis hadn't forgotten the day she'd heard the rumpus outside her window and peered out in time to see the stooshie at the well, and that fair-haired lad nearly losing his life. The Polish detective had arrived, and sorted it out, no question. But it was the man who'd arrived with her that had made Mavis's blood sing in her ears. She knew that gait and the way he held himself. Although his face bore the marks that time inflicts on everyone, she'd had no difficulty recognising him. What had the lass said his name was? Tam Adie. Aye, that was it. She'd mentioned he'd been a local worker. Although Mavis had told her she couldn't remember all the names of the lads who'd worked thereabouts, it wasn't true. She had an excellent memory. And no one called Tam Adie had ever worked anywhere near the Sangster estate.

At the time, she couldn't understand why Watson was masquerading as someone else. Why hadn't he come forward? As Logan's eldest son, Sangster Hall and the surrounding land was his. And, knowing how the estate functioned, he'd make a better fist of running it than Kirstine ever would. He must have had a good reason for keeping quiet. And who was she, Mavis Welles, to betray his secret?

But it had given her a jolt seeing him after all this time. And, as she thought about the past, a memory returned of something she'd hoped was long buried. Aye, and it was always those deep memories that had a habit of slithering up to the surface. She gripped the arms of the chair, her knuckles white, as she recalled that afternoon in June, all those years before.

She was alone in the south wing, dusting the furniture. Everyone was out on the estate. Or so she thought. A sudden rammy from the next room caused her to tiptoe across and peep round the half-open door. Eddie was waving the captain's old army revolver and shouting at Fraser. She couldn't make out all the words, but it had something to do with the estate. Fraser was shouting back, his face hot and red. Finally, Eddie lost it, and no mistake. He threw the revolver on to the table and turned away. Even now, Mavis shuddered as she remembered how the noise of the shot had thundered off the walls. Fraser slumped to the ground with a cry, clutching his stomach. Eddie wheeled round. His face was the colour of ash.

Her instinct was to rush in and try to help. But there was something in the way Eddie stood motionless, staring at his brother's outspread body, that stopped her. His expression changed. It was no longer one of compassion and regret, but of grim determination. He snatched up the revolver and, for one sickening moment, she thought he was going to finish his brother off with a bullet to the head, but he played with the catch and then thrust the firearm into his belt. He reached down and, after several tries, hoisted Fraser over his shoulder. Then he staggered out of the room.

Mavis crept after him, seeing him disappear through the south wing's back door. He left it open, which gave her the opportunity to spy on his movements. At first, she thought he was going to push Fraser into the old well, and the way he paused suggested he was thinking on it, and no mistake. But his glance must have fallen on the wheelbarrow, because he dropped Fraser into it, covered him with the tarpaulin, and then trundled the barrow away. He took the path across the meadow towards the woodland.

She guessed that Eddie would have to make Fraser disappear in such a way that no trace of him would ever be found. And, in that instant, she knew what he planned to do. She waited until he was halfway to the trees, then, running frantically, took another route to the wood. Minutes later, she was hiding in the bushes behind the old ice house. She didn't have long to wait before she heard the creak of the wheelbarrow.

She watched, her nerves strung to breaking point, as Eddie tugged off the tarpaulin and tipped his brother's body on to the ground. A loud groan pierced the silence, causing the corbies to launch themselves into the air, flapping their ragged wings. Dear God, the lad was still alive! Ignoring Fraser's appeals for help, Eddie gripped his brother's arms and slowly dragged him towards the ice house. It took him several goes to get the door open because, with the paint peeled off, the wood was swollen. Without

369

ceremony, he heaved Fraser inside and threw the revolver in after him. He stood looking around, as if unsure of what to do next. Then his expression cleared, and he started to gather branches, which he tossed into the ice house. Finally, putting his weight behind it, he rammed the door shut. He gripped the handles of the barrow and disappeared. The sound of the wheels faded into the distance.

Mavis stole out from behind the bushes and pulled at the door, but she lacked the strength to shift it even an inch. Already, Fraser's cries were growing fainter. She slumped to the ground and covered her face with her hands. Unable to move, she lay on the damp leaves, her mind in turmoil. She had no idea how long it was before she heard footsteps. Was this Eddie returning? Instinct made her crawl back behind the thicket. She peered through the branches. Eddie was fastening a huge padlock to the ice-house door. Before he left, he took a final look round the clearing. As his gaze fell on the bush where she was hiding, he paused, and for one terrifying moment, she thought he'd spotted her. But then he looked away. A moment later, he marched off.

Mavis dragged herself to her feet and retraced her steps, reaching the meadow in time to see Eddie disappear into the Hall. She waited until he'd be deep inside the building before daring to creep in herself. As she stole past the room where the revolver had gone off, she glanced through the half-open door. Eddie, bent over, hands on thighs, was inspecting the wooden floor. Surprisingly, there was little in the way of staining, and what there was would easily be cleaned away. Not wanting to be caught snooping, she sloped along the corridor towards the kitchens. She sat slouched at the oak table, trembling, her thoughts churning. If she called the police, they might well get Fraser out in time. But Eddie would deny everything. Maybe he'd even have her disappear into the cold ground. So, she held her wheesht. And by so doing, she condemned Fraser to his cruel, lonely death in the depths of the ice house.

She returned to the clearing only once, a few days later, to find Eddie planting trees round the circular building. In a short while, the ice house would be hidden from view, guarding its ghastly secret. Aye, and there Fraser would lie until the Day of Judgement. Although it would be Eddie and herself who would be judged. And found wanting.

At the time, Mavis had followed with great interest the story of Fraser's apparent suicide, and that malarkey about his clothes on the Tay Bridge, and Eddie's appeal on the telly. And when Watson had disappeared, she'd been convinced that Eddie had had a hand in that, too. She'd often asked herself if his body lay rotting in that ice house alongside his brother's. But she'd had the good sense to keep her mouth buttoned. And then, years later, he'd returned when she had least expected it. Maybe the time would come when she'd tell him about Fraser. Although what good would that do? Eddie was in his grave, the good Lord having finally decided to take him and send him to where he would burn for all eternity. Aye, but still, it would be nice to see Watson and have a natter about the old days. But he hadn't come to call on her, either at the Hall, or here. For that matter, neither had Kirstine. It was always Scott who'd made the effort. Och, they'd been grand, those wee chats they'd had about the history of Sangster Hall, and the whisky they'd consumed while they were at it. He'd been particularly interested in her photo album. It irked her that she'd mislaid it. It hadn't turned up even when Kirstine had been cramming her few belongings into that old leather suitcase before showing her the door. It wouldn't have surprised her if the woman had decided to keep the album for herself. After all, the folk in the photos were now her kin.

Aye, the care home wasn't a bad place to spend her final years. But it suffered from not having a place where you could pray. Yet the Lord would forgive her absences at Mass, as He had done for many years. She still missed her visits to the chapel at the Hall. In the way that one thought follows another, her mind harked back to the day – how long ago was it now? – when she'd been kneeling telling the rosary. She'd lifted her head as the sun's rays had burst through the clouds and slanted in through the window, illuminating the tabernacle. It wasn't the brilliance of the gilt that she'd noticed, however, but something else. Something *inside* the tabernacle. Something that winked and sparkled. Curiosity had made her leave the pew and, after genuflecting, she'd leant over the altar and pulled open the tabernacle's tiny doors.

A number of pretty glass stones lay inside. They were heart-shaped and pink in colour, and she wondered why she hadn't spotted them before. It had to be the light. It would need to strike the glass doors at precisely the correct angle to fall on those wee gems. And how often did that happen? She reached inside, her fingers closing on the stones. With a glance over her shoulder, unnecessary as she was the only one who visited the chapel, she scooped them up and spread them on the altar. She counted eighteen. And they were so bonnie! The glass had been cut in such a way that, however you moved the stone, the light always caught one of the tiny surfaces.

But hadn't Rhona Sangster had one like this? Aye, it was on a chain, and she'd slipped it round her neck whenever she wore a pink gown, which was often, as she had a number of designer dresses in that colour. In fact, she'd worn the necklace when she'd sat for that portrait in the ballroom of Sangster Hall.

So, what were these glass beads doing in the tabernacle? Were they an offering to the Lord? Unlikely. Perhaps Captain Sangster had been playing a game with his wife, hiding the beads and making her look for them. Mavis smiled as she remembered the two of them, very much in love and always playfully affectionate with each other. Aye, she reckoned that must be it. The captain had hidden the stones in the tabernacle, and something more important had taken his attention, and he'd forgotten about them. But he and Rhona were long gone to their graves. What would it matter, then, if Mavis took the stones for herself? They were only glass, right enough, and somehow it didn't seem proper leaving them in a tabernacle, which, after all, was the house of the Eucharist.

One of the men on the estate was a metal worker, who offered to set them into silver. But the price was an afternoon of hochma-gandy in his wee cottage. It had been worth it, though. He'd been a strapping lad and knew his way round a lass's body well enough. And he'd done a fair job of setting the glass beads into a double necklace.

Mavis gazed out over the river. The care home was so near the shore that seagulls often flew close to the windows, tipping their wings as they took the curve back to the water. The grandfather clock against the far wall struck four. Ach, where was her brew? And her scones? The home was renowned for its afternoon tea, and visitors came specifically at this hour to partake of it with their loved ones. Not that anyone came to visit her. With Duncan and Grace singing with the angels, and Scott rotting in prison, she was on her own. It was true what the priest had told her: alone we come into this earth, and alone we shall leave it. But what did that matter? She'd spent much of her life alone. A couple more years were neither here nor there in the grand scheme of things. And the other residents liked a wee blether, now and again.

A noise made her turn. Finally. Afternoon tea was arriving. Her hand drifted to the necklace, which she always wore now. Today, it was under the lavender jumper, hidden from prying eyes. She ran her bony fingers along the stones. Aye, they were hers now, and they would never leave her. A smile crept on to her lips. She'd rewritten her will so that, when her time came – not long now – she would wear the necklace when they lowered the coffin into the ground.

AUTHOR'S NOTE

Readers interested in the story of how Amsterdam's diamonds were smuggled to London under the noses of the Germans in 1940 might like to read David E. Walker's book *Adventure in Diamonds*. Although I have drawn on this account, there is no evidence that the characters of William Sangster and Hennie Manderfeld ever existed.

ACKNOWLEDGEMENTS

Heartfelt thanks go to my agent, Jenny Brown, and publisher, Krystyna Green, for their ongoing support, and for suggesting ways in which this novel could be improved. My thanks extend to Charley Chapman for all her help with editing. And I am also deeply grateful to Amanda Keats and the team at Little, Brown for their hard work in getting the novel to publication.